ORCHESTRA OF TREACHERIES

A LEGENDS OF TIVARA STORY

JC KANG

This is a work of fiction. Names, places, characters, and events are either fictitious or used fictitiously. Any resemblance to actual events, locations, organizations, or persons, alive or dead, is entirely coincidental and unintended.

Copyright © 2017, 2021 by JC Kang
http://www.dragonstonepress.us
jckang@jckang.dragonstonepress.us

All rights reserved, including the right to reproduce this work or portions thereof in any way whatsoever except as provided by law. For permission, questions, or contact information, see http://www.dragonstonepress.us

Cover Art by Binh Hai
Maps and Cover Layout by Laura Kang
First Edition: June 2016
Second Edition: January 2017
Third Edition: April 2021

To Romain, who planted my geek seeds.

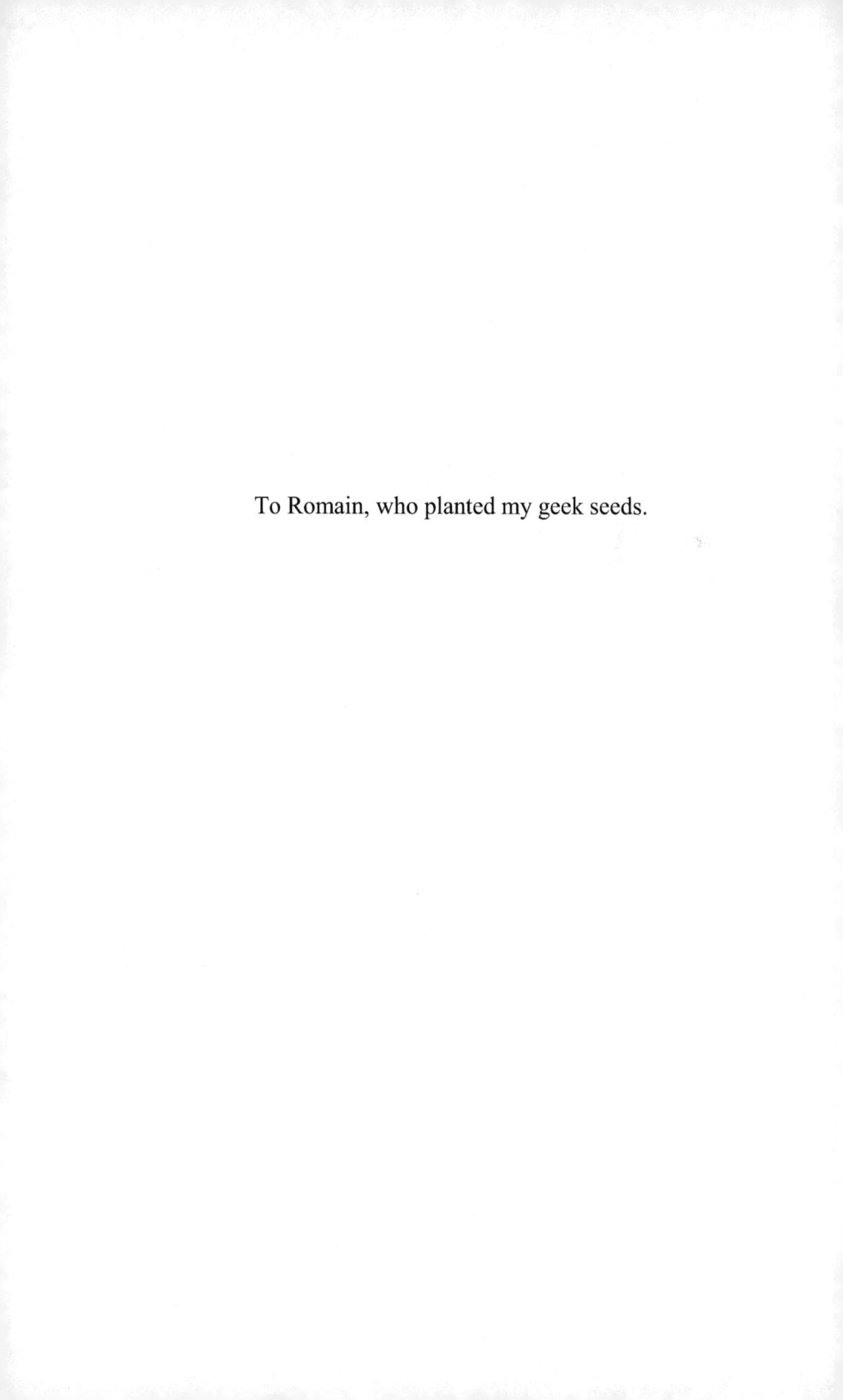

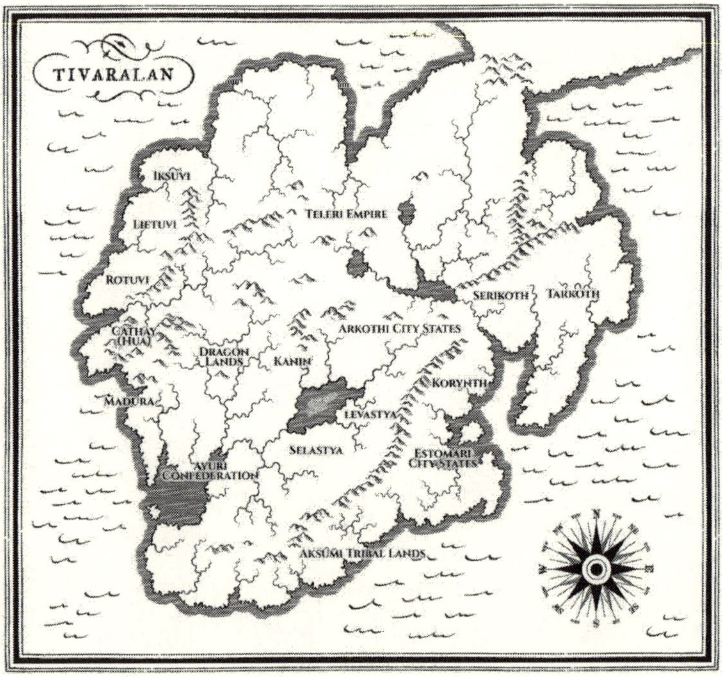
TIVARALAN
IKSUVI
LIETUVI
ROTUVI
CATHAY (HUA)
MADURA
TELERI EMPIRE
DRAGON LANDS
KANIN
ARKOTHI CITY STATES
SERIKOTH
TARKOTH
KORYNTH
LEVASTYA
SELASTYA
ESTOMARI CITY STATES
AYURI CONFEDERATION
AKSUMI TRIBAL LANDS

Map of Cathay

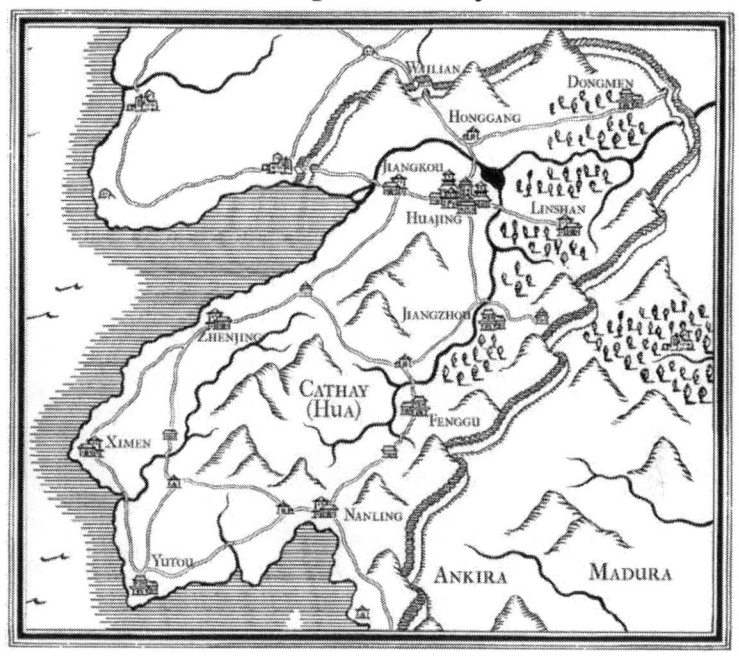

Who's Who in Orchestra of Treacheries

Imperial Family
Wang Zhishen, the Tianzi (Emperor)
Wang Kai-Guo, the Crown Prince
Wang Kai-Wu, the Second Prince
Wang Kaiya, princess
Wu Yanli, wife of Kai-Wu, from Zhenjing Province
Zhao Xiulan, wife of Kai-Guo, from Ximen Province

Kaiya's Friends
Lin Ziqiu, Kaiya's cousin, from Dongshan Province
Wang Kai-Hua, Kaiya's cousin, married to the heir of Jiangzhou Province
Han Mei-Ling, Kaiya's Handmaiden

Kaiya's Mentors
Lord Xu, Elf Lord of Haikou Island
Doctor Wu, Taoist from Haikou Island

Expansionist Lords
Jiang, Lord of Nantou Province
Lin, Lord of Dongshan Province
Peng Kai-Long, nephew of the *Tianzi*, Lord of Nanling Province

Royalist Lords
Han, Lord of Fengu Province
Liu Yong, Lord of Jiangzhou Province
Wu, Lord of Zhenjing Province
Zhao, Lord of Ximen Province
Zheng Han, Lord of Dongmen Province
Zheng Ming, Kaiya's main suitor
Zheng Tian, Kaiya's childhood friend

Ministers
Fen, Council Minister
Geng, Treasury Minister
Hong Jianbin, Minister of Household Relations
Song Henglin, Minister of Foreign Affairs

Tan, Chief Minister

Conspirators
Leina, half-Ayuri from Ankira
Liang Yu, former Black Lotus Fist
Song Xingyuan, Liang Yu's apprentice

Soldiers
Chen Xin, captain of Kaiya's imperial guard detail
Li Wei, Kaiya's imperial guard
Ma Jun, Kaiya's imperial guard
Xie Shimin, mounted archer from Huayuan Province
Xu Zhan, Kaiya's imperial guard
Yan Jie, Black Fist spy, Kaiya's bodyguard
Zhao Yue, Kaiya's imperial guard
Zheng Jiawei, General of the Imperial Guard

Foreigners
Aelward Corivar, Prince of Tarkoth
Ayana Strongbow, Prince Aelward's bodyguard
Benham, Levastyan Empire ambasador
Devak, Paladin elder
Dhananad, Prince of Madura
Gayan, the Oracle's apprentice
Hardeep Vaswani, Prince of Ankira
Mehal, Paladin elder
Piros, Teleri ambassador to the Ayuri Confederation
Sameer Vikram, Paladin apprentice
Sabal, Paladin master
Thielas Starsong, elf prince

Legendary Figures
Aralas, elf angel
Avarax, Last Dragon
Celastya, Guardian Dragon of Cathay
Yanyan, founder of musical magic

Kaiya's Relationships

The Imperial Family

- Wang, Kai-Hua
  Cousin
  18
- Peng, Kai-long
  Cousin
  Nanling P.
  24
- Lin, Ziqiu
  Cousin
  Linshan P.
  14

Wang, Kaiya
18

Wang, Zhishen
Tianzi, Father
54

Wang, Kai-Wu
Second Prince
Second Brother
24

Wu, Yanli
Sister-in-Law
Zhenging P
23

Zhao, Xiulan
Crown Princess
Sister-in-Law
22

Wang, Kai-Guo
Crown Prince
Eldest Brother
25

Han, Mei-Ling
Handmaiden
19

Imperial Guards
Chen, Xin
Li, Wei
Ma, Jun
Xu, Zhan
Zhao, Yue

Black Lotus Clan

Yan, Jie
Half-Elf
Black Lotus Clan
31

Zheng, Tian
Childhood Friend
Dongmen P.
20

Zheng, Ming
Love Interest
Dongmen P.
23

PROLOGUE:
Rude Awakenings

Waking up without wings perplexed Avarax even more than the purple light that flashed at the entrance to his cave. The glimmer danced among the precious metals and gemstones, which towered above his uncharacteristically small size. A rumble shook the cavern walls, punctuating the rude awakening.

It had been a pleasant nap. Now someone would die for disturbing him.

He looked among his horde, searching for his most valued treasure.

The girl was gone.

Her scent lingered, yet in impossibly minute traces.

He thought back. Her voice had resonated with the universe, harmonizing with the vibrations of his own life force. Its vibrant tempo, like the torrent of river rapids, lulled to the dripping of a melting icicle. Heavier and heavier…

She must've sung him to sleep! But how?

He wrapped his consciousness around The dragonstone in his core, the near-infinite source of energy all dragons had. Its pulsations meandered lazily, like a winter stream before the spring melt.

It didn't seem possible for a small human to affect him so much, no matter how special her voice.

And why?

Surely she'd adored him, as much as he did her.

It was time to learn the answers to this question, even if required more conventional means of drawing them out. Uttering a word of magic, his bipedal form morphed. His size swelled as arms bent into forelegs, and wings sprouted. Hands and fingers became talons, while his tail thickened and elongated.

Ah, it felt great to be a dragon again! He stretched his limbs and spine to work out tight muscles. Sufficiently limbered up, he snaked towards the cave opening. Night hung over the land, cloaking the world in darkness.

Another flash lit up the sky. He tracked it to its source, hundreds of miles to the southwest. A column of purple fire streaked down from the heavens, annihilating stretches of a sprawling port city of domes and minarets.

A city that had not been there when he went to sleep.

How long had he slumbered? Shrugging his shoulders a few times, Avarax loosened his wings. His claws tore into rock as he coiled his hind legs and then vaulted skyward. Higher and higher he flew, reacquainting himself with a land drastically different from the one he remembered.

Cities and towns. Hundreds of them within his far-reaching sight, oases in wide expanses of farmland. Not ghastly orc outposts, which glared out from the mountains, nor even the graceful spires of elf citadels melding with their surrounding forests. But rather, the centers of human populations he had seen as a younger dragon, back when their civilization was upgrading from collections of mud huts.

Their rebellion against their orc masters must have succeeded. Like all bottom feeders, humans had a way of proliferating when left unfettered.

The dragonstone in his chest sank. There was no way they could've expanded so fast within the girl's lifetime. Given how little of her song echoed in the pulse of the world, hundreds of years must have passed. The one whose voice connected with him more than any other must be long dead and withered to dust.

Still far in the distance, another blast of energy pulsed down on the city, obliterating the levees restraining the Western Ocean.

An inexorable tide crawled across the low-lying lands and swallowed up towns and villages.

Hell rained down from the heavens. Destruction and suffering. Avarax laughed, belching blue sparks from his snout.

In that moment, he caught a faint whiff of her, in the direction of her homeland. Maybe, just maybe, if he could recover a strand of her hair, or a bone, he could recreate her.

He accelerated northwest, in the direction of her scent.

Flight! The cool night air streaked over his wings. The last time he had flown, he'd held her in his claws.

Over the mountains he soared. In the distance, a town had risen up where her village had been.

There, to the left, was Celastya's lair. From the scent, the only other dragon in the world still lived. Even if the slave girl's ward on his dragonstone allowed him to draw on a trickle of energy, he was more than a match for Celastya. He would rip her open and swallow the flaming pearl that was her dragonstone.

The thought had crossed his mind over the millennia. Instead he had regularly mated with her and ate her clutch of eggs to gradually increase his potential power. He did not have the luxury of time now.

Ignoring the sporadic flickers of purple in the skies behind him, Avarax scanned the landscape below. The plains first rose into rolling hills before vaulting higher into mountain crags. Nestled in a valley, Teardrop Lake glimmered a pale blue, even in the dark of night. The light from the three moons gamboled in its ripples, the reflections dancing across Celastya's hidden cave entrance.

He hovered by the opening. Stronger or not, it would be foolish for him to fight in her lair. He would have to coax her out with sweet words.

His voice echoed across the valley, shaking the mountains. "Celastya, out with you! It is time to mate again."

She was inside. Avarax could hear her shrink back, smell her fear. He would roast her alive and pick through her charred remains for her Pearl. He took in a deep breath and belched into the cave.

Only a few sparks fizzled out— enough to incinerate a human, but only a tickling to a dragon. His frustrated wail sent the mountains shivering. He clawed at the cave mouth, ripping rock away.

A burst of reds and oranges erupted high in the heavens, just above the Iridescent Moon. A roar tumbled across the lands, the shockwave pushing him back from the cave.

Celastya darted out. She glanced at him with her luminous blue eyes. Her wingless, slithering form undulated past as she levitated close to the ground. Light from the White Moon sparkled off of her silvery scales before dark clouds billowing out from Mount Ayudra blotted out their sheen.

Avarax gave chase, the gusts from his wings splintering trees below. He barreled into Celastya, sending her careening into the loathsome Tivari pyramid still standing by the shores of the lake.

Its stones cracked as she rebounded off the walls. He drove his claws toward her, but she darted away, and he ripped into the pyramid's masonry instead. His talons lodged into something deep in the rock, sending a searing shock through body. Curse the Tivari for ever building the vile structures!

Avarax tore his claws free and resumed his pursuit. Celastya flew over the mountains and towards the shore, and then skimmed the ocean as she streaked towards Jade Island.

The fool thought she could channel the energy from the island's istrium deposits.

Of course, he could, too. Perhaps it would energize his dragonstone, reinvigorating it a little more.

Mountains along the closed end of the horseshoe-shaped island shielded a port town at the head of the bay. A smooth metal arch, engraved with runes of elven magic, spanned the mouth of the harbor. Celastya coiled herself around the arch. Her eyes glowed a brilliant blue.

As he approached, she unwrapped herself, freeing herself just in time to avoid a swipe from his foreclaw. With a graceful spin,

Celastya twisted around him and tangled up his wings. The air dropped out from beneath them. Wind roared past as the ground rushed up to meet their tumbling bodies.

They crashed into the shore with a jolt that shook the island. Her strangling grasp around him eased. She seized his forelegs in her own claws, but Avarax was still much stronger.

He raked a talon across her neck. Bright blue blood spurted out. They struggled for dozens of minutes, toppling statues and buildings as they thrashed around.

"Avarax!" A bold voice called his name, and he turned to see a puny elf. He radiated power far out of proportion to his size.

Though smaller than one of Avarax's fangs, the golden-haired elf dared to lock gazes with him. He began to chant. The vibrations of his voice, similar yet different to that of the slave girl from before, rolled over him.

The power of the dragonstone lurched inside of him. A dull ache blossomed into searing pain as his bones broke and reformed. Hulking muscle shrank and impenetrable scales softened. His forelegs and claws withered into arms and hands, his hindquarters transmuting into legs.

Several excruciating minutes of transformation later, Avarax rose on wobbling humanoid legs, a scant head above the elf whom he had dwarfed just minutes ago. He looked down at his naked, frail body.

A human! The most pathetic of sentient beings.

Avarax scoffed. The silly trick might buy them time, but he would pay them back tenfold. He uttered the words to restore his dragon form.

Nothing happened.

What? His morale melted away. Instead of a roar that would compel a mortal to obey, his voice merely shouted. "What have you done?"

"Made you wish you had stayed asleep for another seven hundred years." The elf whipped out a narrow longsword.

Avarax felt its power, knew that it held a magic enchantment. His new tiny heart rattled against the narrow confines of his scrawny chest. Was it in fear? He had not experienced that emotion in several millennia.

He closed his eyes as the tip pushed into his chest.

The blade made a divot in the thin flesh covering him, not even cutting the skin.

It barely tickled.

A magical elvish blade should have slid through a human with ease. Avarax held the elf's shocked gaze.

In that second of silence, Avarax sensed the dragonstone inside of him. It pulsed as feebly as before, yet it still held all the potential energy of a dragon. He spoke a word of power, sending the elf hurtling back into the sand.

He spun to see Celastya bearing down on him. He slammed his fist into her swiping claw. She recoiled and winced.

Avarax laughed. Even in this pitiful form, he was still a dragon. He punched again, hitting nothing but air.

Celastya, the elf, and the horseshoe island were all gone, replaced by wind-driven snow on a mountain top. Ice sizzled and melted beneath his feet.

He evaluated his dragonstone. The elf's ward dammed it up. The trickle of vitality would not sustain his dragon form, at least not for more than a few minutes.

Condemned to be a human!

No matter. *Find opportunity in disaster*, the tribe of black-haired, yellow-skinned humans said. Before him lay a new world infested by inferior beings. Even without his dragon form, his superior intellect would allow him to rule over a weak-willed, borderline intelligent species.

And when he did, he would find the slave girl's bones and recreate her. With her unique voice, he'd teach her how to evoke magic through music. And then, she'd unlock the ward on his Dragonstone.

Celastya snaked her head around. A second before, she had been ready to rip Avarax's human form apart; the next, he and the elf were gone. Before she had time to consider what had happened, the elf reappeared out of thin air. He collapsed into the sand.

"What happened?" she asked.

The elf staggered to his feet. "We were lucky to take him by surprise. I froze time and transported him to the other side of Tivaralan. Though I forced him into human form, he still has all the vitality of a dragon. It took all of my energy to move him."

Celastya scratched her whiskers. She never imagined a mortal could be so strong. "He will return."

"Yes, but he will have to walk. It will take him years, unless he finds a way to unlock his dragonstone."

A shudder sent ripples down her serpentine form. Nothing left in this world could stop Avarax at full strength. "And when he does?"

"Let us hope I have time to teach someone with the right voice to sing him back to sleep."

CHAPTER 1:
Chance Meetings

Princess Kaiya fled Sun-Moon Palace, hoping to escape the dragon's imminent arrival. Not Avarax, who supposedly heard the magic in her voice from afar; but rather General Lu, a human who could pass as a cold-blooded lizard. What the self-proclaimed Guardian Dragon of Cathay lacked in height, he compensated for with an ego that cast a long shadow over her mood.

Her identity hidden by a hooded cloak that roasted her on this unseasonably warm day, she wandered through the busy city streets. Well, not exactly wandered, since she had a destination in mind.

Her five most trusted imperial guards, likewise disguised, kept hands on their *dao* hilts. Chen Xin walked a few paces ahead, ensuring no citizen got too close. More grey streaked his black hair now, perhaps because of such frequent forays into the city. From the way their eyes darted back and forth, one would've thought a new insurrection was brewing.

Covering a giggle with a hand, Kaiya beckoned them to a stop in a quiet intersection. "Chen Xin, if it were dangerous out here, the Ministry of Appointments would have never let us out."

Two years ago, they wouldn't have, but Father had given her some leeway after her role in putting down the rebellion in the North with the power of the Dragon Scale Lute.

"*Dian-xia*," he said, using the formal address, "We should turn back. Your meeting with General Lu…"

Kaiya suppressed a shudder and looked up at the Iridescent Moon Caiyue, never moving from its reliable spot to the south. It waned past its second crescent. "What time is the meeting?"

"Just *short* of the third crescent." Ma Jun grinned, emphasizing his boyish looks.

Chen Xin's lips pursed. "If we turned back now—"

"We'd still fall *short*." Ma Jun stared at the sky, ignoring the elbow Zhao Yue jabbed into him.

She scanned the surroundings, trying to get her bearings. It couldn't be much further. If only she had a better sense of direction. Had they gone straight there… "Just a few more minutes."

Ma Jun shook his head. "General Lu has a *short* temper."

Whether or not the Guardian Dragon deserved ridicule, it wasn't appropriate to mock him. She fixed Ma Jun with a glare until he cast his gaze down. Satisfied, she found the Iridescent Moon again. If it was to the south, that meant east—

"That way." Zhao Yue jutted his prominent chin at the next street corner.

Heat rose to her cheeks. Of course they knew the destination. To hide her embarrassment, she headed in the way he indicated.

At the intersection, sunlight enveloped her in warmth, a reminder that spring was only a week away. It'd been two years ago, around this time, when Prince Hardeep had begged for her help. Her hand strayed to the lotus jewel, Hardeep's token, under her sash.

Heart fluttering, she hummed. With the resolute pulse of the world beneath her feet, she raised the volume. The sounds of walking feet, haggling merchants, and gossiping housewives guided her as she used the hum to bring harmony to the disparate sounds. Around her, commoners going about their daily drudgery smiled. Even dour Chen Xin's stiff shoulders loosened.

Her chest swelled. After two years of practice, her mood flitted through her music. It affected a larger audience now, even without the use of a musical instrument. Perhaps she could finally help Prince Hardeep liberate his homeland from the Madurans. *Once you have grown in your music, I am sure you will come for me*, he'd said. If only there was a way to convince Father.

The scent of turmeric wafted from a street up ahead. They were close. The bright yellow, orange, and red streamers beckoned her. They turned another corner into the Ankiran ghetto, where angry cacophony drowned out her hum.

"You brownies go home!" a male voice bellowed.

"Leeches!" said another.

"Steal someone else's job."

Two dozen burly Cathayi men, muscles bulging from threadbare shirts and pants, massed in a boisterous wall of antagonism in the middle of the street. On the other side, a group of darker-skinned Ayuri folk, mostly women and children, cowered.

The guards formed a protective shield around Kaiya, even as she craned her neck to get a better view.

A lanky fellow in fine silk robes pushed to the front of the Cathayi men. His slicked-back hair contributed to an appearance oily enough to lubricate a dwarf siege engine. A union boss. "Look here, we don't care what kind of work you do, just as long as you stay out of the construction of the outer wall."

A middle-aged woman pressed her palms together and bowed her head. She spoke in fluent but accented Cathayi. "Kind sir, that's all our young men can do. We would starve—"

He waved a hand at the surrounding row houses, painted in lively purples and blues. "Maybe you should use your money for food instead of ruining our city with your garish customs."

The woman touched her ear, an Ayuri sign of apology he wouldn't understand. "We were only able to beautify our neighborhood with the generosity of Lord Peng and Princess Kaiya."

Kaiya twirled a lock of hair, loosened from where she'd already removed gold pins, the ones she regularly gave to Prince

Hardeep's people. It was good to know Cousin Kai-Long had been generous with them, too.

The union leader apparently had different ideas. He threw his hands up. "You see? The *Tianzi* allowed your kind to live here, and now you waste money taken from our national coffers."

Three young Ankiran men jostled their way to the front line. One jabbed a finger into the union boss' chest. "It's your country's fault we are refugees. The least you could do—"

The leader punched the teen in the jaw, and then jerked his thumb toward the homes. "It's about time we taught you freeloaders a lesson. Men, ransack the place."

Kaiya's eyes widened. This couldn't be happening. Not in Huajing. She started forward.

Chen Xin blocked her way. "*Dian-xia*, you cannot risk revealing yourself. There are only five of us to protect you."

With their swordsmanship, two was more than enough. She gestured toward the construction workers, now shoving through the women. "The city is safe. The only violence in the last three hundred years was the attack on these refugees two years ago! You saw the aftermath." Dozens had been murdered in cold blood.

Chen Xin dropped to his knee, fist to the ground. "*Dian-xia*, please." The other imperial guards followed suit. If they were trying not to reveal her identity, they weren't doing a good job.

With the guards bowing down, she had a better view. The young Ankiran men lay on the ground, curling up against kicks. More of the hooligans ripped down the streamers and decorations that marked the Ankiran ghetto.

"Stop!" Kaiya yelled.

She might have been a statue for all the attention anyone paid. Not a single Cathayi or Ayuri even looked in her direction. And if the fighting didn't stop soon, the ruffians would ruin the refugees' efforts to make their Cathayi houses feel like an Ayuri home.

Two years.

It'd been two years since she'd used a Dragon Song for anything of consequence. This situation might pale in comparison to a rebellious lord slaughtering unarmed young men, but these downtrodden foreigners' livelihoods were at stake. The screaming grew louder.

Do not use magic as a crutch, Father had said. Even more ominously, the mysterious elf Xu claimed that powerful musical magic was a beacon for the dragon Avarax. Yet right now, there was no other recourse.

Through her slippers, she gripped the pavestones with her toes. The resolute pulse of the earth coursed into her, rising though her core as she straightened her spine. She raised her voice in song. *Spring Festival*, a favorite for this time of year, celebrated magnanimity. Her notes merged the rhythm of her countrymen's angry jeers with the cadence of the Ankirans' sniffling cries. Her arms grew heavy and her legs wobbled.

The commotion silenced. Everyone turned and looked at her, their eyes glazed over in reverie.

"Please," Kaiya said, catching her breath. "The Ankirans are our guests."

The guild boss shook his head, sending his oiled hair into disarray. The sharpness returned to his eyes. Chest puffed out, he strode over. "Who are y—"

Dao rasped out of scabbards as her guards rose. Their cloaks swooshed open, revealing their distinctive breastplates. The etched lines of the five-clawed dragon flashed in the sun, evoking awe in those not used to seeing it. Save for their leader, the Cathayi workers skittered back, dropped to their knees and pressed their foreheads to the ground. The Ankirans set their palms together and lowered their heads.

The guild boss' face shifted from her to the others and back again before he, too, dropped to his knees. "*Dian-xia.*"

Identity compromised, Kaiya lowered her hood and adopted a tone of imperial authority. "Citizens of Huajing, I understand your concerns. I will present your case to the Ministry of Works."

The leader pressed his forehead to the ground. "Thank you, *Dian-xia*."

"You may go." She waved a hand, dismissing them. Such a flashy motion. Father could have accomplished the same effect with a mere tilt of his eyebrows, no words required.

"Yes, *Dian-xia*." With a jerk of his chin, the boss guided his men away.

Head still bowed, the Ankiran matron stepped forward. "Your Highness, thank you. Men like that harass us on a daily basis."

Daily? Kaiya's stomach tightened. How awful it must be to be far away from home, treated like vermin. She'd never know. She switched to the Ayuri tongue. "I will speak to the city watch." The day's itinerary now included visits to the Ministry of Works, the city watch, and General Lu, not necessarily in that order. To think that two years ago, her only duty had been to get married.

One of the young men spat. "You'd *better* talk to the watch. It's your fault we are stuck here. If you hadn't sold firepowder—"

Whether they understood the Ayuri language or not, the imperial guards stomped forward. The man shrunk back.

"Enough, Ashook." The matron waved him back. "Do not blame the princess for a decision made before she was born. She has tried hard to support us."

"Not hard enough," he muttered under his breath. Quiet, but loud enough for Kaiya's keen ears to catch.

She turned to the matron. "We no longer sell firepowder to Madura. Maybe with the help of the Ayuri Paladins, Ankira will expel them."

The matron teared up as she shook her head. "The Paladins are too afraid of Avarax."

The Last Dragon's name sent a quiver down Kaiya's spine. He guarded against anyone gaining the power to sing him to sleep, like the slave girl Yanyan had done before the War of Ancient Gods. After Kaiya's use of the Dragon Scale Lute, Father had sent spies to keep an eye on Avarax's lair. In the last two years, he had yet to leave the Dragonlands. She shook the worries out of her mind. Perhaps he hadn't heard the lute—now destroyed—or he knew her paltry music was no threat to him.

Behind her, a door to one of the row houses slid open. The guards tightened their circle around her. She spun around.

Standing in the doorway of a house near the end of the block was Cousin Kai-Long's courier. The rugged soldier from Nanling Province delivered Prince Hardeep's secret messages. What was he doing in the Ankiran ghetto? His eyes met hers and widened. He dropped to a knee, fist to the ground. "*Dian-xia*, I was just coming to see you. I have a letter from… Lord Peng."

Kaiya's stomach fluttered. That letter most certainly wasn't from Cousin Kai-Long. She shuffled over to the messenger and, casting a glance back at the guards who trailed just a sword's reach away, received the folded paper cover in two trembling hands. She pressed it against her heart, which pattered like spring rain on roof tiles. The ink's scent invited her to rip the cover open and look.

No, not in front of prying eyes. She turned to Chen Xin. "General Lu must be waiting. We must return to the palace posthaste."

If her guards' jaws could hang open any wider, Avarax himself might grow jealous. Ma Jun opened and closed his mouth several times before he found his words. "Such *short* notice…"

CHAPTER 2:
Love Letters

The shuffling of the imperial guards outside the Hall of Righteous Hearts barely registered in Kaiya's ears as she pressed the latest letter from Prince Hardeep against her chest. Her grasp of the Ayuri language had improved through their regular correspondence, and the poetic imagery of his words became more vibrant with each note. Her stomach twisted in pleasant knots, imitating the graceful loops and whorls of his script.

She looked down and read it again.

Kaiya, my love, I gaze across my war-torn homeland and see immeasurable suffering. The only thing that gives me hope, brings me joy, is the memory of you. The fullness of the lips so close to mine. The gentle curve of your chin which I still feel beneath my fingers. And your voice, so melodic that it still carries me now. Alas, how I wish I could be at your side. The liquid brown eyes that truly saw me.

If only he *could* see her now. She was no longer an awkward, lanky girl with enough pimples to make a topographical map of Tivara. He'd—

"*Dian-xia*," an official outside the door called. "General Lu is here."

Kaiya stuffed the letter into the sash behind her back and squared her shoulders.

The doors opened. General Lu stepped over the ghost-tripping threshold and into the hall. Glossy black hair framed his oval face, and his light complexion, chiseled jaw, and nose all spoke of Cathay's north. He would have cut a dashing figure in his formal blue court robes if he weren't so short.

Behind him, her handmaiden Meiling and imperial guard Ma Jun exchanged raised eyebrows, while a secretary from the Ministry of Household Affairs bowed low.

"*Dian-xia.*" General Lu dropped to his knee, fist to the marble floor.

She nodded, allowing him out of the salute. "General, please forgive my tardiness."

"The princess has important matters to deal with." Though he lowered his head in respect, his acerbic tone suggested otherwise. No doubt he still held a grudge from two years before, when her music had reduced him to tears; and then, not a day later, she'd put down the rebellion in the North with the Dragon Scale Lute before his own nearby army even arrived. Behind his back, some even called the Guardian Dragon the Sleeping Dragon.

She knew. He knew she knew, and yet, the annual ritual continued. As if one day, she'd finally relent and he'd succeed where all the other suitors had failed. She conjured a smile as contrived as his tone. "General, I understand you have kept the North tranquil."

A grin formed on his lips, even as his gaze strayed to her cleavage. "You have followed my exploits?"

Using muskets to defend fortified higher ground against barbarians armed with primitive single-shot crossbows hardly constituted an exploit, but there was no need to antagonize him. She crossed an arm over her chest to brush an errant lock of hair from her face. "I heard that you rebuilt Wailian Castle."

His eyes shot up to meet hers. "Yes. The main keep no longer stands above old mines. We won't have a repeat of the last invasion."

Her hand strayed to the lotus jewel at her hip, concealed by a sash. Prince Hardeep's token. He'd rescued her from the burning castle before it collapsed into the network of tunnels. The magic of the Dragon Scale Lute had ignited the firepowder stored down there. "You undoubtedly learned from Lord Tong's mistakes."

"Well, I was the one who suggested he store the firepowder there, just in case we would ever have to take it from him." He flashed a smug grin as he took credit for her accomplishment. "The castle was only impregnable in name before; now it is fact."

Kaiya kept from pursing her lips. Like all her other suitors, the general's favorite topic was himself. The only men who ever cared about what she thought were Prince Hardeep and her childhood friend, Tian. Who knew where either were now?

She met the general's gaze. Prompt him along, and perhaps he'd use up all his allotted time bragging without bringing up marriage. She said, "I understand the *Tianzi* plans to elevate you to *Yu-Ming* status and grant you full authority over Wailian County."

His smile spread even further, the edges of his lips nearly reaching his ears. "The citizens are content, the borders secure. The saltpeter mines surpass quotas. All the castle needs now is a lady."

Kaiya cringed. He'd weaseled his way into broaching the topic of marriage. She'd virtually given him the opening, and no doubt his military mind seized the advantage. It was time to redirect. "Many eligible girls are coming of age this year. Chen Meili, Fei Qing, Chu Yingying are beautiful *Yu-Ming* daughters. They'd all be appropriate brides for a newly-appointed *Yu-Ming* lord."

"The *Tianzi* suggests I aim higher." If only his focus, fixed on her chest again, aimed higher.

She made a show of pondering, scrunching her forehead and nose. "*Tai-Ming* Lord Lin's daughter Ziqiu, Lord Peng Kai-Long's sister Naying or Lord Liu Yong's daughter Lili are all eligible." Ziqiu was sweet, if flighty, though Naying was something of a bully, and statuesque Lili stood a head taller than General Lu.

His eyes lifted and bored into hers. "I had someone else in mind."

Kaiya looked up at the dwarf-made water clock. "Oh! General, forgive me, but I have an appointment with my doctor."

"At half-past the fourth crescent?" General Lu cocked his head.

In her haste, she hadn't actually noted the time. At least the appointment was real, even if it was much later. She raised her voice in hopes that the officials, her guards, anyone, would hear her. "It is back in the castle, and I have to change."

Wrong words. His gaze roved over her body, likely plotting out a battle plan with her curves as the terrain. How much easier life had been two years ago, when she was flat and acne-ridden. At least then, the suitors didn't leer at her like yellow wolves.

General Lu sank to a knee. "Princess Kaiya, I have asked the *Tianzi* for permission to marry you."

How presumptuous! It was all Kaiya could do to keep from gaping. Hopefully, Father had not promised anything. He had, after all, given her plenty of leeway in this matter since the fall of Wailian Castle. She placed a hand on her chest. "General, I am flattered by your request. However, I am afraid there is another." Hardeep, whom Father would never approve of, but this half-truth would at least extricate both of them with dignity intact.

"I was unaware of a leading candidate."

She flashed a smile. "As the Founder said, *Knowledge of a combatant's disposition is the key to victory.*"

"*Which can only be obtained with use of spies*," he finished. "The *Tianzi* has the best spies in the world, and yet, he is apparently as unaware of your disposition as I."

Kaiya searched his expression. His roundabout responses suggested Father hadn't promised her hand. No, General Lu was baiting her. She tilted her head, intentionally exposing the side of her neck, and covered a contrived giggle. "The secrets of a woman's heart could not be uncovered by even the fabled Black Fists, let alone the *Tianzi's* spies."

He snorted. "Probably because the Black Fists are too busy kidnapping naughty children. In any case, the *Tianzi* said he would be amenable to a union of our families. I humbly request that you take the proposal into consideration."

She dipped her chin. "I am honored by your attention," now on her breasts again, "and I will consider it."

Considered and denied. Though if Father had said *amenable*, perhaps she no longer had the choice. It might very well be a done deal.

Her reply letter to Prince Hardeep could wait. First, she'd visit Father to discern his intentions.

Sitting on the bloodwood chair in Sun-Moon Castle's Jasmine Room, *Tai-Ming* Lord Peng Kai-Long poured another cup of tea for the *Tianzi*. Imperial guards stood by the sliding doors, which opened out on a terrace overlooking Sun-Moon Lake. Annoying bird chirps twittered in on a warm breeze, which presaged an early spring. A historically monumental spring, if his plans went well.

Hand trembling, the *Tianzi* reached for the kettle. "Nephew, please drink."

Kai-Long shook his head. Using the formal address, he said, "*Huang-Shang*, I wouldn't dare. This tea is reserved only for the Imperial Family."

"No need to stand on ceremony." The *Tianzi's* laugh devolved into a coughing fit. "You are my sister's son and grew up with my children."

Which gave him a close-up view of their incompetence. Kai-Long bowed. "I am of your blood, but I do not belong to the Wang line."

"It would be a shame if you never tasted the imperial tea."

Kai-Long suppressed a smirk. At the end of spring, he would. For now, though: "In this, I must refuse your invitation."

"And if I command it?" Phlegm rattled in the *Tianzi's* throat.

Kai-Long withdrew his curved dagger. Hand on their *dao* swords, the imperial guards strode forward, only to freeze and melt back when he set the blade on the table. He lowered his head again. "If you give such a command, *Huang-Shang*, I will cut my own throat."

"My most loyal vassal." The *Tianzi's* laugh came out as a labored wheeze. He was only the husk of a once-great man, and wouldn't last much longer. Perhaps no more than a year, even if Kai-Long didn't arrange for an earlier death.

A good thing, too, since Cathay grew weaker by the day under his increasingly timid leadership. Once Kai-Long ascended the Dragon Throne, he would strengthen the nation through economic and military reform, just as he had his own province. Just as the *Tianzi* had done a generation ago, before age and sickness sapped his vitality.

The door slid open, revealing a kneeling minister. "*Huang-Shang*, Princess Kaiya requests an audience with you." He pressed his forehead to the ground, revealing the princess, who knelt behind him.

"Enter," the *Tianzi* said.

Cousin Kaiya rose with the grace of a weeping cherry and glided into the room. How elegant she'd become. And beautiful, too. Just two years ago, she'd been woefully plain and flat, though that had done little to stem the tide of ambitious suitors. Her gaze met his and a smile quirked across her lips for a split second before her attention shifted to the *Tianzi*. She sank to her knees and pressed her forehead to the floor. "*Huang-Shang*."

"Rise, my daughter."

She straightened. "*Huang-Shang*, I met with General Lu. He informed me that you are amenable to a marriage between our families.*"*

Kai-Long hid his shock. Her tone was too neutral, with no hint of defiance. Perhaps she'd grown used to the magic in the letters she believed came from Prince Hardeep. And the *Tianzi* was *amenable*. That might as well have been order.

The *Tianzi* locked his gaze on Kaiya. "Your brothers have yet to conceive an heir. I would rest assured knowing your future son would be third in line to the Dragon Throne."

Third in line—the position Kai-Long currently occupied based on the patrilineal laws of succession. He kept his face impassive. After all…

"You have one month to choose an appropriate suitor," the *Tianzi* said. "Otherwise, you will marry General Lu."

Kaiya's lips trembled for a split second. Then her eyes darted to all the guards, and her expression settled. She bowed. "As you command, Father."

One month. Her obedience to dear Uncle trumped even the magic of the fake letters. All the plans Kai-Long had set in motion two years prior might crumble around him. If he couldn't keep Kaiya from marrying, he'd have to get rid of her for good.

And with his foresight, he had a plan in place to accomplish that.

CHAPTER 3

Challenges

Kaiya stared blankly out one of the solarium's dozen windows, distracted by thoughts of Father's ultimatum and Prince Hardeep's recent note. With Cousin Kai-Long's help, they'd secretly exchanged letters for a year. Their relationship had matured through their correspondence, and at eighteen, she now realized how idealistic and lovesick she'd been as a sixteen-year-old.

Now, it would never be. Not unless she found a way to make it happen.

"*Dian-xia!*" Doctor Wu's voice rattled her out of her thoughts.

Kaiya blinked, her focus shifting to the grey-robed woman. Nobody knew Doctor Wu's age, though some speculated the Master of the *Dao* had discovered the secret to immortality.

Pulled up into a tight, austere coil, her long silver hair had a faint bluish tinge to it, perhaps reflected from her eyes when the light hit it just right.

Those eyes, unlike any other Cathayi woman. Luminescent blue, like the Blue Moon, Guanyin's Eye, itself. Their depth and serenity evoked a soothing calm rivaling Sun-Moon Lake on the clearest of days.

Kaiya probably deserved the reprimand for daydreaming. She bowed her head, contrite.

"Recite what I just said," Dr. Wu said.

Orchestra of Treacheries

Kaiya twirled a lock of her hair. What *had* she said? Something about the Tivari, who had enslaved humans for millennia until the War of Ancient Gods a thousand years ago. "Altivorcs and tivorcs have an extra energy point on their Conception Meridian, between... between..."

Doctor Wu poked two points on Kaiya's belly. "Between these acupuncture points, *Juque* and *Shangwan*. What happens if it is blocked?"

Why did it matter? The Tivari were now little more than disorganized bands of mercenaries. Since Father had expelled them after they'd conspired to attack the imperial wedding two years ago, Kaiya would probably never see one. She shook her head.

"Nausea. Vomiting. Headaches." Doctor Wu's tone remained calm, devoid of accusation. "You are more distracted than usual. Your thoughts are scattered, unfocused. You will meditate."

And by meditation, Doctor Wu meant standing in an unladylike stance and staring out the window. They'd done it so many times in the last decade. Kaiya obediently rose and strode over to the spot facing east out the latticed windows toward Jade Mountain.

"Now, focus on your breathing, anchor yourself with the energies of Mother Earth."

The same words, as always. Kaiya sank into a deep horse stance, thighs parallel to the ground, spine straight and gaze locked forward on the snow-capped peak. As ugly as the posture was, the stance had helped her channel the magic of Dragon Songs.

"Still not right after all these years." Doctor Wu furrowed a brow. With a nudge of a hand, she lifted Kaiya's chin to further straighten her back. Her voice softened. "Now breathe. In through the nose, letting your stomach expand; out through your mouth, pushing your stomach in."

Kaiya could have quoted the words verbatim.

Doctor Wu afforded her a cursory glance. "Good. Now visualize your weight sinking deeper and deeper into Mother

Earth as you exhale. Draw her life-giving energy through the *Yongquan* points in your feet as you inhale and bring them to your *Dantian* below your navel."

Slowing her breath, Kaiya settled her mind. Her toes gripped the stone floor through her shoe soles. Thoughts of marriage and foreign princes melted away as the resolute vibration of the earth filled her.

A snort came from the right, just outside Kaiya's peripheral vision. "My dear doctor, shouldn't the princess be nurturing musical talents instead of playing with energy fields?"

Kaiya fought the urge to turn and look, lest she invite a rebuke from Dr. Wu. Still, the voice and flippant tone could only belong to the elf, Lord Xu.

He walked around and faced her, blocking the view of the mountain. His glossy gold hair sparkled in the sun. It'd been two years since he'd last appeared, yet his fine, ageless features remained the same. Youthful, even if his eyes glinted with wisdom.

And perhaps, mischief.

Concentration broken, thoughts of Hardeep's written words flooded back. And it wouldn't do to let the elf see her in such a crude pose. She straightened and bobbed her head in a show of respect.

He didn't return the salute and looked her directly in her eyes. "After all," he said, "she has shown a knack for Dragon Songs."

"Perhaps you should teach her," Doctor Wu said with a hint of amusement in her voice. "Just as Aralas taught his Cathayi lover, Yanyan. Princess Kaiya will be singing dragons to sleep in no time."

Xu laughed, his tone mocking. "Aralas was Elestrae, an elf angel sent by the Sun God Koralas. She was—"

"*He*," Doctor Wu said.

"Yes. *He* was master of all magic and none like him have walked Tivaralan since."

Doctor Wu scoffed. "Then if you can't do it, you must trust me to teach her to connect with the energy of Mother Earth. Just because the elves did not teach humans about the *Dao* does not mean it's useless."

Kaiya's eyes shifted between doctor and elf. The barbs they stabbed into each other sure *sounded* mirthful, but who knew? Xu seemed affable enough, but he was still a high lord and could order Doctor Wu's execution for her impudence.

"But she is a busy girl," Xu said, "and I would think her time would be better spent fusing magic into her music."

"What is magic, but a link to the energy of Mother Earth?" Doctor Wu's tone sounded like a verbal jab to the elf's ribs.

Xu scoffed.

The doctor flashed a playful grin. "A wager then, my Lord. Show us something you think is beyond our princess' musical abilities, and if she cannot replicate it, I will give you one herb from my collection of rare tonics. But if she does, you will acquiesce to one of my requests."

Both their eyes turned to her, all but forgotten until now. The argument over her training had been mundane enough until this challenge. How could she possibly compare to the powerful Lord Xu? "But Master, my skills are trifling com—"

Doctor Wu silenced her with a hand. "You recently held an entire audience enthralled by your *guzheng* zither performance. What is the connection between performer and audience, if not a manifestation of energy?"

Kaiya shook her head. "You should not gamble on something beyond my small abilities."

The old woman winked. "Lord Xu will be kind with his challenge, and I won't ask for something like a Starburst when you win."

"A Starburst?" Kaiya gaped incredulously. Though if anyone had one of those mythical relics from when elves and orcs battled for supremacy over Tivara, it would be Xu.

Lord Xu laughed. "Shall I ask her to invoke another Hellstorm? Or the Wrath of Koralas?"

With a grandmotherly grin, Doctor Wu rubbed her hands together. "Lord Xu is having delusions of grandeur. Does he think he is the equal of Archangel Aralas?"

Kaiya's mind swam. Everyone else spoke in awe of the devastating magic that'd obliterated a mountain and ripped a new sea in the continent. Lord Xu referenced it with the same nonchalance as the as he'd flippantly mentioned the genocidal vengeance of the elvish sun god—magic that was never invoked during the War of Ancient Gods. Meanwhile, her teacher bandied about the name of the elf hero from that conflict as if he were a dear acquaintance.

Doctor Wu offered her a reassuring pat on the shoulder. "Easy, *Dian-xia*. This is just idle banter among old friends."

"Old friends, indeed." Lord Xu snickered. "As long as we understand the stakes, I will keep my challenge simple." He beckoned the imperial guards Chen Xin and Ma Jun, conveniently tucked away in the background. "You two, over here."

Neither so much as flinched, their attention set forward.

Kaiya covered a laugh. "If that is all, then it is quite easy. Chen Xin, Ma Jun, please come."

The two guards dropped onto a one-knee bow, fist to the ground. "As the princess commands," they shouted. They stood up and marched over in unison.

Chen Xin eyed Xu. "Do you wish us to remove the lord?"

Unsurprisingly, Lord Xu ignored the threat and sang in the musical words of elf magic. The melody might have been a chorus of angels, and her heart soared.

At the end of the five-second chant, Chen Xin and Ma Jun both started sniffling. Blinking, their lips twitched in a futile attempt to contain emotion. Within seconds, both sobbed uncontrollably.

Lord Xu turned toward the doctor with a smug expression. "Can your breathing exercises accomplish something like that?"

"*Dian-xia*," Doctor Wu said, "make them stop. Use your flute."

How did one stop magically-induced crying? Kaiya withdrew a four-inch *dizi* flute from the folds of her robes. Playing a joyous tune, she looked up.

Her guards still sobbed. Uncertainties grew. Her melody wavered.

"Focus," the doctor said. "The nature of grief is metal, which cloys the lungs. It can be tempered by the fire of the heart."

Heart. Fire. High stances and erratic tones. Kaiya nodded, shifting in her stance and letting her weight sit lightly over her toes. She shook her hair out, sending the precious gold, silver, and jade clips and pins jingling to the floor. Her music became more volatile and whimsical as she drew her breath from her heart.

Ma Jun and Chen Xin's crying came to an abrupt stop. They organized their expressions into their typical stoicism.

Lord Xu clapped. "Nicely done, *Dian-xia*. I concede there is something to what the doctor says. Had you not broken my spell, they would have continued blubbering until I released them or they died of starvation. Perhaps you can move beyond parlor tricks and actually replicate the exploits of your Dragon Singers from the War of Ancient Gods."

Kaiya's heart fluttered. She might have grown in the lost art of Dragon Songs, but... "Stopping men from crying is trivial compared to singing the Last Dragon to sleep."

"Do you think Yanyan's first feat was confronting Avarax?" He favored her with a raised eyebrow. "And yet when she did, he slept for seven hundred years, setting the stage for humans' ascendance after overthrowing the orcs."

Kaiya cocked her head. Avarax had only woken three decades before. Surely the powerful Lord Xu could do simple math. "But Avarax slept for a thousand years."

Doctor Wu scowled at Lord Xu, and then laughed. "*Dian-xia*, Lord Xu has lost his edge in his old age."

"Yes, I was thinking of the Hellstorm. To think, not even a rain of fire roused him."

Doctor Wu poked him in the ribs. "In any case, my Lord, you lost your wager."

"Indeed, I did. Since I gave the princess an easy task, I hope your demand is of commensurate value."

Easy? Kaiya shuffled on her feet.

Doctor Wu chuckled. "Am I anything but fair, my Lord? I ask that you teach the princess *The Ear that Sees*."

Kaiya snorted. A fictitious technique from fanciful martial arts novels, *Seeing Ears* allowed boogeymen spies to fight in the dark. The stories might be fit for entertainment or scaring little children, but not much else. "I don't see how that will help my music."

The elf chuckled. "In the beginning stages, *The Ear that Sees* is simply a means of separating all sounds from each other." He nodded at the doctor. "Perhaps it is not such a bad idea. I've always implored this girl to listen."

Kaiya fiddled with a lock of hair. What was the use of such a skill? But Doctor Wu had recommended it, so…

Lord Xu flicked a wrist at the guards. "Send your men out."

When Chen Xin and Ma Jun left the room and took up places outside of the doors as Kaiya commanded, she searched Lord Xu's eyes.

What would she learn this time? His lesson on the castle wall two years before had opened her ears to the possibilities. She'd since surpassed all her teachers and was now considered one of the best musicians in Cathay. No one else could evoke magic through sound.

And here Xu was again, suddenly interested in her development, after not so much as mentioning Dragon Songs since.

He opened his hand and spoke a melodious word of elf magic.

Kaiya gasped as a long musical instrument appeared in his hand. The *sanxian* was ancient by the look of it, perhaps magical. An unknown animal skin stretched over the round resonator. Three strings ran over the fretless wooden neck.

"This belonged to your ancestor," he said with a wistful tone, "Queen Yuxiang, the consort of the founder of the Wang Dynasty, and later Regent." His fingers danced over the strings, the short melody a flittering combination of short pentatonic notes, ending with a long note. "She adored the sound of it, brought it from her home on Jade Island. It is my gift to you." He held it out.

Kaiya hesitated before reverently taking the priceless artifact in her hands. It was light, the resonator rough and the neck smooth. Unlike the Dragon Scale Lute or Yanyan's *pipa*, it didn't seem to pulse with a life of its own. "I do not know how to play this."

"Which is exactly why I gave it to you. Now, pluck one of the strings and listen."

Kaiya did as she was told and a deep, rich hum emanated from the instrument. It was hard to believe such an ancient *sanxian* could create such a crisp twang.

His hand swept over the room. "Do you hear how the sound fills the room? Play more and ponder how that compares with the acoustics of the Hall of Pure Melody."

She thought back to all the performances there in the past two years, in the hall's acoustically perfect room. And of course *that* time, with Hardeep. She plucked different strings, experimenting with the notes as she pressed on the neck.

He made a subtle gesture and a chair whispered across the floor of its own volition, stopping right in front of her. "Concentrate on how the sound wraps around the chair and reflects back."

Tearing her attention away from the chair, which no one had touched, Kaiya obediently plucked the strings.

Her eyes widened. The quality of the *sanxian's* sound had changed, albeit subtly, from the seat's new position.

The elf nodded at her. "Your ears are keen. You understand. Now close your eyes and play long, slow notes."

Strumming, she peeked through narrowed eyelids. Objects flew through the room: the desk, chairs, cushions, scrolls and wall hangings. In the corner of her vision, she saw Doctor Wu, yawning as if the orchestra of flying objects was no more than a street illusionist's trick.

"Close your eyes!" Lord Xu barked from behind. "Focus on the sound."

How had he seen her eyes? Kaiya acquiesced. The subtle changes in the *sanxian*'s vibrations became clear. Some objects seemed to create their own sounds while others reflected or absorbed the notes. After several minutes, the tone leveled off. The suddenly steady modulation startled her into looking.

Xu had rearranged all the furnishings with the expertise of a *Feng Shui* geomancer. The room sounded acoustically perfect, like the Hall of Pure Melody or the Temple of Heaven.

"Do you understand?" he asked.

"I think so."

He peered at her. "Do not think. *Feel*."

"I will try."

"There's no trying. You either do, or you don't."

Doctor Wu scoffed. "I've heard *this* before. Maybe you're a Daoist, after all. "Xu chuckled, then looked at Kaiya. " Today, I just wanted to open your ears to the possibilities. This somewhat resembles the way bats in the night sky and dolphins in the ocean depths can sense things around them."

Such preposterous statements! Kaiya twirled a lock of her hair.

The elf turned to Doctor Wu. "Is my wager sufficiently fulfilled?"

The doctor flashed the same devilish grin as before. "No, you will teach her more."

He laughed. "Very well, when I return to the capital before the New Year."

Kaiya nodded politely to Lord Xu, and then bowed toward the doctor. "Thank you both for your lessons."

Her sixteen-year old cousin Lin Ziqiu poked her head into the solarium, her face bright. "Hurry up, Kaiya! Lord Peng's messenger is here with a letter for you!"

Orchestra of Treacheries

CHAPTER 4
Theoretical Conspiracies

Minister Hong Jianbin's dark blue court robes absorbed the heat of the late winter sun, warming his old bones as he hobbled through a garden in Sun-Moon Castle. The carefree laughter of young ladies flitted out from beyond a grove of weeping plum trees. The emerging blossoms formed parasols of white fluff, blocking his view.

He followed the blissful chatter, which beckoned him through a wide terrace covered in red tiles. Beyond a white latticework guardrail of interlocking round and square patterns sat five of the realm's most beautiful ladies.

They gathered around an hourglass-shaped pedestal of red porcelain, painted in a gold carp motif and topped with a glass disk. Four were settled on bloodwood chairs, whose gently twisting lines and thin struts belied structural resilience.

Crown Princess Xiulan stood, holding a calligraphy brush in her right hand, and the hanging sleeve of her gown with the left. She finished her work with a flourishing twist. The other ladies leaned back and clapped. A dozen handmaidens joined in the applause.

Ignoring the Crown Princess, Hong fixated on Princess Kaiya, the most stunning of the five. She covered her full lips with delicate fingers as she shifted in her seat and laughed with her friends.

In the two years since he had last seen her, when he had taken the plain and gangly girl to meet the Ankiran delegation, she had blossomed. Gone were the blemishes, leaving her natural complexion as flawless as a pearl. Her curves filled out, borne with a nonchalant grace. Lustrous black locks rippled down to her waist.

Her gaze found his as he shuffled toward them, her dark brown eyes so large a doe would envy them.

Two imperial guards blocked his way. The magic etched into their breastplates' five-clawed dragons radiated out. His legs wobbled beneath him and his hands trembled.

The ladies fell silent as their stares bore down on him.

"Minister Hong." Princess Kaiya's melodious voice stopped his heart, making him forget his dread.

She knew his name. His knees protested with a pair of hollow popping sounds as he sank down into a kneel. "Princesses. Forgive my intrusion. The Chief Minister summoned me here."

"Rise." Crown Princess Xiulan spoke as the highest ranking of the five.

The imperial guards parted. Hong clambered to his feet and hobbled toward them. He caught the Crown Princess' withering glare from the corner of his eyes when he admired her calligraphy.

The script for *spring*, written in a brisk, wispy style tangibly whispered over him like a cool spring breeze. The calm stood in stark contrast to the time he saw her Dragon Script on the army's banners. The character for *fear* had evoked an uncontrollable urge to cower.

The Crown Princess turned back to her writing, but Princess Kaiya beckoned him.

"Do you wish to join us while you wait?" She extended a hand with the refinement of a dancer, offering a paintbrush. Her red outer robe with gold embroidered borders flashed open with the motion, revealing a high-collared white inner gown held together with a broad pink sash.

How he longed to receive the brush and perhaps innocuously graze a finger against the smooth skin of her hand. He looked down at his own dry and gnarled hands and thought the better of it.

The other noblewomen's expressions proved less inviting, though none as hostile as sixteen-year old Lin Ziqiu, who regarded him with a disdainful glare. The imperial cousin's scrunched up nose and curled lip marred an otherwise beautiful face, and proved even more of deterrence than the Crown Princess' banners or the imperial guards' breastplates.

He bowed. "Thank you for your kind consideration, but I must beg off your invitation."

Lin Ziqiu blew out a long breath, and the weight of the princesses' stares lifted.

"As you will." Princess Kaiya flashed him a demure smile.

Hong's heart hopped erratically like a tentative rabbit. Repeatedly bobbing his head, he shuffled backward off of the terrace and turned. He ambled toward one of the plum trees, congratulating himself for his lie. *He* had requested Chief Minister Tan to meet him there, knowing the princesses gathered in the adjacent garden, and hoping to catch a glimpse of Princess Kaiya.

He afforded himself this last look at her as a gorgeous young woman. The curve of her neck, the slender high nose, and those eyes. The next time he saw her, he would think of her as a mere tool for his plans.

"Hong, my friend, you asked me to meet you here, of all places?" Chief Minister Tan called from the garden path.

Hong bowed. "Yes. The *Tianzi* ordered me to vet another potential suitor for Princess Kaiya. I cannot join you in the Floating World tonight."

The Chief Minister laughed. "Ah, old friend, had I known your promotion to Minister of Household Relations would eat so much into your time, I would have never recommended you!"

Hong bowed again. "Of course, I am grateful for—"

Orchestra of Treacheries

because the elves did not teach humans about the *Dao* does not mean it's useless."

Kaiya's eyes shifted between doctor and elf. The barbs they stabbed into each other sure *sounded* mirthful, but who knew? Xu seemed affable enough, but he was still a high lord and could order Doctor Wu's execution for her impudence.

"But she is a busy girl," Xu said, "and I would think her time would be better spent fusing magic into her music."

"What is magic, but a link to the energy of Mother Earth?" Doctor Wu's tone sounded like a verbal jab to the elf's ribs.

Xu scoffed.

The doctor flashed a playful grin. "A wager then, my Lord. Show us something you think is beyond our princess' musical abilities, and if she cannot replicate it, I will give you one herb from my collection of rare tonics. But if she does, you will acquiesce to one of my requests."

Both their eyes turned to her, all but forgotten until now. The argument over her training had been mundane enough until this challenge. How could she possibly compare to the powerful Lord Xu? "But Master, my skills are trifling com—"

Doctor Wu silenced her with a hand. "You recently held an entire audience enthralled by your *guzheng* zither performance. What is the connection between performer and audience, if not a manifestation of energy?"

Kaiya shook her head. "You should not gamble on something beyond my small abilities."

The old woman winked. "Lord Xu will be kind with his challenge, and I won't ask for something like a Starburst when you win."

"A Starburst?" Kaiya gaped incredulously. Though if anyone had one of those mythical relics from when elves and orcs battled for supremacy over Tivara, it would be Xu.

Lord Xu laughed. "Shall I ask her to invoke another Hellstorm? Or the Wrath of Koralas?"

33

With a grandmotherly grin, Doctor Wu rubbed her hands together. "Lord Xu is having delusions of grandeur. Does he think he is the equal of Archangel Aralas?"

Kaiya's mind swam. Everyone else spoke in awe of the devastating magic that'd obliterated a mountain and ripped a new sea in the continent. Lord Xu referenced it with the same nonchalance as the as he'd flippantly mentioned the genocidal vengeance of the elvish sun god—magic that was never invoked during the War of Ancient Gods. Meanwhile, her teacher bandied about the name of the elf hero from that conflict as if he were a dear acquaintance.

Doctor Wu offered her a reassuring pat on the shoulder. "Easy, *Dian-xia*. This is just idle banter among old friends."

"Old friends, indeed." Lord Xu snickered. "As long as we understand the stakes, I will keep my challenge simple." He beckoned the imperial guards Chen Xin and Ma Jun, conveniently tucked away in the background. "You two, over here."

Neither so much as flinched, their attention set forward. Kaiya covered a laugh. "If that is all, then it is quite easy. Chen Xin, Ma Jun, please come."

The two guards dropped onto a one-knee bow, fist to the ground. "As the princess commands," they shouted. They stood up and marched over in unison.

Chen Xin eyed Xu. "Do you wish us to remove the lord?"

Unsurprisingly, Lord Xu ignored the threat and sang in the musical words of elf magic. The melody might have been a chorus of angels, and her heart soared.

At the end of the five-second chant, Chen Xin and Ma Jun both started sniffling. Blinking, their lips twitched in a futile attempt to contain emotion. Within seconds, both sobbed uncontrollably.

Lord Xu turned toward the doctor with a smug expression. "Can your breathing exercises accomplish something like that?"

"*Dian-xia*," Doctor Wu said, "make them stop. Use your flute."

Tan waved a hand. "I jest, of course. We have come a long way together. I just feel sorry that Princess Kaiya is so… particular. I do not envy your duty of finding a suitor for her."

"It is my honor. Again, I apologize about tonight."

Tan clapped him on the back. "Always responsible. That is why I have always supported you. Well, I have another meeting to attend. Perhaps another time?"

"Yes, sometime soon." Hong watched as Tan strolled back through the garden. He owed his title to the Chief Minister's patronage over the years.

After five years of waiting and watching, he had the unenviable task of repaying kindness with betrayal. With all conditions aligned, Hong just needed Tan to start a cascade of events which would leave the Chief Minister position vacant.

Once Hong claimed the highest office a commoner could achieve, he might even dare to ask the *Tianzi* for Princess Kaiya's hand. When their future son ascended to *Tianzi*, a fishmonger's son could rule as regent.

Heavily cloaked to hide his identity, *Tai-Ming* lord Peng Kai-Long jaunted through the Guanshan Temple grounds with a confident gait. A particularly cold winter now gave way to unseasonable warmth, and his fur-lined coat was stifling. As if to punctuate the heat and the early start of spring, *tianhua* flowers burst free from the confines of their dark green sepals, carpeting the garden borders in cloying white fragrance.

It was the perfect setting for the exotic young woman there. Her features bore a slight roundness, unlike the more angular lines of typical Cathayi women. She wore an inner gown resembling the gray luminescence of the White Moon Renyue; and above that, an outer robe with long hanging sleeves. Its sapphire color was reminiscent of the Blue Moon Guanyin's Eye, accentuating her cinnamon skin—the union of the honey-toned Cathayi and the walnut colored Ayuri people.

She knelt on a cushion by a knee-high marble table, across from Minister Hong Jianbin's repugnant form. The servile old man sat, gnarled hands on knobby knees, as he contemplated a chess board. Sallow cheeks hung on a face which might have resembled a weasel had it not been so wrinkled. Wisps of white hair clung to his mottled scalp. Hong easily appeared two decades older than his fifty-some years. His presence sullied all the beauty of the meticulously landscaped garden.

Kai-Long lowered his hood and leveled his eyes at the repulsive man. "Minister Hong, I have come in secret at your request."

Hong turned on his porcelain garden seat and bent his aged frame low. The beauty placed her hands in her lap and lowered her head, revealing the smooth curve of her nape.

Kai-Long's attention lingered on her before a quick glance at the chessboard. A sad imitation of Cathay's own chess, the Northerner's game was the latest fad gripping the aristocracy. He'd taken little interest—foreign barbarians had nothing to offer Cathay's great empire, beyond land to occupy and resources to control.

His focus settled on the old man. "Rise."

Hong creaked out of his bow and met Kai-Long's stare. He ran his hand through his thin white hair. "Lord Peng, I am honored you came. I trust you are enjoying this wondrous late winter evening?"

Peng Kai-Long had not become the youngest provincial ruler in their wealthy nation by wasting time on idle talk. He withdrew a metal-rimmed monocle with curved grills running through one half of it, and held it up toward the Iridescent Moon Caiyue, floating inexorably in its reliable position to the south. "A new timepiece, dwarven make. The convex glass magnifies the image to accurately measure a fifth of a phase of Caiyue. I grant you five minutes of audience and suggest you not waste it on useless pleasantries."

Hong bowed again. "Forgive my disregard for your valuable time, my Lord. I understand why your fellow *Tai-Ming* respect you so. How long has it been now since you inherited Nanling Province?"

A better question would be, *when would the fawning stop*? Kai-Long fidgeted with his sword hilt. "It has been two years since the Madurans ambushed my father and brother on the docks of Jiangkou."

Of course, no one left alive knew his arrangements with the late rebel, Lord Tong: in exchange for convincing the *Tianzi* to give Kaiya to the lord as a bride, Tong would had the Water Snake Black Fists kill his father and brother. Everyone still believed it was the Madurans.

The exotic woman cast her gaze down, shoulders trembling.

Hong shook his head sympathetically. "Forgive Leina. She is from Ankira, her Ayuri mother left behind and slain when her Cathayi father fled the Maduran invasion."

"Then we are kindred spirits." Kai-Long leaned over and lifted the beauty's chin. Rude in polite circles, for sure, but he was a high lord, and she was just some half-breed bastard. In the corner of his eye, he saw Hong's obsequious smile slip into a frown for a split-second. "With the *Tianzi*'s permission, I hope to one day lead my armies to liberate Ankira and avenge my father and your mother."

Hong spoke, his flattery knowing no limits. "You are the *Tianzi's* favorite nephew, the son of his beloved sister, and the most accomplished of the *Tai-Ming*. But even if the *Tianzi* tolerates your disregard for centuries' old laws, I do not believe he would condone open conflict with Madura."

Flatterers, like rats, tickle first, then bite, or so the old proverb claimed. Kai-Long continued with his demonization of Madura, his regular strategy for hiding his true goals. "We cannot stand idly by and continue to repel Madura's incursions against us without retribution."

Hong shook his head. "But you will not change the mind of the *Tianzi*. His thirty years of rule have been marked by policies of free trade and non-aggression, leading to unprecedented peace and prosperity."

Kai-Long stifled a snort. Hong would hum to the tune of whoever was singing. These little men all wanted something, and sometimes it took the right song to draw it out.

"Everyone," Kai-Long said, "from the *Tianzi* and the *Tai-Ming* lords down to the commoners has grown fat on trade and gold, secure with our guns and the Great Wall. We have fallen into complacency. Cathay stagnates while the Teleri in the North and Levastya in the South build their empires. It will only be a matter of time before one or the other appears on our doorstep."

Hong nodded repeatedly. "The Royalists on the council are too strong, convincing the *Tianzi* his policies are right."

Kai-Long regarded the minister, thinking back to his meeting with Chief Minister Tan two years before. Hong was Tan's toady, who in turn was secretly invested in the Expansionist faction.

It this interview was a test, it was time for a patriotic monologue: "We are the only naval power in the West, and through trade, we have brought all of the best ideas to Cathay and made them better. We have improved upon the repeating crossbows of the Eldaeri in the east. We forge steel as strong and sharp as the dwarves. We grow bumper crops on otherwise barren mountainsides."

Leina scowled. "And you monopolize the secret of firepowder."

"There is nothing keeping us back from expansion," Hong said.

Kai-Long ignored the venom in Leina's words, and instead feigned excitement as he held Hong's gaze. "Yes! Old Hong, for the longest time, I had believed you to be just another one of the sycophants currying the *Tianzi*'s favor."

Hong bent over. "I have only the best interests of the motherland at heart."

All it took to get a nightingale to sing was a little seed. Kai-Long decided to reveal some of what he knew. "So these secret meetings with the *Tai-Ming* Lords you have been holding... are

Orchestra of Treacheries

they meant to garner support to petition the *Tianzi*?" He raised an eyebrow. "Tell me, how do we change the mind of my dear, but stubborn uncle?"

Minister Hong lowered his voice to a whisper. "To paraphrase the Five Classics, sometimes it is harder to change the mind of a *Tianzi* than to change a *Tianzi* altogether."

There it was, the offer clearly stated. Or a trap.

Kai-Long placed a hand on his sword, just in case it was the latter. "What are you suggesting? It sounds like treason."

Hong shook his head, his eyes wide and defensive. "Patriotism. You would make a stronger *Tianzi* than either of his sons."

Kai-Long suppressed a smirk. He'd spent plenty of time in his youth with cousins Kai-Guo and Kai-Wu, and agreed with the minister's assessment. Though the two princes were undoubtedly intelligent, the elder suffered from indecision and the younger displayed little interest in national affairs.

Kaiya was the proverbial mystery egg. The ugly duckling had transformed into a swan.

Kai-Long couldn't allow her to become a phoenix. He'd manipulated her fragile emotions with forged letters from a man she'd only met once; but with her imminent betrothal it was time to take more drastic measures. It might very well tie into what Minister Hong tacitly proposed. He shook his head, pretending to need convincing. "I do not aspire to such a lofty position."

Hong sunk to his knees again. "You are the only one of the *Tai-Ming* to have met an enemy in battle, and in just two short years, you have diversified the economy of your historically modest province. We need a man like you, a man of vision like the Founder. Somebody who can guide our country by marrying our technological innovation with our cultural refinement."

Kai-Long laughed to himself. The old man's words echoed his own self-evaluation. "Hypothetically speaking, if I were *Tianzi*, what would you be?"

The corners of Hong's lips almost connected to the crinkles around his eyes. "Hypothetically speaking, I would be Chief

Minister." After a pause, he added, "And I would also like the hand of Princess Kaiya. Hypothetically speaking, of course."

Kai-Long inwardly cringed, trying not to envision the decrepit old man bedding Cousin Kaiya, whose beauty was said to come along once every three generations. "You have obviously already expended a lot of thought on the hypothetical. I wonder if you have a plan in place?"

Minister Hong lowered his gaze and spoke. The meticulous details, including steps starting five years before, plans within plans and conspiracies hijacking others' plots— it was all impressive. It worried him, even, because the old man somehow knew bits of Kai-Long's own scheme. He concluded their talk with a newfound respect for Hong, and assurances that he would play his part.

Smiling to himself, he could guess the eventual, untold outcome of Hong's plot. As someone who'd engineered the demise of his own father and brother, Kai-Long had a nose for treachery. Nonetheless, the first part of the plan was a good one; it just needed a few changes toward the end to make sure *he* sat on the Dragon Throne and Lord Hong was left hanging.

After a quick glance at the chessboard, Kai-Long surmised the treacherous minister would never recognize his own peril. After all, Leina was disguising her inevitable victory in a losing position.

Leina watched as the young *Tai-Ming* lord disappeared down the path. She turned her attention back to the chessboard. With a trembling hand, she moved her Knight into danger, faking a careless attack on Hong's king. "Check."

"Ha!" Hong Jianbin pounced on her diversion, capturing her knight with a pawn.

It opened a path in his line, and she slid her queen through. She clapped her hands together with a delighted squeal. "Checkmate!"

Jianbin's mouth gaped, his wrinkled brow furrowing even more. With eyes darting from her to the board, he used his crooked finger to trace the sequence of moves that led from an apparent victory to sudden defeat.

While he shook his head in disbelief, she thought back to their discussion before the clandestine meeting with Peng. Jianbin had prattled on about Cathay's incomparable resources and ingenuity, eldarwood trees and the need for a great leader.

To her, it was a soulless nation without morals. Their sale of guns and firepower to Madura had led to the occupation of her homeland. If the *Tianzi* ruled with the Mandate of Heaven, then the gods must have a sick sense of humor.

Leina had spared herself the boring history lesson by prompting the old man along, ignoring his biased conclusions. The Wang Dynasty's history, as told by men, always extolled the genius of its founder. Wang Xinchang had invented the gun and taken advantage of the chaos following the Hellstorm and Long Winter to pacify All Under Heaven. Little did the historians talk of his consort, who set Cathay on the road to prosperity during her eighty-year rule as regent after his death.

Now after observing Peng Kai-Long's interaction with Hong, she wondered. Was he indeed the caliber of leader Hong believed? To her, he was just another man who spent too much time admiring his own reflection.

Hong still contemplated the board. Just like in chess, he missed the glaring flaw in his plan to seize power: it relied on a stupid opponent.

"You are right," she said. "Lord Peng is a dynamic man. But would you really allow him to become *Tianzi*?"

Old Jianbin looked up and laughed. "Dear Leina, you may be good at the Northerner's version of chess, but you do not have an eye for real strategy."

"Of course not, dear Jian." Leina hated having to feign stupidity and affection for the wretched old man. It was nearly as bad as being his lover. "Then why do you need him at all?"

Jianbin favored her with the same patronizing smile which she always pretended not to notice. "Because he has what I do not. Youth, handsomeness, charisma, and more importantly, the right bloodline," Hong virtually spat the word. "He is the figurehead who can rally our allies. He also has a motive to murder the *Tianzi* and his sons, and will be the perfect scapegoat after the firework show."

Leina crinkled her nose. Lord Peng had surely seen through Jianbin's plan, but that was something the old minister need not know. Because if she manipulated the situation correctly, both men would be dead, and the nation thrown into chaos. She only hoped that once she'd fulfilled that task, her employer would keep his promise and free her mother.

CHAPTER 5:
Change of Heart

Kaiya usually found the absolute silence in the Hall of Reflection's inner sanctum almost as unsettling as the countless crisscross coffering on the walls, floors, ceiling, and door. Acoustically, it was the exact opposite of the Hall of Pure Melody, the Yin to its Yang.

Yet now, even after the whimsical sensation from Xiulan's calligraphy had worn off, even with Father's ultimatum to choose a husband, even inside the otherwise unnerving chamber, Hardeep's latest letter sent her heart skittering to the same frequency as his lotus jewel in her sash.

Cousin Kai-Long's messenger stood outside the building, rarely used among the nine thousand nine hundred and ninety-nine rooms on the palace grounds. Her cousin had been generous in facilitating the clandestine written exchange, and it wouldn't do to let his personal courier wait so long.

Setting the letter down, she took up a brush and jotted a hasty response. How excited Hardeep would look when he read it, that broad smile beaming, those blue eyes sparkling. She scanned the page, searching for any mistakes.

Perfect.

She stood and poked her head out the door with the note in hand, heedless of her own mischievous grin.

The smile melted.

Second Brother Kai-Wu, Yanli's husband, plucked the letter out of her hand. Behind him, a minister bowed. Several imperial guards, including her own Chen Xin and Li Wei, along with Peng's messenger, all knelt on one knee. The Hall of Reflection's sound-absorbing qualities had masked their approach, even from her keen ears.

Kaiya reached to take the letter back, but Second Brother thrust it behind his back.

His eyes narrowed. "What is this?"

"Nothing important. Just a message to Cousin Peng." As always, she'd written Kai-Long's name on the cover sheet, so it wasn't exactly a lie.

To her dismay, Second Brother unwrapped the cover and unfolded the letter. His gaze raked over the text, his brow furrowing. "You are writing to Peng in Ayuri?"

Kaiya tried to snatch the letter again, but Second Brother passed it back to the minister. She clenched her jaw. Hopefully, the minister could not read the foreign script.

Oh, no. The official's shifting eyes widened. He looked up at her before dropping his chin. "*Dian-xia*. It is a, uh… note… to whom, I do not know, but the message is… well…"

Kaiya's heart lurched in her chest as she clenched and unclenched her clammy hands. Her year-old secret, carefully concealed from all but Lord Peng, exposed.

Second Brother stared at the minister, who withered under her brother's glower. "Speak."

"*Dian-xia*. It is a love letter."

Kai-Wu's mouth dropped open. He turned to the imperial guards. "Take Peng's courier into custody. Find Lord Peng and command him to present himself before me at once."

"As the prince commands!" The imperial guards snapped to attention before hurrying to fulfill his order.

Second Brother took Kaiya's arm and pulled her back into the hall's inner sanctum. He closed the doors behind him and leveled his glare. After several long minutes, he spoke, the chamber rendering his voice oddly flat. "Is this why you have rejected so many suitors? For some secret affair? I pray to the Heavens you have not given yourself to a man."

Kaiya's cheeks flushed hot. Did he just… as if… "No… no, of course not."

"So you are not having an inappropriate liaison with the messenger?" Brother Kai-Wu asked.

The messenger? Her breath caught in her throat. "No. Of course not," she repeated.

Searching her eyes, Kai-Wu exhaled sharply. "Very well. A rumor circulates among the palace servants that you have been secretly meeting with one of Lord Peng's men whenever he visits the capital. If not him, then who is it?"

Kaiya sighed. There was no use in hiding it. They would find out soon enough. "Prince Hardeep."

Brow furrowing, Kai-Wu cocked his head. "Who is he?"

"The Prince of Ankira."

"Ankira? Aren't they in a war or something?"

Kaiya nodded. "Occupied. Prince Hardeep leads their resistance."

"So, a foreigner. This is most inappropriate."

It was true. Yet up to now, the suitors all saw her either as a stepping stone to greater power and influence or, since her blossoming into a woman, an object to possess.

Only Prince Hardeep had ever *seen* her, starting from their fated meeting two years ago and growing through their furtive correspondence. None could match his wit or charm. She pressed the lotus jewel in her sash, feeling its steadfast warmth against her waist.

A slot in the door opened and a voice called in. *"Dian-xia.* Lord Peng is here."

Second Brother's brow furrowed. "You are to end this relationship. We will find you someone appropriate." He then pushed the door open. "All of you, enter."

Lord Peng strode in with a confident gait, followed by the imperial guards, the minister, and the messenger. All sank to one knee.

"You may face me." Though the otherwise aloof Kai-Wu rarely used it, his voice carried the tone of command bred into the Imperial Family. When all looked up, he raised the letter. "Lord Peng, explain this."

Peng bowed. "*Dian-xia.* I have long been in contact with Ankira's Prince Hardeep, since his embattled nation shares a border with my province. I send the Ankiran resistance supplies. I have passed messages between the foreign prince and princess for a year now."

"You did not deem it inappropriate?"

Kaiya started to speak, but Second Brother held up a silencing hand.

"They could be writing about anything," Peng said. "It is not my place to judge the Imperial Family."

Of course Cousin Peng would sacrifice her to protect himself. What had she expected? Kaiya bit her lip. She was by herself in this.

Second Brother's voice rose just a little. "Lord Peng, you will cease your intermediation between Princess Kaiya and the foreign prince."

Peng lowered his head again. "As the prince commands."

"The rest of you: you will not relate what occurred here today. The *Tianzi* must never find out. Am I understood?"

All of the assembled men bowed and spoke in unison. "As the prince commands."

A wave of relief washed over Kaiya. At the very least, Father wouldn't have to worry about her exposed secret.

Second Brother gestured the men out of the room. "Shut the door and wait outside."

The men rose and shuffled out.

When the door closed behind them, Kaiya spoke. "Thank you, Second Brother."

"You are lucky Eldest Brother did not find out about it. He has a good heart, but he lacks discretion as much as you."

Kaiya bowed her head, contrite.

"Now, forget about this Prince Hardeep. There are many great lords in this land who will make fine husbands. In fact, I have someone in mind."

Hardeep's lotus jewel's near inaudible buzz seemed to intensify as Kaiya held it over the bloodwood box. It hadn't left her person in the two years since their parting, even when she slept or bathed.

Her heart squeezed. She couldn't do it. She couldn't put the jewel away. It felt too much like giving up on Hardeep.

No, giving up on *herself*.

When everyone had scoffed at her music, he'd been the only one to believe in her potential.

She'd proven herself. She'd grown in power with Lord Xu and Dr. Wu's lessons. As much as she wanted Hardeep, her music was her own. Putting the jewel away wasn't giving up.

She picked up a smooth river pebble, the one Zheng Tian had given her years ago. Its cool surface felt reassuring.

Settling in Dr. Wu's horse stance, Kaiya gripped her bedroom's wood floors with her toes. She took a deep breath. The cool night air filled her lungs. Outside, birds chirped and frogs trilled. The symphony of spring calmed her thoughts and eased the dragonclaw on her heart.

Prince Hardeep had encouraged and inspired her, but now it was time to sing with her own voice. She would free Ankira, not because she loved Hardeep, but because it was the right thing to do.

She had thirty days.

Kaiya waited until the light breeze off Sun-Moon Lake subsided, then loosed the arrow. The man-shaped straw target standing thirty feet downrange had nothing to fear. Indeed, it seemed to be enjoying the view of melting snow caps reflected in the lake's placid surface on this unseasonably balmy afternoon.

She sighed as the arrow missed by the worst margin in years. Her hand strayed to Hardeep's lotus jewel.

Gone.

Right. It hadn't been easy leaving it on her make-up table four days ago, after Second Brother uncovered the relationship. Each morning it beckoned her, sending her heart racing and palms sweating. She needed Dr. Wu's breathing techniques to resist its tug on her heart. She now plodded back to the communal quiver, head tilted down to avoid the gazes of her four friends.

Crown Princess Xiulan looked back as her shot brushed over the target's armored shoulder. "Thinking about your meeting with Lord Shun yesterday?"

Kaiya shuddered. "He was boring." And not a fraction as amazing as Hardeep.

"But he *is* handsome." Her cousin, Wang Kai-Hua, stroked her fingers through an arrow's fletching. The glow of her recent marriage to Young Lord Liu, the heir to Jiangzhou Province, had yet to wear off. She seemed even more radiant these days. It was good to see her happy, at last, after two years of family misfortunes.

"Oh, Lord Shun is delicious," squealed her other cousin, Lin Ziqiu. The naïve sixteen-year-old stood beside Kaiya, her eyes wide. "I could watch him all day and not grow bored."

All the other ladies covered laughs with their sleeves, hiding their amusement at the girl's youthful bluntness. Yanli glowered at her, though Ziqiu didn't seem to notice.

"There's more to a man than his looks," Kaiya said. "He could not hold a conversation beyond one-word answers."

Xiulan giggled. "A handsome face can sometimes be ruined by too much talking. That's why the Crown Prince and I rarely discuss anything of deep import."

Ziqiu loosed an arrow, which joined her others in the target's head with a dull thud. "That's because you talk with your hips."

Yanli scowled and poked Ziqiu. Sleeves flashed up again, this time covering laughs *and* blushes. If Xiulan's cheeks could burn any brighter, it might seem like a recurrence of the Year of the Second Sun from antiquity.

A smile tugged at Kaiya's lips, though she fought it off. With her chambers next to Eldest Brother's, there was no arguing with Cousin Ziqiu's assessment.

"If you want someone who talks," Ziqiu prattled on, "then maybe you should consider my cousin Lin Ziqiang. He never shuts his mouth! I know my father has been discussing it with the *Tianzi*."

A rumble of galloping hooves interrupted the girl's blabbering.

Kaiya spun around.

A soldier in dark green court robes bent down from his warhorse and pulled a few arrows from the communal quiver as he cantered by. His glossy black locks whipped behind him. Was that the scent of *shouwu* berries? Like most ladies, she used them herself to maintain healthy hair.

All eyes followed the newcomer as he put two shafts between his teeth, fitted an arrow, twisted back and shot.

The arrow lodged dead center in the target's head.

Kaiya turned back to the rider, just in time to see him shoot again.

It hit the target in the center of its chest, driving through the leather cuirass.

The man wheeled around and spurred his horse back toward them. He floated the last arrow upwards. She tracked its lazy arc into the target's neck.

The horse slowed as it approached and the rider swung out of the saddle. His large eyes briefly met hers before veering toward the ground as etiquette demanded. Who was he? There was something familiar about him.

It might've been easier to remember without Ziqiu's tight clutch squeezing the sensation out of her arm. The girl pressed up against her shoulder. "Who is that?" she whispered, breathless.

The archer strode over, his posture straight. His beautiful hair, which rivaled her own, obscured the family crest on his left breast.

A dozen imperial guards, who undoubtedly appreciated his showmanship more than the princesses' mediocre archery, now interposed themselves with hands on swords.

A deep voice from the opposite direction drew her attention away from the visitor. "The *Tianzi*! The Crown Prince and Second Prince!"

Father and both brothers, all wearing official blue riding robes, approached on horseback. Dozens of imperial guards trailed them, their burnished breastplates flashing in the late afternoon sun as they jogged in exacting formation. At their head, iImperial guard commander General Zheng held the Broken Sword, a symbol of the *Tianzi*.

Father hadn't ridden a horse in years. Nor did he ever come to this section of the palace grounds, generally limiting his visits to the Hall of Supreme Harmony. If not for affairs of state, he would've sequestered himself across the moat in the castle. Now, he slouched in the saddle, wheezing.

In unison, the princesses smoothed their practice robes down to their shins and dropped to both knees. Spreading their arms out horizontally to straighten out the sleeves, they placed open hands at the front of their knees and bowed their heads at the approach of the *Tianzi*.

"Rise," he said.

Kaiya looked up.

Orchestra of Treacheries

Age hadn't treated Father kindly. Whenever she saw his many care lines, wispy white hair, lusterless eyes, and listless gait, a lump formed in her throat. Kaiya knew well the other culprit.

His thirty-two-year reign had been marked by unprecedented prosperity for Cathay, spurred by his benevolent wisdom and policy of expanded foreign trade. In recent years, some of the *Tai-Ming* lords had let their newfound affluence transform into avarice, and the *Tai-Ming* Council had become increasingly divided by the lords who wanted to expand the national borders and those who were content to maintain the status quo.

Expansionists versus Royalists. The final arbiter and decision maker, the *Tianzi* had been physically and mentally drained by the contentious situation. After the death of Kaiya's mother two years earlier, he'd declined rapidly.

As the *Tianzi's* gaze brushed over them, his burdens seemed to melt away. He nodded at each, his eyes speaking of fatherly admiration. His voice wheezed. "My daughters, it looks like it will be a beautiful evening with both the White and Blue Moons looming large in the sky tonight. I would be pleased if you would join me in the *Danhua* Room for dinner, so I can enjoy myself before next week's council meeting."

It wasn't a request, and Kaiya and the others bowed again in acquiescence. As senior, Xiulan answered for everyone. "We would be honored to join you, Father."

"Rise." The *Tianzi* motioned toward the horseman, who shifted from a kneel to a one-knee, one-fist salute. "This is Captain Zheng Ming, the heir to Dongmen Province. He is visiting the capital from the northern border to defend his archery title at the New Year's Tournament. Rise, Young Lord Zheng."

Zheng. Zheng Ming was the eldest brother of her childhood playmate, Tian. They had met once, ten years before, while she and Tian practiced swordsmanship together.

He stood and now met Kaiya's gaze again. His complexion hinted at time spent in the sun. Strong, chiseled features rivaled

General Lu's handsomeness, though he stood a head taller. It probably made him even more of a narcissist.

A sweep of Zheng Ming's head sent his hair over his shoulders with a whiff of the *shouwu* scent again. He almost purred when he spoke. "Princesses, it is my honor to meet you."

The five ladies nodded in acknowledgement, though young Ziqiu followed a split-second late, and her face flushed. She batted her lashes at him.

Ziqiu's reaction might be amusing, but Kaiya forced herself not to roll her eyes. The lordling was just the latest among the dozens of handsome lords and generals she'd met over the last two years, with nothing beyond a title and a pretty face to distinguish them. None could compare with Hardeep.

"Young Lord Zheng came to visit Kai-Wu," the *Tianzi* said. "When I heard you were all practicing archery, I commanded him to come share his expertise with you."

Zheng Ming bowed. "*Huang-Shang*, I hope my poor skills can meet your expectations."

The *Tianzi* let out a shallow, breathy laugh. "Your bow has defended the realm against Lord Tong's rebellion and the Kingdom of Rotuvi's incursions. You have earned numerous distinctions. I have no doubt my daughters will benefit from your guidance."

Such praise, as if it would impress her. Kaiya nodded with the others nonetheless.

"Now, I have other matters to attend to." The *Tianzi* turned his horse around.

All bowed low and held the position until the sound of his horse and marching imperial guards faded.

Xiulan smiled, exchanging knowing glances with the others. "Well, I must freshen up before we dine." She motioned for her imperial guards.

Zheng Ming bowed. "Perhaps I will have the honor to speak with you another time, Crown Princess."

"I, too, must be getting ready." Yanli winked at Xiulan and beckoned her guards. She glared at Ziqiu, who had missed the tacit message and still gazed at the dashing cavalry officer.

"And I, too, must be returning to my own residence," added Kai-Hua. "And so should you," she growled lightly at Ziqiu. "You should be getting back to your father's villa before dusk. A lady should not be out after dark, lest she be mistaken for a common streetwalker."

Zheng Ming laughed, a warm laugh. "What a shame. I am always surrounded by soldiers and yes-men, and never by so many beautiful ladies."

Ziqiu's brows furrowed, an annoyed look falling across her pretty face. Her attention still lingered on the handsome soldier. "I am certain the page will call me when my guards arrive."

Xiulan took Ziqiu's hand. "You can wait in the main courtyard. I will accompany you."

Frowning, Ziqiu offered a reluctant bob of her head. The dancing colors of a dozen vibrant handmaiden robes departed like spring blossoms blown from the trees.

After a few minutes, Kaiya was alone with Young Lord Zheng, save for the imperial guards Chen Xin and Li Wei.

Such a blatant set-up. Zheng Ming was probably the lord Brother Kai-Wu wanted to introduce, with Xiulan and the others complicit in the *chance* meeting.

With no time for her to prepare.

In all of the previous appointments with potential suitors, Kaiya had worn the finest silken gowns like armor to protect her from the choreographed farce. Now, training robes and wits were her only weapons against this new opponent. She bowed her head, deferring to the man as convention dictated, waiting for him to speak.

His lips curved upward like the stroke of a calligrapher's brush, sweeping away the awkwardness of the situation. "You may not remember, but we have met before, when you were still a child of seven."

"I do remember, though not clearly."

He nodded. "You shared the same swordmaster as my younger brother Tian. You were fencing with him at the time. And beat him, if my memory serves me well."

"It does." She smiled at the mention of Tian's name and the fond recollection. "He was a dear friend… until that unfortunate misunderstanding. I have not heard from him since he was sent to the monastery. I trust he is doing well?"

"I have only spoken to him once in the last several years. My mother tells me he is a trade official, serving at our embassy in the Nothori Kingdoms."

She covered her laugh with a hand. "Fancy that, a monk becoming a diplomat. But enough about Zheng Tian. I am sure my father did not bring you here for us to reminisce about your brother."

Zheng Ming grinned. "Nor to teach you the finer points of archery, I presume."

Kaiya tilted her head, placing a hand on her chest in mock indignation. "Do you presume to know the mind of the Son of Heaven?"

He pressed his hands over his own chest in exaggerated contrition. "I know the mind of a father with unwed daughters."

She raised an eyebrow. "So you are an expert at this type of meeting?"

"If rumor is to be believed, the princess is much more experienced than I in such matters." Zheng Ming stared at the sky.

Heat rose to Kaiya's cheeks. She lowered her head to hide her blushing. "Rumors proliferate like spring blossoms after a storm."

"Unfortunately, for every blossom there are a dozen weeds."

Kaiya maintained a demure smile, stalling. The weeds *had* to refer to all the lousy suitors. Right? *She* was the one who usually had *them* on their toes.

This blossom, however… he spoke like a poet, reminding her of Prince Hardeep's written words. Yet whereas the prince's script simmered for months between new letters, Zheng Ming's wit had a fulfilling immediacy to it. She tilted her chin toward her guards. "The imperial gardeners carry sharp shears."

Zheng Ming ran his hand back and forth over the side of his neck. "I empathize with the palace weeds, then."

The palace bell tolled, and both looked up to see the Iridescent Moon waxing toward half. The nine-star constellation of E-Long, the evil dragon, seemed to wrap around it.

Kaiya lowered her hand. Heavens, she was playing with a lock of loose hair.

"I am afraid I must depart. I dine with the *Tianzi* tonight. It seems like we will have to cut our discussion of landscaping short."

Zheng Ming lowered his gaze, peering up through half-lidded eyes. "I would not be averse to continuing our debate over the merits of flowers and weeds at some other time."

Up to now, no suitor had survived her questioning, let alone asked to meet again. Kaiya's heart skittered a few beats. For the past two years, she'd held on to an idealized memory of her meeting with Prince Hardeep. Zheng Ming was here and now, and her belly's summersaults felt real. She looked up at him through her lashes. "I would not be averse to considering it."

His grin slipped for a split second, but returned, brighter than before. "I might be inclined to wait here for a more definite answer."

Kaiya smiled coyly, lifting her chin toward the imperial guards. "Do I have to summon the gardeners?"

Zheng Ming dropped to one knee and brushed his hair to the side to expose his neck. "You decide."

CHAPTER 6:
Seeds of Insurrection

After picking out the distinct breathing patterns of fourteen different men, Liang Yu flung open the sliding doors to the private room. Now at middle age, his eyes adjusted slowly from the bright lights of the Phoenix Spring Inn's common area to the candlelit interior room.

Even before the thirteen dark shapes at the knee-high table came into focus, he already smelled the mix of sweat and weapon oil. He was greeted by the rasping of five broadswords, two straightswords, and four knives from their sheaths, as well as the cocking of two repeating crossbows.

Liang Yu admired their enthusiasm. Once upon a time, he would have gone to any end to impress his master. But when he was presumed killed on a mission thirty-two years before, had his master even cared?

He reassured the rugged men with a secret hand signal. All bowed in response, rustling their dark clothes as they returned to their knees. Without looking back, he slid the door to an exact, silent close with a quick sweep of his walking stick.

"Thank you for coming. Make yourselves comfortable." Liang Yu surveyed the former Cathayi soldiers as they shifted from their knees to sitting cross-legged. With their experience in the army and later as mercenaries, their skillsets were suited to the upcoming task. He shifted his attention to the one man, the disowned son of a minister, who had remained calm as he entered. "Little Song, why didn't you reach for your weapon when I entered?"

Song bowed. "I heard you outside the door."

"You knew it was me?"

"Yes, from the walking stick on the floorboards."

Liang Yu nodded. The young man had shown potential when they'd first met two years ago, where the late Lord Peng and his heir had been murdered on the docks of Jiangkou. He'd sharpened his skills under Liang Yu's tutelage. "Very observant. And a cool head is a sign of discipline. You will lead the attack."

Song shifted up to a one knee, keeping his gaze lowered. "I am honored."

Straightening his black robes, Liang Yu sat cross-legged at the head of the table. He passed out several sheets of folded rice paper. Each bore the sketch of a handsome young man, with words written in the Ayuri script.

As the men unfolded the paper, he leaned over the table and spread out his crudely-drawn map of the capital. It did not do justice to Huajing's precise gridded layout, designed by Feng Shui masters at the behest of the Queen Regent three hundred years ago to ensure national prosperity.

Liang Yu indicated the Phoenix Spring Inn on the map, in the northwest near the city's walls. "We are here."

He then tapped his finger on a narrow bridge nearby, which arched over a stream. Houses with first-floor shops lined the street near the bridge—bustling during the day, but almost everyone would be retiring or already asleep when they attacked. "Our target is Captain Zheng Ming, the heir to Dongmen Province. He will be passing over this bridge on his way back from a meeting with Minister Hong Jianbin. My sources say he has two guards with him."

One man grinned. "This should be easy if he only has two guards."

Song shook his head. "Don't underestimate him. He is an excellent, battle-tested archer."

Liang Yu nodded. "We can't let him past this bridge." He pointed out several landmarks near the bridge, assigning hiding spots for each of his men. He then traced a line of approach that would flush Lord Zheng into an alleyway where Liang Yu himself would be waiting.

The men smiled, heads bobbing at each point. Of course they were impressed; his planning skills had once earned him the nickname the Architect. At his side, Song's gaze shifted over the map, undoubtedly drinking in the details. Sharp mind, that kid. Maybe as observant as the other pupil Liang Yu had recruited at about the same time, two years earlier.

"Young Lord Zheng must not be killed," Liang Yu said. "I leave the guards to your discretion, though we should avoid unnecessary bloodshed of our own countrymen. Regroup here after the mission."

All the men bowed again. They stood and departed.

Liang Yu relaxed and called to the proprietress for some rice wine. In two hours, it would be time to incite a war.

Zheng Ming studied Minister Hong Jianbin and decided a monkey would look more dignified wearing blue official robes. Nonetheless, he bowed to the knobby-kneed minister as protocol demanded. The old man struggled to his feet and tottered across the receiving room's dark wood floors.

Ming sighed, his mind swimming with Hong's requests. The minister had revealed Peng Kai-Long's plans to take punitive actions against the Kingdom of Madura. Without significant pressure and resources from the *Tai-Ming* lords, the *Tianzi* would never approve. Hong wanted Ming to convince his father to switch sides to the Expansionists.

Ming should've never come to Huajing for the New Year Tournament. Unlike past years, court intrigue was eating up all the time meant for carousing with the more sophisticated and promiscuous women of the capital.

It was too much of a headache. Perhaps he could still withdraw from the tournament and return to his cavalry unit in Wailian. With the possibility of dying in combat looming over each day, *they* knew how to have fun.

Emerging from the secluded official pavilion, he looked up to the south at the Iridescent Moon Caiyue, never moving from the same position in the sky. It now waxed to its fourth gibbous, just two bells before midnight.

Much too late to be discussing politics, but perhaps not too late to pay a visit to one of the ladies he'd captivated with his charm.

He walked out into the courtyard, now bathed in the pale blue light of Guanyin's Eye. It struck an odd hue with the dark green court robes on his two waiting guards. Both had sheathed swords tucked in silver sashes. One bowed and presented Ming's cavalry saber, the other his bow and quiver.

Ming glanced back to the pavilion.

He could almost hear Minister Hong's joints creak and pop from the way he bent into a plain wooden palanquin. A dozen guards surrounded it— quite a lot for the capital, and overkill for the always safe nobles' quarter.

Blowing out a long breath, he motioned for his men to mount up and set out for the ride back to the Dongmen provincial villa.

He rode with little focus, his mind wandering over the meeting and Hong's appeals. The obsequious toad lacked ambition, so someone must be pulling his strings.

The old man did, however, have a level of influence as Minister of Household Relations. In return for Ming's support, Hong had promised the hand of Princess Kaiya.

Ming chuckled. The princess had rejected over two dozen fine suitors. Though beloved by the general populace, she'd acquired the nickname *Ice Princess* among the young noblemen. Theories abounded, with rumors ranging from a secret liaison with a servant, to her desire to dally with ladies rather than marry a lord.

As much as Ming might enjoy his defenses being flanked by a coordinated onslaught from Princess Kaiya and another beauty, he doubted the validity of *that* rumor. No, if anything, she probably still harbored feelings for his youngest brother Tian, the black sheep of the family. The two had shared some foolish romance as children.

He snorted. Regardless of her reasons, it had become a virtual rite of passage for the young lords, to be offered up as fodder for the Ice Princess. One friend alluded to his meeting with her as akin to a torturer's interrogation. Another compared it with going into battle; never mind that the closest he'd come to a battlefield was the first Wang Emperor's treatise on the Art of War.

With that in mind, Ming had taken his own meeting with the princess a few days before as mere formality. He played her game, with the expectation of adding the most interesting story of rejection to the rumor mill.

Now, Hong suggested he could not only arrange a second meeting, but almost guarantee a betrothal. As the obsequious toad insinuated, marriage to the *Tianzi*'s daughter would place his own future son somewhere in line to inherit the Dragon Throne of Cathay.

Ming laughed out loud. Not that the rules of succession mattered to him. More interesting was the challenge of melting the heart of the Ice Princess. She would—

The horse in front of him screamed. The guard tumbled from the saddle as it collapsed.

A crossbow bolt protruded from the flailing horse's neck. The beast lay squirming, obstructing his path forward off the bridge... bridge? When had he reached it? He reined back his own mount, only to find the rear guard struggling with his own horse.

"Back off the bridge!" he bellowed, as if it would make his retainer move faster.

The rhythmic clicks of repeating crossbows echoed from nearby buildings. Bolts lodged into his guard's horse in quick succession. Both collapsed. Several men swarmed toward the bridge from both sides, brandishing broadswords.

His mount panicked, its head thrashing about as it looked for a means of escape. If only he'd ridden his own reliable warhorse instead of a skittish palfrey borrowed from the villa. Another bolt whistled by, missing his face by a ridiculously safe margin.

"The watch," he yelled, "Call the watch!" Trying to control his lurching horse, Ming unslung his bow. Though the court robes restricted mobility, he nocked an arrow and let it fly. It hit its mark, dropping one of the men. He loosed a second arrow, but the pitching of his horse sent it flying errant.

Unfazed, Ming took aim at one of the four assailants hacking at his lead guard, who was pinned under his horse. If not for his panicky mount, Ming might've targeted the man's eye. Instead, he shot the arrow into his center of mass, knocking him to the ground from point-blank range.

As he withdrew another arrow, he glanced around. Lights flickered and shutters opened as the commotion drew the attention of curious citizens.

Ming drew his string for another shot. The palfrey reared. The arrow slipped from his fingers as he swiped for the reins. A bolt hit his mount's flank, just barely missing his own leg. Another lodged into the beast's skull.

The horse tumbled. Ming leaped from the saddle to avoid getting crushed, and landed hard on his side. He rolled out of the way of flailing hooves.

Sword raised, an attacker bore down. Ming rolled, then staggered to his feet. Though more accustomed to fighting from horseback, he swept his blade out with a smooth rasp, cutting into the assailant before the man could start his chop.

The narrowness of the bridge trapped Ming, but also slowed the advance of his foes. In front, two tried to skirt by his sprawling horse. He glanced back to see his rear guard injured, but standing his ground. The four attackers held back, goading the guard to pursue them off the bridge.

Another several bolts thwacked into the bridge, and then abruptly stopped. These had to be the worst crossbowmen ever.

An assailant in the front clambered over Ming's dead horse. Before the man found his footing on the other side, Ming cleaved him shoulder to chest with a two-handed cut. He yanked the saber free.

Click, click, click. The crossbows resumed their barrage, persuading him to kneel beneath the cover of the guardrails.

His guard's harried voice rasped, "We are surrounded, *Xiao-ye*. Jump off the bridge and escape."

The ambushers held back, affording Ming a momentary respite. He shuddered at the potential blow to his reputation. Stories of his brave death would live on forever. Soldiers would raise their cups to him, and women might dream of him while they lay with their men. On the other hand, abandoning his guards for a midnight swim would brand him a coward well past a quiet death at old age. What woman would have him?

The ones attracted to wealth and power. Ming's family had plenty of both. He gritted his teeth. Time to throw himself over the bri—

"The watch, the watch, fall back!" The villains scattered, leaving their dead and wounded behind.

Ming caught his breath. He'd survived unscathed. Both he and his reputation would live on. A quick survey of the scene revealed his lead guard lying dead among four foes. At the rear, one attacker had perished, and another crawled away. His surviving guard fought to remain standing as blood spurted from a gash to his leg. Ming loped over and knelt. Tearing a strip of cloth from the man's robe, he bound the wound.

"*Xiao-ye.*" A commoner bowed low before him. "Allow me to help."

Ming looked around. Townsfolk emerged from their homes, with several racing over and others calling for help.

He rose and strode over to the survivor. "Who sent you? Why did you attack me?"

The man stayed silent, feebly lifting his sword in defiance.

Credit the man for courage. Ming might do the same, even if he ultimately planned on surrender. "I am asking politely, but I am sure the *Tianzi* has many a good man who can get an answer out of you with much less courtesy."

Too late did he recognize the man's look of resolve—that of a soldier facing certain death. Ming thrust his saber forward to interpose it between the man's sword and neck. It arrived a fraction late, as the man jerked the blade across his own throat.

"Smart Son of a Turtle," Ming said. Better to die quickly now than slowly and painfully.

Rifling through the man's possessions, he found some silver coins stamped with a scorpion and crown, and a crumpled sheet of paper with a very accurate drawing of himself.

Not bad at all! Making sure no one was watching, he stashed it into his robe. Although he couldn't read the foreign script, he recognized it as Ayuri, the language of the South.

Of the countries in the South, only the Madurans would engineer such a brazen attack. As much as he would have liked to believe they had targeted him for his value as a leader, he assumed there must be another reason.

Perhaps they knew of Minister Hong's efforts to start a war against them.

Liang Yu strolled through deserted streets back to the Phoenix Spring Inn. People stuck heads out of windows as patrols of the watch scurried toward the scene of the attack. He kept to the shadows, secure in his stealth.

The plan had worked as intended. Without adversity, he could never effectively evaluate the mettle of his recruits. Those that escaped would emerge stronger for their troubles. Some of them might be worthy of further training. Little Song had survived, saved from Young Lord Zheng's aim by his careful angle of approach. He might make a fine lieutenant, to go along with his special pupil.

Too bad neither of the two would ever begin to compare to his former brothers and sisters-in-arms of the Black Lotus Clan. Nonetheless, his men were skilled enough for the scare tactics he planned to orchestrate over the next several days. The attacks on the nation's ruling class would implicate the Kingdom of Madura. Fearing for their pitiful lives, they would be clamoring for a punitive invasion.

No doubt the *Tianzi* would mobilize Liang Yu's former comrades first, before rushing to war. If the Black Lotus knew he was alive, the mindless pawns he once called friends would label him a traitor.

He saw himself as a patriot.

Sometimes, a patriot had to sow seeds of insurrection, lest the nation succumb to its own complacency.

And if pressure from the nobility couldn't sway the *Tianzi* to act, perhaps the assassination of the beloved princess would.

CHAPTER 7:
Dragon in the Room

Kaiya listened to the warbling songbirds in the adjoining garden. If only she could be out there, instead of stuck in the stifling council of hereditary lords. Unlike daily administrative functions held across the moat in the Hall of Supreme Harmony, this quarterly meeting convened in Sun-Moon Castle.

As the residence of the *Tianzi* and his family, the castle was Kaiya's retreat from official responsibilities. Now, the *Tai-Ming* and *Yu-Ming* lords invaded her refuge. Her ancestor had established the tradition, before his consort and later Queen Regent commissioned construction of the surrounding palace grounds.

The only woman to attend these meetings since the Queen Regent, Kaiya's too-conspicuous place next to her brothers invited the only slightly less conspicuous glances of the three dozen great lords facing her. Dressed in court robes, they sat cross-legged in a three-row semicircle, some peeking at the curves she'd lacked just a year ago.

She tightened her outer robe over her bust. Unlike the Queen Regent, or the *Tianzi*, she couldn't order a lord to take his own life with the curved dagger resting on the floor in front of him. By the time the Queen Regent died at the unprecedented age of one hundred and twenty-four, her figure might not have attracted many leers, anyway.

The sliding doors of the Celestial Flower Room stood open to the garden, taunting Kaiya with a cool spring breeze off Sun-Moon Lake. To be out there…

The *Tianzi* cleared his throat. He slouched on a bloodwood chair encrusted with jade fish and mother-of-pearl bats. His yellow silk robe, embroidered with symbols of health and prosperity, sagged from his gaunt form. A long necklace of jade ornaments hung from his neck, and a square black hat with dangling jade beads adorned his head. His voice rasped when he spoke. "What is next on the agenda, Minister Fen?"

Throughout the morning, the minister had avoided the topic on everyone's mind: the recent ambushes in the capital. He now bowed from his place at the end of the first row, where the nine *Tai-Ming* lords sat. "*Huang-Shang*, we are receiving an envoy from the Eldaeri Kingdom of Tarkoth. The Foreign Ministry has vetted their request."

Kaiya perked up and looked to the interior doors, curious to catch a glance of the visitor. Though human, the Eldaeri had escaped to a distant continent and mingled with elves five millennia ago. With ships rivaling Cathay's, they had returned to Tivaralan in the chaotic aftermath of the Hellstorm and occupied much of the Northeast. Tarkoth maintained a trade office in Huajing, and usually conducted businesses through lower ministries. The only time a Tarkothi of consequence had visited in Kaiya's lifetime was two years ago, when their prince attended Second Brother Kai-Wu's wedding. Kaiya had missed that on account of the rebellion at Wailian Castle.

Murmurs broke out among the great lords. They apparently didn't share her enthusiasm for the guest.

Father silenced them with a raise of his eyebrow. "I will receive Tarkoth's emissary. Send them in."

The doors to an antechamber slid open. Foreign Minister Song strode in and bowed low. He spoke in perfect Arkothi, the common language of the North. "I present Lady Ayana Strongbow, representative of the Eldaeri Kingdom of Tarkoth."

Strongbow? A strange name for the Arkothi-speaking Eldaeri. To get a better view, Kaiya shifted as much as decorum would allow. The lords turned craned to face the antechamber.

A slender old woman with sharp features and pointed ears glided in.

An elf? They rarely left their secluded realms. Lord Xu was the only one Kaiya had ever seen. The lords all whispered among themselves in wonder.

The emissary floated across the room in a light blue gown and diaphanous green shawl. Her dull gold tresses and fair complexion stood out among the black-haired, honey-skinned Cathayi. A corded rope of silver hung around her waist, and a matching silver anklet graced a bare foot. A twinge of jealousy pricked at Kaiya. How could someone so old still be so ethereal and beautiful?

With delicate grace, Lady Ayana curtseyed in the manner of the North. "Greetings, Your Imperial Highness. Thank you for receiving me." Her voice sang like a nightingale as she spoke lilting Arkothi.

The *Tianzi* answered, his own Arkothi heavily accented. "Greetings, Lady Ayana. How is it that an elf comes to represent the human Kingdom of Tarkoth?"

"Your Majesty, I am in the employ of Prince Aelward Corivar of Tarkoth, captain of the Tarkothi Royal Ship *Invincible*. The prince sent me because I can travel much faster than anyone else aboard his ship, which is currently anchored in the port city of Sodorol."

The elf's voice carried a resonance, similar to… the conspicuously absent Lord Xu. Perhaps she could pop in and out of places, just like him. While the lords murmured about how she'd gotten here, Kaiya fought the urge to speak out of line.

Foreign Minister Song bowed and presented a parchment envelope. "The Tarkothi trade mission presented Lady Ayana to the ministry yesterday. The wax seal on her missive matches our records."

Ayana nodded. "May I present Prince Aelward's request?"

The *Tianzi* waved for her to continue.

"The *Invincible* will be provisioning at your port of Jiangkou in about two weeks, and Prince Aelward requests an audience with the Emperor." She gestured toward the *Tianzi*. Kaiya clenched her jaw at the impudence.

He leveled his gaze at the elf. "It will be close to the New Year Festival, and your prince is welcome to join the other dignitaries that will celebrate in Cathay at that time. I cannot promise I will have time to meet with him."

Ayana took a step forward. "Prince Aelward wishes to discuss an alliance. Tarkoth's nemesis, the Teleri Empire, is allied with your enemy, the Kingdom of Madura. The prince will be conducting raids and supplying insurgents in Madura. He hopes we might coordinate our efforts against our mutual foes."

Murmurs broke out among the lords. All eyes turned toward Father. Kaiya sucked in a breath. The Expansionists would jump at the opportunity. If only they had been so enthusiastic two years ago, when Prince Hardeep needed it.

Kaiya's stomach... did nothing. Once upon a time, just thinking about Hardeep sent it into flutters. And she hadn't even thought about him for the last few days. Had the charming and heroic Zheng Ming so quickly replaced Hardeep in her heart? And here she was, daydreaming while the lords discussed sending men to kill and die.

The *Tianzi* raised his hand and the room fell into silence. "Lady Ayana, I was not aware that Madura was our enemy. Cathay's position for the last three hundred years is one of neutrality. Tell your prince we do not take sides, and we trade with all. We only resort to arms when attacked."

Cousin Kai-Long rose from his seated position to one knee. "*Huang-Shang*," he said in the Cathayi tongue, "Madura has created troubles at your borders for years, even while we sold them firepowder. They slip raiding parties in, circumventing the Great Wall and ignoring your law. Certainly it would be wise to join forces with the Tarkothi and squelch this threat."

Orchestra of Treacheries

Lord Liang of Yutou Province and Lord Lin of Linshan Province both rose into one-knee salutes. "*Huang-Shang*, we agree with Lord Peng."

Chief Minister Tan scowled. "Order! Sit."

Cousin Kai-Long continued undaunted in Cathayi. "My armies in Nanling stand ready to descend from the Wall. We could liberate the Maduran-occupied Kingdom of Ankira in two weeks, especially if Madura's troops are diverted to the south by the prince's ship."

Ankira, Prince Hardeep's homeland. Kaiya's hand strayed to the lotus jewel's place in her sash. Left on her make-up table. Forgotten. Yet no matter what her feelings for him, his people still suffered because of Cathay's past trade agreement with Madura.

"And what of the Golden Scorpions, Little Peng?" boomed Lord Han of Fenggu. At sixty-five, he was Father's brother-in-law and a staunch Royalist. "As castoffs and traitors to the Ayuri Paladins, they are a formidable army."

"Not even a Paladin can dodge a bullet," Chief Minister Tan said from his place at the other end of the first row.

"Fool," Lord Han muttered under his breath, though loud enough for everyone to hear it.

Kaiya bit her lip. Lord Han was a grandfatherly figure who spoke his mind, oftentimes forsaking etiquette. She looked toward Chief Minister Tan, whose face burned red, marred by a nasty frown.

Zheng Ming's father, Lord Zheng Han, rose to one knee. "We must not spread our own armies too thin. The Kingdom of Rotuvi also threatens us, especially Wailian County outside of the Wall."

Kaiya shifted uneasily. Her role at Wailian Castle two years ago was the only reason she was in this council. Rotuvi's armies had forced General Lu to hold his position, robbing him of glory.

Lord Liang scoffed. "We have guns."

With an emphatic nod, Lord Lin said, "We can free occupied Ankira and bring them the prosperity we enjoy."

Kaiya twirled a lock of hair. Hardeep had prophesized that she would liberate Ankira with a Dragon Song. The Expansionists proposed military might, at the cost of blood and gold. And ultimately, the Ankirans would trade one occupier for another.

Crown Princess Xiulan's father, Lord Zhao, wagged a finger at the Expansionist lords. "You will exploit their resources as the Madurans do. We know that is your goal, coming from such a poor province."

Lord Lin rose to his feet, and many others followed suit. General Zheng edged forward to the *Tianzi's* side, the Broken Sword in hand. The rest of the imperial guards closed in, hands on their swords.

Such disorder in the *Tianzi's* presence was unheard of. A quick glance at Father revealed his face flushing red. Kaiya prodded Kai-Wu, hoping he'd intervene, only to find him dozing off. On the other side of the *Tianzi*, Kai-Guo wrung his hands as his head swept back and forth over the unprecedented commotion.

If only she'd been born a boy. Her brothers, both kind and doting, provided no leadership. It only increased the burden on Father, who now aged before her eyes. If neither spoke…

The tension in the room sounded like a thick taut chord, vibrating in a slow bass, drawing in anger from all the men. Altering that could change the tone of the room.

"My Lords," Kaiya sang, , modulating her words to unwind the underlying tension.

All eyes turned to her, wide with wonderment. Lady Ayana cocked her head and narrowed her eyes.

Kaiya pressed her forehead to the floor in a show of apology, though also to conceal her fatigue from using magic. Mentally framing her rebuke innocuously so as not to make it seem like an accusation, she straightened. "My Lords, forgive me for breaking protocol and speaking out of line."

The men stared at their feet. One by one, they settled back onto their cushions.

Kaiya switched to Arkothi so Lady Ayana could understand. "The prince of Tarkoth has asked to meet the *Tianzi*. The Classic of Rites expects the ruler to provide hospitality for foreign nobility. The *Tianzi* has two weeks to decide whether or not he wishes to grant an audience. After that, he has more time to decide—with your wise counsel—how he will approach Tarkoth's campaign against Madura."

Chief Minister Tan nodded. "Princess Kaiya speaks with wisdom beyond her years. Might I suggest we defer our decision to meet until the *Invincible's* arrival in Jiangkou?"

The *Tianzi* coughed before speaking in a wheeze. "Sound advice, Chief Minister. Lady Ayana, return to your prince and inform him of our disposition."

"Thank you for considering our request, Your Highness." Lady Ayana curtseyed again. Then, she met Kaiya's gaze and bowed her head. "Farewell, Dragon Singer.".

Kaiya's chest swelled, even as the lords murmured among themselves.

Once she'd drifted out of the room, the *Tianzi* cleared his throat. "We will adjourn for the day and conclude the council meeting tomorrow morning."

Kaiya searched his eyes. Hopefully, Father was only rebuking the lords for their outburst, and not exhausted by the commotion.

"*Huang-Shang*," Lord Peng said, "what of the attacks in the capital?"

The *Tianzi* pushed himself out of his chair and to his feet. "Tomorrow, Little Peng."

All in the room bowed low, holding their position until the *Tianzi* left with his imperial guards.

Minister Hong Jianbin kept his attention on the floor along with the rest of the councilors, until the princes and Princess

Kaiya departed. His back protested when he straightened. Around him, the Royalists and Expansionists stood and gathered in clusters.

Hong pushed himself to his feet and took a step toward the garden where he had requested to meet the princess. Over the last few days, he had worked to gain her trust, running her little errands and gathering information about the council members' political leanings. Now he had some news to share.

"Minister Hong," came a familiar voice behind him.

Hong turned around. Lord Peng Kai-Long stood alone by a window, beckoning him. After a quick glance toward the garden, Hong tottered over.

Lord Peng leaned in. "See how easily the princess diffused the tension? She may only be a girl, but she could disrupt our plans."

"Maybe. In order to get what we want, we must find a way to temporarily remove her from the picture. I may have a way, though it might take a couple of weeks to arrange."

Lord Peng rubbed his chin, his face a study in stoicism. "Well then, I won't keep you." He turned and joined the Expansionists Lin and Liang.

Peng was hiding something. Clenching and unclenching his fists, Hong headed toward the garden.

He found the princess waiting under a budding pear tree, with two imperial guards hovering nearby. He creaked into a low bow. "*Dian-xia*, I have found out what you requested."

The princess glanced back at her guards and then drew closer. His muscles locked up as she leaned in and whispered, "Please tell."

The heat of her closeness sent his heart lurching. She was beautiful and enchanting, forcing Hong to remind himself to see her as a mere tool. "Young Lord Zheng Ming is quite famous for his wit and charm. He has enticed many a young lady into his bed. And he has been particularly busy since his arrival in the capital a week ago."

A half-truth, but one which the princess believed, if the curling of her full lips into a frown was any indication. After a second, she spoke, her voice hitching. "Thank you, Minister Hong. You may be excused."

Hong bent as low as his body allowed, hiding his grin by staring at her feet. "As the princess commands."

He looked up after he heard her robes rustling away, deeper into the garden. Each time the princess had met an eligible bachelor, Hong worried she might agree to wed. Up to now, he had nothing to be concerned about.

Young Lord Zheng was the only suitor the princess had ever shown any interest in, and he seemed to be doing his best to disqualify himself.

This afternoon, Hong would make sure to remove Zheng Ming from the picture altogether.

Peng Kai-Long stewed in his palanquin as he rode back toward his compound. Like the other great lords, he now travelled with an escort of three dozen guards, even if he knew he was safe. Façades had to be maintained. Nonetheless, their noisy boots rattled his concentration.

Minister Hong apparently had a plan to remove Princess Kaiya from the picture temporarily, but Kai-long preferred a more permanent solution. Now that she'd moved on from Prince Hardeep, she was beyond his control.

He slid open the window and called for his aide-de-camp. "Little Yi. Initiate Operation Scorpion."

The Ayuri thugs whose services he retained through several layers of intermediaries would finally earn their keep. With them, and the disaffected insurgents he anonymously funded, he could use suspicions of Madura to get rid of Princess Kaiya *and* guarantee war.

He just had to lure dear Cousin Kaiya out of Sun-Moon Palace.

CHAPTER 8:
Second Chances

The last time Zheng Ming crossed a bridge accompanied by two guards, he had ridden unawares into an ambush. This time, staring at the arched stone bridge between the Sun-Moon Palace grounds and the *Tianzi*'s castle, he *knew* he was walking into an ambush, albeit one of a different kind.

He looked up to the sloping, tiled eaves of the fortress across the moat. It loomed seven stories above him, standing in silent vigil over the capital and surrounding plains. With tiers and vaulting eaves, its triangular shape stood out from the rest of the imperial compound's standard block buildings of white plaster walls and blue tile roofs. If the rest of the palace suggested organized elegance, the central bailey boasted military might.

In the late morning, Minister Hong had sent him an urgent message. The old man had called in several favors and arranged a formal invitation to meet Princess Kaiya. Up to now, no suitor had ever been invited back for a second visit with the Ice Princess.

With a deep breath, Ming smoothed his formal robes and donned his battle face. His two guards followed as he strode across the bridge.

A palace valet, flanked by eight imperial guards, waited on the other side. The valet bent at the waist. "Welcome to Sun-Moon Castle, Young Lord Zheng. Your guards must wait here. Please allow me to care for your sword."

Ming bowed his head and offered his sheathed *dao* to the valet.

The man bent at the waist and received the weapon in two hands. "Follow me. Princess Kaiya awaits."

Narrow paths between steep walls wound clockwise and upwards toward the central bailey. Arrow slits, murder holes, and battlements gave defenders an insurmountable advantage. Even if an invading army made it through the palace grounds, assaulting the castle would result in devastating casualties. Proof of the Founder's genius. Though in these times of peace, it was little more than a relic from the turmoil following the Hellstorm and Long Winter.

At last, without even entering the main keep itself, he came to one of the gardens and emerged onto a veranda. The mottled trunk of a weeping *danhua* tree curved up thirty feet, its willowy branches cascading downwards in strands of red blooms. Almond blossom bushes formed a circle around the tree, their own pink flowers pooling at their bases. A fragrant scent wafted through the air, borne by petals drifting on the early spring breeze.

The blossoms seemed to slow their descent, as if listening to the bright and rapidly varying notes fluttering from the *pipa* nestled in Princess Kaiya's lap. Similar in appearance to the lute played in the North, it was a hollow, pear-shaped wooden instrument with ridged frets along its neck and upper body.

Her long fingers swam swiftly across its four silken strings. Some sounds roared like a pouring rain, others whispered as the sweet secrets passed between lovers. Sitting at the edge of an ornate bloodwood chair, surrounded by three handmaidens and two imperial guards, the princess appeared lost in her music. She wore a light blue inner dress under a dark blue outer gown with hanging sleeves. With her eyes closed and an angelic expression, she appeared oblivious to his arrival.

Mesmerized by the sound and snowing blooms, Ming's steps faltered. A cool calm washed over him as he drew near. The perfect curve of her lightly rouged lips edged upward into a dainty smile, like a benevolent spirit.

He'd conquered many women in the past with his looks and charms, including several since his near brush with death on the bridge; but in that instant, he regretted his past, and swore to make himself a better man, worthy of her.

After a moment, he woke from the whimsical reverie. The emotion of the music changed. Unease and uncertainty crept over him.

As she neared the end of her song, Kaiya noted the change in the *pipa*'s sound. It wrapped around a newcomer on the veranda, whose own breath fell in step with her rhythm. With the fleeting bond between performer and audience established, she smiled.

Kaiya looked up through a half-lidded eye. Young Lord Zheng Ming stood on the veranda. What was he doing here, uninvited? Her throat tightened and the music's power slipped from her fingers.

A couple of days before, she'd felt an instant attraction, like none other since Prince Hardeep. Perhaps it'd been the full White Moon Renyue clouding her judgment. With that in mind, she'd sent Minister Hong to find more about him.

His reports of Ming's philandering should've come as no surprise. All strapping young lords engaged in such behavior. Why was it so… disappointing?

Minister Hong's confirmation of these reports only strengthened her resolve. She wouldn't be just another conquest, no matter how handsome and charming he might be.

Nevertheless, there was no reason to be uncivil.

No sooner did Kaiya finish her song than Zheng Ming dropped to his right knee, right fist to the ground. "*Dian-xia*, thank you for sharing your practice with me."

With a nod, she allowed him out of his bow and beckoned him over. She passed the *pipa* to the handmaidens, and then motioned them to withdraw to the veranda. "Thank you for listening, Young Lord Zheng."

He strode over, withdrawing a kerchief from the fold of his robe. He held it at her forehead. "May I?"

Audacious. Charming. Her stomach fluttered. At her nod, the imperial guards relaxed. Zheng Ming dabbed her skin.

Heat stirred within her. "I… you are first to hear me play this piece, *Eye of the Storm*. Can you offer me any critique?"

He pressed the kerchief into her hand. "Unfortunately, I am just a simple soldier, and I have no technical skill in music, and—"

"Surely you have some artistic talent? The Five Classics implore the gentleman to be skilled in both the sword and the arts."

"I consider myself a decent poet, though you did not give me an opportunity to show off last time we met." He grinned.

Intrigued, she flashed a smile. "Here is your chance. Tell me what is on your mind."

He dropped to his knee again. "As the princess commands." He looked up, his eyes sparkling with mischief. "But I implore you not to be too critical!"

Kaiya caught herself playing with a loose lock of hair and abruptly dropped her hand. She covered a laugh, which sounded too flirtatious to her ears. "I am no more a poetry expert than you are a music critic."

Zheng Ming took a deep breath and his gaze swept over the garden. He then spoke:

"Storm clouds gather on the horizon,
Dark shades of fear and pain.
Travelers lost without direction
Pelted by unforgiving rain.

A melody hums through somber shade

A shining beacon to guide their way
The path ahead opens to sheltered glade
Beckoning back those led astray."

Heat warmed her cheeks. He must be alluding to her and the state of the nation. "Is that poetry or politics? You must have heard what transpired in the council this morning."

"*Dian-xia*, you said you would not be a critic!" His lips drooped into a facetious pout, sending a swarm of butterflies fluttering in her stomach. "You *did* command me to say what was on my mind."

"It weighs heavily on the minds of all the hereditary lords and ministers." And poor Father. Kaiya sighed. "And on the *Tianzi*'s as well."

He plucked a flower and tucked it behind her ear, sending a shiver up her spine. "We stand at a crossroads, facing uncertainty for the first time in the three hundred years of Wang family rule. The intrigue of internal politics has intersected with the machinations of foreign powers. It is a shame that the *Tai-Ming* have sunk to infighting and scheming instead of rising to ensure stability."

"I believe all the *Tai-Ming* have the realm's best interests at heart," she said. "Unfortunately, they do not agree on whose policies will ensure future prosperity."

"As long as the Wang family controls Huayuan Province, the *Tai-Ming* will have no choice but to obey the decisions of the *Tianzi*."

Kaiya stopped fiddling with her hair. "I wonder." The audacity of the lords during the council meeting suggested otherwise.

He nodded emphatically. "It is quite simple, really. With the exception of Huayuan, all of the other provinces are economically interdependent. None could survive on their own."

Kaiya's lips pursed. Cousin Kai-Long's domain had broken conventions. Nanling province could sustain itself. Luckily, none could question his loyalty.

"Furthermore, since Huayuan has half the number of soldiers as all of the other provinces combined, it would take most of the *Tai-Ming* allying against the *Tianzi* in order to pose a military challenge. And the *Tai-Ming* can only meet together in the presence of a council minister. This is how your illustrious ancestor Wang Xinchang established stability in the realm. The political climate may be unsettled, but we are far, far away from a tipping point."

She looked up at him through her lashes. "I did not think a simple soldier could have such deep thoughts."

"Even a carp dreams of becoming a dragon." Zheng Ming's lips twitched.

"Perhaps that is why you were targeted the other night. I am glad you managed to fight off your attackers."

He raised an eyebrow. "Because if something happened to me, you would have one less person to discuss politics with?"

Her belly buzzed like a dragonfly's wings. Why did he have to be so witty? He would be so much easier to dislike if he were stupid. She placed a hand on her chest and tried to imitate his sarcastic tone. "No, because you are a key witness, and we need to uncover who is behind all of these recent attacks. The capital is on edge."

Zheng Ming flashed a disarming smile. "Well then, based on the evidence gathered by the watch, those who attacked me the other day were financed by the Ayuri Kingdom of Madura." Doubt weighed in his voice.

Madura occupied Hardeep's Ankira, as well. "But you do not believe that is the case."

"No. There was too much evidence, and no motive for the Madurans to attack me. I suspect there is something more insidious. I had just met with Minister Hong Jianbin, who wanted my father to support the Expansionists. Then I was ambushed. It leads me to believe the Royalists tried to silence me."

She leveled her gaze at him. "So where do you stand, Young Lord Zheng? Royalist or Expansionist?"

His eyes widened in mock surprise. "So direct! Usually, my peers try to coax me into revealing my affiliations with wine and sweet words."

She found herself playing with her hair *again*. Bad girl! Kaiya straightened, lifting her chin. "I am the princess, and command you to speak." Despite her order, her own lips quivered as she fought to suppress a grin. "Where do you stand?"

Zheng Ming bowed his head. "I stand on the Great East Gate of the Wall in my home province, and look out on the vast untamed lands of the Kanin Plateau. Its pristine beauty, so unlike the manmade splendor of this palace, seems to be a metaphor for our debate. To expand into it means to tame and bring order; but that in itself will destroy what makes it beautiful."

"Spoken like a politician!" She caught herself exposing the side of her neck with a tilt of her head. "I want a straight answer, Simple Soldier."

His lips quirked up. "The Wall protects our land borders, our dominant navy defends our shores from a sea invasion. I see no need to expand as long as the people are content. Enlarging our borders beyond the Wall means stretching resources thin to protect them, as I can tell you firsthand from my experience in Wailian County. So you can say I am an anti-Expansionist though not necessarily a Royalist."

"Is that supposed to be a straight answer?"

He laughed. "Had I known we would be discussing politics, I would have come better prepared. I was led to believe that we would share poetry and tea." He gestured toward a gazebo overlooking the lake. "Shall we?"

Led to believe? He wasn't supposed to be there at all. Still, poetry and tea in the gazebo sounded appealing. She looked up at the Iridescent Moon. Hopefully, time constraints would give her an excuse to get away from him before she forgot all about his reputation and succumbed to his charm. "Alas, I am afraid I must beg off your invitation. Lord Peng invited me to watch a shower of shooting stars from his pavilion tonight. I do hope the skies clear."

"All of the great hereditary lords and their families will be there," Zheng Ming said. "Perhaps I will see you."

Her jittering stomach leaped into her chest, and words slipped out in spite of her better judgment. "Then maybe you would ride with me? An escort of three dozen imperial guards will surely offer better protection in these unsettled times."

"I would be honored. I shall meet you at the moat in two hours."

Kaiya clapped her hands together. "I look forward to it. It will be my first time leaving the palace grounds since all the chaos started."

CHAPTER 9:
AUDACITY

The nearly-full White Moon Renyue hung low in the early evening sky, lighting Liang Yu's path to *Jianguo* Shrine. To think, a shrine dedicated to national peace was where he received instructions that undermined the *Tianzi's* authority.

Such paradoxes didn't matter to a patriot. Cathay had grown complacent and weak. As the Founder once said, *the gourd that rots within is easily smashed from the outside.* The Expansionists must prevail, lest foreign powers enslave the motherland.

As Liang Yu walked, he took mental note of the changes since his last visit: Fewer birds now nested in the plum trees. The scent wafting from the shrine spoke of cheap incense. The white pebbles' scatter pattern suggested the groundskeeper had been distracted when raking the path. Had he skimped on incense quality, pocketing silver to afford a gift? A new lover, perhaps?

This ability to notice a thousand details and draw connections between them resulted from years of rigorous training at the Black Lotus Monastery. Though famed for churning out scribes and accountants, the temple really trained the mythical Black Fist warriors who, according to frustrated mothers, would kidnap disobedient children in the middle of the night.

In reality, they were the *Tianzi's* fiercely loyal spies, whose skills in stealth and swordsmanship bordered on the impossible. One of the three most talented Black Fists in his youth, Liang Yu had been betrayed and left for dead during an operation in the Ayuri City-State of Vyara thirty-two years before.

He'd returned to Cathay five years ago as an importer, under an assumed name. It turned out spying skills translated well to business, and Cathay's aggressive trade policies didn't hurt either. Yet it also exposed him to the dark underside of immoral mercantilism: the bribes, corruption, and greed that would drag the country into decline.

Now forty-nine, Liang Yu pondered these things, all the while assessing potential danger along his route. Nothing amiss. He continued until he reached the grove of plum blossom trees that surrounded the temple grounds. The flowers had passed peak, and now only a few stragglers desperately clung to limbs as they watched their fellow petals fluttering like warm spring snow. Hundreds of pieces of folded paper competed with the blossoms for space on the low branches, tied by those who hoped their written wish would come true.

He silently recited the one-hundred-twenty-third verse of *The Sword Saint and the Night Fox*, a five-hundred year old poem from the Yu Dynasty. Comparing it with a numbered code his anonymous employer had provided, he came to the correct tree and branch and looked for the specific type of paper his benefactor always wrote on. He retrieved the correct note and squirreled it in the folds of his robes, then set a brisk pace back to the Phoenix Spring Inn.

Liang Yu found the inn especially empty this night. With few prying ears, its location made for a perfect meeting place. That, and the attractive proprietress who sometimes shared her bed with him.

A glance around the common area revealed nothing suspicious. He continued on to the private room. Settling on one of the cushions arranged around the table, he unfolded the paper and read the first few words of the sloppy script.

The scare tactics have not done enough. It is time to make a louder statement with an assassination implicating Madura...

He continued reading. His employer was moving quickly, ready to take a bold step. An actual kill. Liang Yu pursed his lips. Not enough resources to make this brash move. Perhaps if he made the kill himself. The order gave meticulous time and location details.

Up to now, all of the missives had been unerringly accurate. Liang Yu, in whom suspicion was well-trained, often wondered how. By consideration of means and motives, he had already narrowed his employer's identity down to eight possibilities. He would find out soon enough.

In the meantime, he had an assassination to plan.

Hong Jianbin peeked out from his palanquin, baffled at Princess Kaiya's weak resolve. He had been certain she would order the imperial guards to expel the philandering Young Lord Zheng from the castle after his unannounced visit. Yet there she was, riding with the fop as the imperial procession made its way toward Lord Peng's pavilion.

Perhaps Peng had been right about women's lack of willpower. The princess went so far as to forgo the propriety and safety of a palanquin to ride by Zheng's side. Had her brothers been there, they would have ordered her to use it; but on this night before the full White Moon, they were most certainly busy in their futile attempt to conceive an heir.

The imperial guards had remonstrated her, citing the unsettled climate in the capital. Zheng Ming also insisted she ride in the palanquin. Even Hong protested, though more for show: he knew of every ambush, and the imperial family was never targeted. Nor were any of the attacks ever fatal to anyone save for a hapless guard or two.

His concerns, along with those of the imperial guards and Zheng Ming, had all fallen on deaf ears.

The princess disguised herself as one of the imperial phoenix riders in court robes. Her decoy, the beautiful handmaiden Han Meiling, rode in the imperial palanquin.

Hong could not help but admire the princess' courage, even if it bordered on recklessness. He slid his palanquin window shut and closed his eyes, thinking of his impending meeting with Royalist *Tai-Ming* Lord Liu in Lord Peng's renowned garden teahouse. He would pledge the princess to Lord Liu's second son in exchange for the Chief Minister position, just as he had promised her to Young Lord Zheng.

Zheng Ming. Just thinking the name brought a bitter taste to his mouth. If the princess still favored the young man even after hearing of his reputation, Hong would have to find another way to remove him from the picture. It was just a matter of timing.

A loud crack jolted Hong in his palanquin. He turned to see an arrow protruding from the wall, the head just inches from his nose.

The grim voice of General Zheng carried over the commotion of men and horses outside. "Ambush. Protect the princess."

Hong fought the rising panic and tried to concentrate. There was supposed to be an attack on Lord Han tonight, not here. This was never part of the plan, nor did it make logical sense. The only scenario he could imagine was the possibility of other disaffected partisans taking advantage of the political climate. That, or perhaps Lord Peng had decided to take things into his own hands.

No, it was still too early for Peng to make a move like this. If the princess were harmed—

A female scream rent the air.

Zheng Ming scanned the line of tiled rooftops where two dozen enemy archers bobbed up, sniping at them. He couldn't believe the audacity of an attack on an imperial procession, let alone the foolhardiness of engaging a contingent of a hundred imperial guards.

His cousin General Zheng remained calm, issuing orders. A column of imperial guards on either side of the procession knelt and loaded their muskets. Others snapped into a protective formation around the princess' palanquin. Her personal detail formed a line around her horse.

She made for an easy target.

She rode high above the rest of the procession, though the archers ignored her. The disguise? He admired her composure, even as her startled doe eyes darted from place to place. A hand strayed to the curved dagger in her sash.

Ming swung out of the saddle and placed himself between their two horses. He reached up to her. "*Dian-xia*, you are an inviting target. Please, come down."

Her gaze settled on his, recognition blooming in her face. She took his hands and slid from her horse. Ming grasped her shoulders. Her slight body trembled.

He gestured downward. "Stay low, between the horses."

Armed only with his own dagger, he pulled the *dao* from her sash. It wasn't much better, given the distance, and he silently lamented the ban on weapons near the Imperial Family. Were he allowed to carry his bow, he could give the assailants a reason to keep their heads down.

A barrage of gunfire rang out, followed by the cracking of wood and tile as musket balls struck them. The horses stirred and shuffled, nearly crushing him and the princess between them. Sulfur hung in the air.

The volley of arrows stopped, and the sound of men skittering across the rooftops faded in the distance.

"Wolf and Lion Companies, pursue the rebels," General Zheng said. "We are not far from Lord Peng's pavilion. The princess' detail, along with the Dragon, Tiger, and Phoenix Companies will escort her there. Captain Tu, run ahead to Lord Peng and order him to send a contingent of his guards to meet us. Commander Ling, take a horse back to the palace with word of this brazen attack, and assemble half of the imperial guards to come to Lord Peng's pavilion. The rest of you remain here, tend to the wounded, and gather evidence."

Ming turned to the princess. "Are you all right?"

Her wide, startled eyes met his. She straightened, her voice firm as she called out, "General Zheng, is Meiling unharmed?"

Ming could not help but gawk in admiration at the sudden transformation from frightened girl to imperial princess.

"Yes, *Dian-xia*," the gruff soldier replied. "Shaken, but uninjured."

"Then let us proceed to Lord Peng's pavilion."

Ming didn't like the idea of splitting their guard. He turned to General Zheng. "Cousin, what if this was merely a diversion, to thin our defenses and draw us into a more dangerous trap?"

General Zheng nodded. "Your concerns are noted. However, Lord Peng is close by and we will be much safer in his compound until the rest of the imperial guard arrives."

Ming only hoped Cousin Zheng was right.

Frogs croaked and trilled in the large pond of Lord Peng's Four Seasons Garden, oblivious to the dangers beyond the compound walls. Having survived an attempt on her life, Kaiya knelt in the teahouse, listening to the serene night sounds in hopes they would calm her rattled nerves.

She'd travelled the width and breadth of the empire, always greeted by an adoring citizenry. To her, the imperial guards were just a formality, a symbol of imperial splendor. Besides the single incident in Wailian two years ago, she'd never considered they might be actually called on to protect her.

Tonight, they had performed admirably, holding a tight protective formation as the procession marched to the Peng's estate. Cousin Kai-Long suggested she sequester herself in the safety of the main keep's inner sanctum; but at General Zheng's insistence, Cousin Kai-Long cancelled his appointment in the garden teahouse so the imperial guards could appropriate it.

Situated on a peninsula jutting into the pond, it was the most defensible position in the pavilion. Her senior-most guards, Chen Xin and Zhao Yue, stood inside by the door, while a dozen others kept watch over the narrow path.

Kaiya's frantic heart slowed as she took deep breaths and wiggled her toes in the slippers Cousin Kai-Long had provided. As her worries over safety faded, other concerning thoughts filled her mind.

Zheng Ming had seen her scared and trembling, the antithesis of imperial grace. She shuddered at the prospect of having to face him, now that he knew she was not a Perfect Princess.

Right now, he might very well be enjoying wine with Cousin Kai-Long—or worse, Kai-Long's pretty sisters—laughing at her expense.

She looked down to find her fists clenched tight around the kerchief he'd given her. She was holding her breath. With a sigh, she closed her eyes and reprimanded herself. Doctor Wu's *Cool Spring Rain* breathing technique quieted her mind.

By the door, Chen Xin's and Zhao Yue's breaths synchronized with each other.

Three other breathing patterns, slow and muffled, emanated from beneath the woven straw floor panels.

Her eyes fluttered open. "Chen, Zhao, intru—"

Two floor panels flung open. Three men emerged just beside her.

Clothed in long *kurta* shirts of the Ayuri South, they all wore expressionless metal masks with eye slits and a nose opening. Each brandished a guardless broadsword with a wide tip resembling a scorpion sting.

The mask, the sting. Madura's Golden Scorpions, the castoffs and deserters from the Paladin Order which defended the Ayuri South. They were banned from Hua, so she'd never seen a Scorpion with her own eyes, let alone been attacked by one.

She twisted to her feet and glided to the side, just as the heavy blade crashed down where she'd been sitting. Another sting whipped toward her neck.

With a technique from the *Dance of Swords*, her foot swept up as she bent back under the swing, and her toes connected with her assailant's chin. Yet the silken slippers Cousin Kai-Long insisted she wear provided little traction. Her planted foot slid out from beneath her.

The collapse to the mats knocked the air out of her. The third attacker raised his blade. Unarmed, fighting for air, there was nothing she could do. She closed her eyes. Tonight, a Scorpion's sting would cut her life short.

A loud clang rang out inches from her nose, followed by cloth tearing and a male scream. To the side, a *dao* whistled through the air and cut through muscle and bone. Two heavy swords and a body part thudded to the ground in quick succession. Someone shuffled across the floor toward the corner.

Kaiya opened her eyes. Chen Xin stood above her, his blade reflecting light from the lamp. One of the Scorpions leaned against the wall, clutching at his spilling intestines. Another lay headless at her side. Zhao Yue held his *dao* raised, ready to fall on the third Scorpion, who pressed his back to the wall.

At the entrance, her guards Xu Zhan and Li Wei rushed in. A third presence breezed in behind them, and Kaiya could hear its quiet breathing. Try as she might, she didn't see anyone else.

As Xu and Li interposed themselves between her and the remaining Scorpion, Chen and Zhao surged forward with a coordinated attack. The would-be assassin huddled down, his sting quivering in a feeble defense. Without a doubt, both of her guards' blades would find their mark.

Their *dao* clinked against metal without reaching the cowering man, though all she could see was a dark blur and a flash of short blades. A shadow darted across the Scorpion with a tearing rasp. The man yelped and his sword clunked to the floor.

"Keep him alive for questioning," the shadow chirped in a girlish voice. A familiar voice, but from where? The shape swept out the entrance before Kaiya could ascertain any other detail.

She picked herself up off the mats with as much grace as she could muster and lifted her chin. "Take the survivor into custody." She waved toward the one man, whose guts hung out of his abdomen, and then met the terrified gaze of a disembodied head.

Her belly lurched and bile rose to her throat. She collapsed to her knees and watched in horror as she threw up.

By the first gibbous, two hours before their planned ambush, eleven of Liang Yu's hired swords had arrived. Song came first, wide-eyed and eager as always; and then a new recruit surnamed Fang who claimed to be a marksman with his repeating crossbow. If he lived up to his boasts, he would be the key to Liang Yu's daring plan, able to eliminate their target from a distance regardless of an army of guards. A clean escape would prove more difficult.

Liang Yu lifted his brush and sketched a simple map on a sheet of rice paper. "Our target is Lord Han of Fenggu, whose heir nominally supports our employer's cause. He could be pushed toward war by his father's death. Lord Han should leave Lord Peng's compound at the fourth gibbous."

He began handing out copper coins from Madura when the sliding door crashed open, causing all to look up. His twelfth man, surnamed Fu, straggled in.

Something was out of place, something wrong about the man's smell: the sweet scent of *yinghua* petals, a contact poison causing intoxication in males.

That flowering weed grew in only one place in the world: the Black Lotus Monastery, home to the Black Lotus Black Fists.

Liang Yu frowned. "Song, go out into the common room and mingle with the other patrons."

With an inquisitive cock of his head, Song left the room.

Liang Yu turned to Fu. "You are late because of a woman, aren't you?"

Fu ran his hand through his dark hair, biting his lip.

"Hurry up and answer."

Fu nodded. "She was such an exotic little sprite, barely yet a woman."

Liang Yu modulated his voice, changing the pitch and inflection to imitate the accent from Cathay's rural South. "Were you able to bed her?"

Fu chewed on his lip.

"She claimed some sort of reason she couldn't, didn't she? Answer truthfully."

Fu's words slurred as he spoke. "She kissed me on the neck, then got up and left."

Liang Yu sprang to his feet, his walking stick already in hand. "Abandon the plan. Regroup at *Long-An* Temple in three days."

An excuse. *If* there were any survivors, they would be followed. He only hoped Young Song had made it out of the room early enough to avoid being associated with the rest.

It was time to recruit a new collection of disaffected soldiers and insurgents. There were plenty, after all.

With confused murmurs and shrugs, his men headed toward the exit. Liang Yu slipped into the low closet door behind him and into the dark. He released the secret exit in the back of the closet and slid into a hidden corridor that ran from the inn to the adjoining bowyer's workshop.

He finished shutting the hatch just as his hurried men opened the sliding doors. The muffled sound of murmurs and ruffling clothes instantly fell into deathly silence.

Suspicions confirmed. A female Black Fist had drugged the hapless Fu with a contact poison; and then a group of them followed him as he stumbled to this meeting. Sudden and precise in their assault, only they could operate with such surgical efficiency and then disappear into the night. Not even the proprietress or other inn patrons would realize what had happened, though it occurred right in front of them.

Liang Yu retreated quickly through the corridor, listening to the silence of the Black Fist. Emerging in the bowyer's workshop, he heard the subtle breathing of one of the warrior-spies, likely assigned to this spot to watch for anyone who might escape out of the inn's kitchen backdoor.

Reaching into his robe, Liang Yu snatched three throwing spikes and flung them at the sentry. The young man contorted himself so that two blades whizzed by, but the third lodged into his throat.

Liang Yu bounded over to both silence his scream and prevent his blood from staining the floor. Too young, too inexperienced, too confident. How unfortunate. The boy might have one day made a fine warrior.

Covering his trail the best he could in the urgent escape, Liang Yu collected his weapons and headed toward his special pupil's home. He could put his gardening skills to use for a couple of days, while hiding in plain sight. The Black Fist would not think to look for insurgents in a *Tai-Ming's* villa.

Then again, the Black Lotus had identified Fu. But how? The only unpredictability in his infallible planning was employer betrayal.

Of course! The order to assassinate Lord Han had been too audacious. It must have been a ruse. His employer had likely decided their group had outlived their usefulness, and needed to clean his hands.

Liang Yu growled. It was time to root out whoever it was and pay him back.

CHAPTER 10:
AFTERMATH

Hong Jianbin passed another cup of rice wine to *Tai-Ming* lord Liu Yong, surprised the aristocrat could be so talkative. The forty-eight-year-old ruler of Jiangzhou province never spoke during council meetings, always siding with the Royalists, always listening to the lecherous Treasury Minister Geng.

Close to the capital, with a cool climate and fertile valleys, Jiangzhou produced bountiful crops of wheat and millet, and its wooded mountainsides supplied timber and silkworms. The Liu family had faithfully served the Wang Dynasty for centuries, and the current lord was no exception.

Hong suspected his support came not from loyalty, but expectation. As a second son who was never cultivated to inherit, the unimaginative Lord Liu did nothing but follow the status quo. Luckily for his province, the systems left in place by his late father, as well as the aggressive trade networks established by the current *Tianzi,* had bolstered Jiangzhou's prosperity.

Liu drained yet another cup. His brand of aristocrat was the most contemptuous: he enjoyed wealth and status by virtue of noble birth, with no appreciable skill of his own. He was, as they said in the North, cut from the same cheap cloth as the *Tianzi*'s two sons. These men would run the nation into the ground.

According to Hong's spy, the man had started his battle with wine right after the council meeting. By the time he joined Hong in a private room at Lord Peng's villa, Liu was already quite drunk.

Liu turned to applaud a young lady dressed in a peach-colored robe. She played the *guzheng*, her hands running over its twenty-one twisted silk strings.

"She is quite good." Hong poured another cup of wine for Liu.

Liu shook his head. His words slurred. "Not nearly as good as Princess Kaiya."

"Nobody in the empire can rival the princess's musical talent," Hong said. "She could probably sing Avarax to sleep."

Lord Liu laughed, raising his wine cup. "A toast to the princess!"

Hong lifted his cup. "To the princess." He then lowered his voice. "Speaking of which, this is the exact reason I wanted to meet with you tonight. Your second son, Liu Dezhen, is of marriageable age, is he not?"

"Yes, he is already twenty-four, and becoming a fine man!" Liu clapped his hands.

Hong forced himself into an enthusiastic nod. If young Dezhen was anything like his father, he still had a long way to go to become a fine *man*. "Just like your first son, who married the *Tianzi*'s niece, Wang Kai-Hua. What would you say if I told you that I might be able to arrange another match with the *Tianzi*'s family?"

Liu's brow crinkled. He tapped the cup.

How dense could he be? There was only one eligible girl. Hong hid his frustration with a friendly smile. "Princess Kaiya."

Lord Liu choked on his wine. "Impossible. She is such a choosy girl. She has already rejected a couple dozen suitors, and Dezhen is only a second son."

Hong shrugged. "Once I am Chief Minister, and the indecisive *Tianzi* faces a united voice from the *Tai-Ming*, he will have no choice but to force his sister to marry your son."

"You, the fishmonger, becoming Chief Minister?" Liu's voice rose in laughter. "I can't imagine that!"

As expected, the dunderhead missed the insinuation. Minister Hong clenched his jaw, promising retribution for the insult. It had been a mistake to make veiled suggestions to such a dense person, especially after alcohol had muddled his mind. "Then imagine this: your grandson, sitting on the Dragon Throne."

Liu's forehead scrunched. "How do you plan to accomplish this?"

"I have secured four of your brethren *Tai-Ming* who will support my candidacy as Chief Minister once Minister Tan retires." Hong continued in a low voice, as if the walls could hear, "The *Tianzi*'s health has deteriorated so quickly in the last few years, I do not believe he has much more time left. His son has little interest in state affairs. He will be easy to manipulate."

Liu cocked his head. "Crown Prince Kai-Guo is sufficiently capable, and certainly takes an active role in the council."

"That is not the son I had in mind."

Lord Liu burst out laughing. "What, you think Prince Kai-Wu will ascend the throne? Then you have my full support, just so I can see if you can make all those pieces fall in place. And of course, I want you to pledge that Princess Kaiya will become Dezhen's bride."

"You have my word of honor, my Lord. In the meantime, I need you to at least nominally support the Expansionists while we set things in motion."

"What will be set in motion?" Liu's eyes glazed over.

Without a doubt, in the debate between the Expansionists and Royalists, Lord Liu had little intellectual depth to consider the merits of either side. He would blindly follow the *Tianzi*, since his province had always benefited from imperial favor. Liu might not even know which side the *Tianzi* supported.

Hong suppressed a sigh. "Troop movements. Huayuan Province troops will move away from the capital and toward the northern border with Rotuvi. Dongmen troops into the Kanin Wilds. And of course, a grand invasion force to liberate Ankira from its Maduran occupiers."

Liu shook his head. "The *Tianzi* will never authorize that!"

So Liu did know more than he let on, though apparently not much more.

"Remember, my Lord, we do not necessarily refer to the wise *Tianzi* Wang Zhishen." Hong again stifled a groan, hoping—perhaps unrealistically—that Liu would at least remember his pledge to support his candidacy for Chief Minister.

The doors slid open, and one of Lord Peng's men entered and bowed. "My Lords, for your safety, please come to the audience hall immediately. The *Tianzi's* agents foiled a plot on Lord Han's life, and there was another attack on Princess Kaiya here, in the compound."

Hong's heart skipped a few beats. More attacks he had not heard of… "Is the princess safe?"

The man nodded. "Yes, Minister."

Hong relaxed his clenched fingers. His entire plan hinged on Princess Kaiya remaining unmarried. And still breathing.

Perhaps he should initiate the second phase of his plot earlier than he intended. Chief Minister Tan's early retirement could not come soon enough.

But before he could do that, he would need to have Princess Kaiya sent away. It would remove her calming influence from the council, *and* keep her safe from whoever was trying to kill her.

Peng Kai-Long mused that his villa's audience hall currently bore all the trappings of a council meeting. With the exception of the enigmatic elf Xu, all the *Tai-Ming* sat there, along with several of the *Yu-Ming*. As host, he relaxed on a cushion at the front of the room, just as the *Tianzi* would in Sun-Moon Castle. As he would, when he became *Tianzi*.

Then, Princess Kaiya glided in.

As protocol demanded, he yielded his seat.

Even if his blood boiled.

The incompetent assassins had foiled a plan he had in place for years. Not only that, they effectively closed the window of opportunity for killing Princess Kaiya, since the *Tianzi* would arrange near-impenetrable security around his family.

He might not even let them out in public at all. The Imperial Family could very well hole up in Sun-Moon Palace until the *Tianzi*'s spies uncovered the conspirators.

Kai-Long did not worry about himself in this matter. His funding of insurgents in the capital passed through many hands, leaving his own clean while falsely incriminating the Madurans.

The princess nodded as she slithered by, wearing the slippers that should've sent her tumbling to her doom. He smiled at her. His cheeks hurt from smiling so much.

No matter; he was safe from scrutiny. Many layers of disinformation insulated him from those pathetic Ankiran boys masquerading as Maduran Scorpions. Indeed, for all the surviving assassin knew, Kai-Long himself was the target in the teahouse. The convincing interrogation performed by the *Tianzi*'s agents would implicate Kai-Long's gardener, a spy for the insurgents whom Kai-Long had hired years ago, just to be sacrificed at a time like this.

The only weak link was Minister Hong, who now tottered in and creaked to his knees. Did the wretched old man still serve a purpose? Kai-Long looked over to meet his ostensible ally's gaze. Minister Hong glared daggers at Young Lord Zheng, the heir to Dongmen Province.

Zheng Ming, in turn, repeatedly exchanged winks and grins with Princess Kaiya.

Kai-Long ground his teeth. Hong had given assurances she would reject Zheng Ming, but that certainly didn't seem to be the case. Kai-Long cursed every orc god and goddess he could think of. Cousin Kaiya was not only alive, but maybe even one step closer to finally choosing a suitor and pushing out an heir.

He consoled himself with the old adage of finding opportunity in disaster. Even if some of his plans crumbled around him, at least other aspects of his scheme were working. With the failed attempt on Lord Han's life, the *Tai-Ming* would make a scene during tomorrow's council meeting. After the princess' own brush with death, even she wouldn't object to punitive action against Madura.

The princess lived, but he would still get the war he wanted.

CHAPTER 11:
Unwelcome Bedfellows

From inside the narrow confines of her palanquin, Kaiya heard five hundred imperial guards marching in tight formation. Like a funeral procession. Perhaps she'd died and now took her last journey in a coffin to a funerary pyre. The walls closed in around her. Her brush with death wove in with the terrifying childhood memory of being locked in a cabinet.

The pitching roiled her stomach, confirming she still lived. A deep breath of hot, stuffy air reassured her of the fact. At least the palanquin allowed for privacy. In the first hour after the attack, she'd forced herself to project an undaunted image. Now hidden from prying eyes, she allowed salty, hot tears to trickle unchecked down her cheeks. She turned Tian's pebble over in her hands, its cool surface reassuring.

The procession lurched to a stop. Kaiya used Zheng Ming's kerchief to dry her tears. Her eyes felt heavy and swollen. Outside, a herald called, and large gates swooshed open. They had arrived at the palace.

"*Dian-xia*," Chen Xin called from outside. "We have passed the palace's front gates. Would you like to alight?"

Her act must have worked, for him to think she'd want to walk the rest of the way to the castle.

Not tonight. The White Moon neared full, ready to cast her vulnerability in its bright light. "No." She cleared her throat. "Take me to the Jade Gate. No need to rush."

Kaiya shuddered. The cracking of her voice revealed weakness. At least the trip from the main gate to the imperial family's residence would provide time to regain her composure. In a way, the ride felt like déjà vu, like the time she'd faced Father after trespassing at the Temple of Heaven with Hardeep.

Just like then, when she had coped with the prospect of certain punishment, she now emotionally distanced herself from near assassination by envisioning the path: Past the Hall of Supreme Harmony. To the Dragon Bridge between the palace grounds and the castle. Through the winding alleys of the castle compound.

The porters stopped and lowered the palanquin to the ground. The doors slid open and a hand—the chamberlain's, from its phoenix feather-like smoothness—took hers and helped her out on to legs as wobbly as a newborn foal's. Imperial guards by the gatehouse dropped to one knee, fist to the ground.

The chamberlain released her hand. "*Dian-xia*. The *Tianzi* will receive you immediately."

With a nod, Kaiya forced herself into a semblance of grace as she crossed the covered stone bridge from the keep to the imperial family's walled-off, hilltop residence. Moonlight sparkled off the gold leaf of the one-story pavilion's tiled eaves. Surrounded by moats, the building was further protected from magical intrusion by an ancient ward.

As she approached the gatehouse connecting the bedrooms to the rest of the residence, her entourage of guards and handmaidens halted and knelt. Ahead of her, eight imperial guards stepped aside to reveal a familiar face.

The old nun from Praise Spring Temple raised a light bauble lamp to Kaiya's face. To guard against magical disguises, like the illusion bauble from Wailian Castle, she spoke in the Imperial Family's secret language to verify Kaiya's identity. "Where did the Founder come from?"

"Great Peace Island."

"What was the Founder's motto?"

"*All Under Heaven Swathed By Might*"

The nun nodded. "What was the name of his castle there?"
A trick question, since he'd had many. "Which one?"
"The last."
"Peaceful Earth Castle."

The gatekeeper turned around and rapped a code—changed hourly—on the heavy ironwood doors. They slid open, revealing nine bowing nuns who straightened and formed up around her.

With them as an escort, Kaiya walked to the *Tianzi*'s quarters. Like her imperial guards, the protection had always seemed like needless formality. Before today.

Her brothers, both kneeling on cushions, met her gaze as she stepped into the bedroom antechamber.

Eldest Brother Kai-Guo motioned her to a cushion. "Doctor Wu is attending to Father."

Kaiya knelt and bowed.

Safe! Truly safe, for the first time in hours. A spring breeze off Sun-Moon Lake wafted in through open windows, cooling her down and calming her nerves.

Father's wheeze rasped from the other side of the gold-painted sliding doors. From her place in the anteroom, she tried listening for his heartbeat. Her own pounding heart drowned out the sound of his.

Sick fathers, assassination attempts. Kaiya looked up to focus on something else. Lanterns with bloodwood frames around paper-thin white jade and dangling red silk tassels hung from the ceiling, providing a soft light from Aksumi light baubles. The ceiling was coffered, with jade insets carved to depict scenes from the Wang Dynasty's glorious history. Lacquered wooden panels with mother-of-pearl inlay adorned the red walls.

The doors to the bedchamber slid open and Doctor Wu emerged. She cast a reproachful glance at Kaiya. "The *Tianzi* is weak. Worrying about his headstrong daughter riding exposed on a horse taxed him further." She passed a scroll to Eldest Brother Kai-Guo. "Have him drink a decoction of these herbs twice a day."

As Kai-Guo withdrew his hand, the old doctor snatched it up and pressed fingers to his pulse. She then beckoned Second Brother Kai-Wu over, who offered his right wrist as well.

Doctor Wu's brow furrowed. "The same toxin courses through all of your veins, though it affects the *Tianzi* differently. I don't know why I didn't feel it in your pulses until today."

Kaiya gasped. A toxin. How, with all the precautions?

Eldest Brother Kai-Guo frowned. "Doctor, I thought you knew everything about the body."

The old woman shook her head. "There is no one thing that could cause this ailment, and I suspect most of the ingredients come from abroad."

Lowering her voice so Father wouldn't hear, Kaiya asked, "What is the *Tianzi's* prognosis?"

The doctor answered in a low whisper. "The stresses of state tire him. He must rest, if he is to see the cherry blossoms bloom next year. You must ensure he does not hear any startling news." With a stern glance at Kaiya, she bowed and slipped out of the room.

Eldest Brother Kai-Guo sighed. "With the New Year's Festival fast approaching and the capital falling into chaos, we must share the burden of Father's duties."

Second Brother Kai-Wu pursed his lips. "We have to convince him to rest, first."

Their eyes turned to Kaiya, prodding her to go speak to him. Her eyebrows knitted together, but her silent refusal was met with chin jerks in Father's direction.

He broke the silence with a throaty voice coming from his bedroom. "My children, enter."

They all rose and approached the entrance to the dimly-lit sleeping chamber, heads lowered.

Father eased himself up into a sitting position.

Hurrying over to help, Kaiya propped him up with cushions and pulled fur blankets to his gaunt chest.

"My children, I am very concerned about your safety in light of tonight's events. I have decided you will have, in addition to your complement of imperial guards, an adept from the Black Lotus Temple accompanying you at all times. This is a secret order known only to a handful of the most senior imperial guards and Praise Moon nuns."

Kaiya's childhood friend Tian had been sent to the Black Lotus Temple, which was famous for training unparalleled accountants and scribes. Mention of it usually tempted her to bring up the taboo subject. However, the idea of a man—even a celibate monk—watching over her sleep invited protest instead. What was the benefit in having a scholar or accountant as a protector? "Father, Chen Xin and Zhao Yue have protected me since youth, and they are unparalleled swordsmen—"

He raised a hand to silence her. "Yes, the imperial guards are the most skilled swordsmen in the nation. However, the Black Fists can recognize potential threats before they happen. I have one with me at all times, yet you have never even noticed."

"*Black Fist?*" Kaiya twirled a loose strand of hair. Was Father jesting?

He wouldn't, not after the attack tonight. Perhaps the legendary thieves in the night were more than a mother's tool for controlling unruly children. Maybe the Black Fist guards explained all the times something sounded out of the ordinary around Father. Or the unexplained bumps in the night. "So they are real."

Eldest Brother Kai-Guo nodded. "Yes, they are a secret only the *Tianzi* and his heirs know of."

Male heirs, at least.

So the Balck Fists existed. The strange shadow at Cousin Kai-Long's teahouse. Perhaps a Black Fist had rescued her. Even so, the idea of one watching over her sleep… She shook her head. "I don't want one in my bedchambers."

Father's brow furrowed. "We suspect these recent attacks are the work of a renegade Black Fist. You need those who understand their methods, even in your room. Your new guard will remain silent unless ordered to speak, or if there is imminent danger."

It made sense. Still, the thought of someone besides her one familiar nun attendant violating the sanctity of her personal space... As if this night couldn't get worse. Father clapped twice as Kaiya started to protest.

Three shadows dropped from the dark ceiling corners, landing soundlessly on the sablewood floors. They sank to one knee, fist to the ground. All were small, wispy figures, wearing black utility suits and masks.

As Father spoke, each of the dark shapes bowed their heads in silent acceptance of his order. "The Crown Prince and Princess will be protected by One. Two, your duty is to Prince Kai-Wu and his wife. Three, you must safeguard the Princess Kaiya. My command supersedes any they might give you."

Kaiya scowled at the Black Fist assigned to her, but Three's body language showed no signs of intimidation. She tried to keep the irritation out of her voice. "Goodnight, Father. Let us speak again about this in the morning."

With a curt bow, she spun on her heel and fled the room, closing the door before Three could follow.

After a quick jaunt through the halls, she came to her sleeping chamber's anteroom. Her usual nun attendant bent at the waist as she entered. Kaiya quickly shut the doors, just in case Three hadn't gotten the message earlier.

With dexterous fingers, the nun untied Kaiya's sash and eased the outer robe off her shoulders. Later, she would take it, and the inner gown, to the private dressing room just outside the restricted bedroom wing.

Kaiya's gaze swept across the room to the stand where her plain white sleeping robe hung. What was that? A flash of black? She turned back.

A girl in black clothes sat in the corner near the door.

The nun gasped and interposed herself between Kaiya and the intruder. She raised her hands in a defensive position.

How had someone slipped in? Tightening the thin inner gown around her, Kaiya glanced toward her bed where she kept a curved dagger. "Who are you? What are you doing here?"

The girl bowed her head. "Forgive me, *Dian-xia*. It was not my intention to surprise you. I am... Three... whom the *Tianzi* assigned to protect you."

Kaiya studied Three. The girl had seemed little more than a tangible shadow in Father's dimly lit room. Now in the bright light, she didn't look to be much older than a young teen, short and lithe. Her dark hair was pulled back to reveal a slight point to her ears and particularly large eyes, reminiscent of Lady Ayana from the council meeting. Though pretty, the girl lacked Ayana's ethereal exquisiteness.

And the voice. It sounded so familiar. "Three, how did you get in?"

"I was right behind you, *Dian-xia*."

Maybe the myths about the child-snatching Black Fists *were* true. "Impossible. I closed the door right behind me."

"Yet, I am here." Three's tone was blunt as a chopstick, with a hint of amusement. From behind her back, she produced a long knife—Kaiya's own.

The nun snapped back into a defensive position, only to tentatively receive the blade when Three offered.

"Remove this from the bed chambers," Three said. "It is something that could be used against the princess. As long as I am here, no harm will come to her."

Such bravado. Kaiya frowned. "You will not always be here. I am going to change into my bedclothes, so begone, until I tell you to return."

"Forgive me, *Dian-xia*. My orders are to be with you at all times."

At least the Black Fist guard was female, but such impertinence! "I will speak to the *Tianzi* about this arrangement in the morning. Do not make yourself too comfortable here. You will be gone by tomorrow night."

Three sucked on her lower lip. "*Dian-xia*, it is for your own protection. If you command it, you shall not even know I am here."

"Then humor me, and at least pretend to leave." With an exasperated sigh, Kaiya snatched up her sleeping gown and went behind a folding screen to change.

On the other side, the Black Fist girl stomped across the room to the door, opened it, stomped out, and slammed it behind her. Her footsteps echoed down the hall.

Once she'd finished changing, Kaiya emerged from behind the screen. No sign of Three. The nun unpinned her hair, allowing her luxurious locks to tumble down to her waist. Taking up the inner gown, the nun bid her goodnight and slipped out the door. As always, a clean inner gown would hang on the anteroom stand first thing in the morning.

Now alone, Kaiya slid her window open and looked out. A cool breeze brushed across her face, and she smoothed her tresses with her hands. The constellation of E-Long loomed high above, a reminder of the evil dragon who supposedly hung over her destiny—if an assassin didn't get her first. Below it, the Iridescent Moon waxed to mid-gibbous. Only three hours to midnight. She would need a good night's rest to deal with the inevitable arguments in the council the next morning.

And the confrontation with Father over the impertinent Black Fist girl.

Blowing out a long breath, Kaiya closed the windows, shuttered the lamps, and rolled into her bed. She drew up the silk sheets and fur covers, allowing them to envelop her. After a few minutes of deep breathing, her annoyance subsided and her mind settled.

She'd been insufferable with Three, and the guilt gnawed at her. After all, Father only wanted her to be safe. And Three had done nothing wrong, save for her tone, which bordered on mocking insolence.

Something felt wrong in the room: an extra sound in the voice of the night. It seemed oddly familiar.

Kaiya called out softly, "Three, are you there?"

Silence was her only reply, and she spoke again. "Three, I command you to speak if you are here."

Three's voice, coming from a mere ten feet away, sounded surprised. "Yes, *Dian-xia*."

"I guess I will not be rid of you, will I?"

Mirth danced in Three's tone. "I am afraid not."

Kaiya sat up in her bed. "Three, come here, and bring a light."

Although Kaiya could always hear most movements in her room, Three reached the lantern and opened its shutters in complete silence. Bright light flooded the room.

Squinting, Kaiya beckoned Three over. "Come. Closer."

Three approached, head bowed. When she raised it, their gazes met.

Kaiya examined the girl's features. "You are very beautiful, although not in a classic sense. It is… exotic. You have elven blood, do you not?"

"Yes, *Dian-xia*." Three answered concisely, though Kaiya had asked in a way that prompted for more information.

"It is not often elves mate with humans," Kaiya said, waiting for an explanation of Three's origins. Elves very rarely left their secluded valley realms. The few half-elves in history were the result of violent circumstances, and usually met tragic ends. To her frustration, the girl remained laconic. "What is your story?"

"It is not what you think," Three finally answered. "From what I have been told, my father is an elf and my Cathayi mother died in childbirth. Since my adventuring father could not raise me alone, I was left in the care of the Temple as a babe long ago."

Long ago? "How old are you?"

Three fell silent again, gaze cast down in avoidance of Kaiya's. She looked up again. "Forgive my rudeness, *Dian-xia*, but may I speak freely?"

Kaiya nodded.

Three sucked on her lower lip before letting it pop. "Do you typically ask your servants their age, even before you know their name?"

Kaiya paused in surprise before shaking her head. "I apologize, that was rude of me. I—"

"How long has your nun attendant served you? Do you know her name?"

Heat rose to Kaiya's face, and she turned her head down and to the side. The way it exposed the curve of her neck would buy her time in the company of men, but the half-elf's eyes merely narrowed. "My apologies. What is your name?"

The girl grinned. "Jie. My family name is Yan, the same as the Master of the Black Lotus Temple, who adopted me. I'm thirty-one."

Yet she appeared no older than twelve, thirteen at best. If the half-elf had spent so much time at the temple, then… "You must know my childhood friend, Zheng Tian. He is a cloistered scholar."

Jie, whose eyes had sparkled with mischief just seconds before, choked on a cough. "Cloistered scholar? There are none of those at the Temple, only Black Fist. Even the cooks and scullery maids can kill a dozen different ways. Tian is a deadly swordsman and an unparalleled planner. The best since the fabled Architect."

Her reference to the Architect meant little to Kaiya, but Tian as a swordsman... The idea would be comical if it weren't so perplexing. As children, he wasn't much better than her with a sword, despite being older and a boy. Her archery skills had surpassed his. Even when Father revealed the Black Fist were real and came from the Black Lotus Temple, Kaiya assumed Tian must've held some clerical role there. How could her gullible, adorable friend be a warrior and spy? "He was like a big brother to me."

"As he is to me, too. He calls me *Little Sister*, even though I'm ten years older, and trained him." Jie's tenor dropped to a drone, but there was a hint of adoration in her voice.

The girl was cute, insolence aside. Kaiya covered a giggle with her hand. "Then we are almost sisters. Very well, Yan Jie, when we are in private like now, I command you to speak freely as my sister. Also, from tomorrow, you'll dress as one of my handmaidens. I'll feel more comfortable that way."

Kaiya rose from her bed and treaded over to her writing table. From an ornately carved rosewood box, she withdrew a jade hairpin and offered it. "We must exchange hairpins to sanctify our bond of sisterhood. It'll make a much more convincing disguise as my handmaiden, as well."

The half-elf tentatively extended her hand, and bowed her head as she received the jewel. She then plucked a flat, tapered pin from her own hair and proffered it in two hands. "This is all I have. Be careful not to stab yourself."

The black-lacquered metal hairpin had a wicked-looking tip. Kaiya tried not to gawk as she received it. "I… I shouldn't take my bodyguard's weapon."

Jie smirked. "There are a lot more where that came from."

Once the princess had returned to bed and her breathing became shallow, Yan Jie settled into an alert meditation. It would allow her to forgo sleep for a while, even as she reflected on the dramatic turn of events.

Just a day ago, she'd returned to Cathay after an unsuccessful two-year mission abroad. No sooner had she stepped of the ship, than she was tasked with rooting out the anti-imperial insurgency. No rest for the weary; at least no more than her current meditation.

This evening had started innocuously enough, with tracking a careless rebel and kissing him on the neck with a contact toxin. That had been followed with her both disabling an assassin posing as a Maduran Scorpion *and* protecting him from certain death at the swords of predictable imperial guards. All in a typical day's work.

And second nature for her, compared to her new assignment.

It was far easier to slink in the shadows than to act like a proper handmaiden. Maybe if she'd received the assignment a decade ago, during her stint as a courtesan-in-training in the Floating World, she could've blended in… but even then, she'd never excelled at etiquette.

Protecting a headstrong aristocrat was already proving to be difficult. Doing so in a dress would be even more so. Hopefully, the princess wouldn't ask who had spoken to her from the shadows two years ago, before the attack on Wailian Castle.

CHAPTER 12:
SWEAT IN TIMES OF PEACE

Zheng Ming watched as his arrow sang through the cool morning air, its path undeterred by a light breeze off Sun-Moon Lake. It smacked into the small wooden target with a satisfying thud, just barely audible over the pounding of his horse's hooves and the applause of watching soldiers.

He looked skyward. Hopefully, the thick clouds would break. He planned on visiting the princess soon, to see how she fared after the ambush the night before. Excitement tingled up his spine as he thought of her, so brave and yet so vulnerable.

Ming turned his horse and trotted back to the starting point on the archery course. His long-time friend, Xie Shimin, waited with several other riders.

Xie grinned. "I see you have kept up with your training since I left the border."

Watching the next rider begin his run, Ming nodded. "As the first Wang *Tianzi* said, *more sweat in times of peace...*"

"*...means less blood in times of war.*"

They both leaned back in their saddles and shared a chuckle.

Xie's laughter settled. "I shouldn't have invited you to practice on my province's equestrian field." He waved a hand at the uninhabited stretch of land in the capital's northwest, nestled among wetlands and manicured parks. "These extra practice sections will help you win the national tournament again this year."

Ming yawned. "I guess I should give your delegation a chance, since you have provided me this opportunity."

"Yes, Princess Kaiya would be happy to see her home province win, wouldn't she?" Xie leveled his gaze at him. "How are things progressing with her?"

"Certainly one of my most challenging campaigns ever."

Xie snorted. "All that sweat, and you are still bloodied. Come now, Brother Ming. You can't expect the Princess of Cathay to easily surrender to your charms like all of your other conquests."

Ming shrugged. Usually, a woman would be warming his bed after an hour of sweet talk. Then again, this was the *Tianzi's* only daughter. "And if she did, I would end up like a Yu Dynasty court eunuch. Nonetheless, a man has urges."

Xie clapped him on the back. "Nothing a discreet foray or three into the Floating World can't solve."

"I have decided to save myself for her." Ming lifted his chin in mock defiance.

Xie grunted. "Let's see how long you'll last."

"It'll be worth it." Ming tracked the next archer.

"If you can accomplish it! But yes, just think about it: your son could be a potential heir to the Dragon Throne."

There it was again, the same bait everyone dangled in front of him. Ming turned to watch a Huayuan Province soldier make his archery run. "That's the least of my worries."

"It should be your foremost consideration, especially if Prince Kai-Guo and Prince Kai-Wu fail to plant their seeds."

Ming gawked. Some things were better left unsaid. He started to respond.

Xie gestured for him to remain quiet. "These are perilous times. If your future son sat on the throne, you could be regent until he comes of age."

Regent? Over the realm? As if ruling his own province wouldn't be difficult enough. "I'm not sure I want that responsibility."

"In times of need, I'd rather trust the unwilling hero who rises to the occasion, than the greedy official who wishes to take charge." Xie locked his gaze on him. "We need leaders to contain the barbarians in the North and an aggressor to the South who seek to carve Cathay up."

Ming's eyes darted about. His friend's words bordered on treason. "In any case, even though the *Tianzi* is in poor health, he still rules. Crown Prince Kai-Guo will rule after him. Even if they remain without child, it would be many, many years before my yet unconceived son would ascend the Dragon Throne."

Xie fell silent, nonchalantly brushing the fletching of one of his arrows.

Ming shifted in his saddle. Enough talk of politics. "Now if there's anyone who needs a wife and child, it's you!"

Xie shook his head. "Unfortunately, a soldier's pay can't cover both the costs of a sick mother's medical expenses and a bridegroom gift for the right bride."

"So your mother's condition hasn't improved?"

Xie sighed. "The herbs are helping to keep her from deteriorating further, but she's not getting any better."

"I'm sorry to hear that. Perhaps she would be heartened if her only son finally married. If you need a bridegroom gift, then let me know how I can help you."

His old friend faced him, blinking away what looked suspiciously like a tear. "I appreciate the gesture, my friend. We're a proud family, and I will not accept charity for this. You need not concern yourself."

Ming placed a hand on Xie's shoulder. "We served together for years in Wailian. It would be my honor to help my comrade-in-arms."

"And I thank you for the offer. But I plan on winning a purse from the national tournament, and taking care of it myself." Xie flashed a broad grin.

"Just know that in this matter, I will not yield." Zheng Ming grinned back. "But otherwise, let me know how I might help. I must be going now; I will soon be engaging another opponent at the palace."

Xie smiled slyly. "I'm afraid I'll have to embarrass you in front of her at the tournament this year."

Peng Kai-Long avoided the downward slash, turning to the side and cutting to his opponent's midsection. The satisfying crack of the bamboo sword on the man's armor echoed through the courtyard.

Both combatants stepped back and bowed.

Kai-Long kept his expression stoic, hiding his satisfaction. He was a fair swordsman at best, using pre-engagement analysis and deceit to compensate for his admittedly mediocre physical skills.

His villa steward shuffled out onto the veranda. "*Jue-ye*, Minister Hong is here to see you."

"I will meet the old man in private. Send him to the teahouse."

The prior night's ambushes had visibly shaken Old Hong. Those who thought they knew everything failed to plan for uncertainties. The minister's lack of foresight and preparation would be why Kai-Long ultimately prevailed once it was time for them to betray each other.

He reached back. One of the squires placed a silk towel in his hand, which he used to dab the sweat off his forehead. More sweat in times of peace.

Peaceful times would be ending soon, for the good of the realm. If only the *Tianzi* and his Royalist yes-men saw it. Kai-Long took his time walking, not bothering to strip off his padded cuirass. Hopefully bloodstains remained on the teahouse mats. That would be sure to intimidate Old Hong.

A servant opened the sliding doors, revealing Hong sitting cross-legged on a cushion. Sweat trickled down his leathery face. He bent over low.

Kai-Long took a seat across from him, taking note of the new mats. "Rise."

The old man creaked out of his bow. "Good morning, Lord Peng. You look well in spite of the chaos here last night."

Kai-Long shrugged. "The *Tianzi's* agents have questioned everyone. From what I have been told, the attackers on the road between here and the palace used arrowheads forged in the south. The assassins were Maduran Scorpions. One was captured alive."

Hong lowered his voice. "You decided to attack the princess?"

So, the old man correctly suspected his involvement. Kai-Long scowled and shook his head. "Of course not. The princess will be yours, as we promised— if we can keep her alive."

Hong's eyes narrowed. "Then this was not your doing?"

Kai-Long glared at the minister, wrapping his next lie in indignation. "No. The prisoner revealed that *I* was their target. They didn't know the imperial guards would appropriate the teahouse for the princess. In any case, I need her alive so that *you* can continue using her as your bargaining chip, and *I* can get what I want."

Hong's mouth gaped. "Are you suggesting there are real Maduran Scorpions in Huajing?"

"It appears so. The *Tianzi's* agents are paying courtesy calls to all of the Ayuri nations' trade offices, to root out infiltrators and spies. I suspect word of the princess' romantic correspondence with the Ankiran prince got out."

Hong nodded, understanding blooming on his monkey face. "That would make sense, then. Killing the princess would prevent her from sealing an alliance with the Ankiran freedom fighters; assassinating you would silence the greatest of our lords and the loudest proponent of punitive action against them."

Kai-Long wondered if the old man was truly convinced. He needed the minister for a little while longer, just until he could get the Expansionist policies approved by the *Tianzi*, as well as measures that would aid with his eventual coup.

Once the obsequious toad delivered on the third stage of their plan, he was a loose thread that could unravel his carefully-knit plans. A loose thread that would be clipped, at the neck.

After wasting time being fitted for her first silk dress in a decade, Yan Jie watched from a covered veranda as her ward shed an extravagant gown in favor of simple cotton robes.

Jie snorted, drawing the stares of the handmaidens beside her. The princess now looked not unlike the young nun who guided the group of noblewomen in their martial arts practice.

Fashionable hairstyles were abandoned in favor of simple pony tails, giving them an austere appearance befitting the White Sand Courtyard. Bordered on the east by the Praise Moon Temple, the courtyard's only defining features were the fine white gravel for which it was named, and a dragon-shaped well.

The Praise Moon nuns practiced a secret style developed by the Founder's consort after witnessing a fight between a snake and a crane. Jie suppressed a yawn. The nuns should probably stick to their duties of harvesting a unique species of tea leaves reserved for the Cathayi Imperial Family.

On this overcast morning, the princess, along with her sisters-in-law, her cousin Wang Kai-Hua, and the yappy Lin Ziqiu, all tied up their sleeves, exposing slender white arms. Wrist-to-wrist, they engaged in the pair exercise of *Sticking Hands,* supposedly to learn how to feel a partner's intention through tactile sensation.

Eschewing elegance, the techniques appeared direct and efficient, not unlike Black Lotus fighting arts. Its economy of motion and relaxed power suited a woman's smaller stature. Perhaps it was a worthy martial style after all.

If only the princesses took it seriously.

Besides the otherwise flighty Ziqiu, they all laughed and chatted, much to the visible chagrin of their teacher. Heavens forbid they would ever have to defend themselves.

"I can't believe the Madurans would be so bold as to attack you," Lady Kai-Hua said as she deftly redirected one of Princess Xiulan's punches.

Princess Kaiya's technique was sloppy as she engaged Princess Yanli. "Cousin Peng believes it is because they feared our support of Ankira."

"Lord Peng would like nothing more than to invade Madura." Crown Princess Xiulan's skill was no less clumsy against Lady Kai-Hua. "The attacks last night may turn the *Tai-Ming* to the Expansionist cause."

Backing away from the Crown Princess, Lady Kai-Hua held up a hand and covered her mouth. "From what my husband tells me, Minister Hong has been working hard to push the Expansionists' agenda."

Lin Ziqiu's lips curled. "Eww. He's gross." Her hands moved like a maelstrom through the nun's defenses, yet never seemed to be able to land a blow as her partner's leisurely, nonchalant movements warded off all attacks. Jie appreciated how the nun cut through Ziqiu's guard and slapped her on the shoulders with both hands like the whipping of a silk sash. Despite the seemingly innocuous movement, the blow struck with a loud hollow thud, sending Ziqiu staggering back four feet.

"Less haste, less emotion," the nun droned with neither haste nor emotion.

Ziqiu stepped back toward the nun, ready to reengage, a frown contorting her otherwise pretty face; but the nun held a hand up, motioning for the ladies to relax.

"We must not judge people by the way they look." Kaiya disengaged and regarded the girl. "Minister Hong is not all that he seems. In fact, I have summoned him to meet with me in two hours."

"Whatever for?" Xiulan and Yanli spoke in unison. If their eyes could open any wider, they might actually be able to see their partner attacking.

"He has been my ears among the *Tai-Ming*."

At Jie's side, the handmaidens all murmured. Jie would make use of the princess' *speak freely* command later to remonstrate her on trusting a minister to do spy work.

From the corner of her right eye, she saw a young page pattering along the far veranda. When he reached the steps, he dropped to his right knee, fist to the ground. His voice was high-pitched. "Minister Hong of the *Tai-Ming* Council requests an audience with Princess Kaiya."

The princess bowed her head at the nun. "I did not expect the minister until after practice. Please allow us to finish early today."

The nun placed a fist into her palm, and all the ladies returned the salute.

"I will receive him here," the princess told the page.

He rose and scurried away, while the nun disappeared into the temple. The ladies straightened out their robes and alighted the veranda on Jie's left. They knelt in a semi-circle with Crown Princess Xiulan at the head, Yanli on her right, and Kaiya on her left. For Jie, it was a fascinating insight into imperial court rituals of rank and seniority.

Presently, Minister Hong tottered along the far veranda with his chin respectfully lowered. His gaze swept over the ladies, lingering on the princess just long enough for Jie to notice. Dirty old man. He reeked of lust and deceit.

He climbed down the steps into the courtyard and shuffled over to where the ladies sat. He stumbled to both knees and bowed. "Crown Princess, Princesses."

Ziqiu rolled her eyes in a look of disgust that Jie needed no special training to discern.

"Rise." As the highest-ranking lady, Xiulan dipped her chin once, allowing the old man out of his bow.

Princess Kaiya afforded him a tight smile. "You are early."

"Forgive me, *Dian-xia*." Hong's straightening resembled a tortuous stretch Jie remembered from her youth. "I wanted to speak to you before the council meeting begins."

The princess opened a palm toward him. "Speak."

"As you commanded, I conferred with many of the hereditary lords last night. Most of them now want war with Madura."

The princess twirled a lock of her hair, a subconscious habit Jie had already seen a few times. It was usually a sign the girl was pondering something. "I hoped we could avoid armed conflict. It puts undue burdens on the citizenry, and little on the ruling class."

Hong's head bobbed like a seal's. "As the son of a fisherman near the border, I admire your concern for the commoners. I believe there may be a way for you to stop the march to war."

"Me? They will not listen to a girl." The princess' already large eyes rounded.

The minister placed a hand on his chest. "You are far more than that. Yesterday, you disarmed angry lords with a laugh."

Only a laugh? Jie favored Princess Kaiya with a discerning eye. She'd been an impulsive, love-struck girl at Wailian Castle. Perhaps she'd grown in the last two years. Perhaps protecting her wouldn't be such a waste of time.

"Even if that is true, what do you suggest I do?" the princess asked.

"The ambassador from the Kingdom of Bijura is an old friend, going back thirty-two years to my first posting, in Vyara City as a trade officer. They have relations with Madura and may be willing to mediate for us. In today's meeting, please offer to negotiate with the Madurans on neutral ground."

At thirty-two years, Hong had been in government service at least a year longer than Jie had been alive! If he wasn't stopped from age, it was the weight of all the bribes he'd probably taken.

The princess twisted a stray tress. "It sounds like a promising idea. Why don't you suggest it yourself?"

Hong placed his hand on his chest. "I am just a minister, one whom the hereditary lords disdain. They will reject it out of hand if I propose it. However, they will listen to you, as will the *Tianzi*."

The princess stopped playing with her hair and let out a deep breath. "If that is the only way to avert hostilities, I will try."

Hong beamed, exposing perfect teeth. "Very good, *Dian-xia*. However, there is still unrest in the capital. I ask that you consider another proposal: allowing the great lords to bring in more protection from their provinces. It will make them feel more secure, and more patient on punitive action against Madura."

"That sounds reasonable," the princess said, even as Jie wondered just how many soldiers Hong considered to be *sufficient*.

Hong bowed low again, forcing Jie to hide a grimace at the motion's ungainliness. "The princess is wise beyond her tender years. With your leave, I must talk to a few lords who may yet be swayed from war."

After Minister Hong's departure, the ladies gathered around the well to wet their throats and wash their hands.

"What did you think about the minister?" Princess Kaiya asked.

Young Ziqiu's lip turned up. "Disgusting! His groveling makes my stomach turn."

Jie couldn't disagree.

Lady Kai-Hua shook her head. "He is adequately respectful, and seems to have the best interests of the nation at heart."

Jie wondered about the accuracy of that. She would send a clan brother to learn more about Minister Hong's comings and goings.

The Crown Princess apparently agreed. "I would not trust him fully."

Princess Yanli nodded. "You must be careful when dealing with him. As the Five Classics say, a wicked heart with good intentions is still wicked."

Princess Kaiya sighed. "For the time being, I will assume the best. His suggestions *do* make sense, after all."

Orchestra of Treacheries

The valet appeared again, dropping to his knee. "*Dian-xia*, Lord Zheng Ming wishes an audience with Princess Kaiya."

Head jerking to the far veranda, the princess shot a hand up to her mouth. She fumbled with her sleeve, trying to loosen the cords that held it up.

The other princesses covered their giggles, trading knowing smiles. Crown Princess Xiulan beckoned in the direction of the royal retinue. "Handmaiden, bring a towel and assist Princess Kaiya."

Jie watched the handmaidens from the corners of her eyes. One of these clueless girls was supposed to respond. None moved.

The Crown Princess' thin-painted eyebrows rose, like dagger points, her gaze stabbing into Jie.

It left little doubt which clueless girl was responsible for Princess Kaiya's towel. Gaping, Jie dropped to her knee, fist to the ground.

A soldier's salute.

It lacked the refinement of a lady's dainty bow at the waist, something she refused to master during her time in the Floating World. The handmaidens exchanged glances which somehow combined shock and amusement.

Heat rose to the tip of Jie's ears. She stood and attempted a bow, which even the stoic imperial guards reacted to with quivering lips.

Jie sucked on the right side of her lower lip as she straightened and descended toward the courtyard. When her foot touched the first of three steps down, her robe's hem maliciously reached over and tangled up her ankle. She took the last two steps with a leaping butterfly twist and landed lightly in a *Dipping Crane* stance.

Who knew working in a dress wouldn't come back as easily as blindfolded tightrope walking? The gown would need modifications to allow for better mobility.

All eyes widened and mouths hung agape, none more so than those of Lady Ziqiu. "*That* is no Praise Moon Fist technique..."

The imperial guards reached for their swords, but were assuaged by Princess Kaiya's glare.

The morning couldn't get any more embarrassing. Jie shuffled over to the princess and offered her favorite silk kerchief, the one with a musky, manly smell.

"Thank you." The princess received it and dabbed the sweat beading on her forehead. The way she cherished that rag...

Princess Yanli favored Jie through slitted eyes. "You are new. What is your name?"

"*Dian-xia*, my name is Jie."

Princess Xiulan also stared at her. "What family do you come from? You do not honor them with—"

"It's all right," Princess Kaiya said. "Please help me with my sleeves."

Jie nodded and moved behind the princess. The delicate knots *looked* impractical, but she pulled the wrong end, causing them to tighten.

"*Dian-xia*, Lord Zheng Ming is here," the page said.

The scent of shouwu berries wafted into the courtyard, though the princess blocked Jie's first view of Tian's eldest brother.

All attention shifted to the handsome lord, and Jie used the opportunity to flick out a knife from beneath her sleeve and slash through the cords. The sleeves tumbled down the princess' thin arms, and Jie let out the breath she'd been holding.

The princess bowed, affording a view of Lord Zheng Ming. He knelt in salute, his topknot hanging over a shoulder. Most ladies would probably find his wolfish grin charming, even if it looked like a wild beast stalking prey.

Though not close to his eldest brother, Tian had always idolized him. After seeing him in person, Jie could not fathom why.

"Princesses, forgive me for interrupting your practice. Again."

"We were just adjourning." Crown Princess Xiulan's tone bordered on flirtatious.

Yanli took Ziqiu's hand. "Yes, we will leave you to speak with Princess Kaiya." Her up-to-now stern voice softened. She, too, sounded enamored.

Zheng Ming bent over in a sweeping bow. "Yet again, I do not get to enjoy the pleasure of all of your company."

Such a fop. Jie caught herself shaking her head in disdain. Luckily, she stood behind the princesses and had her back to the rest of the entourage. No one would see it. Her cover disappeared as all present but Princess Kaiya's own imperial guards made their way to the veranda like a Spring Festival procession.

The princess leaned over and whispered. "We need to work on your etiquette. For now, go change into your utility suit and stay in the shadows."

"I am supposed to be with you at all times, *Dian-xia*."

The princess' lips quirked. "And your skill is compromised in that dress. I am sorry to put you through this."

Jie shook her head, almost contrite. "I have embarrassed you."

"Not at all," the princess said. "Go, change. I doubt Lord Zheng is a threat."

Threats came in many forms. Not all of them caused physical damage. Jie shot a quick glance at the beaming lord. "Better for me to practice in this gown now, while there is no real danger."

The princess narrowed her eyes. "I command you to change."

To obey both the *Tianzi* and the princess, Jie would have to change right there.

It was a good thing she wasn't shy about nakedness.

CHAPTER 13:
THE BEST LAID PLANS

Hong Jianbin admired the princess seated on the dais beside the vacant Jade Throne. She looked beautiful as always, despite her ordeal the night before. After years of finding and sabotaging potential suitors, all of his planning would give him the standing to marry her himself.

A thump jolted Hong from his reverie.

Seated on the floor with the other hereditary lords, Lord Peng slammed his palm on the floor in an unsightly breach of etiquette. The young man must have been a stage actor in a previous life. His contrived rage at last night's ambushes would be convincing to anyone unaware of his likely involvement.

"Perhaps," Peng said, "the attempt on Lord Han means nothing to you. Nor the plan to take my life. But how can you ignore the targeting of your own sister?" He nodded toward Princess Kaiya.

Had he been present, the *Tianzi* would have cowed Peng or any other lord into silence with a tilt of his chin.

Crown Prince Kai-Guo, sitting at the front of the council next to the *Tianzi's* empty throne, adamantly shook his head in a slip of imperial comportment. "The Five Classics say we are all children of the *Tianzi,* and he treats us as such. He does not place his daughter above you in his policy-making decisions."

Lord Han, always a supporter of the throne, now jabbed an impertinent finger at the prince. "Pretty words, but the Five

Classics also say a ruler's actions must reflect his thoughts. What does the *Tianzi* plan to do about this?"

Prince Kai-Guo stared at Lord Han for a few seconds until the old man lowered his gaze. "He will pursue punitive action once we know who to punish."

"Is it not obvious?" Lord Liang of Yutou, an Expansionist, snarled. "The perpetrators of the princess' attack used Ayuri-made arrows. One dropped a purseful of gold coins stamped in Madura. Maduran Scorpions targeted Lord Peng and ended up attacking the princess. We *know* who the enemy is."

"Excuse my impropriety in speaking out of line." The princess' voice carried over the murmurs, a melodic wave which drowned out all others. She bowed her head as the hereditary lords turned to face her. "I appreciate Lord Liang's concern for my well-being. However, I will be the first to say Cathay must tread with caution. My father's spies foiled an attack perpetrated by our own people."

"As were the other ambushes, starting with the one on Lord Zheng's son," Peng said, tilting his chin toward Lord Zheng. "Plenty of evidence indicts Madura. Madura's money is behind this. As the Founder said, *Cut off the head, and the demon will die.*"

Prince Kai-Guo shook his head in an unsightly fashion again, making Hong wonder if the boy would ever have the composure to be *Tianzi*. "There is almost too much evidence. If we assume Madura is behind this, we may be overlooking something more insidious."

"Forgive me, Cousin, for contradicting your wisdom," Lord Peng said. "Only the paranoid ignore the obvious in favor of conspiracy theories. Again, I say, allow me to take my armies into Madura."

The Crown Prince's face burned an angry shade of crimson. He opened his mouth, but no words came out.

"No." The word flitted off Princess Kaiya's tongue like the warble of a songbird, again calming the room. "My father's legacy is one of peace. He would never stand for war if it could be avoided. He has commanded me to negotiate with the Madurans. Minister Hong, I understand you have a contact who can help arrange a meeting in Vyara City, a neutral site."

How sweet his name sounded on her lips! Hong's chest tightened. How could the girl have such an effect on him? He could only nod in response.

More murmurs rumbled through the room, as the Royalists and Expansionists considered the impact of this new measure on their position. It didn't matter. As long as they perceived his support of their cause, Hong would benefit.

Chief Minister Tan cleared his throat. "Minister Hong, while we appreciate your enthusiasm, it is hardly the role of the Household Minister to make such arrangements."

The princess raised a hand, looking every part the *Tianzi*, even as she sat by his empty throne. The effect was the same. The room fell silent and all attention turned to her, a girl of only eighteen. "My father has already approved the measure. He deemed Minister Hong appropriate because of his experience in the Ministry of Trade. You were Minister of Trade back then, and specifically commended his performance, did you not?"

The Chief Minister stared at her a few seconds before bowing a fraction. "Yes, *Dian-xia*. However, surely you can appreciate that each ministry has specific duties and roles. This task should be the provenance of the Foreign Ministry."

The princess locked stares with him and placed a delicate hand on her chest. "Forgive my poor understanding of government, Chief Minister. I had always believed that all duties and responsibilities were the provenance of the *Tianzi*, delegated at his pleasure. Was I wrong to assume he could assign this task to Minister Hong?"

Hong squeezed his lips shut to keep from gaping. The girl had outsmarted one of the most seasoned, highest officials in the realm. He stole a glance at Chief Minister Tan, whose mustaches quivered. His old friend was barely containing his anger.

The Chief Minister bowed, lower this time. "The princess is correct. However, we should not honor the Madurans by sending a scion of the Son of Heaven to discuss a matter that is beneath her."

The princess brought her slender fingers to her lips, covering an innocuous laugh. "I did not think maintaining peace was beneath me. Is that not the primary mandate of the *Tianzi*?"

The hereditary lords demurred, with even the Expansionists nodding.

Lord Peng met Hong's gaze and raised an eyebrow, yet otherwise his expression remained inscrutable. Peng must have been behind the attack on the princess, but if the young lord was disappointed his quarry would escape his reach, it didn't show.

Then Peng spoke up, his voice transformed into anger. "Negotiation? Will we wait again for another attack? Who will be targeted next?"

Lord Han, a longtime Royalist, bobbed his head. "How long will it be until you meet with the Madurans? In the meantime, something must be done to ensure not only the safety of the *Tai-Ming* and their families, but also to prevent the citizenry from descending into chaos."

"If I may speak?" Unlike the others, Lord Zhao asked to be recognized, as protocol demanded.

The Crown Prince beamed and nodded, again forgetting the dignity of the *Tianzi's* office. "You may, Father-in-Law."

Such familiar terms were meant to stay outside of official functions. Hong would have rolled his eyes, if not for the need to stay in the Crown Prince's good graces. For now.

Lord Zhao said, "Regardless of what action we take, we must increase security around the capital."

Hong congratulated himself for not only convincing the Royalists to push his plan, but getting them to believe it was their own. He was further reassured when Lord Liu, drunk during their conversation the night before, spoke up.

"If I may speak?" Lord Liu waited for the Crown Prince to recognize him with a tilt of his chin. "In the three hundred years of the Wang Dynasty, the capital has never faced security issues. The general populace is already uneasy because of these unheard-of attacks, and there may very well be a new insurgency brewing."

"There has been some discussion among the *Tai-Ming*," Lord Lin of Linshan said, speaking out of line. Perhaps the princess' young friend Lin Ziqiu had learned impertinence from her father. "In these unprecedented times, we wish to petition the *Tianzi* to allow each province to bring five thousand of our own soldiers to the capital. They would assist in our personal security and help the watch maintain order."

Hong peeked at the Crown Prince, who gawked in a manner unbefitting the future *Tianzi*. Always suspicious, the Founder had stipulated that the *Tai-Ming* could bring no more than two hundred soldiers into the capital at a time. Although five thousand soldiers—a number that Hong himself had whispered into the ears of the Royalist *Tai-Ming*—would never pose a serious challenge to the national army garrisoned in Huajing, the suggestion bordered on treason.

The princess, too, regarded Lord Lin with an unseemly gawk. Apparently, her support for Hong's request earlier that day only went so far. Despite her apparent shock, her voice remained serene. "Lord Lin, the defense of Huajing is the responsibility of Huayuan Province, the jurisdiction of Prince Kai-Guo. A sudden, dramatic increase in outside provincial troops would certainly raise the anxieties of the people."

Hong had underestimated her. Nonetheless, he could find opportunity in failure. The best-laid plans rarely survived first contact with the enemy. As long as all sides got what they wanted in the end, he would still benefit from a change in tactics.

"If I may speak?" Hong said, and waited to be recognized. "It is two weeks until the New Year Festival. There will be increased shifts of the watch and more soldiers from other parts of Huayuan Province deployed to the capital to maintain order. Perhaps more could come?"

From the corner of his vision, Hong saw Peng trying to get his attention, his eyebrows clashing together. This new suggestion would be perceived as a betrayal.

The Crown Prince dipped his chin a fraction, the motion more becoming and regal. "A good suggestion, Minister Hong. We can divert an extra two thousand men from the Rotuvi border, and another three thousand from Jiangkou. The *Tianzi's* spies are also mobilized. We will make the capital safe."

All anger drained from Lord Peng's voice. Perhaps the man had a touch of insanity to go with his flair for drama. "What would the *Tianzi* think of a compromise? Allow the *Tai-Ming* to increase their military presence by five hundred men, limited to the city's northeast?"

True to form, the Crown Prince wavered. The princess silently prodded him with her eyes, yet she remained quiet. Good, a sign that she remembered a girl's place beneath her brother. At last, he nodded, again the motion coarse and unbecoming. "Very well, start making arrangements, though the *Tianzi* will have to approve the plan himself."

Hong ran calculations in his mind, pondering the timing of all of the plans in place. Some would have to wait until after the New Year's Festival, when the princess departed for Vyara City. In the meantime, he would need to keep her out of Peng's reach, without Peng realizing that was his goal.

The next step of his scheme, to become the princess' groom, now ran well ahead of schedule. It was almost time to oust Chief Minister Tan.

Just after the council meeting adjourned, Peng Kai-Long excused himself before any of the other Expansionist lords could corner him. Now he lay in wait, ready to ambush Old Hong on his predictable visit to the privy. The treacherous minister, likely knowing of Kai-Long's involvement in the attack on Cousin Kaiya, was now trying to protect his ultimate prize.

With the *Tianzi's* spies lurking in the shadows and increased imperial guard presence, the girl was out of harm's reach anyway. Kai-Long had already committed himself to a less satisfying backup plan: rendering her infertile with a steady dose of the right herbs. Or, if he did not want to get his own hands dirty, perhaps push for the marriage with the soon-to-be Chief Minister Hong. The wretched old man's repeating crossbow probably had an empty magazine anyhow.

No, the princess marrying and conceiving a son was the least of his concerns right now. More pressing was whether or not he could still count on Hong in other aspects of their plan. Especially after the outrageous proposal to move more of the *Tianzi's* own men into the capital.

The old bastard turned the corner, and stopped in his tracks when their gazes met. The minister's fearful look was immensely gratifying.

"So old man, are you backing out of our arrangement?"

"What?" A broken smile appeared on Hong's face. "Of course not."

Kai-Long scrutinized Hong's expression for any sign of a lie. "We did not discuss any of what you proposed in council."

Hong shook his head. "We underestimated Princess Kaiya. I had to adjust our strategy in light of that."

Kai-Long glared at the minister. "When she meets with the Madurans, she will learn they have nothing to do with the attacks." Not to mention she might meet with Prince Hardeep and find out their year of correspondence was all a lie...

"We can always incriminate the Kingdom of Rotuvi, which has threatened us for years, and is a weaker opponent anyway. It will also give you reason to move your armies north. Most importantly, she will be out of our way in two weeks. It will be easier for us to attain our final goal."

"I wonder if we are speaking of the same goal." Kai-Long noted that Hong was regarding his own expression with just as much scrutiny.

"Of course. You as *Tianzi*, me as Chief Minister. We will do great things for Cathay."

Kai-Long pursed his lips. At least Hong got half of it right. "Regardless of whether or not Cousin Kaiya is around, five hundred of my best men are not enough to stage a coup. Especially with all of the additional Huayuan troops you proposed."

"Your men just have to be present for contingencies. Once everything has played out, you will be the legitimate heir. Then you will have a new five hundred best men: the imperial guard."

It did make sense, except for how Hong undoubtedly planned on betraying him in the end. Kai-Long forced a smile. It was two weeks until the New Year Festival. After that, Cousin Kaiya would leave. With her out of the way, everything would fall into place.

CHAPTER 14:
Resonance

By the second night, Kaiya could lie in her bed and reliably pick out Jie's breathing from the chorus of spring sounds. Like a shallow whisper, each of the half-elf's inhalations lasted over a minute, followed by an equally-long exhalation. Try as she might, Kaiya couldn't replicate the marathon breath cycle.

Kaiya fiddled with Zheng Ming's kerchief, unable to sleep. As intrusive as the Black Fist girl was, it was still nice having someone there. "How do you breathe like that?"

Jie's breathing returned to normal. "It's part of our training. It's called the *Viper's Rest*. At the highest levels, we can slow our heartbeat so as to appear dead."

What a strange technique, with little obvious use. "What other special skills do the Black Fist possess?"

Pride radiated in the girl's voice. "We are masters of stealth. We can infiltrate an enemy. We make excellent information gatherers. If need be, we can be untraceable assassins."

"You will not need to make use of *that* skill in my service." Kaiya shuddered. To think, sweet little Tian, sneaking around in the dark, murdering. Maybe some things were best left unasked.

Apparently, Jie would be answering those unspoken questions. "It's not something I've had to do. The clan cultivates us according to our abilities. The best assassin in recent memory was the Surgeon, who died thirty-two years ago on a mission in the city you will visit soon. His friends, the Architect and the Beauty, perished with him." Awe carried in her voice. "Tian might be as good a planner as the famed Architect."

Kaiya had a good idea where this was headed. "And you?"

"Like the Beauty, in more ways than one." The girl had to be grinning. "My specialization is infiltration and information gathering."

"What information did you gather from watching the council meeting?"

"May I speak freely?"

"Speak, my Insolent Retainer."

"Then forgive my audacity, but I fear the Crown Prince is not ready to be *Tianzi*. The Second Prince, even less so. He ignored the entire meeting."

"Kai-Guo has plenty of time to grow into the role." Did he? Kaiya tried to sound convincing. Father might not have much time left.

"He'd better have. Lord Peng waits in the wings."

"Cousin Kai-Long? He has always been my father's favorite nephew. Even if he is intent on invading Madura, he does so with the country's best interests at heart."

Jie's silence spoke loudly about her distrust of Lord Peng. When she voiced her concerns again, it had nothing to do with Cousin Kai-Long. "Be wary of Minister Hong. When you're not paying attention, his eyes undress you."

After enduring the lewd stares of boorish suitors, it didn't come as a surprise. "Most men are governed by their base desires."

"Yes, but the minister goes beyond leering. He hides it so well, it makes me wonder what other treacherous thoughts bounce around in his head."

Kaiya shuddered again. Hong was old enough to be her father, perhaps even grandfather. Nonetheless… "He has proven reliable up to now. Unless your elven senses detect something else?"

"The only legacy of my elf blood is a father who abandoned me." Whereas Jie had spoken in an objective tone about treacherous cousins and lecherous old men, her voice now sounded like she'd taken a bite of raw bitter melon.

How awful! Kaiya propped herself up on her elbows. "There must have been a good reason." She beckoned her bodyguard over. Court conventions might frown on physical contact, but here, in the privacy of her room, she would give Jie a reassuring hand squeeze.

Not moving from her seat, Jie sighed. "According to the note he left, it was because he couldn't care for a baby while he adventured. Little good elf-blood has done for me, beyond making me look a third my age. I—"

A cackle broke out in the corner of the room. "When you are ninety, you will be happy for that."

Kaiya shot straight up. A third presence in the room had evaded her hearing. She fumbled for the knife hidden under an extra pillow.

Gone.

Of course. The nun had removed it at Jie's order. She tightened the sleeping gown around her. As if that would help.

Jie leapt to her feet and flung something, or perhaps several things, in the direction of the laugh. Something flashed in her hands as she interposed herself between Kaiya and the intruder.

Then the half-elf froze in place, her defensive stance silhouetted by light from the full White Moon Renyue.

Kaiya peered past her to where a dark shape stood.

Jie felt like a disembodied soul. She had no command over her muscles, nor could she feel a thing. Yet all of her senses worked.

Her elven vision clearly painted the cloaked intruder in olive shades as he walked around her. A thin longsword hung at his side. He smelled of cherry wood.

A male voice invaded her mind. *You can also thank your elven blood for the vision that allows you to see me now.*

The same voice spoke aloud. "*Dian-xia,* your *Ear that Sees* improves, yet it still did not detect my arrival."

The renegade Black Fist! Perhaps the one who taught the rival clan she'd unsuccessfully tracked for two years.

His presence evaded even Jie's own keen senses, and he spoke of *Seeing Ears*, a Black Fist technique that helped adepts fight in the dark. The great masters could paralyze an opponent by merely touching energy centers, and there were supposedly secret techniques of striking an enemy without actually making physical contact. Yet, projecting thoughts was beyond even fanciful legends.

The lamp shutters flapped open, throwing the room into bright light.

The princess stumbled over her words, her tone a mixture of fear and anger. "Lord Xu. This is my personal chamber. How did you get past the magical wards?"

The elf lord! Not a Black Lotus traitor. If only Jie could see the interaction behind her.

"Who do you think put them in place?" Xu's tone sounded harmless enough, and he had no reason to attack the princess.

Try as she might, Jie couldn't turn.

"What did you do to Jie?" the princess demanded.

"I had to protect myself. Her barrage of spikes and stars almost hit me, and I would wager she is handy with those knives... and probably all of the other weapons she hides."

Jie would've shuddered if she could. Perhaps nakedness *did* bother her. And she was fully clothed.

"Release her." The princess' tone of command, bred into the imperial family, would make most people think twice about disobeying.

Jie wasn't one of those people.

Apparently, neither was Lord Xu. He came back around and stood in front of her, examining her with dispassionate eyes. How satisfying it would be to gouge them out. And then spill his guts for good measure.

He looked over her shoulder to the princess. "Your bodyguard wants to dig my eyes out with the hilt of her knife, and spoon out my intestines. You will have to command her to behave."

If Jie could gawk through her paralysis, she probably would. Her first up-close experience with a real elf was proving to be quite memorable.

"Jie, I command you to leave Lord Xu alone."

It is for your own safety. Xu's smug voice grated.

As much as that order begged to be disobeyed, what chance did anyone stand against who'd paralyzed her as an afterthought?

You are still young. Perhaps with more experience and training.

He was listening to her thoughts. Jie blanked her mind, using an anti-interrogation technique.

Lord Xu chuckled, and then uttered a foul-sounding syllable, worthy of an altivorc oath.

The sudden return of sensation nearly sent Jie tumbling to the ground, yet she managed to regain her balance before suffering further injury to her ego. Now if only Lord Xu would get out of her mind.

My apologies. I will not violate your privacy again, unless you attack me. "Now, withdraw from the chambers. I have secrets to share with the princess."

He was unravelling her, puncturing even her mental armor. Jie crossed her arms. "I cannot. My orders are to remain with her at all times."

Lord Xu's almond eyes, almost a mirror of her own, narrowed. "I *could* teleport you to the other end of the realm, but you would probably just kill yourself for dereliction of duty. It would be a waste of such talent." He walked past her to stand at the head of princess' bed.

Such arrogance. Add arrogance to abandonment to the long list of elven shortcomings. The princess retreated to her headboard and glared at him. "So why do you invade my room at this late hour?"

The elf grinned like a schoolboy. "You will be negotiating with the Madurans. I thought I should teach you one more skill beforehand."

"Can't it wait until morning?" The princess pulled the covers up higher. It was tempting to join her beneath the blankets, like Jie's favorite dog at the Black Lotus Temple would.

"I am to perform a ritual magic spell when Renyue is full. I will be returning to Haikou as soon as I am done teaching you."

With a low sigh, the princess bowed her head. "Yes, Master." She pushed her legs over the side of her bed.

Still smiling, the elf drew his longsword. Jie reached for her knives. Before she drew them, he tossed his weapon toward the princess, hilt first.

The princess cowered back, moving out of its flight path, but the sword suspended itself in mid-air, just outside her reach.

Jie and her charge gasped in unison.

Recovering from her shock first, the princess tentatively seized it by the hilt. The nonchalance with which he performed these impossibilities didn't seem to be simple theatrics.

The show continued. Lord Xu reached behind him, and a lute from the anteroom flew across the bedchamber and into his grasp. He turned it over in his hands, examining it. "None the worse for its tumble onto the castle parapet two years ago. Now, *Dian-xia*, place your hand on the sword blade, so as to be barely touching it."

When the princess had done as she was told, the elf strummed several notes. He peered at her as he did so. "Can you feel the change in vibrations?"

She nodded.

"Sound can be a weapon," the elf lord said, "as deadly as the sword you hold."

Jie snorted. To a Black Fist, almost anything could be a weapon. But sound?

"Though perhaps even more deadly is the heart," he added. "Half-elf, come here."

She crossed her arms over her chest. No way would she surrender any more of her pride to this pompous ass.

"Your loss." Xu shrugged before gliding over to the princess' bedside. He took her hand and placed it on his chest.

She recoiled, her head shyly tilting to the side. "That... This is inappropriate."

With a chuckle, Xu jerked his chin in Jie's direction. "It's either me or her. Your choice. Or hers, as the case may be. Or, just lose the chance at a valuable lesson."

The princess looked up at Jie, her eyes pleading. The expression was reminiscent of that temple dog waiting for attention. At least the princess hadn't commanded it. With a harrumph, Jie strode over.

Xu smirked. "Good girl. Now, *Dian-xia*, put your hand over her heart."

The princess did as instructed. Her hand felt cold, even through Jie's shirt.

"Now, feel the change in your little friend's heartbeat." Xu improvised a long series of notes on the lute.

Little friend, indeed! The elf lord could take his little—

As understanding bloomed on the princess' face, her hand resonated against Jie's chest. The vibration changed as the elf picked up the tempo. Maybe a Black Lotus master's delayed death strikes worked in a similar manner.

"You understand, too, don't you, half-elf?"

Jie hesitantly nodded.

"And you, *Dian-xia*, have you experienced a connection with your audience when you play? Something you *knew* was there, even if you did not know exactly what it was? Of course you have, when you saved the boys from slaughter two years ago in Wailian. Here is how: everything has a unique resonance, which can be changed by the cleaving of a sword or something simple as the right musical note. Now sing."

Her eyes glazing over, the princess lifted her voice in song. Both the vibration of Jie's heartbeat and the princess' hand sped up. Joy and happiness welled up in her.

"If you can make that connection, you can bend a sentient being to your will. Now, withdraw your hand and sing a one-word command."

The princess' hand dropped away, her fingers relaxing into gentle crescents. "Sit." The word trilled out like an opera singer's line.

Her voice washed over Jie like a rolling wave, compelling her muscles to obey. She found herself seated at the edge of the bed. The temple dogs again came to mind. Perhaps this was what they experienced. Unlike the dogs, however, she was not rewarded with a tasty treat.

The princess' shoulders slumped, and she gasped for air.

Xu clapped his hands. "Very good, *Dian-xia*. It will feel draining at first, but as you get better, you will be able to string longer commands together with less fatigue. Lesser beings and those of dim wit" —he grinned at Jie— "will succumb easily to your voice. But with enough practice, you might one day be able to affect even Avarax."

Sucking on the right side of her lower lip, Jie glared at the elf.

He returned her stare with a wink. "My, my, if looks could slay a dragon..." *Listen well, Little One. Now that you know how it feels, you can counteract the effect by knowing how to control your own heart's frequency. You may very well need to resist the Siren's Song in defense of your princess. I am sure she will give you many opportunities to practice.*

"Practice more, *Dian-xia*." His gaze bored into Jie. "You will need it soon."

The air popped and Lord Xu was gone.

The princess met Jie's eyes. "I wonder how *soon* soon is."

CHAPTER 15:
Another Foreign Prince

The last time Kaiya greeted a foreign prince, the duty had been foisted on her at the last minute. She fell hopelessly in love and was taken advantage of. Now two years older and wiser, she went armed with feminine wiles and ten days of practice using the power of her voice. If anyone would have the upper hand in today's engagement with Prince Aelward of Tarkoth, it would be her.

She examined her smooth complexion in the mirror of her dressing room. Though the supposed Once-In-Three-Generations beauty batted eyelashes back at her, the gangly, hesitant teen hid beneath.

Perhaps a touch of rouge would help.

The faint sound of a rustling gown was followed by a brief flash of color in the mirror. She turned to see Jie slinking toward the door, dressed in a court robe. Embroidered in a spring flower pattern, the extravagant silk befitted an imperial handmaiden.

However, the lines of the gown had been awkwardly modified, with raised hems and jagged stitching.

Kaiya covered her gawk with a hand. "Who altered your gown?" The tailor would face reprimand for ruining the beautiful dress.

Her Insolent Retainer cast her gaze down. "I did. It constrained my mobility and I needed to sew in hiding places for weapons."

Kaiya raised an eyebrow. "Have you ever stitched before?"

"Only wounds." Jie shrugged a shoulder out of her inner gown and turned to reveal a thin scar, barely noticeable, above her shoulder blade.

Kaiya tried to banish the unsettling image of the half-elf sewing up her own laceration. However… "That is immensely better than what you did to your clothes."

The edge of Jie's mouth quirked up. "How would I reach the back of my shoulder? Someone else stitched that one."

Her hand strayed to the people in her sash. "Tian?"

Jie burst out laughing. "He's far better at cutting flesh than stitching it back up."

Yet another childhood memory of her gentle friend, ruined. She patted Zheng Ming's kerchief, tucked away in her outer gown's pocket. "In any case, we cannot have you seen in *that*. There is not much time to fit you with a new dress, so it looks like you will have to be my shadow again today."

Relief danced across Jie's face before vanishing as quickly as it appeared. "As the princess commands."

"I will need your eyes when we venture out into the city."

Jie nodded. "To watch for danger, I know. That is my job."

"The danger I speak of is the Prince of Tarkoth, and his weapon will be his words."

Hiding in the shadows of the princess' dressing room, Jie shed the annoying gown and slipped into her stealth suit. The princess' primping was so meticulous, her tone so grave when referring to the visiting dignitary.

Jie tried to keep a straight face. From her mission to the East, she knew all three princes of Tarkoth, one carnally. Only one was a particularly dangerous diplomat; but as Crown Prince leading a war effort, he wasn't going to be the one travelling all the way here. Nor would it be the second prince, whose heart she'd broken.

No, it would be the bastard, Aelward, and no amount of the princess' feminine charms would work on him. It would be so fun to watch her try.

After having not seen the princess since the attempt on her life nearly two weeks prior, Zheng Ming looked forward to a quiet chat over tea. Instead, she invited him to accompany her on a carriage ride to the Huajing's West Gate, to greet some foreign prince.

Ming had never heard of a member of the Imperial Family leaving the palace to receive an envoy. A foreign dignitary climbing the steps of the Hall of Supreme Harmony to bow before an imperial representative was standard protocol, a symbolic gesture of subservience to the *Tianzi*.

Waiting for her by the palace carriage house, Ming admired the glossy finish of the two imperial coaches. The stable master and his assistants hitched the covered carriage to four jet-black stallions, imported from the horse-breeding Kingdom of Tomiwa.

"We will take the open coach." The princess' melodious voice caused Ming's legs to buckle.

Still, even though the ambushes on the hereditary lords had abruptly stopped, it was an insane order. He turned around.

Stunning in a light blue dress with a cloud design, the princess glided through the courtyard,. Two handmaidens and several imperial guards followed.

Ming dropped to his knee, fist to the ground. "*Dian-xia*, perhaps the covered carriage would be safer."

The stable master and imperial guard captain nodded in agreement.

The princess tilted her head. "Young Lord Zheng, thank you for your concern. However, there has not been an attack in ten days. On this glorious spring morning, we should reassure the populace with our confidence."

Ming bowed. "*Dian-xia*, please consider your safety."

She covered a laugh with her hand. "My Lord, we must be considerate of Prince Aelward as well. He should be able to see our city at its finest, just before the Spring Festival." She locked eyes with the stable master. With a sweep of her hand, she gestured to the open carriage. "Switch," she said, the single syllable warbling out as a song.

To Ming's surprise, her straight posture sank for a split second, and she reached out to a handmaiden for support. Her thin eyebrows knitted together.

The stable master, on the other hand, gawked at her before looking at the captain for permission.

Frowning, Kaiya sung her order again. "Switch… rides."

She wobbled, and Ming stepped forward, ready to catch her if she collapsed. He couldn't let her fall, even if it meant tempting the death sentence for touching a member of the Imperial Family uninvited. "*Dian-xia*, are you all right?"

The imperial guards looked askance at him, but did not reach for their swords.

The stable master, on the other hand, bobbed his head, and motioned for his assistants to help him re-hitch the horses to the open carriage.

"I will be all right. The fresh air will help." The princess offered him a weak smile.

He helped her into a seat and sat across from her. Two dozen mounted imperial guards formed up around the vehicle, bearing the sky-blue banners of the Wang family and the Cathayi Empire. At the driver's command, the carriage set off, passing through the main gates of Sun-Moon Palace.

Ming's eyes darted back and forth, constantly looking for danger as they travelled down Prosperous Cathay Boulevard, the main north-south thoroughfare, lined with now-blooming cherry trees. At Grand Square, they turned west onto Eternal Peace Boulevard, where past-bloom plum trees boasted their purple spring foliage.

His concern for the princess' safety, and the constant clopping of horse hooves, made conversation difficult. His words faltered as he tried to identify potential threats among all the colorful New Year's preparations.

Strings of red paper lanterns fluttered along all the major streets. Shops hung red scrolls of auspicious poetry over their doors. The smell of burning incense percolated throughout the city, combining with the sweet aroma of New Year's pastries cooking in almost every home. Huajing's population swelled as local soldiers and merchants returned home to spend time with family for the most important holiday of the year. Those not tidying up their homes swarmed the streets as they paid off debts, visited public baths, and got their hair cut to start the New Year on a lucky foot.

Throngs gathered at the side of the road, bowing as the carriage rolled by. For the last couple of years, the citizenry had speculated about whom their beloved princess would choose as a husband. They now pointed at Ming and whispered among themselves. As excited rumors passed ear-to-ear, he would probably go from unknown provincial heir to household name by the end of the day.

Thirty-six *li* and two hours later, they arrived at the West Gate. There, Cathay's Foreign Minister Song chatted with the Tarkothi ambassador and his contingent of embassy guards. The latter all wore green surcoats over chain hauberks. A silver, nine-pointed star—the shared symbol of the Eldaeri Kingdoms of Tarkoth, Serikoth, and Korynth—was emblazoned on their chests. Ming stifled a yawn.

Minister Song and the several dozen Cathayi soldiers flanking him all dropped to a knee in unison. The Tarkothi crossed their fists over their chests and bowed their heads, showing deference to their host's ruling family.

Outside the gatehouse, the sound of horns and marching feet approached. The billowing green flags of Tarkoth came into view as Prince Aelward's party marched through the urban outskirts of the city. Commoners lined the streets, pointing and chattering about the brown-haired men.

Ming chuckled. The prince clung to white horse, led by several walking Cathayi officials and followed by two dozen Tarkothi marines in dark green coats. At his side rode a matronly elf, the first of their kind Ming had seen up close.

The entourage came to a stop just outside the gate. All of the Tarkothi crossed their fists over their chests. The Cathayi, with the exception of the princess, bowed when the prince dismounted, though he nearly got tangled in his stirrup.

The Tarkothi ambassador cleared his throat. "May I present Prince Aelward Corivar of Tarkoth, Captain of the Tarkothi Royal Ship *Invincible*."

It was Ming's first experience with foreign royalty. At the edge of his visual field, he saw the princess' eyes widen, rapt with interest. He gave the prince a thorough examination, wondering what intrigued her.

Sure, he was good-looking, with a bronze complexion and long brown hair tied into a pony tail. His sharp, refined features and shorter stature was typical of the Eldaeri—long-lived humans who had intermixed with elves in millennia past, on a distant continent.

From what little Ming knew of them, they had arrived on the northeast shores of Tivaralan not long after the Hellstorm, on daunting black ships. With those ships and an ingenious repeating crossbow, they had taken advantage of the Long Winter chaos and carved out their own empire. They treated their Arkothi and Estomari subjects as second-class citizens.

Foreign Minister Song spoke in what sounded like flawless Arkothi, the language of the North. "I present Princess Kaiya Wang, daughter of the Son of Heaven."

In Arkothi fashion, Prince Aelward dropped into a rigid bow, reminiscent of his inept horse riding.

"Greetings, lass." He took her hand and pressed his lips to it, making Ming cringe at their uncouth customs. "You're even more beautiful than the stories say."

The princess tilted her head and looked shyly away. She then curtsied with the grace of a weeping willow bending in the wind, surprising Ming with her knowledge of the foreign etiquette. "I am delighted to meet you, Prince Aelward. This is my escort, Lord Ming Zheng."

Ming stammered with his poor Arkothi. "Pleased to meet you, Prince Highness."

The foreign prince grinned and turned to the elf woman. "This is my bodyguard, Ayana."

With no visible weapons and a frail build, it didn't look like the old elf could guard much more than a rocking chair. Whoever these people were, to deserve the attention of an imperial princess, was beyond Ming.

The princess curtseyed again. "Prince Aelward, it is my honor to conduct you to your audience with my father, the Son of Heaven." She extended an open hand toward the carriage. "Please join me in this carriage, a gift we received from Tarkoth ten years ago."

Taking her hand in one of his and gesturing with the other, the prince bowed again. "In our culture, a lady boards first."

With a dip of her chin, she accepted his help stepping into the carriage. Ming rolled his eyes, glad the prince wouldn't be able to see him.

Not to be outdone, Ming took the old elf's hand and helped her onto the seat next to the princess. Prince Aelward slid across the bench opposite Kaiya, and Ming followed last, facing the elf.

When the carriage set off, the prince stared at the architecture and people with wide an unseemly gawp. The princess played the perfect hostess, pointing out landmarks and their history. He would nod, say a few words, and smile. She would smile back.

The prince's Arkothi was downright unintelligible when it wasn't uncouth. Yet the princess tilted her head and looked up through her lashes at him.

Ming sat there, all but forgotten. He could only put on his best face, leaning back with his arms crossed. Even if he barely spoke the language, he could certainly best this arrogant prince in archery or swordsmanship. As a prince, and one who showed neither royal comportment nor riding skill at that, this Aelward probably got his officer's commission as a result of his high birth.

Even though only two phases of the Iridescent Moon passed, the ride back to the palace felt like it took ten. On the order of a palace official, Ming waited at the first moat before entering the palace grounds. He could only watch as prince and princess strolled over the bridge to the front gates, laughing like lovers.

CHAPTER 16
HALF-TRUTHS AND MISDIRECTIONS

With two-year-old scars firmly in her mind, Kaiya had steeled herself to resist more manipulation. Prince Hardeep had entranced her with his golden tongue and hypnotic eyes, each poetic word of their encounter sparking foolish dreams.

Prince Aelward, on the other hand, had barely spoken at all on the carriage ride back to the palace.

When she pointed out landmarks and spoke of their history, he only responded with one-word grunts. Maybe he didn't understand her accented Arkothi. She turned to Ming for help, but the usually witty lord seemed preoccupied with staring off into space.

Even her body language, which typically mesmerized men, failed to capture the prince's attention. A shift of her foot exposed a bare ankle, yet he never looked down. She tilted her head and batted her eyelashes as she spoke. He seemed more interested in the scenery.

As she guided his entourage toward the bridge over the first moat, Kaiya cast a glance over her shoulder toward the carriage. Zheng Ming stared back at her with a most curious expression. Perplexed, she pressed his kerchief beneath her sash. Maybe Jie, slinking somewhere unseen, would have more insight. Then again, the girl probably had little experience in the game of courtship.

Orchestra of Treacheries

Kaiya turned back to Prince Aelward. He'd paused a few steps behind her, in the middle of the gently arching marble bridge that crossed eighty feet over the first palace moat.

She followed his gaze to the towering white-plaster front walls, looming fifty feet above, capped with dark blue eaves and stretching nearly five thousand feet from east-to-west.

From her study of his homeland, she knew the curiously-shaped Tarkothi castle was miniscule by comparison, with rounded towers and elliptical footprints. Small, but an architectural marvel all the same. "I am embarrassed to say that our palace is not as unique as yours," she said.

He harrumphed. "Bah. I rarely go to that court of stuffed shirts, sycophants, and backstabbers."

She covered a laugh. Perhaps on the inside, the Tarkothi castle wasn't so unique.

On the other side of the bridge, they came to the marble plaza running eighty-eight feet from the moat to the base of the walls. Following the protocol of a royal visit, two hundred imperial guards drew their *dao* swords and held them over the left side of their chests.

Prince Aelward was awfully quiet.

Kaiya guided him and his retainers on the central path, lined with guards and gold-plated dragon statues. The front gates were painted dark blue, with hundreds of silver nubs. Above the gates hung a black sign, emblazoned with the words: *Gate of Heavenly Justice*.

Prince Aelward looked up at the sign and then lowered his head. Penned by a master calligrapher hundreds of years before, the magic imbued in the Dragonscript evoked a sense of awe and reverence in those unaccustomed to seeing it. The prince couldn't possibly read it, yet his shoulders trembled.

Kaiya gestured him through the gates. On the other side, she swept an open hand toward the central courtyard, where petals from hundreds of espaliered fruit trees drifted across the white flagstones. "Please forgive the unsightly appearance of Sun-Moon Palace as we prepare for the New Year."

The palace bustled with activity. Servants wiped down the floors, walls, ceilings, windows, and doors. Craftsmen came to repair or refurbish anything that might have broken over the year. Gardeners worked hard to ensure the palace landscaping looked its best. Seamsters sewed up tears in cushions and bedding. Somewhere in the palace, Crown Princess Xiulan directed all of these duties. In two days, every building within the Sun-Moon Palace grounds would sparkle in its full glory.

Prince Aelward gawked as he spun in place, his gaze raking from the imperial archives on the right to the Hall of Pure Melody on the left.

"Come with me to the Hall of Supreme Harmony, where the Son of Heaven will receive you." She dipped her chin toward the enormous stairway, rising up over a hundred feet. Ministry buildings flanked the stairs at tiered landings.

At the top of the one hundred sixty-eight steps, before the doors to the Hall, Prince Aelward hunched over, panting. "Damn, lass, no wonder yer so thin."

Kaiya gestured north. "Only one structure in the realm stands taller: Sun-Moon Castle, on the other side of the Hall of Supreme Harmony. It was originally the centerpiece of the capital, providing a full view of the surrounding basin."

With an open hand, she pointed him toward the entrance, where the doors had been flung open to greet the warm spring breezes. Prince Aelward bowed and continued walking, with Ayana and his ambassador at his side. He nearly stumbled over the high threshold, meant to trip malevolent ghosts if they dared enter.

Inside the Hall, the prince walked down an aisle formed by dozens of bowing ministers, officials, and nobles. Father sat on the Dragon Throne, flanked by her brothers, as well as General Zheng with the Broken Sword. It was the first time the *Tianzi* had been seen in public for weeks. After regular acupuncture and herbal tonics, he looked a fraction healthier.

Still too pale. Kaiya came around and stood on the other side of Father, opposite her brothers.

Prince Aelward and Ayana bent over low, holding the bow until the *Tianzi* signaled for them to rise. When he straightened, Aelward recited words in Arkothi at a dignified, measured cadence, so different from the way he'd spoken to her. "Your Highness, I bring greetings and wishes for your health from my father, King Elromyr of Tarkoth, and thank you for receiving me today."

Father's faint voice wavered as he answered in his accented Arkothi. "Welcome to Huajing, Prince Aelward Corivar, youngest son of King Elromyr. Your eldest brother visited us ten years ago, your second brother, two. I remember them very well."

Prince Aelward clenched his teeth. "My half-brothers. I'm the unwanted get of a mistress, n'er raised with royal graces." He paused to take a breath. When he spoke again, it was reminiscent of young boys, reciting proverbs by rote. "As I am sure you are aware, the Teleri Empire has spread like a disease through what was once the ancient Arkothi Empire, subjugating the Arkothi people under its tyrannical reign."

Kaiya's ears twitched at the sudden switch from sailor slang to diplomatic jargon.

Father's eyes narrowed in the tone of his response. "I shall be blunt. Did your own ancestors not do the same three hundred years ago?"

The prince stared at his feet. Having studied Tarkoth's history and customs in preparation for the visit, Kaiya knew the conquering Eldaeri had seen other humans as inferior and ruled with an iron hand.

Prince Aelward raised his head. "Aye, I can't deny it. But Tarkoth has changed. Its rule is considered benevolent, and both Arkothi and Estomari folk within our lands have the same opportunities as the Eldaeri."

Kaiya searched his expression. He spoke in half-truths. A century ago, clashing views on racial purity led to civil war, sundering the Eldaeri Empire into three separate kingdoms. Perhaps the same disagreements would tear Cathay apart. As the

Founder wrote, *A nation divided within falls victim to predators without.*

Prince Aelward lipped several syllables, then looked up to meet Father's gaze. He again fumbled over obviously-rehearsed words. "The Teleri's First Consul Geros Bovyan has focused his attention toward our peaceful nations. His armies now occupy a quarter of our sister Kingdom of Serikoth."

Eldest Brother Kai-Guo leaned over and whispered to Father, "Serikoth has changed very little. It still has a rigid class system that benefits the Eldaeri at the expense of other humans living there."

Never shifting his gaze from Prince Aelward, Father raised his hand to silence Eldest Brother. "These are affairs in the East. They have very little bearing on Cathay's peace and prosperity."

Prince Aelward turned to his ambassador, who nodded. "The Teleri Empire has formed strategic alliances with the Levanthi Empire, cowed the Nothori Kingdoms into subservience, and bought off the Ayuri Kingdom of Madura. It will only be a matter of time before they attack Cathay. I am in the Western Seas to form mutually beneficial alliances on behalf of Tarkoth."

Kaiya tried to picture a map of Tivaralan in her mind, to no avail. Still, Cousin Kai-Long saw Madura as an immediate threat; and of course they'd invaded and occupied Hardeep's Ankira.

"We are well apprised of the state of international affairs," Father said. "Since we trade with all, including the Teleri, it is of the utmost importance that we remain fair and neutral. We can only extend the same hospitality to you as we do to all of our trading partners."

Prince Aelward opened and closed his mouth, his eyes staring up. "Your true enemy is the Teleri Empire. Madura and Rotuvi only threaten you at their bidding."

Father tilted his head a fraction, the equivalent of a shrug. "These countries are small. They are no more than a nuisance, one we will be dealing with shortly via diplomacy."

"I hear you will be negotiating with Madura in Vyara City soon," the prince said.

Her assignment. How had he known? The gathered officials and nobles murmured among themselves. Only the *Tianzi* remained unfazed.

Cousin Kai-Long, up to now hidden among the rest, stood up, cutting into the clamor. "*Huang-Shang*," he said in the Cathayi language. "As I said before in council, this is a perfect time to end the threat from Madura once and for all, by sweeping into the occupied Kingdom of Ankira. Although I oppose our meeting with the Madurans, I suggest that if talks break down, we ally with Tarkoth."

More murmuring, though Prince Aelward's blank expression suggested he didn't understand their tongue.

Father's tone provided no hint of what he was thinking. "Nephew, your suggestions are better suited for the *Tai-Ming* Council. In the eyes of our distinguished guest, we must always show a united front."

Kai-Long dropped to his knee, fist to the ground. "Forgive me, *Huang-Shang*."

Father raised a hand. "I will speak with Prince Aelward alone, with only my children in attendance. The rest of you will withdraw."

The assembled audience again broke out in low whispers. Father very rarely entertained a foreign guest alone, and usually in one of the palace's pavilions. It was unheard of for him to do so in the Hall of Supreme Harmony. Nevertheless, they all filed out without protest.

Kaiya looked around. With only the imperial guards, Prince Aelward, Father, and Brothers Kai-Guo and Kai-Wu, the cavernous room felt virtually empty. Jie and her Black Lotus brethren were likely hiding somewhere as well.

Father turned to Prince Aelward. "Our traditions stipulate we must act with propriety lest Heaven forsake us. We cannot forego negotiation. Yet if history is any lesson, the Madurans will reject our peace overtures. If our talks fail, we will provide material support to Tarkoth's cause."

Kaiya stifled a gasp. Father was sending her to foreign lands, with the expectation she would fail.

Father lifted a hand. "Would you consider as act of Tarkoth's good will, to take my daughter to Ayudra City on *the Invincible*?"

Kaiya's brow furrowed. The imperial flagship, the *Golden Phoenix*, might not rate with the Eldaeri black ships, but it was still a symbol of Cathay's wealth and power.

Prince Aelward bowed deeply. "Aye, it'd be my pleasure. Not only that, but the *Invincible* can't navigate the Shallowsea between Ayudra Island and Vyara City. I offer my own personal guard Ayana as protection for your daughter when she transfers to the Shallowsea skiffs."

"Her transport will be conducted in the utmost secrecy." Father smiled, breaking imperial decorum. "The meeting is set for when the White Moon waxes to full, just over fifteen days from today. In the meantime, please enjoy our hospitality, especially during the festive New Year season. My daughter will guide you to your guest house after I speak with her. You may be excused."

Prince Aelward bowed to the *Tianzi* and stumbled out with the elf and the Tarkothi ambassador.

Father motioned for Kaiya and her brothers to step off the dais and face him. "My children, you are wondering why I asked the Tarkothi prince to take Kaiya to Ayudra. It was actually the suggestion of Minister Hong Jianbin, and his logic is sound."

Kaiya looked to her brothers to see if they shared her shock. Minister Hong had gained favor with Father, bypassing regular channels to his ear. She turned back to find Father's gaze bearing down on her.

"First," he said, "there are those who would seek to derail the peace talks in hopes of promoting Expansionism. They would never expect you to go aboard *the Invincible* while we send the rest of your entourage on the *Golden Phoenix*. If there is any treachery, you will be safe."

He rose to his feet and swept his hand through the empty hall. "Secondly, we do not know who is behind all of these attacks.

As much as I want to trust the *Tai-Ming* lords and ministers, I will take all precautions with your safety."

The *Tianzi* returned to his seat. "Finally, I wish to see the extent of Tarkoth's good will. Our trade routes must remain protected. Remember that when the elf appeared before the council, she said that Prince Aelward is here to harass Teleri's allies. If we continue trade with the Teleri, perhaps the *Invincible* will target our ships."

Kaiya's mind spun. "*Huang-Shang*, am I being sent to Vyara City, not to push for peace, but rather to ensure war with Madura?"

Father shook his head, something he would only do around his family. "No, Kaiya. I have faith that you will avert war. However, in order to get Prince Aelward to agree to take you, I had to make it seem like failure was the inevitable outcome."

"You lied, then." Kaiya couldn't keep the accusatory tone out of her voice. Heat rose to her face.

Father's lips formed a tight line. "No. I said that *if history is any lesson*. I trust you have the wit to rewrite history."

Eldest Brother Kai-Guo nodded. "The last week administering national affairs in Father's stead has shown me that the *Tianzi* must make decisions in the best interest of the nation. If those choices are not the most moral, they must be articulated in half-truths and misdirection."

Kaiya gawked at Eldest Brother. Such cynicism. Her eyes shifted to Kai-Wu, who as always seemed to be busy with his own thoughts.

Father's gaze still fell on her, reading her. Did he really expect her to succeed against the odds, or was that just encouragement wrapped in a half-truth and misdirection?

She looked back toward Prince Aelward, who waited outside of the Hall. If anyone knew about his agreement with the *Tianzi*, he could very well be Madura's next target.

CHAPTER 17:
Patriot Games

Jie tugged at her dress, almost satisfied with the tailor's alterations. Cut from bright red silk with gold embroidery, the gown allowed her to blend in with the aristocracy gathered to watch the New Year's Tournament. They milled among the stone-tiered seating on the western side of Qingjinghu Amphitheatre, chatting and pointing at contestants.

Unlike the nobles' garments, Jie's afforded plenty of mobility and had several secret pockets for tools and weapons. She was better armed than the dozen imperial guards surrounding the Imperial Family's box. Their *dao* were tucked in golden sashes, which matched their festive red robes.

Replacing the conspicuously absent *Tianzi*, Crown Prince Kai-Guo presided over the final day of the tournament. His wife and siblings joined him in the box abutting the grassy field in the three hundred-foot basin. Across from them, tens of thousands of commoners covered every last inch of the basin's grassy slopes, cheering for their favorite competitors.

Jie shifted her attention from Princess Kaiya to the adjoining box, where foreign dignitaries sat. Yappy young Lin Ziqiu circulated among them, flirting with handsome men.

"Kayane elestrae arasti tu?" called a flitting voice from behind.

Jie spun to meet the gaze of the matronly elf woman Ayana. She responded in Arkothi. "Excuse me?"

The elf leaned back. "I was asking your name, Little One."

Jie glared at the old hag. "It is *not* Little One."

Ayana placed a hand on her chest. "Forgive me, our forms of address do not translate well into Arkothi. Please believe me, in our language, it is a term of endearment for young elves."

Lord Xu had used the same address, but he didn't come off as particularly endearing. And after three decades of life, the constant references to her tender years grew annoying. "I am not as young as you think."

The right side of Ayana's lips quirked up. "I was a child during the Hellstorm. To me, you are quite young."

"It shows." Jie regretted the words as soon as they left her mouth. She bowed. "I'm sorry. I am so used to being called *little* and *young* by people younger than me."

"It is to be expected. You are one of us, living among humans."

Jie pursed her lips. She'd *never* be one of them, but she forced herself to mind her manners. "My name is Jie Yan. How may I be of service?"

The left side of Ayana's lips joined the right in forming a smile, sending rays of fine crinkles by her eyes. "I was just curious. My magic tells me this basin is called Clear Crystal Pond. I don't see any water."

Jie sucked on her lower lip. How did the history go? "It was once a reservoir. The Founder used castles to stimulate urban development and economic growth. As the city grew—"

"It needed water."

Jie pointed to the north end of the basin. "A streambed paved with rocks fed into the reservoir."

"What happened?"

What did it matter to an elf? Jie's forehead scrunched up. "I think an earthquake damaged the streambed and choked off the water supply. Grass took over, and now it's used for recreation, military training, and events like this tournament."

Ayana nodded. "Ah, humans and their competitiveness." She pointed to the horses gathered in the field. "Is this a polo?"

A polo? Jie chuckled. For someone three hundred years old, Ayana should've been an expert in Arkothi grammar. "No, these events are military in nature. Fencing, archery, wrestling… right now it's mounted archery. That's why Princess Kaiya is here."

"Yes, Kaiya has a special rooting interest." Lin Ziqiu appeared at her side, giggling.

The princess glared back. "Lady Ayana, you mustn't believe my naughty handmaiden or cousin."

Naughty! Jie stared back in a subtle show of insolence.

Prince Aelward, seated beside Ayana, leaned over and grinned. "Aye, she is. Put 'er on my ship, and we'll have 'er scrubbing the decks. That'll teach 'er to mind 'er tongue."

"Scrubbing the decks?" Jie snorted. "Maybe using your tears."

Princess Kaiya gawked. "Jie! Your manners."

"Ye can put a pretty dress on the girl, but it won't dull 'er sharp tongue."

"I'm sorry, Your Highness." The princess bowed low. "My handmaiden—"

"Is far more than a handmaiden." Aelward laughed. "The little sprite and I well acquainted. I owe her a favor."

"Or three," Jie said. At least three. The journey to Arkos had been dangerous.

The princess favored her with a raised eyebrow.

"So about that special rooting interest that you've here for?" Aelward asked.

Princess Kaiya covered a laugh. "I merely enjoy watching mounted archery. Even as muskets supplant bows in our armies, there is still an elegance to a man who can shoot a bow from horseback."

Jie coughed. A man. Riiight. *The* man. Her eyes strayed to the kerchief clenched in the princess' hands.

A dark-haired, ruddy-skinned man in the same box as Prince Aelward chortled. He wore a flaxen coat with tassels of braided horsehair along its borders. Brightly-colored bird feathers adorned his hair. A Kanin plainsman from the Kingdom of Tomiwa, he spoke Arkothi with a rich accent. "If you want to see *real* mounted archery, come to my homeland. Our children can ride a horse without a saddle and still shoot."

The princess tilted her head a fraction. "Is that an invitation, Prince Tani?"

He winked. "Only as my bride."

Jie pointed out in the field. "Young Lord Zheng Ming might have something to say about that."

The princess' cheeks flushed a red to match her gown, but her gaze followed Jie's finger all the same.

A parade of the twenty-seven archers, three from each province, circled the green in single file. As reigning champion, Lord Zheng rode in the lead, wearing a light tunic of pale green with the golden circle *wen* emblem of the sun rising over twin mountains on his chest and sleeves. He waved at the crowd to raucous cheers. With the rumors swirling around the capital, the dashing lord's ego had likely swollen large enough to shift the tides. The three moons would be jealous.

He approached the royal box as per custom, to be greeted by the Crown Prince. He drew close, and Princess Kaiya leaned forward and tied a white silk ribbon with the sky-blue stitching of the imperial dragon around his forehead. The break in tradition sent the audience into louder applause. Even if Zheng received it with cool calm, her blush could've competed with the sun. Jie just yawned.

When all the contestants finished saluting the Crown Prince, they gathered at one end of the field. From there, they would circle the course and shoot at twenty wooden targets of different sizes. The number of targets hit would determine the winner, with the quickest time on a dwarf-made water clock as a tiebreaker. Zheng, the reigning champion, would ride last.

Jie scooted forward, rapt with interest. On firm ground, she was a fair archer at best; and she and horses didn't get along. Maybe mounted archery was impractical, but it certainly took skill.

The event started to loud cheers. Each participant seemed better than the last, hitting more targets in faster times.

The princess sat at the edge of the imperial box, right next to Prince Aelward in the adjoining box, pointing out the riders and describing their home provinces. On occasion, her regal demeanor would slip as she gasped and clapped her hands.

At Prince Aelward's side, Kanin Prince Tani shrugged. "What's the challenge in riding around in a circle?"

A rider in a light blue tunic came to the line. With her sharp eyes, Jie picked out the silver *wen* crest of a nine-petal flower, symbol of Huayuan Province. Smiling, the princess rose to her feet and clapped. Prince Aelward, looking at her, followed suit.

The princess gestured with an open hand. "That is Xie Shimin, a decorated soldier and provincial champion. He is a crowd favorite, a strong contender every year."

Xie spurred his mount forward, shouting a salute that carried across the basin. None of his first shots came close to their targets.

Prince Tani scoffed. The crowd buzzed with talk of the hometown hero's poor performance.

Jie sucked on her bottom lip. Something felt wrong.

Besides the imperial guards and her two Black Lotus brothers, none of the spectators had weapons. The contestants, on the other hand…

Jie inched forward, straining to get a better view of Xie Shimin as he rounded the final bend. He urged his horse into a full gallop, no longer even looking at the remaining targets. The audience pointed and shouted, many launching jeers at their own soldier.

With an arrow fitted, Xie approached the center of the tiered seating, far past any of the clay targets.

Around Jie, the imperial guards surged past her toward the front.

Xie leveled his bow, took aim and let his arrow fly.

The audience let out a collective gasp as the arrow streaked toward the dignitaries.

Jie reached across the stone divider into the adjacent box and snatched the arrow out of the air with her left hand, just before it could hit the unsuspecting Prince Aelward. With her right, she whipped out a throwing star from her sleeve and hurled it at Xie.

The would-be assassin had already nocked another arrow and shot just as the star lodged in his gut.

In Jie's peripheral vision, Lady Ayana raised her hand and spoke a guttural syllable. The air in front of them shimmered like a hot summer haze. The arrow careened into an invisible barrier and fell to the ground.

In front of her, the imperial guards Chen Xin and Li Wei formed a protective shield for Princess Kaiya, their naked blades held at the ready.

Xie took aim at a target higher up, seemingly unfazed by the throwing star in his belly. Jie followed his line of sight.

Chief Minister Tan stood alone, unprotected, sweat trickling down his forehead and drenching the armpits of his robes.

The arrow smacked into the stone wall behind him with a loud thwack.

Jie spun back to see Xie fit another arrow. He aimed at Lord Peng Kai-Long, who stared impassively at the instrument of his own impending doom.

Zheng Ming spurred his horse into a full gallop across the field. He'd watched his friend Xie's bizarre run, wondering about the challenge Xie had promised on the practice field several days before. Each of his shots had been sloppy. On the final stretch, he didn't take a shot at all.

At least, not until his friend started shooting into the dignitary box. Not once, but twice.

Leaning from his saddle, Ming plucked an errant arrow from the ground as he closed the gap. He whispered a prayer to any god that would listen and let his arrow fly.

It struck Xie in the back of his left shoulder, just before he loosed his fourth shot. The shock of the blow jolted him forward. The bow skidded from his hand and snapped back into his face. The arrow dropped to the ground.

Wobbling in his saddle, Xie withdrew one last arrow and placed the edge on his neck. Ming closed quickly. He would never reach his friend in time.

"Stand down." The princess sang the words, her voice carrying across the field and above the chaos of frightened spectators.

Xie hesitated.

The elf woman pointed a finger at him and grunted something.

Xie slumped in his saddle, the arrow slipping from his fingers. He pushed against the neck of his horse, his body rocking as he righted his balance.

On the slopes, the watch swam through the panicked audience toward the field. The nobles and ministers in the seats pushed and shoved their way toward the exits. Several imperial guards spilled over the balustrades and charged toward the horse and rider with weapons drawn.

Crown Prince Kai-Guo pointed at Xie. "Take him alive!"

Zheng Ming trotted up to Xie's horse and seized its reins. The imperial guards pulled the limp man from his saddle.

Splotches of red spread from his abdomen and shoulder, his complexion pale as they laid him on the ground.

Crown Prince Kai-Guo climbed down, surrounded by wary guards, and pushed his way to the would-be assassin.

Behind him, the exotic little handmaiden pulled on Princess Kaiya's sleeve, even as the princess slipped between her two imperial guards. She glared at her handmaiden, and the servant relented.

Such courage! Not only that, she could make something as awkward as jumping from the stands look graceful. Ming dismounted and came to her side.

The Crown Prince stood over Xie. "Why did you attack the Tarkothi prince? Who sent you?"

Xie Shimin, his eyes fluttering, choked on his words. "Forgive me, *Dian-xia*, I am sworn to secrecy. It was not treason. I did it to protect our great nation."

"Protect the nation?" The Crown Prince gestured back to the stands. "You attacked a foreign dignitary. How will that do anything but tarnish our great name? I command you to answer. I would prefer not to subject one of our soldiers to an interrogator."

An imperial guard shook his head. "*Dian-xia*, he will not survive this wound, let alone interrogation."

Ming made his way to the circle of men surrounding his friend.

"*Dian-xia*." Xie coughed blood as he spoke. "These are not times for talk, but for action. Foreign enemies seek to swallow up Cathay."

The princess touched Ming's arm. "What can you tell me about Xie Shimin?"

Ming bowed. "We served in Wailian County at the border. His father passed away several years ago. His only family is a sick mother. He has no siblings, no wife."

Without any acknowledgement of his words, the princess pushed forward through the guards. Even as they tried to stop her, she knelt by Xie's side and took his hands in her own. "Brave soldier of Cathay," she said, "you have been misled by those who seek to destroy our peaceful country from within. Please, let us know who your co-conspirators are, and I will personally ensure that your parents' graves are tended to."

Xie looked up at her, inner struggle mingling with pain on his face.

"Tell me." She sang her words again.

Xie's shoulders relaxed. "I have sworn on my family's grave not to reveal the origin of the order… When you go to my barracks, you will find a lot of evidence meant to mislead you…"

That answer was no less a riddle than anything else Xie had said. Ming exchanged glances with the others gathered around. Eyebrows were raised, lips were pursed. At least he wasn't the only one who was confused.

Crown Prince Kai-Guo straightened and addressed the guards. "Reestablish order, calm the citizenry. The tournament will be cancelled for now. Send someone to the soldier's barracks and gather all of his belongings. The *Tianzi* must not be told about this. I will not worry him more before New Year's prayers at the Temple of Heaven on the morrow."

Ming dropped to his knee. "*Dian-xia*, please allow me to accompany your investigator to Xie's barracks. He was my friend, and never once did he say anything treasonous."

The Crown Prince peered at him for a few seconds before nodding. He motioned for a member of the watch. "Accompany Young Lord Zheng to the Huayuan Provincial Cavalry barracks."

Ming turned to check on the princess. She would be shaken from yet another attack, and a few sweet words would comfort her. He'd reassure her he would ride with her during tomorrow's New Year's procession.

She already stood at the base of the stands, smiling and chatting with the Eldaeri prince.

Kaiya still felt the cold of Xie Shimin's grasp, even as she held a low bow before Prince Aelward. She hadn't wanted to release the dying soldier's hand, but the prince's choking in the stands was a poignant reminder of her duties as an imperial representative. If a foreign dignitary died at the hands of an assassin, the repercussions could range anywhere from trade embargos to war. It would also scuttle her own mission of peace, perhaps leading to more unnecessary deaths in Cathay.

She did not deign to meet Prince Aelward's eyes. "I cannot apologize enough for this breach in security."

"It's okay, lass," he said, voice gruff. "No need for theatrics."

With effort, Kaiya straightened. After expending the energy needed to get Xie to talk, her limbs felt like dwarf anvils, and a haze fogged her mind. Such power came with a price, apparently, and the limit of her commands seemed to be two syllables. "Again, I am sorry. I hope you are uninjured."

"Aye, lass. Only a scratch when I slipped on the step. Your chippy handmaiden has quite the hands. Saved me from an arrow." He nodded toward Jie, whose sleeves concealed her hands, and who knew what else. "I owe you a blood debt."

Jie started to drop to one knee, but twisted with the grace of a cat into an Arkothi-style curtsey. "That's four, now."

Kaiya clenched her jaw. "Perhaps we should retreat to the safety of the palace now."

"Nay, I think I've enjoyed enough of your country's festivities. I'll be heading back to the *Invincible*. She'll be ready to sail when you embark on your mission."

From the embankment on the opposite side of the basin, the renegade Black Fist Liang Yu used a dwarven magnifying scope to watch the dying soldier. He had to twist and crane his neck to get a good view through the swirling crowds.

Though he did not know of this plan, he had suspected his former employer would strike here. Without Liang Yu to do his dirty work, he had blackmailed Xie Shimin, using the leverage Liang Yu had uncovered months before.

He sighed. Alas, yet another patriot sacrificed, all to ensure Cathay's continued greatness. Certainly the *Tianzi* would now move beyond purely defensive measures and take decisive action.

His special pupil flashed a hand signal, confirming Liang Yu's suspicions. Snapping the dwarven scope shut, he rose to his feet. He now was certain of the identity of his former employer. Once the war started, he would exact his vengeance for the betrayal at Jade Spring Inn.

Near the back of the stone seats, Minister Hong Jianbin feigned panic, even as he struggled to hide joy at his luck. Even if his spy had bungled, his plans might work out better than he imagined. With the princess to depart on her trip to Vyara City in two days, he might very well be Chief Minister in less than a week.

CHAPTER 18:
Idle Pursuits

Zheng Ming lay awake on silken sheets, in a room whose luxury might have rivaled an imperial pavilion. Not that he'd know.

He stared at the ceiling tiles, admiring how the late afternoon light played on the intricate dragon and phoenix carvings. His thoughts wandered, bouncing between the investigation into his friend Xie Shimin, and the princess' affection for the foreign prince.

A search of Xie's personal effects earlier that day revealed Maduran coins and a letter in Ayuri script. Though Ming couldn't read it, he had little doubt it had come from Madura as well. Yet Xie had also told the princess something about not believing all the evidence.

Ming rolled over, only to be pulled into the bare arms of some minister's daughter or niece or something. The walnut-toned beauty, who looked to have some Ayuri blood in her, had virtually thrown herself at him after his exploits at the tournament. He'd succumbed to her charms, having grown frustrated at the princess' coy flirtations. After several weeks, a man needed release, after all.

It hadn't taken much to coax the exotic young woman into joining him at this high-end establishment, which specifically catered to discreet meetings. A frequent visitor on his trips to the capital, Zheng Ming often wondered what secrets the proprietress knew, given the patrons included all manner of lords and high officials.

Yet right now, even as the girl kissed his neck and ran her hands over him, all he could think about was his guilt. Of course the princess would not be like other women. She was too bound by court conventions to openly shower affection on a man. Her token before the tournament was already a bold statement on her part.

And here he was, with a girl whose name he couldn't even remember.

Her kisses stopped abruptly and she pushed him away. She pulled the sheets up to hide her magnificent nakedness, eyes glinting in accusation. "You are thinking of *her*."

Ming flashed a well-trained smile at her. Her lips quivered. A strategically-placed finger on those full lips caused her to inhale sharply, eyes closed.

"If by *her*, you are referring to our motherland of Cathay," he said, "then yes. I'm thinking of her. I'm sorry. But if you are implying some other woman, then the only one I'm thinking of is you."

His response was so glib, he almost believed it himself. He kissed her forehead. Her hands reached into his hair. The sheet covering her slipped, forgotten.

So naïve, these city girls. Ming tried to ignore the guilt tapping on his shoulder, and focused on pleasing her. The afternoon ambled on, their lovemaking leaving him spent.

When he awoke, the woman was gone. All his worries and guilt flooded back to him. He dressed and slipped out of the guest house. Above, the Iridescent Moon waxed to its fifth crescent, giving him an hour before the New Year's Eve feast began at his provincial compound.

The streets bustled with people rushing home for their own holiday feasts. With his *dao* tucked in his sash, most recognized him as a lord and made way. He ground to a halt just before he reached the stable where he'd left his horse.

A dozen members of the city watch were questioning the stable boy. A couple of other men milled among them, nodding and pointing.

Just when Ming was about to approach, a plainly-dressed man with a walking stick barreled right into him, nearly knocking him to the ground.

Ming growled. "Hey! Are you blind? Watch where you're going!"

The boor just snickered and kept walking. The gall!

The horse and commotion could wait. Ming spun around and jogged to catch up with the man. "I'm talking to you! Do you know who I am?"

The man's shoulders shook as his pace quickened. The bastard was laughing!

Indignation rising, Ming followed the man around a corner.

He found himself dumped onto the ground. A knife pushed against his throat. Ming's eyes darted around to get his bearings. He'd turned into an alley, never suspecting a trap. After all, who would attempt such an audacious attack in broad daylight, in a fairly busy part of the city?

"Young Lord Zheng Ming," the man whispered. "That should answer your question, I *do* know who you are. I am going to let you get up, and I want you to follow me. Swear to me now you will not call for the watch."

"I swear," Ming whispered his answer, now more intrigued than angry or frightened.

His assailant had long black hair with streaks of silver, and worn features that bore evidence of a hard life. Besides that, he was incredibly plain. He offered a hand, and Ming took it.

Pulled to his feet, Ming followed the stranger deeper into the alley. Who was this guy? And what did he want? With the man's back turned, it would be easy to run away, call out—though not for the watch, since he'd sworn—or even attack—

"You will be dead before your sword leaves its scabbard."

Ming's hand had unconsciously strayed toward the hilt of his *dao*. He thrust his hands behind his back.

The man chuckled. "Do you know with whom you have been sharing a bed?"

Heat burned in his cheeks. "Have you been following me?"

The man looked over his shoulder at Ming. "I am watching you for your own sake. You, my friend, are being set up. What do you suppose will happen if your pretty princess finds out you are spreading your seed while actively courting *her*?"

Ming shrugged. Years of smooth talking yielded a lie he almost believed himself. "It doesn't matter. It's over between us."

The man grinned. "Good. Now that we've gotten that out of the way, don't you wonder why you were set up? Or did you just assume your handsome face was enough to get any girl into bed?"

Ming had, in fact, assumed that. He bit his lip. "Why?"

"If you knew *who*, then the *why* might be easier to guess."

"Would you stop talking in riddles?" Ming glared at the man.

The man's smirk deepened. "My problem is I know *who*, but not *why*. Maybe you can help me."

Ming threw his hands up. "Just say it!"

"Minister Hong Jianbin. The girl is his pawn. Or maybe even his lover."

Ming winced. Had he just slept with… "Hong's lover?"

Another chuckle. "I can only surmise. If I were in your boots, I'd be more concerned that Hong was setting you up."

Ming's mind swam. "Whatever for?"

"And we circle back to the first question. I would think he is either trying to ruin any chances you might have with the princess—"

"He *wanted* me to court her." Ming scratched his head. Maybe there was more to that.

"—or use it as leverage against you," the man continued.

"What kind of leverage?" Ming asked.

"Almost certainly not the same *I* am going to use on you."

Ming reached for his sword, but found the walking stick pressed against the guard, preventing him from drawing it.

"Young Lord Zheng, you have much to live for. Don't throw your life away in this alley. I can make your death look very embarrassing."

Ming hid his cringe. The idea of death did not seem particularly appealing. Dying with everyone thinking him a coward— or worse—, even less so. He spoke through gritted teeth. "What do you want?"

The man raised a silencing hand. He then reached and plucked a red envelope from the folds of Ming's robe.

"Hey!" Ming swiped for the packet, but the man shifted just out of his reach. It was only a poem he'd written for the princess before the tournament, a gift for the New Year's procession tomorrow. Hadn't he given it to one of his men to take back to the compound? Now some stranger had his dirty paws on it.

The man withdrew the folded paper and snapped the letter open. His eyes darted over the script before he looked up. "Love letters—to the Crown Princess, no less."

Crown Princess Xiulan? That would be a capital offense. Ming snatched the letter from the man's willing grasp and read. "This isn't even my handwriting." Not to mention... "The poetry is horrible."

The man shrugged. "Has the princess ever seen your script?"

No. Ming clenched his jaw. "Why would Hong do this?"

"Scuttle your budding relationship with the princess? Have you branded as a traitor? Undermine the Crown Prince and Princess?"

"Hong is going to pay for this."

The man held up a hand again. "Young Lord Zheng, let the Founder's words guide you. *Knowledge is power.* Perhaps Hong is up to something more insidious. If it were me, I would make Hong think you have fallen into his trap and see how he reacts. You might very well dig up more than you imagined."

Ming closed his slack jaw. "So you want me to give this to the princess?"

"No, just don't meet with her at tomorrow's procession. Hong will think she spurned you."

Ming's heart sank, even if he kept his face impassive. Standing the princess up would destroy any chance of winning her back from Prince Aelward. "No, I have to go."

The man grinned. "Well, let's not forget about my leverage. I have means of reaching the princess. I will expose your infidelity myself. I know where you went and who you were with."

This man was some mousey commoner. How did he have access to the princess? Perhaps it would be better to risk exposure of his dalliances. After all, young lords were expected to have an occasional tryst or three.

The man shook his head. "If that's not enough persuasion, let me give you another reason to heed my advice. I can make you a hero."

Liang Yu sat quietly at the Jade Teahouse, his new meeting place in the Floating World in southeast Huajing, close to where he'd ambushed Zheng Ming.

Stealing the poem from the young lord's messenger outside the amphitheater had been easy. Planting and then revealing the fake letter was even easier, like pulling a coin from a child's ear. Liang Yu took only mild offense at Zheng's insult of his poetry and handwriting.

He leaned back from the table and chuckled. The provincial lord's naïveté was amusing. Even an initiate Black Fist could have seen through Zheng Ming's pathetic attempts to hide his emotions. His affection for the princess and his own vanity made him simple to manipulate. Promised with the chance of again being the hero, he'd willingly embarked on a trail which would—with Liang Yu's help over a few weeks— expose his former employer.

Of course, it meant keeping Zheng Ming in Cathay until the betrayer pushed the war with Madura to inevitability.

The only uncertainty was whether or not Young Lord Zheng's servant would confess to losing the poem. A betting man would gamble that the man would not come forward with his guilt, and the naïve young lord would assume Hong's woman had swapped the letters.

Gambles only won wars half the time. The messenger would be yet another necessary casualty for Cathay's greatness.

The door to the teahouse opened. His special pupil stood there, back from spying on Minister Hong.

Minister Hong Jianbin looked at his naked form in the full-length mirror, not really liking what he saw. It had little to do with the sagging leathery skin, sallow complexion or thin whitening hair that came with his advancing age. Rather, he wondered when and where he had become obsessed with power, willing to do almost anything to obtain it.

He was not ambitious by nature, but his family had sacrificed much to get him into the civil service and on the path to rapid social mobility. He had been a good government bureaucrat at every level, quickly rising through the ranks and gaining the trust and friendship of the man who would become Chief Minister.

Hong turned around and studied his back, all covered in splotches. When had his inside become as horrible as the outside?

Chief Minister Tan had brought Hong up with him. At each level, from dutiful provincial clerk to trade official, and now to Household Minister, he had tasted new heights of wealth, power, and privilege. He might have been satisfied, had the opportunity to progress even higher not serendipitously tumbled into his hands.

"My Lord," a sweet voice sang from outside at the sliding door.

Hong smiled, gathering his robe around him and forgetting his misgivings. One of wealth's perks was the keeping of a concubine. "Come in, come in."

The doors slid open, revealing Leina, his half-Cathayi, half-Ayuri beauty, now wearing a translucent vermillion inner robe. The hot bath they'd shared together left a pink flush on her walnut cheeks. With no family in the capital, he would spend New Year's Eve with her. She closed the doors behind her and swept across the room to a low table where she kneeled again. Her every movement reminded him of the graceful fluttering streamers of the ribbon dance. Tonight, she practically sparkled with bliss.

Leina poured some tea for him. "My Lord, are you ready to play chess?"

Minister Hong tottered over to the table. He eased himself down into a cross-legged position, his old knees protesting. "I have never beaten you, have I?"

"No, my Lord, neither in Northern nor Cathayi chess. But there is always a first time." Leina beckoned him with an enticing lift of her eyebrow. "You look particularly naughty this evening. Perhaps you should take the black pieces while I take the white."

As always, her sense of humor made him forget his own troubles and uncertainties. He admired her delicate elegance as she glided her pieces across the board in response to his own moves. Her intelligence and charm just added to her exotic beauty, and Hong often wondered if he should just give up his plans, forget about Princess Kaiya, and take Leina as his official wife. Of course, she continually pressed him to pursue the princess, claiming it would make her the second most important woman in Cathay.

Leina shifted her chariot into a defensive position. "Sending the princess to meet with the Madurans will be disastrous to your prospects of becoming Chief Minister. She'll learn they had nothing to do with the insurgency. The Expansionists won't get their war."

Hong tried to concentrate on the implications of her move. Although Leina rarely used the same strategy twice, or any strategy for that matter, the one constant was her lulling voice. "I had to send her away," he said, "or Lord Peng would kill her."

"You will never have her if you cannot become Chief Minister in the first place."

Hong sighed. He realized the limits of his ambition when he placed the princess' life ahead of his own plans. "I gambled that I could push the Chief Minister issue before the princess meets with the Madurans. The Expansionists would still support me because I have done everything they asked. The attack on the foreign prince all but guarantees the war they want. I also have the backing of the Royalists, who want the princess as a bride for their sons."

The rise of Leina's thin eyebrow prompted him to continue.

Hong grinned back. If she had to think it out herself, she would be less focused on her game. His first victory was close at hand.

At last, she shrugged.

Hong laughed. He could always outwit her in conspiracies, even if he could not beat her at chess. However, that string of defeats looked to change in a few minutes. "It won't be long before the *Tianzi's* agents learn about Xie Shimin's immense debts from paying for his sick mother's treatment."

Tears glassed over her eyes; the sentimental weakness of women. "Oh, the poor thing."

"Yes, the honorable Xie Shimin, duped into believing there was patriotism in assassinating a foreign dignitary under the *Tianzi's* protection, and exploited by his financial needs. The trail will lead back to the mastermind, and I control the timing."

"What a stroke of genius!" Smiling, Leina clapped her hands together. Then her perfect brow crinkled. "But by sending the princess to Vyara City, you are putting your prospect of marrying her into jeopardy. No telling what the treacherous Madurans will do, especially if they are unjustly accused of meddling."

"Dear Leina, you mustn't let your own biases cloud your judgment." Hong used the distraction to put pressure on one of her advisors, which would open up a line of attack for his elephant. "I know your mother was Ankiran—"

"But my father was from Cathay, the trade official to Ankira," she interjected, a wounded look in her dark eyes.

Hong looked up from the board to contemplate her exotic features. He knew her history well: her father had been posted in Ankira for many years, arranging official sales of outdated, first-generation muskets to Ankira; her mother an Ankiran dancer whom he had taken as a lover despite his family back home. Leina had grown up in Ankira. When Cathay ultimately closed its trade office after Madura's occupation ten years before, she had been left behind and her mother killed. How horrible life must have been for her before escaping to Cathay two years ago in search of her father. "Would *you* rather marry me instead?" he ventured.

She threw her head back in laughter, such a refreshing show of emotion compared to reserved Carthayi ladies.

Heat rose to Hong's face, maybe enough that the redness showed through his thick, tough skin. "I... I would be honored to take you as my wife."

"And give up on your ambitions?" Her amusement carried an underlying tone of rebuke. "I would be selfish to have you do that. After all, you are just one move from becoming Chief Minister, two moves from marrying the princess."

"And three moves from finally beating you!" Hong smacked his cannon down in direct line to her general. "*Jiangjun!*" Check.

"No, just one move from losing," Leina said, moving her rider back between his cannon and her general. It opened up a line for her chariot toward his general, where his own cannon had just vacated. "Checkmate," she exclaimed with girlish excitement. She had unwittingly disguised her offense and defense, and he had stumbled into the trap.

Again.

He reached across the table and placed his hand on hers. "Let us celebrate your victory, the New Year, and my imminent appointment as Chief Minister."

If Hong Jianbin weren't already so dismissive of her, Leina would feign stupidity and play strategy games to lose. As it was, beating him time and time again provided small consolation for having to tolerate his patronizing.

She now peered through the darkness at him, fast asleep from their long and vigorous lovemaking. His always surprising virility had allowed her to close her eyes and imagine it was Young Lord Zheng again.

Maybe in Zheng's mind, she was just another conquest. Still, he could dissemble convincingly enough with his pillow talk to stir a rush of excitement.

And she'd sacrificed him. A lump formed in her throat.

Hiding out as they were in the Floating World, news of Zheng Ming's arrest wouldn't reach old Hong's ears until the next morning. She'd hidden a letter in the young man's scabbard, implicating him in the insurgency. The city watch, tipped off by her informants, would find it when he went to get his horse.

She rolled over to face the window, away from Hong. He would never know of her involvement, and yet he would benefit: with Zheng out of the picture, the princess would remain unwed just a little longer, and Hong would stay motivated.

At the same time, Leina would move closer toward completing her assignment of weakening Cathay from the inside. All the easier with Princess Kaiya about to leave. Without her soothing voice balancing out rivalries, the hereditary lords would be at each other's throats.

She sighed, considering Hong again. For so long, she'd stoked his ambition, helping him overcome his natural lack of motivation and tenacity. She'd manipulated him, making him believe her scheming was his own. Though he showed remarkable adaptability to Peng's change in plans, his lack of foresight validated her choice of him as a tool.

Just as in chess, when playing a long game, forward thinking and planning overcame reaction and countermeasure. As Chief Minister, Hong would never foresee the long-term implications of the decisions she made for him. With two and a half years left in her assignment, his actions would leave Cathay weak, ripe for invasion.

In the meantime, sharing the old man's bed was the price she would pay. It was far preferable than staying in Ankira, to be used by countless foreign soldiers. She could only hope that when everything was said and done, her employer would hold up his end of the bargain and free her mother.

CHAPTER 19:
It Will Be a Good Year

For Kaiya, the staccato bursts of firecrackers in the distance punctuated the most somber New Year's Day she could remember. The *Tianzi's* annual procession to the Temple of Heaven was her favorite ritual and usually a lively affair. In previous years, crowds had lined the streets to watch and perhaps catch a glimpse of the Imperial Family among all of the lords and ministers.

Given the current security concerns, the city watch and national army kept the citizenry blocks away. Storefronts, while bedecked in celebratory red, remained shuttered and idle. Strings of lanterns and banners hung limp and lifeless. Without cheering crowds, the procession seemed like a wedding banquet with no guests.

No spectators enjoyed the one-hundred-and-sixty-eight-foot dragon, embroidered in gold silk and borne by eighty-eight of the most handsome imperial guards. The only people to see the flashing colors of silken robes and horse brocades were those marching in the parade.

Kaiya sighed. Perhaps in the distance, the citizenry could hear the beating drums or tinkling saddle bells. They would certainly see the imperial aviary's eight earth phoenixes circling above the procession. Nearly fifteen feet with a wingspan of twice that, they made for an impressive sight, despite being a tenth the size of the mythical phoenixes. They had heads that resembled pheasants, but tails that fanned out like peacocks. Their legs stretched long like cranes, while their wings flapped like swallows. Brightly colored gold and silver feathers sparkled in the sunlight.

Female imperial guards rode astride the phoenixes. Like all imperial princesses past and present Kaiya had trained to ride, but with her fear of heights, she was happy her New Year's duties kept her on the ground.

Father rode in an open carriage. The High Priest of Cathay's patron god, Yang-Di, sat beside him; though Jie had told her that today, the man was the half-elf's adoptive father, Master Yan of the Black Lotus Monastery, who sometimes posed as a minister at court. In any other year, the citizenry would sink to their knees and press their foreheads to the ground as the *Tianzi* passed, wishing him a life of ten thousand years. Today, there was no one.

The rest of the Imperial Family followed the carriage in gold-painted palanquins; though at her insistence, Kaiya rode a horse, as she had for years. Her vantage point provided an excellent view of the inactivity. Her keen hearing told her that beyond the confines of the main boulevard, New Year's Day went on as usual for everyone else.

People flocked to the temples to wish for health and prosperity, and neighbors visited each other bearing auspicious gifts of fruits and candies. Despite the Cathayi people's worldwide reputation for frugality, not even beggars went hungry this day, as they were given leftovers from the feasting the night before. After all, generosity on New Year's Day would be repaid tenfold throughout the year.

Martial artists performed lion dances in front of stores and homes to scare away evil spirits. The sounds of drums and children laughing floated on the winds. Kaiya even imagined she could smell the burning incense drifting in from afar.

And here, the imperial procession marched, detached from the vibrancy and vitality of the annual celebration. Were these precautions really necessary? No one would stage an attack during the Spring Festival—nobody in Cathay would use anything sharp on New Year's Day, for fear of cutting their luck during the coming year.

Kaiya looked to her side, where her senior-most imperial guard Chen Xin rode awkwardly in the saddle, his knuckles white around the reins. It should've been Zheng Ming beside her, the invitation having been extended and accepted weeks before.

She pouted. As if the funerary atmosphere of her favorite holiday wasn't bad enough. She *liked* him. *Really* liked him. Problems dashed every opportunity to meet. Assassination attempts. Gruff foreign princes. Now sickness.

She pressed at his kerchief, stashed in the fold of her robe. A courier had arrived earlier that morning with news of Zheng Ming's illness. He'd been fine just the day before, when he heroically saved ministers and lords from assassination at the hands of his own friend. If illness kept him from accompanying her to Vyara City tomorrow, it would be at least a month before they met again.

"Halt!" The announcement by the Minister of Rites jolted Kaiya out of her thoughts.

She scanned the area. The procession had arrived outside the walls of the Temple of Heaven, an eight-tiered stupa. Painted red with blue gables, it housed a chunk from a fallen star, brought to Cathay by the Wang Dynasty Founder at the bidding of the Gods. It was here, two years ago, that she'd played the Dragon Scale Lute for Prince Hardeep.

The *Tianzi* descended from the carriage with the help of Ming's cousin, imperial guard general Zheng Jiawei. With an entourage of ministers in tow, he plodded through the gates and onto the Temple grounds.

Kaiya and her brothers followed at a respectful distance. It was only two years ago, after her exploits at Wailian, that she was allowed to enter. The white marble walls followed the elliptical outline of dragon bones, with the temple itself at the far focus. It stood on a circular, three-tiered marble base. She'd played the Dragon Scale Lute on the identical base at the near focus. Father negotiated the steps to the base with some difficulty before disappearing inside the stupa.

Vibrations, strong and rapid, emanated from the tower. She'd first noticed them when she came with Prince Hardeep, but now… the frequency sounded so clear, and a slower, deeper pulse harmonized with it. How had she never noticed it before? Lord Xu said sounds changed based on their relative location; but now, no matter where she stood, the resonance sounded the same. If not for the solemnity of the rites, she would've raised her voice in song.

Instead, she gazed into the heavens. At exactly noon, when the Iridescent Moon Caiyue disappeared from the sky for a few fleeting moments as it phased to new, on this day of the Spring Equinox, the *Tianzi* would pray to Cathay's patron god Yang-Di for the nation's continued prosperity.

To mark the time, the Minister of Rites struck a standing gong, which rang much louder than it should have given its size. The *Tianzi's* voice emanated from inside the stupa, sounding as awe-inspiring and powerful as she remembered from her youth.

Despite her earlier melancholy, Kaiya's spirits rose. Every fiber of her being resonated with excitement. This *would* be a good year. She would make it so. Starting with a visit to sick Zheng Ming, whose villa was fairly close to the temple.

From her place behind the princess, Jie found the *Tianzi's* voice pleasant, in an almost fatherly way. If her real father had ever sung to her, it might have sounded something like the Emperor's prayer.

Why everyone else seemed genuinely enraptured by his words, Jie couldn't fathom. She made a mental note. Give—no, proffer—a handkerchief to the princess so she could dab off the drool.

The princess' eyes glinted with a new focus. If Jie's experiences from two years ago were any guide, there was an idea forming in that pretty head, and thus far, nothing good had ever come of her impulses. Riding in open carriages, jumping into the fray surrounding the would-be assassin Xie Shimin, riding a horse today—the princess always got her way. It was a miracle she was still alive.

Jie watched her charge with a careful eye, recognizing a subtle fidget as the entourage departed the temple grounds.

As when they left Sun-Moon Palace, Chen Xin dropped to all fours to allow the princess to use him as a footstep to mount her horse. No sooner had she settled in the saddle did she spur her mount out of parade formation and into a fast lope.

Insane princess!

While the rest of the procession gawked, Jie pop-vaulted off Chen Xin and onto his horse. She urged it into pursuit.

Now who was insane?

Though Chen Xin's riding had been laughable, Jie had next to no experience with a horse. One of those rare occasions had been two years ago under the similar circumstances of rescuing an impulsive princess.

This impulsive princess. The gown, while modified for fighting, further hindered her questionable equestrian skills. She clutched the reins, her balance keeping her from bouncing out of the saddle and into an embarrassing—and potentially dangerous—rendezvous with the ground.

Despite her misgivings, Jie quickly got the hang of it. Luckily, the crowds of well-wishers made way for the princess, giving their horses a relatively straight path. Jie ventured a quick glance behind to see no one else giving chase. Above, the phoenixes still circled over the Temple of Heaven.

She quickly banished the wistful thoughts of riding a phoenix— *that* would never happen. It was up to her to protect the princess. Their direction left little doubt as to where they'd end up. There, Princess Kaiya would face a threat beyond Jie's ability to defend.

Sure enough, the princess slowed her horse to a stop outside of the Dongmen provincial villa. She gingerly dismounted, and Jie followed. Her foot nearly caught in the stirrup, causing her to stumble. Her thighs burned and her rear ached, just from the ten-minute canter. Forget phoenixes. If she never rode a horse again, it would be too soon.

The princess approached the solid wooden gate. "I am here to see Young Lord Zheng Ming."

The gate guards gaped and bowed. Perhaps they recognized her, but even if they didn't, her regal carriage and tone commanded respect. One raised his head. "The young lord is not here right now."

The princess raised an eyebrow. "Is he not convalescing? Open the gates."

The guards looked among themselves, confusion creased into their brows. The same one as before bowed again. "Do you have an invitation?"

Jie snorted, only to be silenced by the princess' glare. Jie composed her expression and stepped forward. "Princess Kaiya gave you an order."

The guards dropped to a knee, fist down. "*Dian-xia!*"

One stood and rapped on the gate. A slot slid open, revealing a pair of eyes. "Princess Kaiya is here to see the young lord." The slot snapped shut, and the guard turned back and bowed.

The gates opened at a tortoise's pace. A middle-aged gentleman knelt at the threshold, his forehead touching the ground. "*Dian-xia*, please be welcome. I am the villa steward. If you would like to wait for Young Lord Zheng's return, allow me to convey you to our teahouse."

The princess looked at Jie, her brows furrowed, before glaring at the steward. "So he is truly not here?"

The steward's face contorted into confusion. "No, *Dian-xia*. He had urgent business to attend to this morning."

"On New Year's Day?" the princess said.

"Yes, *Dian-xia*."

The princess spun on her heel, all excitement drained from her face. She wobbled toward her horse.

Jie's belly hollowed. Until this moment, she never empathized with a noblewoman over trivial matters of courtship. She reached her hand out, for once at a loss of words. The princess was making her soft.

The steward hurried to the princess' side. "*Dian-xia*, it is not safe in the city. Please come inside the compound and I shall send a messenger to the palace."

Ignoring him, the princess put her foot in a stirrup and climbed onto her horse.

The reality of Jie's assignment quashed her short-lived sympathy. By now, word of Princess Kaiya's mad dash could have reached whoever wanted her dead. They were out in the open, with no protection. She dropped to her knee, fist to the ground. "*Dian-xia*, please listen to the steward. You must not risk your life."

The princess looked down from her mount, her expression forlorn. "I do not wish to be here when Zheng Ming returns."

Jie rose and took the reins, holding firm even as the princess tugged back. "Lord Steward, please send your messenger to the palace. We will wait here."

The princess' eyes narrowed into a deadly glint. "Yan Jie, I command you to let go."

Jie turned and started leading the horse into the compound.

"Let go." The princess sang the order. Her angry voice seemed to shake the walls, and the guards dropped their spears. Even the old woman tending to a small garden down the street by the Linshan provincial villa dropped her walking staff.

Having experienced the power of the princess' voice several times already, Jie let it ripple over her and continued walking toward the gates. Glancing over her shoulder and seeing the princess slumping in the saddle, she waved toward the wide-eyed steward. "Prepare that tea. If your young lord returns, I would suggest—"

Guards murmured and pointed. Jie followed their gazes.

Down the street, Zheng Ming rode side-by-side with a plain young woman, chatting and laughing and oblivious to the unexpected visitors ahead of him. Hopefully, the princess hadn't seen them. Jie hazarded a glance up.

Sitting stiffly, the princess scowled in Zheng's direction. With a jerk of the reins out of Jie's limp grip, she turned the horse around.

Zheng Ming looked up and brought his own horse to a stop. If his mouth hung any wider, a fist would fit in it. It was a tempting thought.

Instead, Jie could only watch as the princess set her chin and rode her horse at a walk toward Zheng. Jie scrambled to catch up.

Zheng Ming bowed his head. "*Dian-xia*. I… I am sorry. But it's not what you think."

The princess didn't stop the horse, or even deign to acknowledge him as she rode past.

"*Dian-xia*. Please, let me explain." He might as well have been talking to the Great Wall.

Jie trotted past him, casting the reproachful glare the princess was too proud to express.

As for the young woman… too much perspiration glistened on her forehead for this cool day, and up close, the smile she wore looked too contrived.

Very little surprised Liang Yu, but the turn of events in the last ten minutes reminded him of how little he could actually predict.

He had been there, pretending to weed a small garden plot at the side of the Linshan provincial villa, just to see if Young Lord Zheng had followed the instructions he provided. Little did he imagine that Zheng would bring Xie Shimin's prospective bride back to the Dongmen provincial villa.

Even more surprising was Princess Kaiya's unannounced visit, with a handmaiden who seemed familiar, despite the fact he had never seen a half-elf up close before. From the way the latter moved, he guessed her to be a Black Fist. She was probably the same one who had saved the foreign prince from Xie's arrow the day before. Curse his old eyes.

Liang Yu looked up from under the brim of his wide straw hat, assessing. His former employer had suggested he might need to assassinate the princess if all of their other plans failed to shake up the ruling elites. Now, she made for an inviting target, guarded only by a handful of provincial guards and a Black Lotus Fist hindered by a court dress. With the city on edge, he wouldn't get a better chance to find her so unprotected.

Her death, if pinned on Madura, would ensure war. Against a Black Fist and a battle-tested, champion archer, Liang Yu doubted he would live to see that war. Maybe he could have overcome them in his youth— though even then, he had been defeated and left for dead by a different elf.

He tightened his grip around his walking stick, ready to draw the blade concealed within. The smooth wood jarred the memory from just a few minutes before. The power of the princess' voice, even from twenty-three feet away, had compelled him to drop his walking stick.

The day before, she'd also braved the chaos and fearlessly approached a would-be assassin. Perhaps the princess was not such an easy target after all. Perhaps she might be a worthy leader.

Liang Yu went back to weeding, wishing his ears had not deteriorated so much with age. What he would give to be able to hear what Zheng Ming would say once he caught up to the princess.

Zheng Ming couldn't believe how quickly good luck could turn bad. His hands shaking on his reins, he waved toward the handmaiden's horse. "Lord Steward, bring the other imperial stallion."

He then turned to Li Feng, the common girl whom his friend Xie Shimin had been secretly courting. "Ms. Li, please accompany my steward into my province's compound. You will be safe there."

Ming took the reins of the imperial horse the handmaiden had left behind and set out in pursuit of the princess.

On horseback, it didn't take long to catch up.

He found them in a quiet alley, where the princess leaned into her horse, one arm draped over its neck and her face in its mane.

His fault. The handmaiden rested a hand in the bend of the princess' elbow, even as her head shifted left and right.

She must've caught a glimpse of him peeking around the corner. Her eyes locked on his and she marched toward him. If his guards were as alert as this girl, he'd never have worry about ambushes. He stepped into the alley.

The handmaiden blocked his way. Her elven features seemed all the more exquisite in her anger. "You have done enough to ruin the princess' New Year."

Ming didn't have time for a girl, even a unique one such as this. He extended an arm to push past her.

His hand never reached her.

She brushed it aside and somehow managed to stay in front of him. He used his other hand, only to find himself spun around with his arm wrenched behind his back. A shove into his shoulders sent him stumbling a few steps.

Ming spun back around, hand on his *dao*.

The insolent girl stepped forward, pressing herself against him, her hand on his wrist. It probably would've excited him had she not been so young. She grinned. "It is bad luck to draw a blade on New Year's Day."

Though not a superstitious man, he hesitated. It would look bad if he cut down an unarmed handmaiden. It would look worse if he were bested by an unarmed handmaiden. He raised his hands and took a step back.

She kept pressuring him backward, only stopping when they reached the main road.

"*Dian-xia*," he called, craning his neck around the girl's omnipresence. "It is not what you think. I will explain on the way to the ship tomorrow."

He scowled down at the half-elf again. She smirked. With a turn on his heel, he stomped back to his compound.

Not far from the gates, a stooped old woman, straw hat concealing her features, stood by a garden plot next to a house. She beckoned him over, and he came to a stop, not wanting to be rude on New Year's Day.

"Did you win your princess' heart back?" Her voice creaked with age. "Or was she too disgusted by your womanizing?"

The impertinence! As a noble, Ming had every right to slap the old hag. Yet it was a New Year. He settled for a glare.

The eyes of his mysterious informant twinkled back at him from beneath the hat's brim.

Ming let out a sigh. "You!"

"Why did you bring Li Feng back here? You deserve the princess' scorn for your stupidity."

Ming's jaw clenched at the insult. "I will explain everything to her tomorrow."

The man shook his head. "No, you won't."

"I made a promise to accompany her to Vyara City." Ming could not believe the desperation in his voice.

"If you want her to live," the man said, "you will have to break that promise."

"Are you threatening her to secure my obedience?"

The man chuckled. "I already have your obedience. No, you will break your promise because in doing so, you will protect her and also come closer to exposing the perpetrator of the insurgency."

CHAPTER 20:

MIRRORS AND WARNINGS

Twenty-year old Wang Kai-Hua looked across the table at Kaiya, Yanli, and Xiulan, all gathered for a special New Year's game of mahjong. They played several times a month, as a pretext for sharing the latest gossip among the hereditary lords. Unlike in the opium-filled gambling dens of the city's seedier parts, where family fortunes could be lost in a drug-induced stupor, the noble ladies typically bet favorite pieces of jewelry or clothing.

Kai-Hua sighed. She missed her father the most around the New Year. The younger brother of the *Tianzi* would have been fifty this year, had he not died from the sudden onset of asthma two years before. Not long after, her two brothers also perished from respiratory illnesses which even the renowned Doctor Wu couldn't treat.

Her mother, the sister of *Tai-Ming* Lord Liang of Yutou Province, returned home in grief, not wanting to stay in Huajing with all the memories of her family. She'd only come to the capital once since, for Kai-Hua's wedding to the *Tai-Ming* heir to Jiangzhou Province.

The Liu family, into which she'd married two years before, was full of obedient but narrow-minded men. Though she hoped her own husband Dezhen, the heir, would spend more time in his province learning how to rule better than his father, Kai-Hua was also happy he resided in the capital. It allowed her to frequently visit Sun-Moon Castle, where she'd grown up with Kaiya and Lin Ziqiu.

The atmosphere of the game room in Sun-Moon Castle felt more like a funeral than the New Year. As expected. Although she hadn't lived in the palace for two years, she knew her cousins' monthly rhythms well—everyone had synced up with Yanli when she moved in two years prior. Without a doubt, another month had passed without the conception of an heir to the Dragon Throne.

Xiulan and Yanli were somber as usual. More surprising was that Kaiya, who usually helped comfort the others, seemed the most downcast. Never looking up from the square bloodwood table, she didn't speak a word through her pursed lips. Perhaps she'd forgotten to take Doctor Wu's herbs that month.

Kai-Hua rubbed her belly, still flat two months into her pregnancy. Even if her friends knew nothing of it, it felt wrong to try to comfort them when the Heavens had blessed her while denying the others.

Through two hours of silence, broken only by clicking mahjong tiles, Yanli won most of the games in ruthless fashion. That was not out of the ordinary, but on any other night, she would teasingly gloat after each victory.

At last, Kai-Hua pushed the tiles in. "It's late, and Kaiya should get some rest before her journey tomorrow. Do we even need to calculate the winners and losers tonight?"

Xiulan wordlessly tossed a jade bracelet into the tiles. Kaiya added an embroidered silk kerchief.

Kai-Hua sucked in her breath. "Isn't that a gift from Young Lord Zheng?"

Without meeting her eyes, Kaiya nodded.

"Is that why you've been so quiet tonight? Did he say something during the procession this morning?"

"He didn't show." Yanli hadn't spoken for so long, Kai-Hua had almost forgotten what her voice sounded like.

Kaiya glared at Yanli before focusing on Kai-Hua. "He lied to me. He was with a woman."

"Are you sure?" Kai-Hua raised an eyebrow.

"I saw them riding together."

Xiulan let out a long sigh. "Oh, Kaiya. Men will do that. Even the Crown Prince. The Floating World wouldn't exist otherwise."

Kai-Hua nodded. Though the Founder's consort had broken with the traditions of previous dynasties by outlawing polygamy and disbanding the imperial harem, laws failed to change male nature.

Kai-Hua allowed her husband an occasional dalliance, just so long as he remembered who his wife was. Especially now, while she was pregnant. Even so, her spy kept careful tabs on just how many times Dezhen visited the half-Ayuri beauty in the Floating World.

Kaiya frowned. "I had hoped he would at least control himself while we courted."

"You're right, Kaiya." Yanli snorted. "I don't know how you two tolerate it. Our husbands should be saving their seed for making heirs."

Heat burned in Kai-Hua's cheeks. Xiulan shot Yanli a scowl.

Yanli threw her hands up. "What? It's true. The *Tianzi* would rest easier knowing there was an heir after our husbands."

"Which is why," Xiulan said with a nod toward Kaiya, "you should give Young Lord Zheng a chance to explain himself. The *Tianzi's* health deteriorates quickly. It would set his heart at ease to see you married before…"

Nobody wanted to finish her sentence, least of all Kai-Hua, who had lost most of her family already. After a brief silence, she spoke up. "Did Young Lord Zheng say anything?"

"He said he would explain himself tomorrow. I don't think I will allow him inside the gates."

"Hear him out." Xiulan turned the kerchief over in her hands before pressing it down in front of Kaiya.

"But make him grovel first," Yanli added.

Kai-Hua chuckled. Despite their shared sadness, Xiulan and Yanli had resumed their roles in Kaiya's love life. Xiulan, the enabler who encouraged her to follow her whims; and Yanli, the practical voice of reason. Kai-Hua imagined them as mirror images of Kaiya's psyche.

Kaiya stared at the kerchief before tentatively retrieving it and sliding it into a fold in her robe.

Silk gowns rustled as handmaidens folded the dresses and wrapped the jewelry Kaiya had chosen to take on her mission to Vyara City. They stacked lacquer boxes near the doors to her dressing room. Porters would take them to the *Golden Phoenix*, even if she herself would travel on the Tarkothi ship *Invincible*. Worried that Jie might make inadvertent alterations to her wardrobe, Kaiya had ordered the half-elf to stand back and take inventory.

Still dwelling on Zheng Ming's betrayal, Kaiya glanced at the brocade box on her make-up table. It sat apart from her cosmetics, next to the table's oval mirror. Holding her breath, she opened it, revealing Prince Hardeep's lotus jewel and Tian's river pebble.

She lifted the lotus jewel and held it up to the lamplight. It seemed to vibrate in her hands, slow and sluggish. So swept up with Zheng Ming's wit, she'd all but forgotten Prince Hardeep in the past few weeks. Cousin Peng had said the prince was in Vyara City. Perhaps she would see him there, and she could apologize for the sudden end to their correspondence. She tucked the jewel into her sash. Though it had always seemed like part of her, it now felt oddly foreign after a long absence from its familiar spot.

With a sigh, she grasped Tian's pebble, the cool smoothness reminding her of his sweet, genuine affection. His had been a childhood love. He never used her as a tool, like Prince Hardeep had; nor as a conquest, like his older brother Ming.

Perhaps *conquest* was too harsh. She played the scene back in her mind yet again, for the hundredth time that day. The girl, cute in her own way, looking up through her lashes at him; Ming, flashing that infuriatingly charming grin. Kaiya couldn't have misjudged the situation. Or had she?

She turned to see Jie, attention fixed on the pebble. Kaiya closed her hand around it. "Jie, what did you think of the girl riding with Young Lord Zheng?"

The half-elf sucked on her lower lip. "Desperate, *Dian-xia*."

It wasn't the word Kaiya would've used. "How so?"

"She was not particularly adept at riding, and she was quite nervous."

"But she was smiling."

"Contrived. Her eyes darted back and forth, and her brow glistened with sweat on a cold day."

Kaiya kept her jaw from dropping. Her Insolent Retainer's ability to notice details and draw connections was amazing. Perhaps it would be worth giving Zheng Ming a chance to explain himself tomorrow.

A male voice said, "You should be less concerned with philandering lords and more focused on important things."

Kaiya jerked her head around.

The elf Xu leaned against a wall, fiddling with a hand-sized rectangular mirror.

One handmaiden gasped, while another dropped a jewelry box. Trinkets jingled on the floor. Others stared wide-eyed at the intruder. Jie's lips tightened, even as her hand, tucked in the fold of her gown, strayed behind her back.

Kaiya glared at him. "Must you always make such dramatic appearances?"

"I am impulsive." Lord Xu yawned. "Here, a sending-off gift." He tossed the mirror at her.

Kaiya caught it in both hands. It was light, lighter than it should be based on its size. It displayed a perfect image of her face, instead of a mirror image. It was rather disconcerting. Curious, she tilted it side to side, and then over. "Thank you."

"You do not seem impressed. It's magic."

She turned it over in her hands. "I assumed so. What does it do, besides reversing my reflection?"

"Brush your finger across it." He pantomimed the motion.

Kaiya raised an eyebrow. "Won't that smudge it?"

"I said it was magic, didn't I?"

Kaiya glanced sideways at Jie. Maybe impertinence was inherited among elves, like their pointed ears. Nonetheless, she did as she was told. Her reflection disappeared, replaced by text written in a skilled hand. She sucked in breath. "What is this?"

"A gift. Rather, part of the bet I lost with Doctor Wu. She bade me to give this to you: a book of songs and music theory. It may entertain you during your voyage."

"A book?"

"Keep brushing it, back and forth, and it will turn the pages. It is a copy of a tome Doctor Wu, with the help of myself and your music teachers, used to treat one of your father's maladies, thirty-two years ago. Unfortunately, it is missing four important pages, lost when three of his best agents retrieved the original." The elf's eyes gleamed through his otherwise inscrutable expression.

Kaiya stared at the book... mirror. "Thank you."

"It does one more thing: If you need me, call my name into it. I will try my best to respond. And as long as you hold it, I can transport you through the ethers if you need to escape danger."

A sudden hope swelled in her. Perhaps she could avoid seasickness in the tight confines of a ship cabin. "Could you just send me to Vyara City?"

"I could." He grinned again. "But that would rob you of the chance to reconcile with Young Lord Zheng."

Heat rose to her cheeks.

Lord Xu's face hardened. "A warning, before I go. Limit using the power of your voice while in Vyara City. Just as I warned you about that power two years ago, the mirror interacts with all the sounds of the universe, rippling out from you. It would be like a beacon to those who can detect it."

In the past, he'd warned her about Avarax sensing the effect of her music from afar. However, the Last Dragon's treasure hoard was rumored to be enormous, so he probably wouldn't care for a little mirror. "Who would be listen—"

The air popped, filling the space where the elf had just stood.

CHAPTER 21:

Bait and Switch

Waiting in the pre-dawn darkness, Zheng Ming finished his mental countdown. It gave his men time to cover the dimly lit inn's side and rear doors. Several others gathered with him at the front. According to his mysterious informant, insurgent leaders converged there, preparing to attack Princess Kaiya's procession to Jiangkou. Their assault would commence once they saw Ming marching in the procession, so as to finally kill both him and her.

He would surprise them with an early appearance. He whipped his *dao* out. "Attack!"

A sheet of paper fluttered away from where it had been wrapped around the base of his blade. He skidded to a halt and retrieved it, leaving thirty of his men to surge across the street toward the building's front entrance.

His eyes widened as he scanned the letter, which implicated him as a traitor. The informant must've set him up! Had he not drawn his sword now, he would've sauntered into the inn, possibly to square off against government troops. But why would the man do this to him? How had he gotten ahold of his sword?

And who was really in the inn? Ming started to call off the attack, but his men had already stormed in. Sounds of struggle broke out.

Letter revealed or not, his own men had just attacked imperial troops. Who else could it be? He took his time slogging toward the main door, savoring his last minutes of freedom. How humiliating it would be, striding into the building in full dress uniform, only to be escorted out in chains.

Inside the common room, his soldiers stood with bared blades. A dozen men knelt with hands on their bowed heads. Ming studied each, scanning for some identifier.

As long as the planted letter remained secret, he could pretend his intentions were legitimate. He turned to his aide-de-camp. "Did they have weapons?"

"Yes, *Xiao-Ye*." His man pointed to a table where broadswords, crossbows, and daggers formed a heap.

Ming stifled a cringe. Maybe those weapons had government marks. He picked up a dagger, checking for any tell-tale sigils. None. He pointed it at the captives. "We have foiled your attack on Princess Kaiya."

They looked among each other, confusion scrawled across their expressions. One murmured under his breath, while another shook his head in response.

If they were government soldiers, they would surely be protesting now. Putting on his best gambling face, Ming stepped forward and glared at one of the men, who looked more like a sailor than a warrior. "I know you are part of the insurgency. Who do you work for?"

Heads drooped in silence. Perhaps they were insurgents after all. He thought back to his encounter with the informant. At no time had he taken Ming's sword. But if he hadn't planted the letter, someone else was plotting against him. Perhaps one of the jealous young lords who resented Ming's success with women.

In the distance, a bell tolled six times. Princess Kaiya's procession would depart the palace very soon. The foiling of this attack on her had taken too much time. There was no way he could keep his promise to meet her at the main gate.

There was still a chance to redeem himself. He turned to his aide-de-camp. "Call the city watch to take these men into custody."

On horseback, Ming might still make it to the palace in time.

Jie looked from the princess to the fog-shrouded Iridescent Moon and back again. Even if she could barely make out the moon, she knew valuable time slipped away. Horns at the main gate blared again, echoing through the early morning quiet and into the palace garden where they waited.

The drums and horns marked the departure of the princess' palanquin, flanked by a hundred imperial guards and followed by her baggage train. It would take the main road to the port city of Jiangkou, where the princess' decoy, Meiling, would board the *Golden Phoenix*.

Jie touched the princess' hand. "*Dian-xia*, we must make haste."

Her focus fixed on the veranda, Kaiya shook her head. "A few more minutes. He will be here. He promised."

Jie exchanged glances with Chen Xin, the senior-most of the five heavily cloaked imperial guards.

With a nod, he spoke: "*Dian-xia*, we have arranged for a cargo boat to take us downriver. They have a tight schedule to keep and will not wait for us."

The princess turned around, jaw set. In her hands, she squeezed the kerchief. "Zhao Yue. Go to the main gate and leave word with the guards there. When Young Lord Zheng arrives, send him to the *Songyuan* quays."

Standing behind the princess, Jie waved her hand to countermand the order. Zheng Ming's flamboyance would certainly attract attention to their clandestine trip.

Zhao's gaze met hers, and he tilted his chin a fraction before dropping to a knee. "As the princess commands." He rose and jogged toward the veranda.

"We shall depart." The princess waved a hand toward a spot on the garden wall.

Chen Xin's fingers probed the wall. He glanced back at the rest of them and then used his body to conceal which stone he pressed. It wasn't too hard for her Black Fist eyes to see past his efforts.

A slab of stones slid back without a sound, a testament to dwarven engineering. Chen Xin disappeared into the opening, followed by Ma Jun and then the princess. Jie went next, trailed by Xu Zhan and Li Wei.

Steep stairs, illuminated by Chen Xin's light bauble lamp, descended into the musty bowels of the castle. Jie counted eighty-eight steps, which placed them about sixty feet below ground.

Ahead of her, the princess walked stiffly, her shoulders hunched as if she were hugging herself. Jie sighed. Unrequited affection was a heavy burden, but one which should never interfere with duty. She should know.

The four imperial guards—five, once Zhao Yue caught up to them—clopped over the passageway's stone floors. Luckily, they were far enough underground that no one would hear them. In any case, anyone who considered foiling their diplomatic mission was probably preoccupied with the public procession.

After ten minutes, they emerged from the passage into a building in the secluded *Tiantai* Shrine, just outside the palace walls in the city's northwest quadrant. The princess let out a monumental sigh, as if she'd somehow held her breath the whole time underground.

Hooded cloaks concealed their faces and the men's short swords. The brittle light of dawn filtered through the cool morning mist, further obscuring their identities. Trailed by a dozen Black Lotus brothers and sisters, they set off on a brisk, ten-minute walk to a freight dock not far from where the Jade

River emerged from Sun-Moon Lake. Despite the secrecy of their departure, Jie maintained careful vigilance.

Princess Kaiya seemed detached, staring down at her feet while they walked through the warehouse-lined streets. When they arrived at the quay, she craned her neck, looking among the dozens of sailors and workers bustling along the wooden docks, loading and preparing cargo boats. There was little doubt whom she searched for.

Jie didn't have the heart to say Young Lord Zheng would not be joining them. It was for the better. Whether she admitted it to herself or not, the princess repeatedly fell prey to his charm. Given a week at sea with his forked tongue beguiling her, it might be more than the waves rocking the ship.

Chen Xin flagged down a middle-aged pilot, who'd been contracted through anonymous intermediaries. His river boat, laden with cargo, would take them through the wide but shallow waters of the lower Jade River to the sea docks in Jiangkou. Two dozen brawny rowers looked over their group with little interest, while the quartermaster kept peering through the mist at the Iridescent Moon.

The princess didn't accommodate him, raising a hand. She spoke in an unmistakably regal tone, which might unwittingly blow their cover. "Wait a moment." Her eyes swept across the docks several times, and then focused on the road.

Jie followed her gaze. Maybe Zheng Ming had somehow found them. No, the philandering lord didn't seem to be among the dockworkers and sailors. She tugged on the princess' sleeve. "We must get underway. Our hosts in Jiangkou are following an unforgiving schedule."

The princess glared at her from underneath her hood, but after a few seconds, turned on her heel and motioned for her entourage to board. With Li Wei's help, she climbed onto to the boat.

Jie held her sigh of relief until the boat pushed off. They would be on time, and she wouldn't have to suffer through Zheng Ming's presence.

Kaiya listened to the oars swishing through the water, following the cadence of the drum situated at the long river boat's aft. Perhaps it wasn't too late to order a full stop and head back. What if Ming had been attacked by the insurgents again? And hurt, unable to meet her in the palace? He'd better be hurt, to not show up.

Forget Zheng Ming. She stared at the lazy waters of the Jade River. Melting winter snows first filled up Sun-Moon Lake before emptying into the wide channel that flowed out to sea. With the river being too shallow for ocean-going vessels, swift row boats and slower pole barges plied the waters, transporting goods and people from Cathay's largest port to its capital.

Since the transformation of Huajing from a muddy fishing village to the national capital, other villages along the river banks had blossomed into towns, catering to the barges as they pushed their way upstream.

For the first time, Kaiya saw these towns from the meandering river. Normally, she bypassed them on the main highway. Merchants sold wares directly from docked barges, while fishermen took small craft out for the day. Women washed clothes in the shallows, sharing gossip with broad smiles and laughter.

Even though she frequently traveled through the country, it was always meticulously choreographed. It was rare for her ever to see the common folk going about their daily lives. How relaxed their lifestyles were compared to the rigid routines of court life! Her hand strayed to Tian's pebble.

The boat arrived at Jiangkou's docks in the early afternoon, and the party disembarked. Ma Jun went to search for the *Invincible* while the rest of the group waited by one of the many large warehouses near the busy docks.

On previous trips, Kaiya had gone directly to a wharf just outside of the city and a little further upstream in a private cove, where the *Golden Phoenix* moored. Now in a public area, she could hardly hear herself think over the buzz of activity as sailors, dockworkers, and merchants all played their respective roles in Cathay's vibrant international trade.

The smell of fish and sweat mingled with brackish water to assault her nose. Her stomach turned at the sight of huge crates writhing with live shellfish, on their way to the sprawling Jiangkou fish market. Perhaps the open sea wouldn't be so bad compared to this.

Thankfully, it didn't take long for Ma Jun to return. He beckoned them to follow, and within minutes, the *Invincible's* sablewood hull and five masts loomed large over the three-masted Cathayi cargo ships around it.

Kaiya had never seen such a gigantic vessel. If only Zheng Ming could be here to experience this! Fair-skinned sailors rarely seen in these waters prepared the ship for departure. They laughed, shouted, and relayed orders as they worked the rigging and moorings. Their Arkothi was laced with colorful metaphors which might as well have been gibberish.

Their catcalls, as Jie approached the gangplank and pulled down her hood, needed no translation.

Better to keep her own hood up. Perhaps for the duration of the weeklong trip.

Four stout marines armed with cutlasses eyed them suspiciously. After the attempt on Prince Aelward's life two days prior, he'd returned to his ship, and it stayed under heavy guard. No supply crates or cargo went unchecked.

Soon the prince, along with the elf Ayana, came to greet them. He took Kaiya's hand to escort her aboard. "Welcome aboard the *Invincible*, lass. I hope to be as fine a host as you were for me."

There was no sarcasm in his voice, despite what had happened at the arena. Kaiya searched his eyes and found nothing but sincerity. She bowed her head. "Thank you. Your ship is beautiful. Though we take pride in our ships, even the Son of Heaven's flagship cannot compare to the *Invincible*."

With grace he couldn't imitate on land, Prince Aelward sidestepped some sea foam carried on the wind. "Impressive as she be, yer *Golden Phoenix* is built fer speed, not fer power. Our ancestors arrived on the Tivaralan coasts as conquerors three hundred years ago in these ships. Even now, they are the technological pinnacle of sea-going vessels. We still build them with sablewood, which is only found in Tarkoth."

Li Wei, known more for his left-handedness and pessimism than his eye for woodwork, ran his hand over the rail. "The wood is beautiful but clearly well-worn."

"The *Invincible* is nearly two hundred years old, one of just eight Intimidator Class ships ever commissioned." Beaming, Prince Aelward patted a bulwark. "None have been lost to battle or to the sea, and the three originals on which our ancestors arrived are still in service."

Kaiya clapped her hands together, in awe at the age of the ships. "I always believed we in Cathay were the best sailors, but it seems that the Eldaeri are masters of the sea."

"Saltwater runs in our veins." Aelward motioned them to follow him across the deck toward the aft. "Now come with me to your quarters."

Xu Zhan pointed at four light cannons, two each at the bow and stern. "You have fitted your ship with guns."

Kaiya twirled her hair. No Cathayi ship was similarly armed. What if Father was right about the Tarkothi being a threat to Cathay's shipping?

"Wrought-iron cannons," Aelward said, gliding across the deck, "bought from your country a hundred years ago. Yer modern cast-iron guns are too heavy and unbalance the ship."

"Our ships don't have guns at all." The pugnacious Xu Zhan never shied from an argument. He might very well get them thrown off.

She bowed her head. "Please forgive my guard."

Aelward laughed. He was a different man on a ship. Relaxed. Confident. "Not at all. Our circumstances are different. Ye have no seafaring rivals in the West, but Tarkoth and Serikoth have been nominally in conflict with each other for a hundred and twenty years. Now we face the even greater threat of the Teleri Empire. We use ships not just for trade, but to project our might from the seas."

They arrived at the door to an aft cabin beneath the poop deck, and Aelward held the door open. "It is very rare that we have women on board." Aelward grinned with what could only be described as nostalgia. It would be worth asking Jie about later.

"Princess Kaiya and her handmaiden will stay in my cabin. I will bunk with the senior officers. Unfortunately, we only have space for your guards in general crew quarters."

Kaiya bowed. "Thank you for your consideration. I am sorry to inconvenience you." Though not sorry enough to bunk in the ship's guts.

Jie emerged from the cabin— Kaiya hadn't even seen her go in—and bowed her head. "It is secure," she said in the Cathayi tongue. "The only thing out of place was a single strand of frizzy red hair."

Red hair. It was unheard of among the Eldaeri, and rare even among other Northerners.

Jie held it up for Aelward to see, eyebrow raised, and he grinned. The knowing nod she gave him suggested they shared more than a passing acquaintance.

Peng Kai-Long mingled in with the peasants on the bluffs overlooking the restricted cove where the *Golden Phoenix* docked. Though Jiangkou city guards kept a watchful eye, he was confident they would not see through his disguise. He regretted, however, that they had confiscated his spyglass at the cordon.

Nonetheless, he saw Cousin Kaiya about to board the *Golden Phoenix* with two of her handmaidens Once it was out on the open seas, he would finally be rid of her.

For good.

Through three layers of agents and influence, he'd managed to get two insurgents on board. Somewhere on their journey, they would ignite the muskets' gunpowder magazine and sabotage the lifeboats, scuttling all hope of negotiations with Madura and forever drowning the secret of Prince Hardeep's fake correspondence. And of course, consigning another source of heirs to the Dragon Throne to a watery grave.

The *Golden Phoenix* sparkled in the sun. How regretful to sacrifice the realm's magnificent flagship. It would have been his once he ruled. No matter, he would commission an even grander vessel, even better than the Eldaeri's *Invincible*.

Below, an imperial messenger, clearly marked by his dragon banners, interrupted Kai-Long's daydreams. The rider galloped toward the cove, kicking up dust along the access road. When his horse reached the dock, the rider jumped off and dropped to a knee before the ship's quartermaster.

He pointed toward the ship and held his arms out as if he were embracing a bear. The quartermaster shook his head, then threw up his hands and traipsed up the gang plank.

Around Kai-Long, the rustics murmured and pointed. Before long, Cousin Kaiya appeared at the gang plank and disembarked.

Had his agents been uncovered? How was it that all of his supposedly foolproof plans failed? Kai-Long loosened his fists, even as heat rose to his ears.

He listened to the chatter of the people around him. Something about sabotaged water barrels. What was happening?

Against his better judgment, Liang Yu waited around to see Lord Peng's reaction to the princess disembarking from the ship. He had not expected to see the lord of Nanling disguised among the crowds of well-wishers, and now wondered what his stake in this game of intrigue was. Up to now, he had only suspected Peng as one of the serious players. Here was proof.

Somehow, Liang Yu had become a player as well, instead of just a somewhat independent game piece. As he surmised, his former employer had hired new agents to scuttle the princess' mission to Vyara City; and Liang Yu had tricked Young Lord Zheng into revealing them.

The results were better than he planned. Negotiations would be delayed. He did not have long to wait now. Once war began, he would trick Zheng Ming into exposing his former employer. In the meantime, it was time to investigate Lord Peng Kai-Long a little more carefully.

CHAPTER 22:
Song of Ayudra Island

With a large porthole looking out onto the sea, Kaiya's cabin was the *Invincible's* most spacious and luxurious. Nonetheless, the tight confines, combined with the rocking of the ship, stirred her stomach to rebellion.

Though Jie and Chen Xin implored her to stay indoors and avoid the foreigners' leers, she spent most of the week on deck. To her relief, the sailors and marines of Tarkoth's elite navy proved to be disciplined, and none so much as spoke to her beyond polite greetings. With no interruptions save for the half-elf's constant nagging over safety issues, she delved into the mirror-book Lord Xu had given her.

Acoustic theory came to life through tales of legendary musicians and their songs. To think music could stir armies into bloodlust or send enemies into a panic. Kaiya might be able to invoke a two-syllable command, yet that paled compared to singers who beguiled large audiences with only their voice.

The book also recounted the first part of Kaiya's favorite story: how the slave girl Yanyan sang the dragon Avarax to sleep. How she would love to learn that song! Unfortunately, four of the pages were missing.

Using what *was* there, and what she'd learned of vibrations and vocal commands, Kaiya experimented on her guards.

Getting Li Wei just to yawn drained her; and even then, it might not have been the impact of her voice, but just the lulling waves.

Such a basic skill, beyond her grasp. How could she ever hope to attempt some of the book's more unbelievable feats, like stirring gale winds or causing the ground to quake?

On the fifth day, the seas pitched with a curious regularity. Kaiya stumbled across the deck to the prow, grasping the cool metal of the cannon to stabilize herself. Facing into the winds, she listened.

The waves sang in rhythmic ripples.

Ears tracking the sounds to their source, her eyes followed a long line of small islets. Their contours curved toward the horizon, finally ending at a large island rising out of sea. It seemed to whisper to her through the symphony of ocean sounds.

"You feel it, too," came a melodic voice behind her. "Ayudra Island."

Kaiya met Ayana's gaze. The elf woman pointed back toward the prow. "Those are barrier islands, which separate the Western Ocean from the Shallowsea. Beyond them, Ayudra Island. On it, the ruins of Ayudra City and the hill that was once Mount Ayudra."

Kaiya knew the history well. Ayudra City had once been capital of the Ayuri Empire, a vibrant and prosperous port of magnificent spires and domes built up around an ancient orc pyramid. The Hellstorm obliterated it, and reduced Mount Ayudra to a hill. The city's levees failed and the hungry ocean swept in, swallowing ten thousand *li* of low-lying farmland and the millions of souls inhabiting it. Those that survived, along with everyone else on the continent, suffered through the Long Winter. Empires fell, chaos ensued. It was in the ashes of the old world that her own ancestor, and those of the Eldaeri and Teleri, forged a new world.

"How is the island *speaking* to me?" Kaiya asked.

Ayana smiled. "One of the pyramids dedicated to the worship of the ancient Tivari gods stood in the shadows of Mount Ayudra.

Even though the Hellstorm annihilated it, the energy of the world wells up there. Some humans can feel it."

"Then elves can hear it, too? What is it saying?"

"I *feel* it," Ayana answered, "but no one experiences the energy in the same way. I can tell you this: our oral histories, ancient even to us elves, say that our civilization sprang up tens of thousands of years ago in the same places where our Tivari conquerors later built pyramids as monuments to their vile gods."

Kaiya nodded. Human civilizations, as well, flourished in these areas. "Why?"

"All those areas resonate with the energy of the world. Especially here, where the physical manifestation of Magius, God of Magic, appeared," she pointed to the Iridescent Moon, floating much higher and larger than usual, "to help my people hide from the Tivari's attempts to exterminate us. That is why the Ayuri Paladins constructed the Temple of the Moon over the ruins. Perhaps you should visit the Oracle there."

A visit to the Oracle… it might answer more questions about this energy bubbling in her core. Kaiya turned back to contemplate the island, which grew larger as the *Invincible* approached. By late afternoon, the island's docks came into view. With seagoing Cathayi ships incapable of navigating the Shallowsea, and the Ayuri skiffs unable to handle the open sea, those docks served as a gateway for trade into the interior Ayuri kingdoms. Hopefully, they could arrange transit and leave enough time for a detour to the Temple of the Moon.

She looked up at the Iridescent Moon to gauge the approximate hour. As when Ayana pointed it out before, it no longer hung in its reliable position to the south. Instead, it floated much higher, almost directly overhead. How bizarre—but not nearly as strange as its hum.

The humming joined with the ever-rising chorus of seagull caws and ocean waves. The finger-length *dizi* flute in the folds of her robe found its way into Kaiya's hand. She played, allowing the harmony of the island to guide her just as she'd learned from Lord Xu two years before during the Wailian debacle.

Orchestra of Treacheries

The flute resonated clearly, its sound louder and fuller than she could imagine. Sailors paused and stared.

Ordered back to work, they returned to their duties, and the *Invincible* lumbered into port. There, the Arkothi-speaking sailors and Ayuri-speaking dockworkers began tying the ship down to the moorings, communicating through the universal language of seafarers.

Oh, to feel solid ground again! Kaiya shifted her weight left to right, peering down a single stone-paved boulevard running several *li* to the broad, low-lying hill. Two-story buildings of white mud bricks topped by flat roofs lined the wide road. Save for the Ayuri architecture, it might have been any street in Cathay for all the bustling activity.

However, on the other side of the buildings lay the ruins of the once-great city of Ayudra, as far as her eye could see. She shuddered. Hundreds of thousands of unfortunate people perished here during the Hellstorm. The piles of rubble stood as their grave markers.

Once the gangplank lowered, Kaiya disembarked with Jie and the five imperial guards. Prince Aelward and Ayana followed with ten marines. Around them, Ayuri dockworkers began unloading cargo under the watchful eye of a harbormaster and the ship's quartermaster and boatswain. The call of sea birds mingled with the buzzing of the Ayuri language, swarming in from all directions.

As the party advanced toward the head of the wharf, they were greeted by an Ayuri man, not much older than her, wearing a lightweight, white cotton tunic that hung to his knees. The *kurta*'s high neck was embroidered with symbols indicating he was an official, and he sported a short beard of coarse black hair. He spoke in heavily accented Arkothi. "Your papers, please."

Prince Aelward produced a scroll with wavy Ayuri script. The official skimmed over it before regarding the group.

"Welcome, Prince Aelward of Tarkoth. You, the elf lady, and your crew may come ashore, but only within six blocks of the harbor." He then narrowed his eyes at the Cathayi. "These people do not look like Tarkothi crew. Unless you can produce proper identification and permissions, I am afraid they will have to stay on your ship, at least until we can arrange escort tomorrow morning."

Kaiya searched the harbor for the *Golden Phoenix*. The faster vessel should've arrived earlier, and certainly they would've made arrangements for her.

It was nowhere to be found.

Uncompromising bureaucrats! There had to be some way to persuade him, even it meant identifying herself. She lowered her hood. "I am Kaiya Wang, daughter of the Emperor of Cathay. I have business at the Temple of the Moon."

Behind her, the imperial guards and Jie shuffled on their feet. She wasn't supposed to reveal their identities, let alone break from their rigid itinerary.

The official paused to gape at her. "We were not informed of your visit, and without any kind of identification, I am afraid I cannot let you off this wharf."

He began to motion for several local soldiers to come over and help enforce his judgment, when an adorable young boy of about ten years scampered up. He wore a white *kurta* with a light-yellow embroidered collar. Kaiya searched her memory, and recalled that his clothes marked him as a trainee of the Ayuri Paladin order.

The boy bobbed his head. "The Oracle wants the Cathayi woman with the flute to visit the temple tomorrow at dawn. The Paladins will allow her to stay in one of the guest houses."

Kaiya looked back at her people, who all gawked at the boy. She turned back to the beaming child and withdrew her flute. "How did he know I was coming?"

The official harrumphed. "He is the Oracle, after all. It is his business to know. Very well, the lady may come ashore. Did the Oracle say anything about her friends?"

The boy stared at Kaiya with wide eyes and shook his head. "He only mentioned the one with the flute."

The official peered at them with a smug grin. "I am very sorry, but only the princess may enter the city."

"That is not acceptable," Chen Xin said in Arkothi. "The princess must be protected at all times."

The official laughed. "This is the spiritual home of the Ayuri Paladins, the greatest warriors on Tivaralan. As their guest, she is safer here than anywhere in the world."

Kaiya summoned her most charming voice. "At least allow me to bring my handmaiden."

The official looked down at her feet. "I am sorry, but we must follow protocol."

Kaiya sang her request. "Let her come." Three syllables, yet it didn't drain her energy at all. The boy's eyes widened.

The official pressed his hands together and bowed his head. "Very well."

"I protest, *Dian-xia*," Chen Xin said in Cathayi. He dropped to one knee. "It is our duty to protect you, always. Please stay on *the Invincible* one more night."

"I will not stay on the ship tonight. I will be safe with Jie and an island full of Paladins." Kaiya lifted her chin and scowled.

Chen Xin immediately stood up, took two steps back and bowed down again. Turning to the boy, she smiled graciously and said in Ayuri, "Please, little friend, take us to our quarters."

Jie barely noticed the smell of the sea mingling with curry and spices. Since the night Lord Xu popped into the princess' bedchambers, she'd felt the power of the princess' voice dissipate around her with no effect.

Yet here, on this island which pulsated at a low hum, the princess' command swept over her like a tidal wave. She stood mesmerized, just like all of the men, and trailed after the princess like an automaton. It took a few minutes of walking in a daze before she regained her focus.

The boy skipped down the boulevard, between warehouses, trading offices, inns, and shops. He, too, seemed to recover his wits and spoke with puppy-like enthusiasm. "This part of the ruins was rebuilt. Ayudra is now a transit point for people and cargo. Lots of merchants, sailors, and passengers. But not everyone is allowed here. And there is a nighttime curfew."

Jie suppressed a cough. For a purportedly safe place guarded by the supposedly most powerful warriors in the land, there sure were a lot of rules.

The crowds thinned and they came to a short stone wall crossing the road. It had an open gate large enough to allow a cart through. On the left stood a handsome young man, on the right an attractive young woman. Both wore the same white *kurtas* as the boy, though their high collars were embroidered in gold. Postures relaxed, their hands rested on the guardless hilts of curved *naga* swords hanging at their sides.

Paladins. Jie eyed them. Had she not witnessed their fighting skills two years ago in Tokahia, she wouldn't have believed their martial prowess. The boy pressed his hands together and bowed his head. "This is the Cathayi lady who is allowed to enter."

The two saluted her with folded palms and stepped to the side.

The princess nodded in response. Jie followed her and the boy past the checkpoint.

"Welcome to the sacred inner city. The spiritual home of the Order of the Ayuri Paladins." The boy waved his hand at the boulevard ahead, which looked just like the harbor side of the city. It continued toward the verdant hill, with two-story, flat-roofed buildings on either side. An occasional dome or spire or minaret topped a few buildings. There were less people here, and all were uniformly dressed in the garb of the Paladin Order.

More evident was the change in sounds. The commotion of commerce gave way to orderly marching footsteps and the rhythmic pounding of metal—all woven into the rustling of the wind in the willowy paperwood trees and the song of the ocean behind them. It should've been a cacophony raucous enough to scare off evil spirits, but Jie found it oddly soothing.

The princess wore a serene expression, perhaps for the first time since Zheng Ming's betrayal. With those sharp ears of hers, she probably noticed the sounds, too.

"You feel it, don't you?" said a male voice from behind them.

Jie's stomach lurched into her chest. Someone had snuck up without her hearing. She whirled around, her hand instinctively reaching into the folds of her cloak for a throwing star. Before she could get her fingers around it, a hand pressed firmly on her elbow, pinning it down. Try as she might, she couldn't free her arm.

"Please, do not be alarmed." The older man's grandfatherly voice rippled through her, calming her nerves and relaxing her muscles.

He had long, graying hair tied into a pony tail, and wore a white *kurta* with a gold-embroidered collar. Unlike the sentries at the wall, his shirt also had gold-embroidered cuffs.

The boy bowed low, hands pressed together. With even the princess bowing, Jie followed suit.

"Master Sabal," the boy said. "I am taking the Cathayi lady to the guest house, as instructed by the Oracle."

The Paladin master waved the boy off. "Run along, young Gayan, back to your studies with the Oracle. I will take them from here."

Gayan pouted, but then pressed his hands together and skipped off down the boulevard toward the hill.

"You." Master Sabal's focus locked on Jie. "Have you come back for more training?"

More training? Jie's brows scrunched up. "I've never been here before."

"You were here two years ago, spying on our training." The Paladin master's lips pursed.

If only. Jie cast a sidelong glance at the princess, and then shook her head. "No, I've never set foot in Ayudra before."

She'd only seen it from a ship on the way to her mission in the North.

"I see." Master Sabal scratched his chin. "Perhaps my old eyes failed me. Still, there aren't many half-elves in this world. Maybe you all look alike."

The nerve! Jie's cheeks must have flushed an interesting shade of red.

Turning from her, the master examined the princess, so different from the way any other man looked at her. "Young lady, for years I have been charged with identifying children who can feel what you feel right now: the Vibrations of the world itself. It is a shame that our mandate only extends to the borders of Ayuri lands, for we will miss rare gems like you. Perhaps one of your parents is Ayuri?"

The princess shook her head.

"Please pull down your hood."

To Jie's shocked disapproval, the princess did as requested.

The old Paladin sucked in his breath. "By the Sun and Moons, I have never seen such a perfect face. Perhaps it is a good thing we never found you. We are still dealing with the repercussions of a beauty who threw an entire class of Paladin students into chaos."

Enough of the princess' beauty, already. It wasn't like Tian hadn't raved about it all the time, even before she was actually pretty. Jie tried not to roll her eyes. "How did you know what my hand was doing?"

"We learn to surrender our conscious thought and let the vibrations of the world guide our actions and amplify our own abilities beyond normal physical limitations. My hand moved to stop you from reaching your weapon, even before I consciously recognized the threat." The man smiled disarmingly.

She would have to try again, though maybe not on a master the next time. He far surpassed the skills of Sameer, the Paladin Apprentice she'd travelled with up North.

"In any case," he continued, "follow me to your lodgings. You will find your answers... or perhaps just more questions... when you visit the Oracle yourself."

He brought them a little further down the boulevard, where they came to one of the ubiquitous two-story mud-brick buildings. Unlike the other structures, the guest house had a metallic domed roof that reflected the swirling colors of the Iridescent Moon, now waxing to its half phase. The sun hung low in the sky, gilding the Ayudra hilltop in gold.

The princess' stomach rumbles joined the other harmonized sounds. Her cheeks flushed red in the late afternoon sun.

"There is food, and a hot bath." Master Sabal opened the door and gestured for them to enter. "Rest well tonight. If you are so inclined, come to the temple before dawn tomorrow to join our morning meditation." With a bow, he bid them farewell.

Jie followed the princess into the two-story foyer, overlooked by a second floor mezzanine wrapping around three sides. Her feet sank into the wool Ayuri carpet, intricately woven in patterns of red, cream, and gold. She walked under a glass chandelier of light baubles that hung from the ceiling, illuminating the room.

Twirling in a circle, she took in the cloying scent of incense. The bright light brought out the colors in two large paintings of pre-Hellstorm Ayudra, which hung on either side of an arched opening.

An older boy, wearing a simple cotton *kurta,* emerged from the opposite archway, between a pair of golden banners with a twenty-one-pointed black sun. He bounded up the flight of steps at the far end of the foyer and beckoned them. "Follow me, mistresses."

When they reached the landing, he motioned to a door with an open hand. "That will be your room for the night. Please let me know if you need anything. We are serving dinner right now on the first-floor room to the left. There is a communal bath off of the room to the right."

Jie looked at the princess. An internal struggled played in her expression. In all likelihood, the hot bath after a long journey would win out over the aroma of roasted chicken wafting out of the dining room.

The princess' eyes drifted to the bathing area, then back to Jie.

If she thought Jie would help her bathe like a real handmaiden, she was in for a surprise.

CHAPTER 23:
What Happens in the Floating World

Minister Hong Jianbin's hands sweated, though not from the warm moisture billowing off the baths and percolating through the halls. The bathhouse was one of many in the Floating World, nestled among gambling dens, theatres, brothels, and teahouses. The district was secret in theory only, providing a haven for those who might seek temporary escape from the rigors of daily life.

Floating and ephemeral, like a waking dream. Commoner and noble alike visited, anonymously brushing shoulders on their way to enjoy pleasures for every budget. While the *Tianzi's* law ostensibly extended into the Floating World, it was more governed by convention and custom. As long as nothing spilled into the *real* world, and the businesses continued paying taxes, the authorities left well enough alone. What happened in the Floating World, stayed in the Floating World.

Or so the maxim said.

The effects of what would happen here tonight would ripple throughout Cathay and usher in a new era of greatness. At least, that's what Hong told himself. Again.

His gaze returned to the dressing room's full-length mirror. His old skin glowed pink from a young woman's vigorous scrubbing. Yet no matter how much dirt and dead skin came off, the blackness of his soul reflected in that mirror. Were power and prestige worth betraying a friend? A friend who had helped him rise through the ranks?

Yes.

It would have never come to this, had the opportunity not fallen into his hands. The impossible aligning of so many circumstances could not have happened unless Heaven willed it.

Years ago, when he was still a minor palace official, he had recommended a new maid for Chief Minister Tan as a favor to an old hometown acquaintance. Little did he know how much the grateful girl would overhear: a plot to start war, in order to rectify the Chief Minister's past mistakes. With the maid as his eyes and ears in the Tan household, Hong knew almost everything.

At the same time, his father's former business connection told him of an exotic weed surreptitiously imported from Ayuri lands, delivered in small amounts to Lord Peng Kai-Long's Huajing estate.

Through a little investigating, Hong found out that the weed rendered a man's seed sterile. He would have exposed Lord Peng's treason right then and reaped a small reward, had he not met Leina. She inadvertently convinced him to keep the knowledge for himself and wait for a more opportune time to reveal it.

Up to now, he had just ridden on the wave of plots and plans, positioning himself to benefit when it crashed. He would have waited even longer, had the bumbling Young Lord Zheng not begun closing in on Tan's treachery.

Hong took in a deep whiff of the flowery air, which did little to cover the stink of betrayal. Peng and Tan were neck deep in seditious moves, with plenty of evidence waiting to incriminate them. Meanwhile, Hong's only treason was testing an herb interaction on the *Tianzi's* brother and nephews two years ago. Nothing linked him to those deaths.

Hong draped a thin robe over his frail body and approached the sliding doors. A scantily clad young woman opened them for him. He banished thoughts of his own treachery and walked across the wooden floors. The hall was empty. In an effort to protect the anonymity of her patrons, the proprietress always ensured that only one customer was in a passage at any given time.

Another door opened ahead of him and he turned and entered a private bath room. Chief Minister Tan was already soaking up to his chest in an enormous wooden tub, two beautiful young women sitting naked on either side of him. The water level tantalizingly hinted at the cleft between their breasts.

"Little Hong," the Chief Minister said, "thank you for inviting me."

"It is always my pleasure, Elder Brother." Hong addressed the Chief Minister as he always had in the many years they had known each other. He removed his own robe and settled into the hot water. One of the women waded across the tub, keeping her soft curves provocatively submerged, and sidled up next to him.

Tan draped an arm over the girl beside him. "It has been years since we enjoyed a bath together with such lovely ladies. To what do I owe the pleasure?"

"I want in." Hong eschewed all secrecy—they could discuss classified affairs of state here, since the ladies of the bathhouse were sworn to confidentiality. What happened in the Floating World, stayed in the Floating World.

Tan yawned. "What exactly do you want?"

Hong leaned forward, out of the arms of the beauty, and kept all hint of accusation out of his voice. "I know Xie Shimin visited you in secret before his unlikely assassination attempt."

"Yes, he did," Tan answered casually, without even a trace of worry or concern. "I suppose my maid told you? What of it?"

So he knew about the maid. "Just that I know. And I support you in your work to punish Madura. I was a part of that trade mission thirty-two years ago, too, and bear the same responsibility for Ankira's occupation. I want to help you."

"You already have." Tan disentangled his arm from the girl and leaned forward, hands steepled to his chin. "Did you ever wonder why so many of the attacks on the *Tai-Ming* occurred after their meetings with you?"

Hong paused, thinking back to each of the attacks.

"It is because you always informed me whom you were meeting with," Tan continued. "But given the circumstances, it certainly does not look good for you."

Blood rushed from Hong's face. Minister Tan had been setting him up to take the blame in the event his plot failed! But why?

Tan grinned. "Do not worry, my old friend. I withheld this piece of information from investigators. I merely wanted to let you know, to ensure your good behavior."

"Of course." Relief washed over Hong. "I only share your vision of Cathay's prosperity."

"Good. Because the prerequisite for being a part of my plan is dedication to our great nation." Tan shook his head. "I am sad I had to go to such great lengths, but the *Tianzi* will not change his ways in his old age, at least not without significant provocation."

Hong hid his scoff. Chief Minister Tan, as one of the *Tianzi's* favorites, probably believed he would be awarded a fief and *Yu-Ming* status if new lands came under Cathayi rule. "If I may ask, why did you want to assassinate the Tarkothi prince? It does not seem to have any relevance to our goals of expanding the nation, and if anything, would make Cathay look very bad in the eyes of our trading partners. And there are those, such as Lord Peng, who wanted to ally with Tarkoth."

Tan waved his hand dismissively. "He was simply a necessary casualty, an expendable target that would not needlessly kill one of our own lords. We needed to create the appearance that nobody was safe; that Madura, Rotuvi, and their allies were meddling in our affairs. That is why we have tried to implicate Madura time and time again."

"Which explains why you had the *Golden Phoenix*'s water barrels sabotaged." Hong feigned sudden epiphany. "To keep Princess Kaiya from travelling to Vyara City. As soon as she talked to the Madurans, she would find out they had nothing to do with our own internal problems."

"Exactly!" Tan said, beaming. "I should have recruited you earlier, since you seem to have an eye for conspiracy."

More than Tan realized. Hong raised an eyebrow. "And all of the attacks on the lords? Your doing?"

Tan shrugged. "All but the debacle in Lord Peng's compound that night. None of my planned attacks, save the attempt on Lord Han, were meant to be fatal; just enough to scare the *Tai-Ming* into pushing for punitive action against Madura. I was worried when you began to propose troop movements, especially away from the borders, since that is where we will eventually launch our expansion."

Sweat beaded on Hong's head. It was hot, and not just because of the steam. "How were you able to recruit the insurgents?"

"Insurgents?" Tan's brow furrowed. "I had nothing to do with them. I procured the services of patriots. There are enough former Cathayi soldiers who are tired of hiring themselves out to foreign armies, who share our vision of Cathay's greatness. All it took was the recruitment of one of the *Tianzi's* agents, a real Black Fist, I believe. He did the rest."

Black Fist? Hong's forehead scrunched. Tan really believed they existed.

The girl massaging Tan's neck paused momentarily and Tan smirked. "Do not worry, my sweet, you have nothing to fear from the Black Fists . They only kidnap babies. And do the *Tianzi's* dirty work."

The girl smiled nervously and returned to her kneading.

Hong lifted his hand, letting the warm water slither off. "So there really is no foreign threat, is there?"

Tan scowled for a split second. "There is no *imminent* foreign threat. However, our neighbors covet our wealth. Mark my words, it will only be a matter of time before the Teleri Empire and its satellites pressure us. We must expand our buffer territory, to protect the Cathayi heartland from their machinations."

"Certainly you have shared your concerns with the *Tianzi*? He is a reasonable man."

Tan sighed. "I have. But he has become too tentative with age. He will not budge in his mindset without significant pressure from the hereditary lords. His sons are too weak-willed to do anything. The realm will stagnate and fall to ruin under them."

"But if the princess negotiates a lasting peace with the Madurans—"

"She will not." Tan slapped his hand down on the water's surface. "She has been ill for two days, and the *Golden Phoenix* would not sail even if she were well."

Ill! Hong's chest tightened. His ultimate prize, sick.

Tan continued, "I have many ways to keep the ship anchored. If we do not show for our meeting with the Madurans, they may take offense. Perhaps they will attack us first."

"When do you plan on pushing Expansionism? The *Tianzi* dismissed the notion at the last *Tai-Ming* Council."

Tan leveled his stare. "The next council meeting, in three months. By then, all of my pieces will have fallen in place, and I will remonstrate the *Tianzi* to come to a resolution."

Hong grinned. Tan had effectively incriminated himself, and it was time to deliver the coup-de-grace. "I would like to remonstrate the *Tianzi*."

"That is not your place as Council Minister." Tan glowered at him.

Hong's grin curved into a toothy smirk. "But it would be, if I were Chief Minister."

"The only way for you to become Chief Minister…" Realization bloomed on Tan's face. He turned to the girl beside him. "Go, summon my guards!"

The sliding doors to the room crashed open, revealing six shadowy figures brandishing lacquered swords. Unlike the brash Young Lord Zheng, who had tried to win all the glory by uncovering one plot himself, Hong had gone to the *Tianzi* and secured the help of imperial agents.

"Yes, the position will be vacant," Hong said. "You, old friend, have revealed enough tonight to seal your fate."

"Ungrateful cur!" Tan bolted up in the tub. "You will not have the satisfaction of seeing my downfall, and I will not have to suffer witnessing a fishmonger's ascension to Chief Minister!" His eyes flashed, the infuriated look of a man whose lifelong dreams had just been quashed. He started to lunge across the tub toward Hong, arms outstretched as if he would choke the life out of him with his bare hands.

Yet before the Chief Minister had even had a chance to launch himself, the young woman beside him tangled up his legs with her own, and he floundered unceremoniously, face-first into the water.

She yanked his head out of the water by his hair, and placed him in an unrelenting choke hold. Tan clutched desperately at her slim arms, frantically trying to break her precise grip, fighting the inevitable shutting down of his brain.

Hong laughed to himself. He would never be allowed in this bath house again. It did not matter. It was time to start calling in the *Tai-Ming* lords' agreements to have him named Chief Minister.

CHAPTER 24:
VISIONS

Kaiya woke to the sound of frog trills and bird chirps outside her open window, still singing in orchestra with the ocean rumbling in the distance. She yawned. How refreshing! Never again would she take for granted a comfortable bed which didn't rock with the seas.

She blinked away the unladylike gunk from her eyes. Outside, the black of night faded to an inky blue at the horizon. Dawn, and with it, the Paladins' morning meditation, fast approached.

Kaiya jumped to her feet and flashed a disdainful eye at her travelling clothes, still inundated with the stench of brine and—she shuddered—sweat. With nothing else to wear, she threw them on nonetheless.

On the other bed, Jie might have been hibernating. The poor girl needed her sleep, and it would take time to wake her, anyway. Precious time. Scarlet lined the horizon.

Kaiya flung the door open and dashed out. She almost careened into a boy on the mezzanine, who nonchalantly sidestepped her just outside the door. Not even the Insolent Retainer could have reacted so fast.

Or could she? Back in the room, the half-elf's feet padded on the floor. Kaiya looked down at the boy.

Gayan, their guide from the day before, stared back with bright eyes. He placed a yellow flower in her hand. "No need to hurry, miss. The Oracle said you wished to speak to him. He sent me to meet you here."

"How did he know?" Kaiya stared at the boy.

He giggled. "He is the Oracle, after all. Come, follow me to morning meditation." He took her hand with a blush.

The touch might have been impertinent if he weren't so cute. She let him guide her down the steps, out the door and into the street.

Outside, Master Sabal towered over a dozen boys and girls, all dressed in white *kurtas*. "Good morning, Your Highness. I am glad you could join us." He pressed his hands together and the children followed suit.

Kaiya imitated the greeting. "Good morning, Master. Thank you for guiding me."

They set off at a brisk walk with Master Sabal leading. He didn't speak a word, and it seemed inappropriate to break the silence. Behind her, the entourage of children trailed like a line of ducklings, so unlike her usual retinue of handmaidens and imperial guards.

After a few minutes, they came to a life-sized statue of a handsome, middle-aged man in the center of the road. Sitting in a lotus position, he held a shattered *naga* sword in his left hand, out to the side with the tip down. Over his heart, his right hand cupped a fist-sized gemstone with countless facets, round at the bottom and tapered on top. The statue itself was made of a greyish blue metal and pulsated with the same energy as the island.

The children each added a yellow flower to the hill of yellow blossoms on the stone base. They then pressed their hands together and bobbed their heads, like pecking baby chicks.

"This is part of our morning ritual: to salute Acharya, the first Oracle." Master Sabal prompted her to add her own flower to the pile.

As she knelt to do so, she saw countless sword shards at the figure's feet. "I did not think an Oracle would need a sword."

"In his younger years, when the chaotic aftermath of the Hellstorm and Long Winter still gripped Ayuri lands, Acharya led a band of *Bahaadur* mercenaries."

The term, to Kaiya's understanding, implied heroism—she'd always associated it with Prince Hardeep, who must have trained at this very island. A mercenary hardly evoked the image of honor. "He fought for money?"

Master Sabal smiled. "In desperate times, people do what they must."

Definitely not the image of heroism. Her lip twitched into a curl. "I guess I had a different understanding of the term *Bahaadur*."

"You speak our language well," he said, "but this word has a long history. It is a thousand years old, from when the elves taught the gifted among our ancestors to channel their *prana* life force into superhuman martial abilities. We used those skills to overthrow our orc masters during the War of Ancient Gods."

"Just as elves trained Cathayi girls how to evoke magic through the arts." Kaiya watched the children shuffle away.

He nodded. "The Cathayi and the Ayuri people share a similar history of consolidation. The *Bahaadur* played a major role in ours. For seven centuries after the War of Ancient Gods, tribal chieftains used them to carve out kingdoms; kings sought them out to build an empire; and the Emperor of the Ayuri organized them in the Hundred Years of War against the Arkothi Empire in the North. To our people, they were heroes."

"Even the mercenaries?" Kaiya pursed her lips.

Master Sabal leveled his gaze at her. "Our life experiences can help us transcend our origins. In his middle years, Acharya made a pilgrimage to this island, where he received his first vision. It inspired him to systemize *Bahaadur* training methods and lay the groundwork for the Paladin Order. It brought peace to most of our lands."

Kaiya contemplated his words. Her own ancestor had reunified Cathay, sometimes through brutal methods. Yet, historians described him as a heroic figure, and she accepted it without question. Who was she to judge the leaders who had lived through the upheaval of the Hellstorm?

Master Sabal gestured toward the *naga* shards. "Acharya took up residence here and became the first Oracle, living to be one hundred and twelve years old. He shattered his own sword, to represent the precedence of wisdom over martial skill. When Paladin masters retire, they shatter their *naga* and leave them here, as well. Our young students are reminded every morning. Speaking of which, look, they have already continued without us. Come, perhaps the current Oracle will tell you more if he sees fit."

It was a short distance to the Temple of the Moon. Cathayi books and scrolls had never described the famed temple itself. Expecting a magnificent structure of spires and domes characteristic of ancient Ayuri architecture, Kaiya was sorely disappointed. She found nothing but a broad stone-paved park facing a flat-topped mesa, with Ayudra hill's cliff face as a backdrop. A semicircle of several dozen megaliths surrounded the plaza. Above her was the open sky.

And the Iridescent Moon, now waning to half. It appeared larger than ever, its soap-bubble colors swirling more vibrantly than usual.

Picking her way through the couple hundred sitting Paladin students, knights, and masters, Kaiya found an open spot and settled into a lotus position. She looked up to contemplate the mesa.

It jutted up some fifty feet. A cone of pale blue light sprayed from the top, upwards toward the Iridescent Moon. This had been the core of the ancient Ayuri pyramid, which originally towered some four hundred feet above the low-lying delta in the shadows of Mount Ayudra.

Kaiya closed her eyes and listened. The Paladins breathed in unison, synchronizing with the wind in the trees, the twittering of birds, and the ocean waves in the distance. She joined her breath to theirs, the thump of her heart slowing to beat in time with the island.

She opened her eyes. Sounds flashed in a multitude of colors, coalescing with one another and painting fleeting images, both beautiful and grotesque. The unworldly pictures should've evoked emotional responses, yet the sounds lulled her into calm.

Minutes passed as seconds, and before Kaiya realized it, morning meditation had ended. The images slipped from her memory. Master Paladins dismissed students, sending them to their next tasks. The handful of Paladin knights talked among themselves.

Beside her, Jie rose to her feet, expression serene. When had she arrived? She'd never looked so calm.

Gayan beckoned. "Come, the Oracle awaits you. Your handmaid must wait here, though."

Kaiya nodded at Jie, giving her the tacit order to stay. Surprisingly, the Insolent Retainer actually complied.

The boy took Kaiya's hand and pulled her along through the dispersing throng of Paladins and students, toward the cliff behind the mesa.

They came to steps hewn into the cliff face and climbed. Halfway up, Kaiya peeked over the edge, only to hug the side the rest of the way. At the summit, a white-bearded man draped in long white robes sat in lotus position.

Looking at him, Kaiya bent, hands on knees, to catch her breath. Cathayi records placed his age at eighty-one, but he didn't seem a day over fifty. Yet when he gazed at her, his eyes bared her soul with an ancient wisdom.

She bowed low, respectful of the mysterious man's dignified aura. He was only the fourth Oracle in two hundred years, and there might not be another in her lifetime.

"Go back to your studies, young one," the Oracle said to Gayan. "Though I know you will be back soon." He laughed with a wink.

Once the boy departed, the Oracle stood with a swirl of his robes and motioned to a stone bridge that crossed over to the mesa. "Come with me, young lady of Cathay."

She followed him over the bridge, to the top of the rock column. From this new vantage point, she saw that the almost perfectly flat top of the rock was about thirty feet in diameter. In its center was a circular hole, the size of her fist, from which the ray of pale blue light emerged.

"You have questions," he said just as she was opening her mouth to speak.

"I feel as if the island is trying to speak to me."

He laughed. "When a Paladin apprentice finishes his service with his mentor, he often comes here to meditate and feel the vibrations of the world. What he experiences becomes a vision of his life's work. Throughout his career, he receives assignments from the Council of Elders of the Crystal Citadel in Vyara City, yet ultimately, it is the vision that guides his path."

"Where does the vision come from? The island?" She waved her hand from horizon to horizon.

He gestured for her to sit near the hole. "There are other places in the world where people have been documented to have received these types of visions. Around all of the pyramids. In the valleys of the two elven realms. Wild Turkey Island on the Kanin plateau. Around Haikou Island in your own country. Supposedly the Forbidden Island of the Eldaeri."

Sitting, she contained a scoff. "Then the Paladins place a lot of trust in architectural ruins, if their vision guides their life."

"What can we trust more than that which comes from within ourselves?" He sat down across from her, on the other side of the hole. The light cast his complexion in turquoise hues.

She must've looked the same to him. Her brows furrowed as she considered her words. Did the vision come from oneself, or from the location?

He smiled and placed his hand over his heart. "The vision is what separates the Ayuri Paladin from the Maduran Golden Scorpion, for power without guidance leads to a selfish sense of superiority and self-righteousness. Even worse is power which is manipulated by dogma. The Bovyan Knights, who inspired Acharya to form the Paladin Order, deferred to the Keepers of the Shrine of Geros, who interpret their progenitor's last will. They are now the Teleri Imperial Army, whose very existence is sustained by institutional rape."

"Is the Paladin's vision so clear? I do not understand what I heard." She stared into the cone of blue light.

"Understanding the vision requires special training in harmonizing one's own life force to the vibrations of the world. All Paladins begin this study when they are children and practice as you saw them do today. Yet even with this life-long training, they oftentimes come to me to help them make sense of what they feel." He ran his hand through the light. "You said the island *spoke* to you, that you do not understand what you *heard*. This is different from how we describe what the Paladins *feel*. What exactly are you hearing?"

They were speaking a different language, it seemed. "All of the sounds around me are harmonized, from the beating of your heart, to my breathing, to the sounds of the ocean waves. It is a symphony of sounds. During the morning meditation, I could almost see these sounds as colors, coalescing into fleeting images."

His lips formed a perfect circle. "This is why you played your flute yesterday. You were answering the call of the island."

"How did you hear my flute from all the way over here?" She gawped at him.

He laughed again. "Have you not been listening? I did not *hear* it, I *felt* it. The notes you played merged with the Vibrations of the world and came to me. So, you saw the sound as colors this morning?"

Kaiya nodded.

"Fascinating. I have heard that in ages past, your people could do astonishing things with the fine arts, whether it was music, dance, sculpture, or painting. This warrants further investigation by the Paladin Order." He reached across and took her hands in his, pulling them into the light. "Now, perhaps I can help you understand your images. Please, tell them to me."

Kaiya's skin tingled in the light. The forgotten images flooded back. The emotional content, lost in her meditative state, now engulfed her like a tidal wave. Tears blurred her vision. Choking with sobs, she crumpled over. "The most perfect lotus flower transformed into a venomous snake. The rest, I can't remember clearly. A plucked phoenix. Scorching sun. Shattered jade."

The Oracle's hands pulled her up. His eyebrows scrunched together. "Is that all you remember now?"

Kaiya nodded. "What does it mean?"

"It is your near future."

Such a terse answer, after all the loquacious stories! Kaiya straightened, trying to regain her composure. Her voice sounded desperate in her ears. "What is my not-so-near future, then?"

His lips and nose wiggled. "Let me preface my answer about the future by telling you about the past. Something that happened thirty-two years ago, not long after my mentor passed on and I became the Oracle."

Kaiya nodded. If nothing else came from this visit, at least she would get a history lesson.

"The dragon Avarax, who had disappeared from history during the War of Ancient Gods a thousand years before, suddenly reappeared and descended upon the Temple of the Moon. He demanded the Lotus Crystal."

"The Lotus Crystal?" she asked.

"The Dragonstone which hovered above the Font." The Oracle waved at the hole in the ground, from which the light sprayed out.

Kaiya shuddered. Avarax! He ruled from his mountain lair in the Dragonlands; the mere threat of his fiery breath kept his subjects cowed. With so many of their numbers deployed at the border with Ayuri lands, the Paladins hadn't been able to assist Prince Hardeep's Ankira when Madura invaded.

The Oracle bowed his head, sending his white hair and beard cascading. "Many Paladins died in its defense that day. He threatened to immolate the island with his breath. I surrendered the Lotus Crystal and he left. Ever since then, Paladin students have needed deeper training to gain a more complete picture of their visions. A beginner cannot possibly sense much, let alone hold on to what he felt."

Was that why she couldn't remember the vision clearly? Did she need more training? Kaiya prompted him with a tilt of her chin.

The Oracle stroked his beard. "What I mean is, in order to see further into your future, you would either need more training, or the Lotus Crystal would need to be returned to its rightful place over the Font."

"So you cannot tell me anything?"

The Oracle shook his head. "I never tell, just guide."

She bowed. "Then guide me, please."

"I believe the lotus flower represents something you treasure. Its transformation into a snake could mean that it becomes something onerous. Or perhaps it never was what you thought."

The Oracle's *guidance* seemed just as perplexing as the image itself. Kaiya conjured her most gracious smile and bowed. "Thank you."

He gazed at her. "Master Sabal will be setting off for Vyara City later today to greet some young Paladin recruits. I will see to it that he takes the same skiff as you, and that he teaches you a simple exercise to help you feel—or hear—the vibrations of the universe. When you are ready, come again and meditate with us. Perhaps then you will get a deeper insight into your future." Without looking back, he gestured toward the bridge. "Ah, here is Gayan to deliver some news."

Kaiya glanced past the Oracle. The boy hurried across the bridge on his short legs. He stopped just short of the mesa. "Master, the Dragon—"

"—is sending an envoy to Vyara City."

The boy nodded. "The Council of Elders wants to—"

"—know if I will take my seat and greet the envoy with them. Young Gayan, surely even without your gift of foresight, you know what my answer will be. What it has always been." He then turned to Kaiya. "Though they do not yet know, the council will be asking you to meet the Dragon's envoy."

CHAPTER 25:
Token from Ayudra

To Kaiya's ears, even the hammering from the dwarven smithy in the distance seemed to beat in tune with all of Ayudra's other sounds. She regarded the stone building with a dubious eye. According to the Oracle, the Blackhammer dwarf clan would help her find a focus—a tie to the energy of Ayudra.

Cross-armed, Jie tapped her toe. Apparently, she agreed it wasn't worth the delay.

Two teenage Ayuri, a boy and a girl, sat outside sharpening their *nagas*. Beyond them, the stone building had an open front, allowing a clear view of the two dwarves in goggles and leather aprons.

Sparks flew as a dwarf with rust-colored hair and beard struck a blue-hot metal rod with a large hammer. A wrinkled, white-bearded dwarf held and flipped the rod over an anvil with a pair of tongs. They both hummed what sounded like a marching tune, the beat set to their hammering.

Kaiya gasped. Dwarves were famous for their inventiveness and craftsmanship, not their music. The sound was beautiful. But what were they making?

"Paladin *nagas*," Gayan yelled over the pounding, answering her unasked question. He waved at the younger dwarf, who paused and lifted his goggles.

Tugging off his gloves, the dwarf stomped over. He stood a head shorter than her, nearly as tall as Jie. Soot covered his face, except where the goggles had protected his eyes. He thumped his chest with his fist. "Ashler Blackhammer, at yer service, lass," he said in Arkothi. "Or should I say, Yer 'ighness?"

Even a dwarf she'd never seen before recognized her. Kaiya returned his salute, bringing her fist to her chest. "Well met, Master Blackhammer," she spoke in the manner of the North.

He favored her with irises as black as coal. "So up the hill we go, t'fetch ye a rock of istrium alloy."

"A rock?" She raised an eyebrow at Gayan.

The boy nodded. "To make your focus."

Master Blackhammer tilted his chin to the elder dwarf and wiped his hands on his apron. He then led them down the street.

At the flower-covered statue of Acharya, they turned right off the main road and onto a side street that ran through the three-hundred-year-old ruins of ancient Ayudra.

Kaiya shuddered. Nothing in Cathay spoke of the Hellstorm like the crumbling buildings and rubble-strewn streets before her. A city built over seven hundred years, reduced to ruins in just a single night. Hundreds of thousands of unfortunate souls, immolated or drowned.

Following a cleared path through the debris, they circled the Temple of the Moon at a distance and began the gentle ascent onto the hill.

The dwarf raked an open hand over the land. "Keep yer eyes open fer somethin' that catches yer fancy, lass." He then started to hum, continuing his earlier war song. Every now and then, he would pick up a stone and thrust it into a coarse cloth bag.

Bewildered, Kaiya looked around at the heap of blue-grey shards scattered as far as the eye could see. She bent over and picked up a smooth pebble.

The dwarf laughed. "That's just a rock, lass."

Kaiya held him in her gaze. "What am I searching for?"

"A rock ye kin feel belongs to ye."

Gayan's head bobbed several times. "When the Hellstorm obliterated Mount Ayudra, the istrium dust fused with iron deposits. Paladin students come here to find a piece that *feels* right to them, and the Blackhammers incorporate that into a *naga*. Rumor has it a Golden Scorpion melts his *naga* sword to make his mask to symbolize their break from the order. Still, it's their connection to the spiritual home of the *Bahaadur*. The Oracle wanted you to have a tie as well."

Master Blackhammer raised a bushy eyebrow at Gayan. "Ye sure she kin do it? She's got no trainin' in yer meditation."

The boy nodded enthusiastically and the dwarf shrugged, going back to his humming.

"Sing," Jie said. "Just like Master Blackhammer's hum. The Paladins *feel*, you *hear*."

The suggestion was as good as any. With a deep breath, Kaiya banished impatience and uncertainties from her mind. She raised her voice in song, letting the orchestra of the island guide her as she improvised.

Around her, shards lit up in soft blue light.

The dwarf stared at her, eyes wide. The boy just grinned ear-to-ear.

Among all the scattered rocks, a cherry-sized stone sang back to her. Kaiya knelt down and picked it up. Its coldness gave the impression of a stream infused with snowmelt.

"That's yer stone, lass," the dwarf said. "Give it t'me, and I'll craft a nice ring for ya. Come t'my uncle's forge next time ye visit so ye kin sing t'it again. Yon voice o'yers will work much better than a pair'o dwarves a'hummin'."

The next time she visited, he said. If the Oracle's predictions were true, a lot would be happening between then and now.

CHAPTER 26:
Song of Swords

The wide sailing barge cut through the Shallowsea's mangrove-dotted expanse, sailing farther and farther away from Ayudra. As the island disappeared in the distance, Kaiya needed to focus harder to perceive the soft wind in the mangrove branches singing in concert with the ripples of the placid waters.

"Concentrate!" Master Sabal's tone had become strict after leaving behind his role as guide and taking up the mantle of mentor. "You can feel, and to some extent control, the Vibrations of the world. You must now learn to surrender to them. You laugh, half-elf?"

Kaiya opened her eyes and whipped her head around.

Jie covered her mouth with a hand. "Sorry, Master. The way you spoke brought visions of one of my teachers."

The master Paladin pursed his lips. "I hope he was handsome."

Jie grinned. "She was."

His eyebrows clashed together as he glared at the Insolent Retainer. "You want to challenge my *naga* skills. You have, since the day we met. Well, let us have at it. I forewarn you, you will get wet."

Kaiya stared from Jie back to the master. The kind man from just a couple of days before was nowhere to be found on this barge. In his place, a strict teacher stood ready to tongue-lash her each time she failed to *feel* the so-called Vibrations of the world. Now, she stood forgotten as he turned his ire toward Jie.

The Black Fist girl placed her right fist in her left palm. A snap of her wrists brought a knife into each hand. "Please teach me."

Kaiya twirled a lock of her hair. The Cathayi politeness before a duel might be lost in translation.

The master pressed his palms together and then drew his *naga*. Made of a bluish-grey metal, the single-edged broadsword had a wide tip and no guard. "After y—"

Jie lunged at him with a torrent of slashes. The older man avoided each one with subtle body shifts before his *naga* whistled toward her in a single horizontal cut. It glowed with a blue tinge.

She barely dodged the blow by jumping backward; but the Paladin pressed the attack. Her next step back sent her over the edge of the barge, flipping head-over-heels into the sea.

Water sprayed upwards with a loud splash. Kaiya flinched. It had all happened so fast. Her ears had captured it all, but her eyes still processed the image.

"You felt it! Good!" The Paladin beamed at her. He then looked toward where Jie had gone overboard. "Not bad on your part either, half-elf."

The imperial guards rushed to the edge. Jie's fingers gripped the rim while she vigorously kicked up water.

Master Sabal laughed. "Try standing, girl. There is a reason we call it the Shallowsea."

The babbling water quieted and Jie's head popped up. Only her pony tail was wet. "It's just waist-high!"

"Yes," the master said. "Just below the brackish waters lie the fertile flood plains that once made up the heart of the Ayuri Empire. Most of the Shallowsea's depth is knee-height. The barge captains follow the old river beds, which rarely go deeper than the height of a man."

Ma Jun helped Jie back on board. Wet clothes clung to her lithe form, outlining several small weapons and tools.

Master Sabal turned to Kaiya. "What you saw me do, Your Highness, is what happens when you surrender to the vibrations of the world. You move—not with intention, but because you are moved. Combat slows down in your mind's eye, and your own motions become subconscious."

Kaiya nodded, even if it didn't make sense. Her music teachers always emphasized the power of intent... though Lord Xu had mentioned something about improvisation before.

"You do not believe me." He motioned for the guards. "You three, attack me."

Xu Zhan whipped his short sword out, ready to take up the challenge. His enthusiasm for fighting might get him killed one day.

Zhao Yue, on the other hand, responded cautiously. He looked over the boat, then back. "When you send us for a swim, I am afraid the ghosts of the millions who died in the Hellstorm will drag us under."

Master Sabal harrumphed. "There are no ghosts. The energies of the living join the Vibrations of the universe for a time, only to be reborn and die again. The cycle has repeated itself many times since the Hellstorm. Now draw your weapons. Fight as if you are defending your princess."

As if defending her? Zhao Yue and Ma Jun turned to her, and Kaiya nodded in silent authorization. Hopefully, they would be careful.

The two joined the more enthusiastic Xu Zhan. They saluted with right fists in left palms, and then bared their blades.

The Paladin pressed his hands together. "Now come at me."

The three imperial guards fanned out as much as the boat would allow, interposing themselves between the Paladin and her. On Ma Jun's shout, they engaged Master Sabal in a synchronized attack that very few would escape alive, let alone unscathed.

The master Paladin whirled in a blur among their buzzing swords. His deadly dance was reminiscent of when Lord Xu had approached her through a cordon of imperial guards on the castle wall years before.

Like Hardeep, as well.

Unable to track his movements, she turned her ear to listen. Jie appeared in her line of sight. The Black Fist's eyes darted back and forth, tapered ears twitching as she watched the melee.

The noises were unlike those of any other duel Kaiya had witnessed. The swishing of blades and bodies through the air replaced the typical clinks and clanks of metal on metal.

When the sound stopped, Master Sabal's presence radiated next to her. She met his solemn gaze.

"Your guards fight in harmony with each other," he said. "Their form is intricately choreographed, with excellent changes according to situation. Nonetheless, it needs to harmonize with the Vibrations of the world if they are to have a chance of defeating a seasoned Paladin."

The three all sank to one knee, heads bowed, swords proffered to her. "We have failed you, *Dian-xia*. If it is your command—"

Kaiya waved them into silence, even as she gazed at Master Sabal. The sounds of the fight replayed in her ears, giving clarity to the blur of motion.

He narrowed his eyes. "Do not just *feel*. Be *moved*."

Kaiya sighed. She'd never felt so inadequate, even as an awkward tween pretending to be Perfect Princess. "I will try."

He jabbed a finger at her. "*Trying* is the first step to failure. Your conscious mind cannot *be moved*."

"I will meditate on it more." She bowed.

The master smiled. "Good. You, handmaiden, get some dry clothes or you will catch a cold."

The journey across the Shallowsea took three days, giving Jie plenty of time to watch and listen to the lessons meant for the princess. It gave her reason to ignore the badgering old elf wizard Ayana, whom Prince Aelward had sent along as extra protection.

At times, Jie would convince one of the imperial guards to play with her at the other end of the skiff, in the games they excelled at.

As much as Black Lotus clansmen mocked the imperial guards behind their backs, the only Black Fist who could go toe-to-toe with one in a swordfight was Tian. She was certainly no match for an imperial guard in a *fair* fight. Which was why she rarely fought fair.

These days, however, with Master Sabal's lessons to the princess taken to heart, Jie refrained from tricks and found herself performing better and better with each successive loss. The master, whose line of sight was blocked by the center cabins from his side of the deck, shouldn't have been able to witness the duels. Nonetheless, he would tell her almost exactly how a fight had unfolded and where she'd gone wrong.

In the afternoon of the third day, she and Chen Xin squared off against each other in a light drizzle. After returning her salute, he surged forward with a quick stab of his curved short sword. She sidestepped and cut toward his hand with a knife, but he raised his weapon to parry.

A stray clump of seaweed on deck begged to be kicked into Chen's face, but that wouldn't be fair. She followed through with a thrust of her other knife. He parried that blow as well and swept his blade around. She stepped back out of reach and sank into a defensive stance.

He was fast, even though he approached middle years for a human.

"Feel his intention," Ayana said, uninvited.

Jie turned to spit out a retort, just as Chen Xin pressed his attack with a lethal combination of slashes. In that second of inattention, she knew everything he planned. His sword seemed to move through honey, and it took little effort to avoid.

She moved in to deliver the winning blow when he paused and looked toward the bow of the ship. She followed his gaze to a sparkle on the horizon.

"The Paladins' Crystal Citadel," Ayana said, "on Vyara City's central hilltop."

Hair matted with sweat, Chen Xin backed away. He put his fist into his palm and grinned. "We'll call it a draw."

She would've won. Nonetheless, Jie ignored him and instead squinted to see a thin line of land in the distance, separating the pale blue sky from the dark green sea. Yet even her sharp elven sight couldn't make out any detail of the famous city-state.

Vyara City intrigued her not for its famous network of beautiful canals, nor for its importance as home to the Paladin Order. Rather, the city played prominently in recent Black Lotus history, when on a mission a year before her birth, one of three young masters perished while retrieving a secret artifact for the *Tianzi*. The other two died within the year; and the next generation of Black Fists conjectured fanciful theories of how the mysterious artifact had been cursed.

The names of the three had been expunged from the monastery records, and all adepts who knew the young masters were forbidden to speak of the mission or their real names. Master Yan had gone so far as to block off the memory of some Black Fists with the *Tiger's Eye* technique. In tales of their other exploits, the three deceased masters were known by the code names Beauty, Surgeon, and Architect.

Though the ill-fated mission had occurred a year before her birth, it always piqued Jie's interest. If circumstances permitted, she would investigate the three-decade-old cold case. Perhaps she could find someone in Vyara City, not bound by the Black Lotus rules of secrecy, who might tell her more.

CHAPTER 27:
A Hot Welcome

A barrage of sound assaulted Kaiya's ears as the barge approached the wharfs, which reached far into the waters like several dozen spindly fingers. Seagulls screeched in lazy circles above, occasionally swooping in to steal fishermen's daily catches. Sailors joked and cursed as their barges jockeyed for docking positions. Even the din emanating from the city itself echoed over the water. If Jiangkou Port had been cacophonous, the Cathayi language didn't have a word to describe the level of noise and chaos of Vyara City's harbor. She rubbed her ears.

Master Sabal laughed. "You will find no noisier place on Tivaralan than early morning Vyara City."

A smile! It befit him better than the gruff role of teacher. Kaiya nodded in time with the gently rocking boat. Jie edged up next to her.

Master Sabal gestured toward the skyline. "Vyara City was already quite a commercial center before the Hellstorm. Located at the confluence of two great rivers, where ocean-going vessels could no longer pass upstream, it prospered as a transit point between the river barges upstream and the sailing ships downstream. In one night, the ocean came all the way to its doorstep and transformed it into a peninsular seaport."

Kaiya tried picturing the city as an inland river city, but the noise addled her imagination.

"Concentrate, young one." The teacher's tone returned, if only for a second. He pointed to other cityscapes in the distance. "When smaller nation states emerged from the ashes of the Ayuri Empire, they established national capitals there, there, and way over there. Each is less than an hour's ferry ride from Vyara's harbor. That is how it supplanted Ayudra as the economic and cultural heart of our people."

Grasping the bulwark, Kaiya looked at the other cities before scanning Vyara's waterfront. Block-shaped, flat-roofed shops, warehouses, and trading offices stretched as far as the eye could see, broken only by canals going inland. People crowded the streets, yelling and gesticulating as they went about their business. The noise rose to a roar as their barge docked. Her heart rattled at the dissonance. Reading about Tivaralan's largest city was so different from experiencing it.

She disembarked, followed by her guards. Humid heat rolled over her almost as soon as her foot touched the quay. Paintings did the city little justice. A hill rose in the background. A single road spiraled its way up the slope, lined by dozens of white mansions with graceful columns and arches, and topped by elegant domes, spires, and minarets. At the very top, the Paladins' Crystal Citadel sparkled in the morning sun.

If the Oracle truly knew the future, Kaiya would be visiting the citadel soon enough. "Why do the Paladin elders meet here, instead of Ayudra Island?"

"Ayudra may be the spirit of the Paladin Order, but Vyara City is its brain. It is in the center of Ayuri lands, within a week's travel of every nation within the Paladins' mandate." Master Sabal gestured to the dock. "Here is where we part ways, Your Highness. It has been a pleasure. I hope our paths cross again."

Hopefully. With the imperial guards drawing up around her, Kaiya pressed her palms together and bowed her head. "Thank you for teaching me, Master."

He returned the gesture and disappeared into the crowds.

Without the foreign ministry official who was supposed to have met up with them on Ayudra, they were on their own. Kaiya drew her hood up, despite the stifling heat.

Jie's shrill voice answered her thoughts. "Shall we go to our embassy?"

"That would be the best course of action," Chen Xin added. "Where is it?"

All eyes turned to Ayana, who shrugged. "It is *your* embassy."

Jie sucked on her lower lip, and then pointed. "Near the hill. We could probably take a canal boat and avoid the masses."

Not another boat. Kaiya shuddered. Her feet were just getting used to solid ground after so many days at sea. People jammed the canal boat stations, making the proposition even less appealing. "We shall walk, since we know the general direction."

Despite their prior instructions, her imperial guards all knelt, fists to the ground.

Jie hissed. "On your feet, dunderheads! Don't betray the princess' identity!"

The men tentatively rose, heads bowed. So much for secrecy.

They set off toward the hill, pushing their way through the mass of humanity. Unlike the unified sounds on Ayudra Island, Vyara City was a disjointed screaming of Ayuri and Arkothi languages, with several other tongues mixed in.

Kaiya's mind spun. Countless light-brown skinned Ayuri people negotiated trade terms with the many darker-toned Levanthi. A handful of fairer Nothori, Estomari, and Arkothi from the North mixed in with the crowd as well. The heavy scent of sweat, fish, and curry powder joined in with the bewildering sights and sounds to overwhelm her senses.

It didn't help being bumped and jostled by people hurrying by, despite the imperial guards trying to provide a shield. Jie clasped her hand, like a mother keeping hold of her frightened young child.

A press of people pushed back from the middle of the streets, shoving her against the walls of a building. A firm hand rested on her shoulder, providing a comforting warmth. She turned to see Ayana looking back at her with knitted eyebrows. Heat flushed Kaiya's cheeks. This three-hundred-year-old survivor of the Hellstorm was handling the crowds better than she.

"Make way, make way." A voice shouted in Ayuri and accented Arkothi, carrying above the quieting crowds.

Kaiya pouted. Had they come with the rest of the diplomatic staff from the *Golden Phoenix*, they would've enjoyed the privilege of right-of-way, instead of being swept along in the tide of people. She craned her neck to see above bodies and heads. Rust-red banners emblazoned with a golden scorpion fluttered in her line of sight.

The Ayuri Kingdom of Madura. The rogue nation behind the attacks in Huajing. The ones who had invaded and occupied Prince Hardeep's homeland of Ankira. She was supposed to meet with them the next day, and perhaps the one riding on the litter was her counterpart.

"Make way, make way for Prince Dhananad of the Kingdom of Madura!" the crier yelled again.

Copper coins rained from above, flung from the procession. Kaiya raised her hands to protect her face, but Li Wei snatched one out of the air. He handed it to her, revealing a scorpion stamped on one side.

She flipped it over. A faded image looked back at her. Despite the lack of clarity, there was something unsettlingly familiar about it.

Despite the scent of incense and spices cloying her mind, Jie recognized the name Dhananad as a piece of the thirty-two-year-old puzzle—a survivor of the Black Lotus plot devised by the famed Architect in their quest to retrieve a secret artifact. She left the princess' side, slipping through the wall of people to reach the front.

The procession stretched half a city block, with a crier at the fore, throwing coins into the crowds. Several dozen soldiers and ministers wearing rust-red *kurtas* followed, surrounding a gold-cloth litter.

Jie snorted. Such ostentatiousness. Still, it didn't begin to compare to the man in his late thirties reclined on his side in the litter.

Long dark hair hung loosely about his shoulders, merging with a pointed beard to frame a somewhat handsome face. Embroidered with gold borders, his rich burgundy robes brought out his light-brown complexion. A curved *talwar* sword dangled from his left hip. Even from this distance, his musky scent assaulted her nose.

At the side of the litter, standing almost a head above the other guards, marched six imposing men, all fair-skinned and fair-haired. Chainmail jingled beneath black tunics with gold-embroidered collars. A yellow sun was embroidered onto each left breast, and straight longswords hung from their sides.

Bovyans: the rulers and soldiers of the Teleri Empire. Jie sucked on her lower lip. After her last mission deep into their homeland, she'd never expected—or wanted—to see one of those brutes again. Descended from the mortal son of their Sun God, the all-male race had devolved into conquering thugs and gang rapists.

One beggar apparently didn't know of their reputation. He stepped toward the litter with an open palm, only to be launched back into crowd with a nonchalant shove of a meaty Bovyan hand.

Jie pulled up her hood and pushed back through one rank of spectators, then knelt to look between the people in front of her.

Interspersed with the Bovyans marched four smaller Ayuri humans. Their grace reminded her of the Paladins' fluidity; but instead of white, they wore open-faced surcoats in a light bronze tone with intricate borders. Dark bronze-colored *kurtas* peeked out from underneath the surcoats. Most distinctive were their featureless masks, made of a bluish-grey metal. The *nagas* at their sides ended in the shape of a scorpion sting.

Maduran Scorpions.

Real ones.

Body language alone suggested they were similar in skill to the Scorpion who'd knocked her out in Tokahia than to the three incompetents in Peng's teahouse. The latter's masks had been cheap facsimiles of the ones she saw now. Who were those three, and who had sent them, if not Madura?

After the procession passed, the crowds thinned enough to provide some breathing room. Jie headed back to where she'd left the others.

Chen Xin's gaze was locked on the princess, his expression contorted with concern. "The princess looks pale. We should get out of this crowded area."

It was a sound idea. There'd been a less busy side-street not far back, and Jie beckoned them. "Follow me. It's only a couple minutes' walk until things clear up."

"If we aren't crushed to death first," muttered Li Wei.

The suggestion proved to be good. They made their way northeast toward the city center, with the density of moving bodies thinning the further they travelled from the docks.

Before long, Chen Xin called for a halt. He was looking at the princess again. He'd served her since she was a child, and even if all the imperial guards adored her, his paternal affection showed in small gestures like this. "Do not worry, *Dian-xia*. Once we reach the embassy, we should enjoy the same right of way afforded other dignitaries. We won't have to wade through the masses."

The princess afforded him a wan smile. It hid whatever silly ideas might be bouncing around in her pretty head.

Jie could guess, though. The princess' expression was similar to when they had walked through the castle's escape tunnel. Jie snorted, and then scanned the area to reorient herself.

White block buildings rose two stories above them, their first floors being storefronts. The Crystal Citadel still glittered from the hilltop, serving as a landmark. The Iridescent Moon hung high and to the southwest.

Ma Jun pointed northeast. "I believe our embassy is only half an hour away on foot."

Li Wei shook his head. "The last time we trusted you with directions—"

Chen Xin shot Li Wei a glance, and all the guards chuckled. Perhaps they had shared some misadventure in the Floating World. Or maybe they were just being men.

Though showing no signs of fatigue in her old age, Ayana threw her hands up. "Have any of you been here before?"

Ma Jun grinned. "If we get lost, *you* can ask for directions. Now, with the princess' permission, I will lead the way."

Just like a man. For now, Jie would have to trust Ma Jun with directions. Her skillset was better used for another problem.

Someone was following them.

CHAPTER 28:
Stalker in the Shadows

Humidity hung in Kaiya's lungs and her heart pounded in her ears as they headed from the docks toward the embassy. Throughout her life, she'd always been shielded from the masses—metaphorically by Cathayi conventions toward their royalty, physically by a line of imperial guards. She was just about wilting from the close quarters and incessant noise. Yet she put on her best face, mortified by the idea of her people seeing her as anything less than a Perfect Princess.

To hide her fatigue, she lifted her chin and lengthened her stride. If she was no longer a living metaphor for nonchalant grace, let them remember her gritty determination. Kaiya channeled her younger self, envisioning the inconvenience as one of the imaginary adventures she had shared with her childhood friend, Tian. A smile tugged at her lips.

With Ma Jun ostensibly in the lead, they stuck to the main streets, crossing several arched bridges which spanned the numerous canals. She observed the Ayuri people going about their daily lives and stole glances at stands outside storefronts.

Women picked through fruits of exotic colors and shapes lying perfectly stacked in bins, making her wonder about their flavor and texture. Young ladies ran their hands through multicolored *sari* dresses that hung from poles, piquing her imagination. Would a dress like that make her look beautiful? Perhaps this negotiating trip wouldn't be so bad, after all.

On a couple of occasions, Paladins walked by, marked by their white *kurtas* with gold embroidery on the cuffs and collar, and the curved *naga* sword hanging at their side. They paid the Cathayi no mind.

Bins of deep green tea leaves lined the front of one store, and a dark trail of smoke billowed from its open door. The merchant standing by the entrance beckoned them in. "Come in, come in! Take a puff of the finest gooseweed you will find in all of the Ayuri Confederation."

Despite their haste, Kaiya approached, curiosity getting the better of her. The dried weed's curled appearance and sweet aroma seemed almost identical to the leaves from the tea shrubs on Jade Mountain, picked by the nuns of Praise Moon Temple for the Imperial Family.

"Do you drink this?"

The man's eyes widened. "No, no. It will kill a man's seed. No. It is for smoking. Very rich flavor, and incomparably relaxing! Come in and try it!"

Images of emaciated addicts straggling out of opium dens formed in her mind. With a bow, Kaiya backed away.

"Please, try!" The man moved to follow, motioning toward her.

Hands on sword hilts, Chen Xin and Li Wei formed a wall between them.

Scowling, the merchant raised his hands and retreated several steps. "Who do you think you are, the Queen of Vadara? Don't smoke, then!"

Kaiya glanced back at him before they resumed their walk. He stood halfway inside the store, talking to someone while pointing in their direction. It was too early in the day to make an enemy.

Almost three-quarters of the way to the Cathayi embassy, Jie inserted herself between Kaiya and Chen Xin. "Keep walking, don't look back, don't act surprised," she whispered. "We are being followed, by someone who knows how to follow without being noticed."

"*You* noticed him." Chen Xin kept his attention forward, but his tone carried an audible smirk.

Jie grinned. "You should know I'm better than he is. He is trailing about a hundred feet behind us, on the other side of the road, trying to keep lots of other people between us. A large Ayuri man wearing a *dhoti* skirt and shawl."

Kaiya fought the urge to look back, and twirled a lock of her hair instead. Someone sent by the scorned gooseweed merchant, perhaps.

Chen Xin nodded. "This is a good time to take a break." He opened his pack and drew out a waterskin, which he offered to Ma Jun. He whispered a warning about the stalker. Ma Jun passed both canteen and message to Li Wei.

Jie sucked on her lower lip. "I am going to find out why he is following us."

"How do you plan on doing that?" Kaiya raised an eyebrow.

The half-elf pointed down the street. "Keep walking and turn onto a quiet side street. In the meantime, I will go back to the last fruit seller, let him pass me, then tail *him.*"

Li Wei coughed. "That seems very elementary. Are you sure he will fall for it?"

Jie shrugged. "Only one way to find out. If it doesn't work, at least he'll stop following us."

Kaiya played with her hair. "Very well. Proceed as you see fit. Meet us at the embassy if we get separated."

Jie bobbed her head and turned back. So cavalier. The half-elf's confidence bordered on foolhardiness.

From the corner of her eye, Jie watched the spy's reflection in a storefront window as they passed each other on opposite sides of the street.

He continued walking with almost admirable stalking skills. From his size, he had to be a Bovyan Nightblade, like the ones she'd faced in Jiangkou during the insurrection two years ago, and later in the North during her mission.

When she reached the fruit store, she took her time choosing a perfect mango from the stands out front, all the while keeping an eye on the interloper. It was time to practice her Ayuri.

And the fine art of haggling.

She scrunched her nose and held a fresh mango up to the vendor. "How much for this rotten one?"

"Rotten?" The man placed his hand on his chest. "It was just picked today. You cannot get any fresher. Ten copper rupayas."

"Ten?" Jie feigned outrage. "This fetid piece of slime would only bring three coppers in Cathay."

"But you can't get it in Cathay," the vendor said with a sly grin. "However, the gods favor the magnanimous. I offer it to you for eight."

Jie spat. "Magnanimous is five. Eight is waterway robbery."

The man wagged a finger at her. "My boy fell down from the tree picking this very mango this morning, and broke his leg. I need at least seven to pay the doctor, or he will never walk again."

A bare-chested boy of about ten skipped out of the door, smiling. "Mother wants me to run to the South Market to pay the mango farm's distributor."

The man's face flushed red. "Did I tell you I have two sons? Six coppers, no less."

Smiling victoriously, Jie handed him an Ayuri silver rupiya, worth ten coppers. Before the man reached into his purse to make change, the spy had almost reached the side street where the princess had turned. Jie hurried after him, mango in hand but change forgotten.

In the game of espionage and counterespionage, the man was overmatched. Jie had learned his trailing and stalking techniques years before, and her smaller size allowed her to melt into the crowds.

Before turning the corner, he looked back toward the fruit seller. His eyes widened as he scanned the crowd. Though his gaze swept over her several times, he didn't seem to have noticed her. He ducked into the alley.

Time to sneak up behind him and choke him into unconsciousness. Jie dashed to the alley and turned the corner.

The man waited there, curved dagger brandished in an underhand grip. He seemed even larger up close, with broad shoulders and square features. Huge for an Ayuri, small for a Bovyan. Just like the Water Snake Black Fists in Cathay; just like the operatives she'd fought in Eldaeri lands.

Jie took a few steps back, hands raised. "Why are you following us?"

The man snarled and slashed down at her.

Jie jumped out of range, and then tossed the mango up in a high arc.

His eyes tracked the fruit, and in that instant, she darted in and yanked the *dhoti* skirt from his waist.

All he wore underneath was a loincloth. A well-bred Cathayi lady would've averted her eyes, but Jie wasn't well-bred. Instead, she twisted the rectangular cloth into a rat-tail as the man recovered from his initial embarrassment.

His cheeks red, he stabbed at her again.

She spun around him, catching his arm in the cloth. In a split-second she was behind him, and yanked so the blade was now pinned against his throat. With another twist, she wrapped one end of the cloth around his free hand and squeezed tight, while stepping into his knee.

He buckled to the ground.

"Now, let's try again," she said in his ear. "Who are you?"

His voice trembled. "I'm sorry, miss. Just a petty thief, casing some unsuspecting victims."

Jie gave the cloth a slight tug and the blade nicked his chin. "I tried to shave my brother's beard like this once, but I ended up rearranging his face. I'm not stupid. Thieves don't choose groups of people to rob."

"Jie!" The princess approached from around the corner, the imperial guards close on her heels. "There is no need to torture him," she said in the Cathayi tongue, "even if he is a spy."

"Forgive me, mistress," Jie answered in Ayuri, to make sure he understood the misinformation she was about to feed him. Then again, *mistress* tasted kind of funny compared to *Dian-xia*. "He won't speak unless given the right encouragement."

Ayana stepped forward and looked the man over. "Teleri Nightblade. They've been trained in your people's art of spying and assassination, and played an instrumental role in the Teleri Empire's invasion of Eldaeri lands."

Chen Xin frowned. "He's a little short for a Bovyan."

"He's Ayuri." Xu Zhan pointed at the man. "Bovyans aren't so dark-skinned."

Ayana shook her head. "No, Bovyans are all male, and they will always look like their mother's race. This one's mother was undoubtedly some unfortunate Ayuri or Levanthi woman." She glared at the man and said, "But you never knew your mother, did you? No Bovyan ever does, because of your despicable rape and breeding programs."

The man spat. "My mother is the Teleri Empire. In time, it will be your mother as well." With a flick of his wrist, he tried to slash his own throat.

Jie jerked part of the cloth so that he missed completely. She launched her knee into his back, right between the shoulder blades, knocking the wind out of him and driving his face into the ground.

"Jie!" The princess scowled at her.

"Sorry, mistress," Jie said without the least amount of sincerity. She twisted the man's dagger out of his hands. "But we had better do something about him."

Zhao Yue pointed. "Bystanders are gathering at intersection to the alley. It would not be good if they called the Paladins to enforce the law here."

Jie withdrew a vial from the folds of her robe and dabbed it on her wrist. A fruity smell almost like perfume wafted through the air.

The princess raised an eyebrow. "What is that?"

Jie wiped her wrist across the back of the Nightblade's neck as he struggled. "It is a contact toxin made from several secret plants. This combination will induce a state of euphoric intoxication in human males."

The imperial guards took two steps back. The spy wriggled for a couple of seconds before relaxing.

Chuckling, Jie loosened the cloth. "Come on, big boy, up on to your feet."

With a ridiculous grin, the spy eased himself into a sitting position.

"Why were you following us?" The princess flashed that infuriatingly alluring smile.

He just smiled back for a moment. "You are such a pretty lady! How about you join me for a drink of delicious Ayuri *thara*."

Jie frowned, lifting her hand to backhand him, but the princess' preemptive lip pursing stopped her. "The toxin is not truth serum. But we can safely leave him here without fear he'll follow."

Ayana shot a reproachful glance at Jie. "I can make him talk without having to resort to barbaric means or unreliable coercion." Chanting in the flowery language of elven magic, she waved a hand over the man's face.

"You could have said so sooner," Jie mumbled under her breath.

The Teleri's ridiculous grin broadened even wider. "My friends! Shall we have that drink now?"

Ayana beamed. "Not now, dear friend. My name is Aya. What is yours?"

"Toran."

"So Toran, could you tell me why you were trailing us?"

"Well, Grandma," he started, drawing a look of ire from the elf, "we had heard there might be some Cathayi dignitaries coming through." He nodded amiably at the rest of the party. "And they might be trying to strike some sort of deal with the Madurans. Our embassy staff needs to know what that deal is, because, well, you know, the Madurans are our friends. We've been staking out the waterfront, keeping an eye on all of the passenger barges coming in."

"We? How many of you are watching the docks? How many staff in the Teleri embassy?" Ayana asked. Whatever else Jie thought about elves, at least Ayana knew what questions to ask.

"Six of us scouring the docks. Eighty-some people working in the embassy."

Ayana smiled at him. "Thanks, dear friend. Now why don't you run along back to your embassy? And just for old time's sake, tell them that we are just merchants."

Toran pouted. Nonetheless, he stood and moped off, head hanging.

Jie sighed. "You should have had him spy for us."

Ayana shook her head. "A charm spell can convince someone to do something they would not ordinarily consider, but it's hard to change their true nature. I didn't want to test the limits. We may still be able to find out more through him if we cross paths again."

Chen Xin watched him turn the corner. "That would be handy. It would be good to know why the Teleri are so concerned about our dealings with Madura."

Ayana wagged a finger at him. "Prince Aelward already told your Emperor: Madura is an ally of the Teleri. They would not meddle in your country unless the action was either condoned or even instigated by the Teleri Empire."

Ma Jun chuckled. "Too bad. I bet he knew the fastest way to our embassy."

CHAPTER 29:
For Every Answer, Two New Questions

Zheng Ming sat cross-legged at his father's seat in the council, warmed by the sun which bathed the *Danhua* Room in morning light. Around him in the hastily-called meeting, ministers and hereditary lords shuffled and murmured among themselves.

Such an influx of youth! Due to the urgent summons, several *Yu-Ming* and *Tai-Ming* lords had been unable to come from their home provinces. Sons living in the capital attended in their stead. Like him, most had never participated in a council meeting, and didn't know whether their position was determined by their fathers' seniority or their own age.

Lord Zhao's son sat stoically, yet sweat beaded on his brow. At the other end, Lord Han's son fidgeted uncontrollably. Even the usually debonair Lord Peng seemed nervous, playing with his sleeves. To think, the assembled faces might well be a preview of the *Tianzi's* future advisors.

They all pressed their foreheads to the ground as sliding doors opened and the *Tianzi* entered, flanked by General Zheng, bearing the Broken Sword, and another imperial guard. He creaked onto the throne between his sons.

"Rise." His voice rasped before being overtaken by a fit of coughing.

Ming straightened, avoiding eye contact as protocol demanded. Nonetheless, he noted that the *Tianzi*'s eyes seemed more sunken, his face more sallow, than just a few weeks before at Ming's first meeting with Princess Kaiya on the archery field.

The *Tianzi's* coughing subsided. "Thank you all for coming on such short notice to this emergency gathering of the *Tai-Ming* Council. Such a meeting has only been called a handful of times in the three centuries of Wang family rule, so I do not summon you here without cause."

Everyone bowed.

"When Cathay is threatened, her sons are ready," Peng said.

The *Tianzi* nodded with a smile. "Thank you, Nephew. Now, I am pleased to report that we have apprehended the mastermind behind the attacks on our lords."

A collective sigh of relief was followed by excited chatter.

"*Huang-Shang*," Lord Peng said, "who was it? Who had so much information that he was able to orchestrate so many attacks?"

The *Tianzi* seemed to age even more with his deflating sigh. "It is my utmost disappointment and sadness to announce it was Chief Minister Tan."

The Chief Minister! Ming steepled his hands to his chin. He'd been so close. With his dying breath, Xie Shimin had referred to his attack as an *order*. His betrothed had mentioned his meeting with a high official before the tournament. The insurgents Ming captured at in the inn had been able to board the *Golden Phoenix* and sabotage the water barrels. All the clues, right there in front of his nose. His informant might as well have spelled it out for him.

Lord Wu shook his head. "Why would he do such a thing?"

"It was his hope," Crown Prince Kai-Guo said, "that the implication of Madura would push us toward the liberation of Ankira. He felt guilty about his role in selling guns and firepowder to Madura thirty-two years ago."

Lord Liu scratched his chin. "But Xie Shimin tried to kill the Chief Minister. The letter of command we found included the order to kill him."

"But he missed," Ming said. On purpose, without a doubt. "Xie Shimin was the realm's second best archer, shooting from point-blank range."

Minister Hong bowed. "It was likely a diversion, so he would not be implicated."

Lord Liang of Yutou, an Expansionist, narrowed his eyes. "I cannot believe the patriotic Minister Tan could do such a thing."

"Minister Tan's patriotism is not to be questioned," the Crown Prince said. "His means were misguided. Never did he order any of our lords killed. He just wanted to scare us into action. Even a gentle dog will bite when poked."

Lord Han's son bent his neck and stammered. "*Huang-Shang*, he tried to kill my father in his treasonous plot. His family should be executed to five generations."

Ming stared at Young Lord Han. With no descendants to follow proscribed rituals, Minister Tan and his ancestors would starve in the netherworld, and be forced to wander the land as hungry ghosts. It was too cruel a punishment, one which hadn't been handed down since the time of the Wang Dynasty Founder.

Heads nodded, accompanied by low murmurs.

The *Tianzi* raised his hands, silencing all. "Chief Minister Tan was a loyal servant. He confessed to his crimes and provided information for rooting out the insurgents. I have commuted his death sentence. He will live the remainder of his life under house arrest."

Minister Hong put his forehead to the ground. "We are blessed by your benevolent mercy."

Lord Peng stroked his chin. "How was the Chief Minister able to organize an insurgency without anyone noticing?"

"He recruited a merchant, who we believe was once one of the *Tianzi's* agents," the Crown Prince said. "Minister Hong laid a trap for him, which he did not fall for."

All attention turned to the beaming old man. Minister Hong would likely reap grand rewards.

The *Tianzi* straightened. "In the meantime, his former clan is piecing together information about him so we can learn his true identity."

Perhaps this was Ming's mysterious informant. If he surfaced again, Ming would turn the tables on him. In the meantime... "Is this renegade a threat?"

Prince Kai-Guo shook his head. "Now that he knows his patron is gone, he no longer has the information he needs to carry out his attacks."

Lord Peng slapped his hand on the floor. "Until the insurgency is completely wiped out, there will always be a threat."

"Yes, Nephew." The *Tianzi* coughed. "The insurgency remains, with or without Tan. In his confession, he claimed he was not behind them, but merely sought them out in hopes of controlling their excesses."

Lord Peng snorted. "As long as the insurgents live, the Madurans may try to use them to destabilize us."

"Chief Minister Tan was behind the attacks, not Madura," the Crown Prince said.

Ming's eyes widened. Of course. "Then thank the Heavens Tan sabotaged the *Golden Phoenix*. Otherwise, Princess Kaiya would be in Vyara City by now, demanding they cease their meddling. If falsely accused, there is no telling what an unreasonable and aggressive nation like Madura would do to her. I do hope she is recovering?"

The Crown Prince looked down at the floor while the *Tianzi* sank forward in the throne. Ming hadn't been allowed to meet with her since the day she'd been supposed to depart. From their reaction, maybe she was more ill than they had let on.

"What?" Peng sucked in a sharp breath. "Is she getting worse?"

The *Tianzi* sighed. "The princess is in Vyara City already."

273

Ruined! All of Peng Kai-Long's plans slipped through his fingers like fine sand in the wind. Princess Kaiya was in Vyara City. When Madura confirmed their non-involvement in the recent attacks, the fake Scorpion attack would raise questions. It might even cast doubt over the circumstances of his own father's murder. Then, if she sought out Prince Hardeep, she would learn he'd never written a single letter to her.

Gaze raking over the council, Kai-Long knew he had to distance himself from any of the plots he'd hijacked to his own purposes. Otherwise, he would need to flee the capital and consolidate his power in the South. "The princess lacks sufficient protection. We must find some way to send word to her not to agitate Madura. They are belligerent and unpredictable." Or so they all believed, thanks to his disinformation.

"Are you not the one who wanted war?" Lord Liu stared at him. The unimaginative sycophant certainly chose an inopportune time to find his tongue.

"Ask Lord Xu." Young Lord Zheng, perhaps the most incompetent buffoon in the room, somehow came up with the best suggestion. "His magic could summon her home."

Crown Prince Kai-Guo shook his head. "My sister is also tasked with visiting the Sultan of Selastya, who lives in exile near Vyara City. She will request that an Akolyte come to Cathay and heal the *Tianzi* with their Divine Magic."

Kai-Long gritted his teeth. If a true Akolyte healed his uncle... "Perhaps Lord Xu could send a message to the princess, warning her against meeting with the Madurans. They did not hesitate to kill my father and brother."

The *Tianzi* sighed again. "I already asked as much. He said it is beyond his power, based on the distance of Guanyin's Eye in the Heavens."

"Then the princess walks into danger." Kai-Long placed a hand on his chest. "I could not bear to see my cousin harmed."

The *Tianzi* beamed at him. "I appreciate your concern, Nephew. But now, I need your advice. All of your advice, for that is the reason I called this meeting."

All bowed, pressing their foreheads to the ground.

"The position of Chief Minister is vacant," the *Tianzi* continued. "I have narrowed my candidates to Household Affairs Minister Hong and Foreign Minister Song."

Kai-Long hid his scowl behind a pleasant smile. Hong had wheedled and cajoled himself into consideration. He needed reminding that his road to the Chief Minister seat depended on Kai-Long being *Tianzi*.

Kai-Long bowed toward the throne. "Foreign Minister Song has served for many years at the highest level of government and proven to be an excellent administrator." He narrowed his eyes at Hong, holding his gaze. "Minister Hong is capable."

Leave it at that; let Hong simmer a little. Both he and Minister Song bowed when Kai-Long had finished his endorsement.

The Expansionist lords followed Kai-Long's lead, praising Foreign Minister Song with glowing praise and leaving nice but less enthusiastic words for Hong. The old man's weathered smile seemed to sap him each time he rose from a bow.

Surprisingly, the Royalists favored Song as well. Although the *Tianzi* would make the final decision, if the *Tai-Ming*'s words held any weight, Hong's candidacy was dead in the water. Just like Cousin Kaiya should've been.

Young Lord Zheng spoke last, all the while staring at Minister Hong. "Minister Hong's hard work led to the arrest of Chief Minister Tan. Despite his lack of experience compared to Minister Song, I believe he has shown creativity and initiative."

Kai-Long studied Zheng. Hong must've promised him something amazing. The upstanding Zheng family was known for honoring its word to the point of stubbornness. Kai-Long had used their sense of honor to manipulate Zheng Ming's youngest brother Tian many times when they were children, and would do so again when Zheng Ming inherited his father's seat.

"Kai-Guo," The *Tianzi* said. "I do not have much time left, so whoever rises to Chief Minister today will likely serve you. Therefore, I entrust this decision to you. Choose well, for the Chief Minister is one of the Dragon Throne's greatest assets."

Such trust! Kai-Long hid his surprise.

In contrast, the Crown Prince's mouth hung open in a manner unsuited to rule. He bowed low. "Thank you for placing this great trust in me. Based on the advice of our esteemed lords, I choose Foreign Minister Song."

Minister Hong was the first to congratulate Chief Minister Song, yet he must've been stewing inside. Two years of maneuvering for naught. In this, the old man could share Kai-Long's despondence. It would make it easier to get him to skip to the final stage of their plan.

The *Tianzi* raised his hand, silencing the hereditary lords. "Chief Minister Song, your first duty will be to ensure the *Golden Phoenix* is ready to set sail for Ayudra Island with a full complement of imperial guards and diplomatic officials."

The new Chief Minister bowed. "As the *Tianzi* commands."

Young Lord Zheng bowed low. "*Huang-Shang*. The princess had asked me to travel with her, and I was unfortunately delayed by the insurgents. I ask to join in on the journey to Ayudra."

Kai-Long considered the implications of Zheng Ming's blooming relationship with the princess. Even if he could convince Hong to go through with the final stage of their plan, he still had to do something about her.

Hong Jianbin's face hurt from forcing smile after smile. His cheeks burned even more than his old knees, which buckled with each step toward the main gates of Sun-Moon Palace.

Orchestra of Treacheries

The day could not get any worse. If only the *Tianzi* had decided himself, instead of leaving the choice to his foolish son, Hong's merits would have reaped rewards. Instead, the Crown Prince caved to the *Tai-Ming* lords, as Hong knew the weak boy would.

Years of planning, all gone to waste. All of the backroom deals, for nothing. Only Young Lord Zheng had kept his word. And how ironic would it be if Hong's role in arranging Zheng's second meeting with the princess actually led to the philanderer winning her?

A hand clamped his shoulder and yanked him into one of the many small buildings on the palace grounds. His heart jumped into his throat as his vision adjusted to the dim light.

Lord Peng. Hong would expose Peng's treason, as soon as he could figure out a new way of doing so without revealing his own complicity.

"*Household Relations Minister* Hong," Peng hissed. "I am sorry things did not work out for you today. However, there is still a chance for your dreams to come true."

Hong searched Peng's eyes. "How is that?"

"When I am *Tianzi*, you will be my Chief Minister." Peng patted him on the shoulder. "Even though things did not unfold as we planned, we can skip to the end of our plot. You deliver stage three of the poison. The *Tianzi* and his two sons will be dead. The Expansionist alliance currently has enough men in the capital to support my nominal claim to the Dragon Throne."

CHAPTER 30:
A Position of Strength

The symphony of peaceful sounds energized Kaiya as her entourage made its way through the upper city. The low strums of the sitar radiated from one mansion, while fountain chimes rang from another. Birds twittered and chirped as they hopped among the hanging vines and flowers on villa walls.

If she had to live outside of Cathay, this is the place she would choose! Unlike the raucous waterfront and downtown, which were virtually devoid of vegetation, this district of Vyara boasted graceful trees and manicured shrubs along the broad avenues.

By mid-afternoon, as the Iridescent Moon had waxed just past its middle crescent, they arrived at Cathay's embassy. At last! Walls nearly twice Kaiya's height connected several adjoining block buildings, each two stories with tiled flat roofs. It certainly wasn't as elegant as the neighboring villas, though it was nice enough not to shame Cathay in the eyes of its Ayuri trading partners.

Two embassy guards, dressed in dark blue robes and armed with broadswords, stood by the main entrance.

Chen Xin stepped forward and displayed the unique silver ring that signified him as imperial guard. "By order of Princess Wang Kaiya, summon Ambassador Ling."

Orchestra of Treacheries

Kaiya lowered her hood and shook out her hair. Though still clad in simple travelling clothes, she brushed off the persona of tired traveler and did her best to project the image of imperial grace.

"*Dian-xia.*" The embassy guards dropped to a knee, fists to the ground. "Welcome to the *Tianzi's* office in Vyara City," they said in unison.

She allowed them out of their salute with a nod of her head.

One jumped to his feet and ran inside. The other beckoned to the entrance and followed them in.

Kaiya took in the foyer with curious eyes. A fusion of several cultures, it didn't resemble any room back home. A mosaic floor of white, brown, and green tiles depicted a map of the Cathayi Empire. An Estomari-style framed oil painting of the *Tianzi* in his youth hung on the wall opposite the entrance. The two scrolls flanking the portrait were unmistakably written in Xiulan's bold hand. The broad strokes of Dragonscript sent a shiver of awe through Kaiya's spine.

The embassy guard guided them to a side room.

Now this felt much more like home! A Cathayi silk carpet with colorful symbols of health, longevity, fortune, and prosperity covered the tile floor. Brush paintings of famous landscapes in Cathay adorned the walls on brightly bordered scrolls.

Kaiya settled on the edge of one of several elegant bloodwood chairs, and ran her fingers through some exotic Ayuri plant that grew in a white porcelain planter with a blue dragon motif. The imperial guards took up defensive positions around her.

Without any invitation, Ayana sprawled into another chair and let out a long breath. So much for the legends of elvish dignity.

Commotion erupted from deeper inside the building. A middle-aged man in dark blue court robes emerged from an arched doorway, flanked by several similarly-dressed officials. It was Ling Xiaomin, a distant relative who had visited Sun-Moon Palace several times in her childhood.

He bowed low. "*Dian-xia*, it is our honor to receive you here in Vyara City. We had originally expected you two days ago, but since we had heard no word of the *Golden Phoenix* ever arriving in Ayudra, we were unsure how to proceed."

Kaiya's heart sank. The *Golden Phoenix* carried her wardrobe, personal effects, and official documents. Negotiating with the Madurans in salty rags would embarrass Cathay, not to mention her.

She allowed him out of his bow. "Thank you for receiving us, Ambassador. We are pleased to be your guests. I would like to receive a briefing on the Maduran situation once my retinue and I have settled in."

"Of course, *Dian-xia*." The Ambassador bowed again. He motioned a girl forward from behind the wall of aides. "This is Meixi. She will take you to the guest house and assist your handmaiden in attending to your needs."

Kaiya glanced at Jie from the corner of her eyes. The half-elf wore a half-smirk that told Kaiya she would be washing herself. Again.

The girl, probably no older than Jie's apparent age, cast her wide eyes downward as protocol demanded. Her hand shook as she extended it toward an arching exit. "Th-this way, p-please, D-*Dian-xia*…"

Meixi kept her head lowered as she led them to a house within the compound. "We reserve this only for important visitors."

Kaiya's second-floor quarters were decorated with bloodwood furniture and fine silk carpets. Fresh, exotic fruit, cut into narrow slices, sat in a bowl on a center table. Narrow windows allowed a glimpse of the street, where activity was now winding down for the day. The house had its own private bath on the first floor, which Meixi had started preparing. Cowed by Jie's narrowed eyes, Kaiya waved the servant off and washed and dressed herself.

Though the simple shirt and dress on hand were more suited to a commoner, at least they were clean. With that small improvement, Kaiya felt a little more like herself. When her reflection in the dressing room mirror looked more like an imperial princess and less like a ragged traveler, she was ready to receive the ambassador.

Her entourage of imperial guards, all looking and smelling clean, joined her in the first house's audience room. Kaiya ascended the far dais and settled on the edge of a central bloodwood chair carved in the shape of a dragon's claw. Unlike a formal room in Sun-Moon Palace, where visitors would kneel on floor cushions before the *Tianzi*, chairs were arranged in a semi-circle facing the dais.

Niches in the walls displayed samples of Cathay's most treasured goods: bolts of silk, porcelain wares, and tins of tea leaves. A second-generation musket, less accurate than the current model and therefore allowed for export, occupied the most prominent spot behind the central chair.

Kneeling, Ambassador Ling motioned toward a slender man in blue robes. "This is my Information Minister, Yi Minshou."

"A Black Lotus brother," Jie whispered in her ear.

How did Jie know? Had she exchanged some secret message with the gaunt, middle-aged man? Kaiya allowed the two out of their bows and motioned them into chairs facing her. "Ambassador, what have you learned about Madura's relationship with the Teleri?"

The ambassador took a seat. "*Dian-xia*, Madura is a staunch ally of the Teleri Empire. Any meeting that occurs between Madura and other nations will invariably be attended by a Teleri advisor."

"Do you believe that the Teleri Empire, not Madura, is behind the unrest in Cathay?" Kaiya asked.

Yi Minshou bowed. "*Dian-xia*, if I may speak. The maharaja of Madura believes he can manipulate his relationship with the Teleri. It certainly seems that Madura has a free rein with regards to its aggression."

Ambassador Ling nodded. "We think the Teleri chose Madura as an ally because of its belligerent nature toward its neighbors."

"However," the Black Fist said, "there is nothing to suggest that Madura instigated any of the trouble in Cathay."

Kaiya twirled a lock of her hair. If it wasn't Madura behind the unrest in Huajing, then who was it? "Are you certain? And if not, how much of a threat is Madura to Cathay?"

Li bowed his head. "We can never be fully certain. We only have limited reach into Madura's inner workings. Their Golden Scorpions root out our spies with ease."

The ambassador unfurled a map. "As for the threat, Madura has occupied Ankira at our border for ten years. Though much of the populace still pines for the return of their own maharaja, the land is mostly subjugated."

Ankira. Prince Hardeep. Kaiya's hand strayed to the lotus jewel, concealed in her sash. Yes, they would make time for a visit to the Ankiran villa here.

The ambassador pointed out locations on the map. "Madura will not directly confront the Ayuri Confederation because of its Paladin protectors. The wild lands to its east between Madura and the Kanin Kingdom of Tomiwa are controlled by the dragon Avarax. Therefore, Cathay is the most available target."

A full-on assault? Unthinkable.

Kaiya straightened. "The Great Wall and thousands of muskets stand between us and Madura. Are their Golden Scorpions so formidable they could breech the Wall?"

The ambassador gave a slow half-nod. "If Madura could deploy half of its two thousand Golden Scorpions, then Lord Peng's provincial army would have a difficult time defending the Great Wall's south gate. However, many Scorpions are stuck in Ankira to suppress a potential insurgency."

Minister Yi raised his hand. "The Teleri have been breeding an auxiliary Bovyan army in occupied Ankira for almost ten years. Within another four or five years, they may have enough numbers to control the populace and escalate the threat to us."

Kaiya shuddered. The Maduran army, bearing down on the Great Wall. Tens of thousands would die on both sides, and if the Scorpions could fight half as well as Master Sabal... And to think Minister Hong wanted to bring so many soldiers into Huajing. She might not have a mind for strategy, but even *she* knew such moves would leave the defenses in the south thin.

She stood and glided over to the map. She ran a finger from Cathay north to the Nothori kingdom of Rotuvi. An aggressive neighbor and independent tributary nation to the Teleri Empire, they had tried several times to recapture Wailian County, where Zheng Ming had served.

Her eyes turned south to Madura, another friend of the Teleri. Prince Aelward had insisted that there was an unholy alliance among the three nations, and Ayana insisted the Teleri were pulling the strings. Their encounter with the spy earlier in the day lent credence to those assertions.

She looked up from the map. "It seems, then, that even if Madura is not a threat now, it may be one in the future. We must gain the support of those who might help us deter Maduran aggression—either current or future."

The ambassador bowed. "The princess is wise. Just remember that it is our national policy not to enter into alliances with other nations, so that we may trade unfettered with all."

"Of course, Ambassador," Kaiya said. "Yet the perception of an alliance can be just a powerful tool as an actual one. Please make arrangements for me to meet with representatives of the Ayuri Confederation." Another thought crossed her mind. "And Ankira's exiled maharaja."

"What about the meeting with the Madurans tomorrow?" the ambassador asked. "You are supposed to dine with their prince at the half-waxing crescent."

If the Madurans weren't behind the insurgency in Cathay... "I do not see the urgency. Let us delay the meeting for one week. By then, my retinue will hopefully arrive on the *Golden Phoenix* and I will have met with potential foreign friends. When we negotiate a non-aggression treaty with Madura, it will be from a position of strength."

The ambassador shifted in his chair. "Prince Dhananad has been pestering us about the meeting for the last several days. It would be unwise to offend him with a postponement."

She twirled a lock of hair. "Then I will have lunch with him, and relay our desire to negotiate a non-aggression pact at a later date."

The ambassador gazed at her, a smile forming on his lips. "As the princess commands. I will send messengers to all of the embassies at once."

Kaiya raised a hand to stop him from leaving. She pulled the Maduran copper rupiya from her sash and passed it to him. "Who is this?"

Ambassador Ling held it up to the light before passing it back. "This is old Maduran coinage. You can tell by how worn the images are. I would guess it is Madura's former Grand Vizier Rumiya."

The name sounded familiar. Kaiya received the coin and stared at it. "Who was he?"

Minister Yi tapped his index fingers together, a symbolic gesture to ward off bad luck. "He was an evil magician who rose to power in the Maduran court a century and a half ago."

An evil magician! As if elf wizards and Oracles weren't enough excitement for one lifetime. Kaiya twirled a lock of hair. "He must have been influential to have ended up on a modern coin."

Minister Yi nodded. "It was his idea to recruit castoffs from the Paladin Order and establish the Golden Scorpions. In a few short decades, Madura tripled in size, until it reached the border of the Paladin mandate."

And then north into hapless Ankira. Kaiya's hand strayed to the lotus jewel in her sash.

"Rumiya himself," the minister said, "used black magic to suck the life force from others to preserve his own. Until thirty-two years ago, he remained young and hale."

Evil magic. Kaiya shuddered. "Then what happened?"

The ambassador paused a second. "He just disappeared."

Disappeared? She rubbed her finger over the image on the coin. Perhaps the familiarity came from having seen it in a history book before. "Do you have any paintings of him?"

"No, but I am sure the Maduran embassy does. He would be a national idol if their current maharaja didn't downplay his role in their history."

Kaiya pushed the coin into her sash, joining Tian's pebble and Hardeep's lotus jewel. She hadn't wanted to request anything of Prince Dhananad in tomorrow's meeting, but she felt compelled to see a painting of Grand Vizier Rumiya.

CHAPTER 31:
EVEN A CARP DREAMS OF BECOMING A DRAGON

Though not an accomplished poet like that fop Zheng Ming, Hong Jianbin felt inspired to compose. It was not the full White Moon Renyue reflecting in the carp pond of his courtyard garden that stirred him, though he watched it as he sat on the adjacent veranda on this warm spring evening. Without a doubt, his muse was the deflating feeling of failure. The poetry he wrote tonight would sing of unfulfilled dreams and monumental disappointments.

The only path he could see to Chief Minister now travelled through Lord Peng. The treacherous lord might very well have him executed instead of promoted. He had always planned on poisoning the *Tianzi* and his sons, but on his own terms, not Peng's.

Now, the *Tianzi* might be the only one who could keep him alive. All those years getting into Prince Kai-Wu's good graces would also be meaningless if Crown Prince Kai-Guo inherited.

Hong let out a long sigh. He was to meet Leina tonight in the Floating World—not for the celebratory lovemaking he had planned, but for advice. He could not count how often great ideas came to him through her idle banter. If the silly girl had an eye for political maneuvering, perhaps *she* would be a high official.

He studied the rocky stream that fed the pond, thinking of the ancient story of the carp that swam up a waterfall and transformed into a dragon.

The position of Chief Minister was still within reach. If he played his game carefully, if he courted the right people and betrayed them before they realized what was happening, he could very well become father of the future *Tianzi*.

"You will need help," the stone dragon overlooking the pond said.

Hong's heart jumped into his throat as he gawked at the sculpture. Had it read his mind? His first impulse was to call for the guards posted just outside his pavilion.

They would think him insane.

"No need to call your guards," a frog on a rock said in the same voice. "If you did, I would be gone long before they arrived."

Hong found his wits. "You are the renegade agent. Tan's asset."

"One and the same," said a just-opening blossom on a cherry tree, forcing the minister to turn again in confusion. "I am impressed you know me."

"Will you stop doing that?" Hong wagged a finger at the blossom.

A painfully plain, middle-aged man with a walking stick melted out of the shadows, a bemused tone in his voice. "As you command, Chief Minister."

"Apparently, your information sources have failed you for once."

The man smirked. "Oh, no. My information is *early*. The title... and all its benefits... can still be yours."

Being beholden to a traitor didn't seem much better than having to trust Lord Peng. "What do you want from me?"

"First, let me thank you. You knew of the former Chief Minister's method of contacting me, and warned me of the trap, did you not?"

"I did not," Hong said, now thoroughly mystified. He had *set* the trap.

The man shook his head. "Oh, but you did, though perhaps you had intended the opposite. No matter. Which brings me to the reason for my visit. I am here to accept your assignment."

Hong's confusion grew, though he tried his best to hide it. "What assignment?"

"The unspoken one." The upturn in the man's lips almost connected to the crinkles at the side of his eyes. "The removal of Chief Minister Song."

Hong stared at the man through narrowed eyes. "How would you do that?"

"First, you must promise to pursue war with Madura once you become Chief Minister."

The man was perplexing. Hong threw up his hands. "Everyone now knows Madura had nothing to do with the insurgency."

"You are a smart man. Make it happen. If you go back on your promise with me, I will not be as incompetent as Minister Tan when *I* try to throttle you."

Was he referring to the bathhouse incident? Hong could not keep the incredulousness out of his voice. "How do you know such things?"

"It is my business to know," the man said. "For example, I know how Peng has been rendering the *Tianzi* and his sons sterile for four years now, by replacing the imperial tea with Ayuri gooseweed."

Hong had learned this from a business associate long ago, which was one of the reasons he had approached Peng with his plot. How did the renegade agent know? Perhaps he would spill his secret. Let him monologue.

"Your contact inside the imperial kitchens orders from your business acquaintances in Yutou province, and that acquaintance in turn procures a certain Levanthi spice through my shipping company, Golden Fu Trading. The otherwise harmless spice,

Orchestra of Treacheries

which goes into the *Tianzi's* longevity elixir, interacts with gooseweed to cause respiratory distress."

The man knew of Hong's actual treasonous actions, even more than Peng did.

"That on your command, your kitchen contact will mix that spice into the palace meals so that the princes will consume it as well. And lastly, you knew the asthma-treating herb *Ma Huang*, when mixed with gooseweed, will cause heart failure."

He *knew*. Did he know about—

"Just as you did to the *Tianzi's* brother and nephews two years ago."

He *did*. Aching face muscles told Hong he must have been wearing the most ridiculous expression.

"You see, Minister Tan's plot was simple; yours more subtle and entertaining. Mine is even more complicated, and ultimately, you will be one of the main beneficiaries if you play along."

Though always ahead of his political opponents, Hong was completely baffled by this man. "What is your stake in this?"

The man shrugged. "I have nothing to gain personally. I only wish to make Cathay strong before its neighbors swallow us. Tan was my greatest hope for success until he betrayed me, which is why I led Young Lord Zheng to him."

Whatever made him think Tan betrayed him? Still, his goals seemed noble enough, and were very much in line with Hong's. He would at least reap benefits until he found a way to tie up this loose end. "Very well. I swear to press for Expansionism once I am Chief Minister. Now, how do you plan on killing Chief Minister Song?"

"Killing?" The man glared. "I have no such plan. He is a good man whom Cathay still needs. But he will resign in embarrassment when he learns his son is an insurgent."

If Hong's jaw could drop any further, he would have to pick it off the ground. "How do you know that?"

"Because he has worked for me for two years."

Hong's head spun. "And what do you need me to do?"

"First, let us remove Lord Peng from the picture. Left unfettered, he is conniving enough to thwart our plans. Go through with your plan to poison the *Tianzi*."

CHAPTER 32:
An Audacious Proposal

Yan Jie's sharp eye caught the small scar on the side of Maduran Prince Dhananad's neck. The Architect's intricate plan from thirty-two years before had called for kidnapping the young prince. The Surgeon had nicked him when the brave boy fought back.

Adult Dhananad covered the mark with a thick layer of cosmetics—part and parcel of a flamboyant package. It did little to compensate for the toll age had taken on a mildly handsome face.

Gold pins held up his hair in a twist the Cathayi would consider feminine. His rust-red *kurta* of fine cotton hung to his knees, embellished with a repeating pattern of gold scorpion symbols. Gold-threaded slippers graced his feet, while a cloying musk hung about him, competing with the sweet incense burning in the brazier. All told, Prince Dhananad's vanity could challenge even Princess Kaiya's.

"Absolutely stunning!" He brought both of his palms together below his chin in a typical Ayuri greeting. "Truly, you have come prepared to impress us!"

The princess covered her laugh with a slim hand. She pressed her palms together to imitate his greeting. "We say, *When in Vyara, do as the Ayuris do*."

Jie suppressed a snort. Although the Cathayi expression was liberally translated, the pretext was a white lie: the princess *had* planned to wear a priceless silk court robe, lost aboard the still unaccounted-for *Golden Phoenix*.

Refusing to meet dignitaries in simple clothes, she'd recruited the young and enthusiastic Meixi, who had grown up in Vyara, to help her choose something local and presentable. At first light, she visited a tailor to alter a local dress to reflect her own conservative tastes.

Even with little fashion sense, Jie had to admit the result was stunning. A *langa* petticoat wrapped around the princess' legs and to her ankles, the most modest part of the ensemble. A long, broad strip of bright blue Cathayi silk, embroidered with white cranes and bamboo, swathed around the princess' waist and draped over her left shoulder much as the local women wore their *saris*. It partially covered a tight-fitting white cotton *choli* blouse with short sleeves and a low neckline. It completely covered her back and midriff, contrary to local fashion trends— thank the Heavens, as if the neckline didn't reveal enough! The unaltered *choli* looked like the Cathayi bust supports Jie never needed, except to stash weapons.

With none of her handmaidens around, and dubious of Jie's hairstyling abilities, the princess let her hair cascade freely down to her waist. That girl certainly loved her hair. How long before she fiddled with a stray lock, *again*?

The prince's eyes roved over her like a starving man at a royal banquet. Jie wouldn't mind helping the princess bathe tonight, if it would help wash off the stains his leer left.

He extended his hand toward two matching chairs made of a maroon wood. Topped by plush burgundy cushions, the chairs stood on either side of a knee-high oval table. The tabletop's pink marble matched the color of the dome above them in the Bijuran embassy.

Following his gesture, the princess glided across the red and gold carpet. If average Ayuri carpets were prized for their craftsmanship and high-quality wool, this particular specimen was fit for nobility. She settled on the edge of the chair while Ambassador Ling stood to her right. Chen Xin, the only imperial guard in attendance, stood behind him. He wore the light blue robes of the embassy guards, his own armor and ceremonial clothes aboard the missing *Golden Phoenix*.

Jie knelt on the princess' left, dressed in a standard *choli* and *langa* that bared her midriff,. A bolt of Cathayi silk matching the princess' wrapped around her as a *sari*. She stole yet another glance at her reflection in the silver lamps.

She looked good! If only Tian could see her like this. Though he'd probably focus more on the numerous small weapons the *sari* concealed.

Prince Dhananad took a seat on the chair opposite the princess. To his right glowered a giant of a man with fair hair and fair skin, dressed in a *kurta* of black with gold embroidery. The size and emblazoned sun symbol marked the brute as a Bovyan from the Teleri Empire. He stood even taller than the prince's escort the day before.

To the prince's left was a Golden Scorpion, obvious from the dark bronze *kurta*. Dark brown eyes stared out from beneath the oval slits of the otherwise expressionless mask. As the Bijurans had stipulated, no weapons were allowed in the embassy, and so the Scorpion didn't bear the curved sting of their order.

The prince clapped his hands together, summoning servants as if they were his own. Several Bijuran girls, dressed in light green *saris,* emerged from the door and hurried over to place food and drink on the table. The centerpiece was an enormous oval dish made of Cathayi white porcelain with four-clawed blue dragons—audaciously denoting *Tai-Ming* status—with two dozen matching rectangular bowls nestled within.

Each held a unique Ayuri delicacy: colorful sauces and pastes filled some bowls, while chicken, pork, rice, and vegetables filled others. Saffron, curry and other exotic spices provided a symphony of delectable aromas. A piece of *roti* flatbread wrapped in a white cotton napkin on a silver dish, a single silver spoon, and a crystal glass graced each setting. A matching decanting carafe filled with a yellowish liquid sat on the side of the table.

"Is this your first time in Vyara City?" The prince flared his fingers toward the dish; according to Meixi's primer of Ayuri etiquette, an invitation to eat.

"This is my first time leaving Cathay." The princess tilted her head and imitated his gesture. Thank the Heavens it was her manners on display instead of Jie's!

"Ah!" He clapped his hands together. He made each gesture intricate, even the crude act of eating with bare hands. "You must allow me to show you around this magnificent city!"

"If time permits," the princess said.

"And sometime, hopefully in the near future, I would like to personally give you a tour of my hometown of Maduras." Dhananad flashed a broad smile of straight white teeth and turned his palms up. According to Meixi, each refined movement denoted some deep meaning, but Jie had lost track of the lesson in the first few minutes. In any case, it would be far more interesting to see if that masked Scorpion could fight as well as the one she'd faced in Tokahia.

The princess predictably brushed a lock of hair out of her eyes. "I have heard that while Vyara City's skyline is a testament to Ayuri cultural beauty, that of Maduras bears witness to Ayuri cultural might. Is it true that your entire capital is a virtual fortress?"

He grinned ear-to-ear. "The fortifications are impregnable. Yet within hides a true architectural gem, befitting a jewel such as yourself. It is certainly worth seeing."

"Yet fortresses hold little interest for me, for I have seen so many crenellations and battlements along our Great Wall."

Jie stared at the princess is admiration. The naïve girl who'd chased after Prince Hardeep two years ago now delicately broached the issue of Maduran aggression.

Prince Dhananad frowned, leading to seconds of palpable silence. He then gestured to the table. "Are you enjoying this fine sampling of Ayuri food?"

She nodded. "It is delicious. By comparison, Cathayi cuisine varies widely by region, and some of the foods in the west have very bold flavor. But most of what we eat in the capital has a very subtle taste. I am afraid you would find it bland compared to Ayuri fare."

"Any food would be like sweet nectar from Heaven when shared with an angel." His grin was as smooth as a baby's bottom, and probably just as toxic.

All discipline lost, Jie shuddered. The silky delivery of his responses resembled Zheng Ming's charming tone. All the more reason to dislike him.

The princess placed a hand on her chest. "Then you should come to Cathay to enjoy our food, for we treat all of our *invited* guests as royalty."

A warning, wrapped in pretty words. Jie glanced at the men across the table. The prince's eyes shifted back and forth, and his lips jiggled into a somewhat gracious smile. The metal mask hid the Golden Scorpion's thoughts, but the Bovyan official's displeasure was evident from his silent scowl.

Conversation over lunch between prince and princess continued along these lines. Seemingly mundane topics about the New Year and weather all carried unspoken suggestions and refusals. Prince Dhananad repeatedly extended invitations for her to visit his homeland; while she repeatedly rebuffed him, packaging her refusal in flowery language. He was either annoyingly tenacious or inordinately dense in his persistence.

Kaiya drew strength from the high whine of the sitar and rhythmic beating of drums, which an ensemble of Bijuran musicians in the far corner of the room played as background music.

Without it, she might have withered under Prince Dhananad's ogling. At least most men tried to hide their peeks. The elegant

Ayuri body language would've been easier to imitate if not for her need to conceal all that the local clothes tried to expose.

As they finished eating, a serving girl came to the table and reached for the decanting carafe.

The prince held up his hand to stop her and motioned for the Golden Scorpion to serve. Agile as a cat, the warrior knelt and poured the yellow fluid into the two glasses, and slid the drinks in front of her and the prince.

Like a happy wolf, the prince bared his teeth. "This nectar is extracted from several different rare flowers, and served only to royalty. Please, drink."

Kaiya took up the wineglass in her hands and lifted it toward him. "In Cathay, it is our custom to toast friendships."

His eyes tightened into slits, but he raised his glass as well.

With a smile, Kaiya brought the carafe to her lips. Her rouge would leave a mark, and there was no telling how the pervert would—

Jie took a step and tripped over her skirt. Her light weight plopped into Kaiya's lap, her *sari* sweeping across the table. Dishes clattered noisily onto the floor. The glass was knocked from Kaiya's hand, its precious contents spilling out onto the fine carpet.

"Clumsy fool!" The prince bolted to his feet, his hand reaching to his left hip, where a *talwar* had hung the day before. Not finding a weapon, he stepped over and cocked his arm back to strike Jie.

The girl cowered, covering her head with her arms.

Recovering from her initial shock, Kaiya leaned over to protect her Insolent Retainer. Jie must've seen something; she was far too dexterous to fall like that.

The prince growled, his glare bearing down on the half-elf. "If you caused such a scene and wasted the nectar in Madura, we would pluck your eyes out. You are lucky your liege is more forgiving than I."

Jie picked herself off Kaiya, took several steps back and sunk to her knees, forehead pressed to the ground. "Please forgive me," she pleaded in halting Ayuri.

Jie could speak better than that. Kaiya extended her hand, which the ambassador took and helped her to her feet. She bowed deeply at the waist. "Gracious Prince Dhananad, please forgive my handmaiden's clumsiness. Let us not allow this unfortunate accident ruin what has thus far been a pleasant afternoon."

The prince pressed his palms together. "As you wish, dearest Kaiya. Your magnanimity is truly admirable." He invited her to return to her seat with a wave of his hand.

So presumptuous, addressing her by name! She settled on the edge of the chair. Jie shuffled back, holding a low bow. Oh, to be able to ask what she saw. But no, one of the prince's entourage might be able to speak Cathayi. It would have to wait.

"So, Kaiya," Dhananad said, "it came as a great surprise when your nation approached glorious Madura through the Bijurans to propose such a high-level meeting. Since our past trade agreement expired, we have had little contact. To what do we owe the pleasure of your visit?" His focus dropped to her bust, which the cut of the *choli* embellished and revealed too much of.

It was no furtive glance, but rather the most unabashed stare yet, less subtle than her childhood lapdog waiting for a treat. Kaiya brought an arm across her chest, feigning to adjust the *sari's* position at her shoulder. Dhananad's gaze shifted up to meet hers.

She lowered her hands to her lap and bowed her head. "Benevolent prince, my father sent me to express Cathay's desire to maintain amity between our peace-loving nations."

Confusion, which could only be genuine, contorted his expression. "I did not realize there was anything but peace between us."

Perhaps Lord Peng's accusations were unfounded. Kaiya searched Dhananad's eyes. "Of course. The Ayuri Kingdom of Ankira—"

The Teleri official cleared his throat, the sound commensurate with his Bovyan size. "Certainly, Princess Kaiya, Cathay recognizes that Ankira is not a kingdom, but merely a province of Madura."

Kaiya's hand strayed to Prince Hardeep's lotus jewel, concealed by the band of her *langa*. It warmed her palm, even through the cloth.

Prince Dhananad nonchalantly waved off the Bovyan's comments. "It goes without saying that Ankira is an indivisible part of Madura."

"And as Princess Kaiya knows, Ankira Province sits at the border of Cathay." The Bovyan's stare bore into her. "You would not come all the way here unless you were concerned about the potential sting of the Golden Scorpions. So perhaps the question should be, what token of goodwill is Cathay willing to offer to ensure lasting peace with glorious Madura?"

The prince laughed and waved a hand. "Our lunch was virtually ruined by the clumsy handmaiden. There is no need to leave a bad taste in our mouths by spewing unveiled threats."

The Teleri glared at Dhananad, but remained silent as the prince turned back to her. "Though our friend brings up a good suggestion: we must certainly endeavor to ensure continuing good relations between our two countries."

Kaiya bowed her head. "I could not agree more with your wisdom. Though our past trade agreement expired, perhaps we could negotiate a new one?" One that didn't involve firepowder.

A devious glint shined in the Dhananad's eyes. "Yes. Perhaps we could trade nuptials among a prince and princess of our realms. I believe this is a custom our cultures share, to strengthen relations via marriage? The Wang family marries its princes and princesses to the sons and daughters of your hereditary lords, does it not?"

Ambassador Ling's robes rustled behind her, and Jie's gaze bored into her back. Maybe they worried she didn't understand the tacit message, though Dhananad left no doubt where the conversation was headed. All of his previous flattery and invitations had been a game to set up this question. With both of her brothers married, there was only one princess to barter.

Dhananad would probably not take no for an answer, and the Madurans hopelessly outnumbered the Cathayi in Vyara City.

Kaiya stole a glance out of the window. From the bright sun and position of the shade, the Iridescent Moon had probably waxed to mid-crescent, and there were only a little more than three hours until sundown. In order to avoid replying to Prince Dhananad's audacious proposal, she decided to mimic Ayana's charm spell the only way she knew how.

CHAPTER 33:
SHIFTS IN WINDS

Peng Kai-Long sat in his tea room, reading and rereading the imperial missive which summoned all *Tai-Ming* and *Yu-Ming* to the palace.

The *Tianzi* was dying, Crown Prince Kai-Guo was bedridden. Prince Kai-Wu was already dead.

Hong's poison, as promised during their secret meeting at Guanshan Temple six weeks earlier, had worked. The old fool's ambition to become Chief Minister must've blinded him to the perils in trusting the soon-to-be *Tianzi*. It wouldn't be the Chief Minister's medallion around his neck when everything was said and done.

Kai-Long unfurled a map of Huajing, picturing where his soldiers and those of his allies were deployed in relation to vital government centers. It was a precautionary measure. Once the *Tianzi* and Crown Prince joined Prince Kai-Wu in the netherworld, he would meet little resistance.

The Dragon Throne was his.

How long would the old man linger? The uncertainty raised other uncertainties. Cousin Kaiya might visit the Ankirans any day now. If Prince Hardeep were there, with no knowledge of his correspondence with her, she was smart enough to realize who was behind the fake letters. Perhaps smart enough to unravel his entire role.

A grin came unbidden. Information travelled at the speed of ships, and the *Golden Phoenix* would depart for Vyara today. It would be best to make sure she remained anchored in Jiangkou for as long as possible, to give him more time to consolidate his power before the girl returned. He already had a hundred men not far from the docks.

Kai-Long hastily drafted a letter. He then rose and threw open the doors to the tea room. A glorious afternoon awaited him, sun shining in the bright blue skies. Surely it was a sign from Heaven. He was destined to rule.

His steward waiting outside bowed. "Your horse is ready, *Jue-ye*."

"Excellent." He pressed his handwritten message into the steward's hands. "Have this letter conveyed to our provincial trade office in Jiangkou. Use our *own* horse relays. Nobody is to see this except Lord Tu."

Dismissing the steward, Kai-Long strode toward the stables and found his horse already saddled. An entourage of his best guards, dressed in formal court uniforms, sat astride their mounts.

He swung into his saddle and beckoned them forward. "Come. Destiny awaits."

The horses trotted toward the main gates. They opened to reveal a heavily-cloaked woman.

Undaunted by the horses, she sank to both knees and set her forehead to the ground. "Lord Peng, might I have a word with you in private?"

That voice, the foreign accent. Hong's concubine, Leina. Likely here to secure her lord's favor in the new regime. It might be entertaining, and rewarding, to see what she might offer for the old man's life. Rewarding enough to delay departure. "What do you wish to tell me that my own loyal men cannot hear?"

She looked up. "You are riding into a trap. Do you want to know why?"

Leina knelt on the tea room mats, recalling what old Hong had told her. In his own clandestine meeting with Lord Peng here, he'd been shaken by the attack on Princess Kaiya. Worried that Peng was ready to betray him.

Not even a month had passed, yet how long ago it seemed. Each player's plot had surged into motion from that point, sometimes hiding in another's shadow, sometimes amplifying, sometimes crashing head-to-head. The first round of winners would soon emerge from the mess of entangled plans.

With one of his underlings kneeling behind him, Peng eyed her like a bird of prey. "Hong had the *Tianzi* and his sons poisoned, did he not? The Dragon Throne sits empty. How am I walking into a trap and not to glory?"

He had less foresight than it seemed. To think she'd picked him out as one of the initial victors. She bowed her head again. "Prince Kai-Wu still lives, unharmed, with the authority of the *Tianzi* vested in his hands until either his brother or the *Tianzi* recovers."

Peng pulled out and unfurled the imperial missive with a whip of his hand. "This says Kai-Wu is dead. It is stamped by the imperial correspondence seal. Do you deny its authenticity? A lie stamped with the seal would mean the *Tianzi* losing the Mandate of Heaven." Despite the outward show of confidence, his trembling voice hinted at uncertainty.

She pointed. "Look carefully. It's a Dragoncarving. The magic of distraction is embedded in the words, so much that you missed that the seal is a fake." As his eyes roved over the page, she continued, "Minister Hong convinced Prince Kai-Wu to send these out to find out who is loyal to the Wang family."

"I *am* a member of the Wang family!"

"But through a maternal line, so your claim is in question. You will be branded as a usurper, taken into custody the instant you try to claim the Dragon Throne."

Peng's eyebrows bunched together. "Not if I don't claim the throne. Not if I swear loyalty to Kai-Wu. The weak-minded boy will be easy to manipulate until I can get rid of him altogether."

She shook her head. "Hong's mole in the kitchen staff fingered you as the procurer of the offending spice, since it came up through Nanling Province, on your ships."

Peng paled, forcing her to hide her satisfaction. His lip quivered. "My province is loyal to me. I will retreat there and reconsolidate my power. Yutou Province is my ally. They can defend the west road into Nanling while my armies defend the north pass."

Men. Always too confident. She shrugged. "Your fief is forfeit. Lord Liang will desert you, making Yutou Province a staging area for an invasion instead of a buffer. That is, if you even make it home in the first place. A full division of the imperial army waits on the road south to capture you."

The young lord jumped to his feet and turned to his lieutenant. "Send word to all of my men stationed in Huajing. Order them to march east to Jiangkou. Have our men already in Jiangkou begin operations to capture the *Golden Phoenix*."

He then glared down at her, the hand on his sword sending a cold shiver down her spine. "Why are you helping me?"

If there was one thing a man believed, it was his own genius; none more so than Lord Peng. As long as she sang the song he wanted to hear, she could deceive him and she would live. "You are a capable leader. If you survive, you will make an unparalleled *Tianzi*."

And create enough chaos inside the nation to weaken it...

It was the only way her employer would free her mother.

Minister Hong Jianbin knelt close to the Dragon Throne, where Prince Kai-Wu sat for the first time. The exalted spot, reserved for the Chief Minister, provided an excellent view of all the other ministers and hereditary lords who sat in rows facing the throne. It made the trip up the steps to the Hall of Supreme Harmony worth the toll it took on his old knees and lungs.

Prince Kai-Wu fidgeted, his attention shifting from person to person. Sweat matted the hair peeking through the *Tianzi*'s hat of office. Never expecting to inherit, the poor boy was in over his head. It was fortuitous—or at least well-planned—that Hong had put himself in the prince's good graces to become his advisor. Once the *Tianzi* and Crown Prince died, his power would know no bounds.

"He will show," Hong said. At least he hoped the soon-to-be ex-Lord Peng would show. It would be far easier to take him into custody inside the palace, unarmed and lightly protected. He looked at the hundred imperial guards deployed around the room, each more than a match for Peng and a pair of guards. Malleable Prince Kai-Wu's first decisive act would be a public humiliation of Peng.

Unless the wily young lord had sniffed out the trap.

Hong had distinguished himself in Prince Kai-Wu's esteem with his infallible wisdom and accurate predictions. To have this plan fail would undermine his credibility, though he had also advised Prince Kai-Wu to surround Peng's compound.

A messenger appeared at the threshold, quieting the murmuring lords. He stepped into the hall and dropped to both knees, forehead to the ground. "*Dian-xia*! Horrible news! Our troops surrounded Lord Peng's villa, but he already escaped. He is moving on Jiangkou Port!"

Blood rushed from Hong's face. "He is going to try to steal a ship. Maybe even the *Golden Phoenix* herself." How could he have not foreseen such a move? Where was the opportunity in *this* disaster?

There it was. Zheng Ming, soon to embark for his reunion with Princess Kaiya, might already be on the *Tianzi's* flagship. Maybe Peng would kill him. Or better yet, hold him hostage and expose him for the weakling he was.

Hong met Prince Kai-Wu's gaze, trying to speak as quietly as he could. "Send word to Young Lord Zheng to defend the *Golden Phoenix* from the traitor's imminent attack."

CHAPTER 34:
The Perfect Dance

As a collector of unique and beautiful objects of art, Prince Dhananad looked forward to possessing this stunning girl, whose every move embodied grace. Even without the use of the intoxicant-laced nectar, Princess Kaiya had fallen for his charm. Yet she still kept up the charade of innocent misunderstanding.

How adorable! She surely understood his wedding proposal. He had made it obvious with the talk of binding royal families.

"As always, you are well-informed," Princess Kaiya said. "My ancestor Wang Xinchang used many methods to ensure civil stability and lasting peace, political marriage among them. He was also famous for the cultivation of the fine arts, especially among our nobility. Beyond economic, political, and military acumen, all of our hereditary lords are well-versed in some form of art. Is that not the same in Madura? I have heard that you are an excellent dancer."

She knew of his dance! He waved a nonchalant hand. "I have been told that my dancing is passable. Certainly not on par with one such as yourself."

Her eyes twinkled mischievously. "It is rude in Cathay to directly ask someone to perform, but I would be honored if you show me an Ayuri dance."

"By all means, Sweet Kaiya." He returned her coy smile. "But it is our custom that if I dance at your request, you must dance for me as well."

She covered her mouth with delicate fingers as she giggled. "This is *not* our custom, but, *When in Vyara, do as the Ayuri do.*"

Dhananad laughed. "Then it is a mutually beneficial situation, much like a union between our two illustrious families would be." He beckoned toward the musicians. "Play *The Scorpion King Vanquishes the Twelve-Armed Demon.*"

The Teleri official—what was his name again?— shuffled petulantly beside him. Cursed with a short life, Bovyans lacked patience. That was why their soulless empire would never achieve greatness compared to Madura. If this uncultured boor could not appreciate fine art, that was his problem.

He stood and sauntered to the middle of the room. The music, which had been barely perceptible while they ate, now resonated clearly in the domed room. The rhythmic beat energized his solo, which he knew to be the epitome of Ayuri male dance: distinct poses with rapid transitions to the music's cadence. Perhaps she would find it jerky, but no more than their dance between the bed sheets would be.

At the end of his display of technical mastery and physical flexibility, she wholeheartedly applauded. "Prince Dhananad, I am embarrassed to follow such an amazing performance."

As she should be; but at the very least, it would allow her dress—irritatingly altered to befit a virgin priestess of Shakti—to expose more of her smooth skin. He grinned. "Yes, but you promised!"

"And it would not reflect well on Cathay if I go back on my promise, would it?" She blinked with captivating eyes. "But since we do not have any of our instruments, please forgive me as I improvise to your music."

Casting him an apologetic smile, Princess Kaiya spun and glided over to the musicians. She approached the drummer, whose various-sized *tabla* hand drums stood in a semicircle around him. She tapped out a long sequence on the drums at a moderate tempo. "Please play this as your *tala* refrain." She then turned to the rest. "And please, let your inspiration guide you."

The musicians nodded, and Dhananad could not help but be impressed with her knowledge of Ayuri music theory.

She returned to the center of the room and bowed. "I will dance *The Loves of Prince Aralas*. It recounts the story of the elf angel who fell in love with eight human girls, thereby establishing the alliances that helped overthrow the Tivari during the War of Ancient Gods."

A dance of love! Albeit with a tragic ending, at least as recounted by the Ayuri storytellers. Perhaps the Cathayi had a different take. At the very least, the theme was obvious: she was dreaming of their marriage!

The girl drifted into a pose, forming an elegant curve reminiscent of an elephant tusk. Her right arm floated upwards with her palm facing to the heavens and delicate fingers gracefully bent. Her other arm sank low as if cradling a giant ball. Both the free end of her makeshift *sari* and her hair cascaded behind her. The shift in the *langa* exposed the perfect arc of her calf, and the *choli* rose to allow her navel to peek out. Had he been sitting in the right place, he could have snuck a glance at the luscious valley between her breasts.

Soon enough.

She gave no signal, yet her movement and the tune started in perfect synchronicity. Had the musicians reacted so fast, or had she been moved by the melody? The flavor of the dance was decidedly foreign, and yet harmonized with the local style of music.

The *langa* around her legs should've restricted her mobility. Yet she seemed to swim through it as she wafted across the floor, like a fluffy cloud on a perfect day, blown by the strumming of the sitar and transforming to the beat of the drums. It seemed gravity itself had paused to admire her, allowing her to achieve impossible feats of balance and flexibility.

The symbiosis between musicians and dancer caused the seconds to blur into minutes, minutes into hours. Dhananad sighed. It was like experiencing the legend firsthand, through the eyes of the dashing elf angel (how appropriate!). His beauty, reflected in the enchanted eyes of the ancient human princesses; the ecstasy among lovers; and at last, the melancholy as they aged and died while he remained youthful.

The music slowed to a stop, guiding the girl to the floor in a tangle worthy of a yoga guru.

Yet it was Dhananad whose stomach twisted in knots. His heart hammered in his chest. A few minutes of utter silence followed, interrupted only by an occasional bird chirp and the shifting of the Golden Scorpion.

Dhananad looked out the arched window toward the Iridescent Moon, which had passed through two phases in the blink of an eye. It would have required a monumental reserve of stamina to dance as the princess had for so long. He rose from the chair, ready to help the girl to her feet.

To his surprise, she spun up unto her toes, appearing as energized as if just waking to the morning sun. When she batted her lashes at him, he knew then he would do anything she asked.

He applauded, followed by the musicians and even the Teleri troublemaker. Dhananad said, "I have never experienced such a dance. You, my lady, give sound a shape, a tangible form."

Sweet Kaiya bowed again before returning to her seat. With dainty grace, she took up a glass and sipped some water. When she smiled again, he thought his heart would stop. She gestured toward the west windows. The sun, now meeting the Shallowsea, flooded the room with red rays of dusk.

"Alas, Prince Dhananad," she said, her very inflection of his name sending sparks up his spine. "Time is short, for I have been invited to dine with the maharaja of Vadara tonight."

Dhananad waved his hand, even if his chest felt squeezed by her imminent departure. "Well then, I look forward to seeing you again."

The Golden Scorpion prodded his back. "The Princess of Cathay did not respond to your proposal," she said, voice silky. "She should not leave until she answers."

Kaiya's eyes widened at the Scorpion before turning back to him, where they belonged. She looked up at him through her lashes. "Matters of peace are important, but please give us some time to consider details."

"No," the Scorpion said. Dhananad hoped it would be now. They could exchange private vows at the local Temple of Surya now, celebrate in each other's arms tonight, and then hold a grand wedding in Maduras within a month.

Princess Kaiya shook her head, sending her voluminous tresses prancing. "My next several days are marked by meetings with officials from other Ayuri Kingdoms to discuss trade and docking rights. Let us meet in seven days, when the White Moon wanes to its half-phase."

The Bovyan wore a stupid grin on his face, nodding. "One week, very reasonable."

One week! It was too long not to be graced by her beauty. Still, waiting made good things even better. "Very well. I had planned to return to Madura before then, but I shall delay my departure."

She dipped her chin. "Then let us host you at our embassy as a means of compensating you for the time you have lost."

Dhananad clapped once. "Of course! I would be delighted to enjoy Cathayi hospitality."

The Golden Scorpion—what was her name?— poked him again. "We will make arrangements to meet here, at the Bijuran embassy."

The Scorpion's voice tugged at him, pulling at the fog in his mind.

The princess shook her head. "We have troubled the Bijurans too much already. We are more than happy to have you as our guests." Princess Kaiya locked her gaze on the Golden Scorpion. Their eyes waged a silent battle of will.

Dhananad wavered. His logical brain understood the Golden Scorpion's intervention: it was better to talk at a neutral site instead of giving the Cathayi a territorial advantage. Yet his heart could not bring him to oppose the princess' will. Finally, he waved off the Scorpion. "The princess is right. We have already asked much of the Bijurans. Let us meet at the Cathayi Embassy in seven days. I hope to hear some good news then."

Sweet Kaiya stood. She motioned for her retinue, and they all followed her lead, standing and bowing. The imperial guard led them out of the room, with the infuriating handmaiden in the rear.

Standing at the window above, Prince Dhananad watched her entire entourage of two dozen guards form up. The haze shrouding his mind lifted. Why had he let the princess dictate terms to him?

He waved toward the musicians, who whispered among themselves as they packed up their instruments. "You, drummer. How did you know when to start playing?"

The drummer exchanged glances with his compatriots. "We were just discussing that, Your Eminence. We felt the princess' movements guided our hands. We may never put on such a wondrous performance again."

The Golden Scorpion and the Teleri official came up on either side of him. Both stared out the window.

"Your Eminence," she said, her voice soothing. "Do you not find it curious that the Princess of Cathay travels with such minimal protection? Among her guards, I can count the truly skilled warriors on one hand."

The Bovyan nodded. "Our spies say she arrived in Vyara in secret, with a very small retinue and no baggage. Usually, Cathayi royalty travel abroad with at least a hundred of their elite soldiers."

Dhananad slapped the window sill. "Curse the clumsy handmaiden. May the many arms of Yama drag her down to Hell! Had my Lotus Blossom drunk the nectar, we would be making wedding arrangements now. It would only be a matter of years before we could take Cathay without drawing a sword."

"It was no accident," the Scorpion said. "The handmaiden intentionally knocked the glass out of the princess' hand."

He turned to the woman, trying to read her expression. "Could she have seen you slip the aphrodisiac into the princess' drink?"

"Only one with natural talent and trained in the *Bahaadur* fighting arts could have perceived the speed of my motion."

Dhananad looked to the Bovyan. "Bring out your Nightblades. Have the princess followed, find out what she is doing over this next week."

"Your Eminence," the man replied. "The Teleri embassy must attend to many issues in Vyara city. We cannot commit all of our resources just to chase this latest infatuation of yours. I will certainly speak to our ambassador about it, though."

Dhananad spat. "Bah. To control Cathay would mean monopolizing the supply of guns and firepowder. Your enemies in the East and ours in the West would soon fall before us. My marriage to Princess Kaiya, combined with your empire's machinations in their country, will put my future son on their throne."

"Do not underestimate the princess, Your Highness," the Scorpion said. "She could very well be Madura's undoing if you do."

Dhananad held her gaze. "That is why you will follow her moves, especially if the Teleri will not."

The Ayuri music still echoed in Kaiya's ears. Her arms and legs screamed to move to the beat of her guards' marching boots. Her energy should've been drained after such an epic performance; but instead, she felt invigorated, as her vitality surged against her corporeal bonds.

The Loves of Prince Aralas was the longest solo dance she knew. The entire suite, when performed by an ensemble of dancers, lasted nearly two hours; the abridged solo version took ten minutes and tested the limits of her endurance.

Yet when the music had started, Master Sabal's lessons on the barge came to her. She lost all volition as the melody guided her body's movements and tangibly held her up in positions she had never achieved before. Each enunciation of a musical note pulled or pushed her, while her classical training allowed her to effortlessly articulate perfect postures.

When at last she had eased to a stop, having decided to leave out the tragic ending in favor of one of bliss and fascination, over two hours had passed— impossibly longer than the stamina of the stoutest warrior. Never in her life had she performed such a perfect dance.

She thought back to her audience, all enthralled by *her*, lulled into complacent reverie. Even the Bovyan, who as a race cared little for mundane pastimes, watched with rapt interest. She'd formed a connection, not with her voice as Lord Xu had taught her, but through motion. The beating of their hearts, nudged into harmony with hers. Just as Ayana had done with her elven magic to the Teleri spy.

Only the Golden Scorpion had seemed bored, and, like Master Sabal's *naga* when he fought, her mask had emitted a soft blue light during the dance. The woman had resisted the connection, shrugged off the enchantment. Perhaps Paladins could do the same. If Madura indeed had two thousand of the Golden Scorpions... What an ingenious move it had been to recruit them.

Kaiya gasped. She'd forgotten to ask to see an image of Grand Vizier Rumiya, the man who had formed up the Golden Scorpion Corps.

CHAPTER 35:

A Prince by Any Other Name

After several days in Vyara City, Kaiya had grown accustomed to the bustling cacophony of its main boulevards. It made the district around the Ankiran maharaja's villa seem quiet and eerie. It was as if they had crossed a bridge into a different city.

Worn boots clopped on the uneven pavement as several dozen soldiers in threadbare uniforms marched around the weathered white walls. The villa's crumbling minarets cast shadows across a fetid canal, making the entire compound appear dark and cold. She tightened the sari around her shoulders, as if it would provide warmth.

In a city of spotless buildings, manicured boulevards, and sparkling canals, it seemed like they were visiting a castle that had been held under siege for the year. Poor Prince Hardeep. He'd come to this ramshackle building to recover from his wounds a year before. From his letters, he was still staying in Vyara City.

Maybe she would see him today. The lotus jewel felt warm at her waist. Her heart quickened and her palms sweated. Had her feelings for him been there all this time, tucked away by Zheng Ming's attention?

A steward in a faded blue *kurta* guided them into a receiving room which spoke of desperate times. Light bauble lamps were three-quarters shuttered, perhaps to avoid illuminating the Ankiran royal family's plight.

The steward pointed her toward a rickety-looking wood chair. Kaiya's bare feet slid across the thinning rug. She gingerly settled on the edge, worried it might collapse beneath even her light weight.

Jie, despite her even slimmer build, eyed her own seat dubiously. Though invited to sit, Chen Xin and Ma Jun remained standing, either from protocol or their own doubts about the chairs.

A girl in Ankiran blue livery, if it could be called that given how dead it looked, brought a large bowl with cracked enamel, filled with *naan* flatbread. She placed it on a low table with splotchy varnish.

Several guards watched her from the periphery of the room.

"*Dian-xia*," the half-elf whispered in the Cathayi tongue. "How much clout do you think the Ankiran maharaja has?"

Kaiya glared at her Insolent Retainer, cowing her into silence. Let her believe it was all about alliance building. Soon, very soon...

The valet called out from the entrance, "His Majesty, Maharaja Bahir II."

Kaiya turned back to the doors. An old man strode into the room, shoulders square and head held high. Just behind him walked a youth whose face looked not much older than Jie, but whose broad shoulders and barrel chest could have belonged to a fierce warrior. He entered the room cradling a middle-aged woman's hand in the crook of his arm. A dozen guards flanked them as they walked to the front of the room and sat.

"Greetings, Princess Kaiya of Cathay," the maharaja said. Like the boy, he wore a royal blue *kurta* with a gold lotus emblazoned on the left breast.

Kaiya pressed her hands together and bowed her head. "Thank you for receiving me, Your Eminence."

The maharaja motioned toward the woman. "This is Queen Shariya."

The queen shifted the blue *sari* on her shoulder. Her eyes narrowed to slits. "We are something of outcasts to Vyara City's high society. To what do we owe this royal visit?"

Cold and blunt. Kaiya sucked her breath in. "I bear greetings from my father, the Emperor of Cathay."

The queen's tone went from unfriendly to downright hostile. "Does he wish to gloat at Ankira's occupation? Your trade mission's decision thirty-two years ago to sell guns to Madura doomed us."

Guilt yanked at Kaiya's heart. The ugly side of unfettered mercantilism enriched Cathay at the expense of others. She would've never considered the implications if not for meeting Prince Hardeep. She folded her hands in her lap and bowed low. "I… We—"

The queen thrust an obtuse finger at her. "And there you sit wearing fine silk and the latest fashions and rubbing our misfortune in our faces. I should have my guards hold you down and rip your dress from you and share you many times over, before cutting your pretty head off and sending it back to avaricious Cathay on a spear so that your Emperor will know how Ankira suffers because of his selfish decisions." The queen panted to catch her breath. Tears ran down her weathered cheeks.

A chill raced up Kaiya's spine. Embassy robes ruffled as the imperial guards tensed. Jie reached into the band of her *langa*. They were hopelessly outnumbered.

Fixing his attention on Kaiya, the boy raised an open hand. He spoke in a deep voice which matched his build but not his face. "Please calm down, Grandmother. You cannot blame the Princess of Cathay for something that happened before she was even born. Princess Kaiya, please forgive the queen. All of her sons were lost in defense of our homeland, her daughters married off to secure alliances which never materialized."

Lost? *All* of her sons? Kaiya met his gaze. The lump in her throat strangled her words, and she had to clear it before continuing. "Does Prince Hardeep still live?"

Orchestra of Treacheries

The queen burst into sobs. The boy prince looked at her with sympathetic eyes.

Oh Heavens, no. Kaiya's spine might have been made of jelly, the way her body wanted to fold in on itself. "I am sorry for your loss." Her loss. She slipped off her chair to her knees and touched her fingers to the rug. Her retainers dropped to a knee as well. "I was very touched by my meeting with him two years ago."

Queen Shariya wiped her eyes and cocked her head.

"That is impossible," the boy said. His brow creased.

Impossible? A presumptuous kid she just met was judging her emotions! Kaiya straightened. "He came to our palace to request an alliance against Madura."

The queen choked on tears. "Two years ago would have been too late, anyway."

The boy whisked his hand to quiet his grandmother. He nodded at Kaiya to continue.

"We exchanged correspondence up until just a month ago," Kaiya said.

Queen Shariya pursed her lips and snorted.

The boy shook his head. "That is just *not* possible."

The gall of the little brat, questioning her emotions. Heat flared in Kaiya's cheeks. She reached into the band of her *langa* and withdrew the lotus jewel. It pulsed with a warmth in her hands. "He gave me this lotus jewel."

The queen and the boy gaped at it. The maharaja leaned forward, squinting. Perhaps now they would believe her.

At last, the boy spoke in a low monotone. "That is *not* a lotus jewel. I don't know what it is, but it is not a lotus jewel."

Kaiya stared at the trinket in her hand. For two years, she'd gazed at it, stroked it, pressed it to her heart many times, all holding on to the memory of her prince. "But what about Prince Hardeep? When did he die?"

The prince cocked his head. "My uncle Hardeep died in infancy. Before you or I were born."

The world spun and Kaiya thrust a hand back against the chair for support. This could not be right. She'd seen the royal registries in the foreign ministry archive herself. No death date for Prince Hardeep had ever been entered. He'd been there, before her eyes.

Who had visited her?

And if Hardeep was dead, who had she been exchanging letters with?

Jie had seen Prince Hardeep from a distance at Wailian Castle two years before, but was curious to see what he was really like. She knew Princess Kaiya had a thing for transparent men like Young Lord Zheng… but a ghost?

She laid a hand on the princess' shoulder. Her trembling body radiated an unnatural heat as she staggered to her feet and slumped back into the chair. Which creaked, but by an act of the Heavens did not collapse into a tangle of firewood and princess.

Jie's focus shifted from the maharaja to the queen and back. The woman crumpled onto herself, crying inconsolably. The old man's face might as well have been frozen, like a Black Fist under interrogation, revealing less than a Golden Scorpion's mask.

The boy was the real king, setting up the old man as the primary target for Madura. Though no doubt, the child was no safer than the decoy. Which was why the royal treasury must have been strained to finance so many guards protect the sole heir to the Ankiran throne.

No point in revealing her suspicions. Jie turned to the old man. "Your Eminence, I am sorry to ask in light of the sad circumstances, but an impostor with full credentials visited Princess Kaiya back then, requesting assistance in your fight against Madura. Who from Ankira authorized the visit?"

The decoy remained impassive, but the boy stroked his beardless chin. "I do not recall any missions to Cathay. Two years ago, it would not have mattered anyway. It could have been anyone looking to make mischief."

Princess Kaiya found her voice. "He had pale blue eyes, unlike any other Ayuri I have ever seen."

The boy maharaja exchanged looks with the others and the soldiers murmured among themselves.

His grandmother set her hand so the pinkie and index finger stuck out, the *mudra* for warding evil. "Only one Ayuri in history has had blue eyes, though he disappeared thirty-two years ago. Madura's Grand Vizier, Rumiya."

Jie hesitantly looked back at the princess.

Her knuckles were white around the armrests. Tears glistened in her eyes. She mouthed *painting*, but only a gasp came out.

Jie bowed toward the old man. "Do you have a painting of Rumiya?"

The boy motioned toward a female servant and pointed toward the entrance. "Go to the library. Retrieve the *Chronology of Madura*."

The girl disappeared and the room fell into a nervous hush, broken only by the princess' and Queen Grandmother's occasional sniffs.

Jie used the awkward silence to ponder the bigger picture. If Prince Hardeep was really the evil wizard Rumiya, where had he been for thirty years before visiting the princess? And who had she been corresponding with? Oh, to be as good as Tian at drawing connections!

Tian. The answer dawned on her and she turned to draw the princess' attention, only to find her looking back, mouthing the same name.

Peng. It fit what Tian had said: several years after the fact, he realized Lord Peng had set him up to take the blame for the horrible mistake that got him banished. Peng was a snake to be sure, and this was certainly the same sort of vicious prank that inevitably hurt others.

Unless Peng had more sinister reasons beyond pure maliciousness.

When the servant returned, the boy motioned for her to deliver the heavy bundle of scrolls into the princess' hands.

Kaiya sat in her room at the Cathayi embassy, fingers trembling as she flipped through the sheaf of yellowing scrolls the Ankirans had loaned her. Her focus settled on an entry.

When the Hellstorm and Long Winter laid low the first great human empires, dynamic individuals forged new nations with strategic skill, diplomatic acumen, or the sheer force of will. In the region that would become the Kingdom of Madura, that individual was Madukant, who had been a captain in the Ayuri Empire's armies.

A masterful military tactician, Madukant made up for his lack of charisma with a combination of brute force and cutthroat political maneuvering. He ensured his soldiers survived the Long Winter by plundering the land of all its value. He set himself up first as a regional warlord. After absorbing nominal friends and crushing enemies, he declared himself maharaja.

His descendants inherited his ambition but not his skill, and had barely expanded the borders of the original Kingdom for a century and a half. That all changed when the sorcerer Rumiya rose to Grand Vizier.

See Illustration on the next page.

Kaiya tightened her hand into a fist. Was it worth seeing what this Rumiya looked like? It was bad enough she wasted two years of her youth pining for an imposter. If that imposter turned out to be an evil wizard…

She closed her eyes and flipped to the next scroll. With a deep breath, she looked down.

Orchestra of Treacheries

The full-color painting captured her Hardeep's dark bronze features just as she had remembered. How often had she dreamed about the line of his jaw and the thin curled beard? And of course, the luminous blue eyes which *saw* her.

The image blurred as hot tears clouded her vision. He had never truly loved her. Her own genuine feelings, wasted. A single drop splattered on the painting, causing the rust-red in his *kurta* to run.

Why had Rumiya come to Cathay? Surely not to free Ankira, as he claimed. Why the interest in her music and the Dragon Scale Lute? And why had he rescued her from Wailian Castle?

Kaiya dabbed the tears, grateful for the solitude of her room. With magic involved, there was one person who might be able to tell her more. She unwound Lord Xu's magic mirror from its silk wrapping.

Her reverse reflection gazed back at her, eyes rimmed in red. It would not do to let Xu see her like this.

After a few minutes, she cleared her throat. "Jie, please bring me some water."

Presently, the door swung open and the half-elf slunk in, a decanter in hand. With a rare look of sisterly concern, she sucked on her lower lip. A squeak escaped when she opened her mouth to say something, but she then fell silent.

The very fact that Jie had actually done something handmaidenly, without protest, made Kaiya feel a little better. She flashed a bittersweet smile. "Close the door behind you, Jie. I want you to be privy to this conversation."

"Conversation?" Jie raised an eyebrow, but turned and did as she was told.

Kaiya waved her hand over the mirror. "Lord Xu, please answer me." She waited until her impatience got the better of her. "Lord Xu?"

At last, her own reflection faded, and the ageless elf shimmered into view. He peered back with half-lidded eyes, and his hair looked as if birds had recently nested in it. "*Dian-xia.* How may I be of service?"

"What can you tell me about Madura's Grand Vizier Rumiya?" Her voice choked on the man's name.

Xu yawned and scratched his head. "He claimed he would expand Madura to Cathay's Great Wall. But Madura spread too fast, and its armies were stretched too thin, suppressing rebellions in its north and defending the east against the Paladins." His brow furrowed.

"Then what?" Kaiya prompted.

Xu eyed her for a second. "When the Dragon Avarax awoke from a thousand years of sleep, many of the Paladins stationed at Madura's border redeployed to the edge of the Dragonlands. It allowed Madura to resume its northward expansion into Ankira. However, Rumiya was not around to see his dreams realized."

Not around? "Where did he go?"

Xu shrugged.

A shrug? Kaiya glared at him through the mirror. "Rumiya visited me as Prince Hardeep. Why didn't you tell me?"

Xu's brows scrunched together. "I know a lot, young lady, but I did not know it was him. He might have cloaked his energy signature. From what I know, his magic resembled the sorcery of the Aksumi humans, which in itself is beyond the capability of an Ayuri human. And much more powerful. No human should wield so much power."

Kaiya sighed. Xu supposedly knew *everything*. Could do virtually *anything*. Yet now, he told her no more than the scrolls.

Xu looked beyond her. "Half-elf, you are smarter than you look, I'm sure. Use that pretty little head to piece together everything you know. A lot happened thirty-two years ago…"

Why did Xu always speak in riddles? Kaiya started to complain when his image faded out, revealing her own perplexed expression.

CHAPTER 36:
Titles Bestowed, Titles Earned

From his command tent near the cove entrance, Zheng Ming counted his blessings. Had he not received the imperial missive to return to the capital, he would've boarded the *Golden Phoenix* and been trapped after Peng's men captured it. The dead bodies of sailors caught on board bobbed in the harbor, a feast for the birds, victims of Peng's brutality.

Now, by order of the acting *Tianzi*, Ming was elevated to *Dajiang* and tasked with the immediate recapture of the flagship. He examined a rough map of the cove and its surrounding bluffs. With Princess Kaiya's escort of a hundred imperial guards, joined by a thousand infantrymen with a hundred guns, they had superior numbers. Yet despite what Prince Kai-Wu might think, numbers alone wouldn't prevail in this situation. If only he had the services of the *Tianzi's* mysterious agents, he could send them aboard under the cover of darkness.

Ming swept his gaze over the officers. Their hard expressions spoke one message: storm the cove, there and now.

Of course, very few of them had actual combat experience. Ming knew better. He'd charged into a situation before, at the inn, only to find he'd been tricked.

Since their initial assault, Lord Peng's faithful soldiers had swelled to five hundred men. At least a hundred occupied the *Golden Phoenix*, while the rest held strategic points near and around the sandy cove where the ship was moored. More importantly, the enemy controlled the cliffs above. The dock was a bottleneck, much like a certain bridge from Ming's recent past.

Ordering his men to assail such a fortified position was practically a death sentence. It was safer to just wait them out. Without a crew, Peng wouldn't be going anywhere. Yet the imperial messenger in the tent crossed his arms and looked askance. Why the urgency on Prince Kai-Wu's part?

Ming stepped out of the command tent and glanced up at the bluffs overlooking the cove. An indeterminate number of Peng's archers held a ridge above the bluff's rear access path. Any chance at victory depended on securing that spot. It would provide a good view of the enemy's deployment and a line of sight to the flagship.

If the imperials wanted a fight, at least Ming could keep them busy with something that wouldn't get many killed. On his command, the infantry commander formed up a phalanx of muskets, three ranks of thirty-three men each, facing Peng's archers.

The first volley from the lower ground did little more than kick up dirt around the archers' entrenched position. Peng's men retreated out of sight and returned an arcing salvo of arrows.

The barrage pushed the musketmen out of range; nonetheless, it had done its job. From the number of arrows, Ming estimated about three dozen men defending the ridge.

He pondered the conundrum. The angle of the rise rendered muskets useless. A charge up the narrow path would only get his men killed. Unless the archers above had a reason to keep their heads down... like the night the princess was ambushed on the way to Peng's. The attackers' barrage had kept them hiding between the horses. "Commander, set your musketmen in ranks of six men—"

"Six men at a time?" The commander looked at him as if was insane. "Not concentrated enough. We won't hit much."

Ming nodded. "That is not the point. Each group will approach, fire their volley, then fall back and allow another group to replace them. I want non-stop shooting to lay suppressing fire. It will cover my horses' charge."

All ten of them. Only the officers rode horses, and Ming doubted their cavalry skills. No one else could lead the charge. What had the Founder said? Men respect a title earned, not bestowed?

Now if only the cover fire would keep the archers' heads down until he led his makeshift cavalry to the top of the bluff. He beckoned a captain of the imperial guard. "I want you to follow our horses and engage any surviving enemy at the top."

The captain placed his fist in his open palm. "As you command, *Dajiang*."

The musket squad commander shook his head. "It's never been done before. I can't guarantee the rebels won't return a volley."

Such insubordination. Ming gritted his teeth. "I will take it into consideration. Now, let us ready our horses. Begin firing on my signal."

When his line of horses and the imperial guards behind him were ready, Ming drew his *dao* and raised it to the sun. "Charge!"

The musketmen discharged a staccato patter of gunfire, six shots every two seconds. Wind rushing through his hair, Ming dared a glance up. Could it be? None of the archers poked their heads up from behind cover, though some took blind shots that flew toward the source of the musket fire.

Ming's horse galloped up the path, rounding the bend and breaking out into the archers' line at the top of the ridge. He charged through, cutting as many as possible with one run.

He wheeled around. The survivors drew swords, even as the rest of the mounted imperial soldiers crashed through them.

Unslinging his bow, Ming cantered back the way he came. With aimed shots in the gaps between his troops, he dropped five of Peng's men.

The imperial guard reached the top of the bluff. Their gleaming breastplates, with their scowling dragons, radiated dread. Peng's surviving men threw down their weapons and cowered.

Ming turned to a lieutenant. "Our losses?"

His aide-de-campe beamed. "Four musketmen killed, seven wounded. Two of your riders were also injured."

Ming nodded. A sad sacrifice, but one made for the sake of superior position. And certainly better than the blind charge the imperials wanted. "Redeploy the musketmen along the bluff, facing the cove. Send the imperial guards to the head of the cove's access road to await my orders."

"What about the prisoners?" His aide lifted his chin toward Peng's defeated men, who knelt in a line with hands on their heads.

Ming strode over to them, twenty-one in all, mostly uninjured. Several prostrated themselves, perhaps hoping to avoid the penalty for treason. But no, the princess had treated the dying Xie Shimin with dignity and kindness. "Soldiers of Nanling. You have risen up in arms against the Son of Heaven. You know the punishment."

One man whimpered. "It was Lord Peng. He ordered us to do so. Said it was for the good of the nation."

"You obeyed orders. For that, I give you two choices." Ming held out his curved dagger. "You may cut your own throat and die with honor. Or, I will organize you into our army." Heaven knew they needed archers, even if the imperials preferred guns.

All twenty-one rose into one-knee salutes.

"Traitors," the imperial commander muttered.

Ming flashed him a sharp glance. "Assign a dozen men to watch over them, ready to run them through at the first sign of treachery. Provide bows only if we need their service."

Lips pursed, the commander placed a hand in his fist. "As the *Dajiang* commands."

Letting out a long breath, Ming turned around and used the new vantage point to reassess their situation. Peng's men held the cove's beaches and the dock. The *Golden Phoenix* remained anchored about four hundred feet away from where he stood,

Orchestra of Treacheries

making it difficult to pick out Lord Peng from the other men on deck.

He turned to the musketmen's commander. "Can any of your sharpshooters find Lord Peng and hit him from here?"

The commander gawked. "Not from this range, no. We would splinter the *Golden Phoenix* with all of the misses."

Ming looked back at the ship. From this range, it was an impossible shot with a bow, even if they could locate Peng among the defenders. He waved toward the newly appointed commander of the archers. "Bring your unit here. When we storm the beach, I want our new recruits to prove their loyalty by raining arrows on the ship's deck."

He then turned to the musketmen's commander. "On my order, lay down volley fire into their units on the beach and dock."

Orders passed from unit to unit. Soldiers brought the command tent to the top of the bluffs. Within two hours, everyone was deployed.

When the fusillade of muskets tore into the beach, many of the enemy threw themselves into the sand or cowered behind the docks' pylons. Arrows from his new archery unit arced into the ship, sending Peng's men below deck.

The imperial guard swept in. Ming had seen combat in Rotuvi before, but never the beautiful but brutal efficiency with which the imperial guard fought. The defenders put up little resistance, many throwing down their arms and begging for mercy.

The beach was theirs in just minutes.

A volley of musket fire roared from the *Golden Phoenix*'s portholes, ripping into the imperial guards' efficient lines. Ming gritted his teeth. There had been no report of Peng's men having guns.

"Sound a defensive withdrawal," he told an officer. "Without a crew, their only escape is by the beach. Have our men fall back and guard the access road. Do not let anyone through."

Another officer shuffled on his feet. "What about the *Tianzi's* command to take the ship?"

Ming sighed. "As long as they have guns, the ship is a floating fortress with one point of access. I will not needlessly sacrifice our men in a futile attempt to take it." Even with his archery skills, the portholes were a near impossible shot given the range and angle. Which left... "How many days of food and water do they carry?"

The officers chattered among themselves before a quartermaster spoke up. "I don't know much about ships, but it takes six days at best to reach Ayudra. If it were me planning, I would provision for ten days."

Ten days. A long time, but hopefully, the stark reality of Peng's situation would set in sooner: a soldier's bravado would last only as long as his stomach was full.

Ming pointed toward the city. "Procure lumber from the port and construct cover fortifications that bring us closer and closer to the ship. Then we will wait."

They waited three days. Ming imagined the ship's occupants must be growing unsettled, wallowing in their own stench and perhaps rationing food.

He drew up a letter:

Brave soldiers of Cathay, your loyalty to your lord is admirable. However, you now stand in rebellion against the Tianzi. Surrender Lord Peng, and your death sentences will be commuted.

He tied the note to an arrow and shot it onto the deck.

Nobody went up top to retrieve it.

He rewrote the letter and had a messenger deliver it under the flag of parley. The unfortunate man made it halfway down the dock before falling to a barrage of musket balls from the ship.

The imperial soldiers shouted and cursed. Ming stared wide-eyed. To kill a man walking under the flag of parley was unthinkable.

Let Peng starve. The *Golden Phoenix* would bake under the sun, all those below deck boiling in a stinking cesspool of disease and misery.

On the fourth day, the enemy soldiers lowered the gangplank and began filing off one by one, weary, unarmed, and hands on their head.

Ming rode down to accept Lord Peng's surrender.

Instead, he found himself talking to *Yu-Ming* Lord Tu, the young heir to one of Nanling Provinces' more prosperous counties.

"Where is Lord Peng?" Ming demanded.

Lord Tu shook his head. "Dead. Killed by one of your arrows on the first day."

Not totally unexpected. Nonetheless… "Why did you not surrender at that time?"

"It would have been dishonorable."

And yet, they had slain a man approaching under the flag of parley. Ming raised an eyebrow. "You surrender now."

Lord Tu cringed. "Your agent onboard murdered several of us each day. I was faced with a mutiny."

Agent? Ming scowled. Why had he never heard of this?

Voices stirred Liang Yu out of the *Viper's Rest* technique and back into the world of the living. He instinctively remained still and kept his breath near imperceptible as he tried to piece through the disorientation and memory loss the technique caused.

At least he remembered his identity—Black Fists who were not true masters like himself might even forget their very name.

Beside him laid dead corpses, cold, but not yet rancid with the stench of death.

The memories trickled back.

He was the one who killed those soldiers.

Days before, he'd melted in with Lord Peng's troops as they marched to Jiangkou.

He made sure he was part of the boarding party that initially captured the *Golden Phoenix*.

That first night, he hypnotized Lord Tu with the *Tiger's Eye* and learned the attack on the flagship was meant as a diversion for Lord Peng's escape over the border into Rotuvi.

Liang Yu focused. Why was that so important to him?

Because he intended to kill Lord Peng, lest he became a threat. Yes, Peng had pushed Expansionism, but according to Minister Hong, it was mostly as a way of garnering support among the Expansionist lords. What he would do after actually capturing the Dragon Throne was anyone's guess.

Though now, it turned out Peng was quite clever. Perhaps he would be worth keeping alive a little longer.

Liang Yu peeked out of a nearly closed eye once the voices faded into the distance. He was still below deck on the *Golden Phoenix*, lined up among the dead. A blade of fading afternoon light cut through a partially open porthole.

He withdrew a slender bamboo reed from his hidden pouch. Though not as supple as he had been in his youth, he could still squeeze out of a sea-side porthole, and then swim below the water, undetected.

He had done as much thirty-two years before when an elf pushed him off a bridge and left him for dead.

Unfortunately, Lord Peng had escaped his reach. And apparently the *Tianzi's* as well.

For now.

CHAPTER 37:
ROGUES GALLERY

P rince Dhananad disliked visiting the Teleri embassy not just because of the vermin inhabiting it, but mostly due to its spartan décor. It seemed that even in Vyara City, a magnet for culture and refinement, the Bovyan Scourge prided itself on its bland lifestyle. The sooner his country ended its alliance with the Teleri Empire, the better.

The huge guards, dressed in black surcoats that must have left them roasting in the South's sun, stepped to the side and let Dhananad and his Golden Scorpion escort pass.

Dhananad stormed through the halls and slammed open the metallic double doors to the audience room. The Teleri ambassador sat straight-backed and cross-legged on a dais, holding audience with several— Dhananad skidded to a halt.

Leisurely nestled in a mountain of cushions was a turquoise-skinned altivorc dressed in a dapper military uniform.

Dhananad knew this particular specimen. Unlike the rest of his kind, this one was handsome, with refined, almost elf-like features. No one was sure how old he was, or even if he was the same person over the centuries. He had first appeared in history a millennium ago (but who was counting?) as his people were losing the War of Ancient Gods. Nobody knew his name, and Dhananad joined everyone else in addressing him as the King of Altivorcs.

Humph. King of what? A pack of ugly humanoids of little consequence. The Tivari might have once controlled all of Tivaralan, enslaved all of humanity; but now they hid away in subterranean cities sprinkled throughout the mountains of the Northwest. Both the altivorcs and their more hideous, stupider cousins, the tivorcs, worked as mercenaries for the highest bidder. Dhananad's homeland of Madura had nothing to do with them. If he had anything to say about it, they never would.

Dhananad avoided the altivorc's gaze, and instead turned to Ambassador Piros di Bovyan. Like all of the Teleri Prospecti—the upper echelon of Bovyans who ruled their empire—he was an imposing man, with dark hair and grey eyes. He had been in Vyara for six years, and Dhananad tired of having to pander to him.

"Is it true?" he asked. "Did Princess Kaiya really meet with the Ankiran insurgents?"

The Bovyan brute Piros shrugged and cocked his head. When he spoke, his Ayuri reeked of the North. "If by insurgent, you mean their former maharaja, then yes. Perhaps you should have paid heed to our advisor, instead of falling for the girl's charm. She was obviously misleading you."

Dhananad spat. "Bah. A meeting with some outlaws means nothing. Perhaps the filth begged her to speak to me on their behalf."

Another familiar face sneered. With Lord Benhan's light-brown skin tone and dark hair, a Northerner might have mistaken him for Ayuri; but Dhananad (and any other Southerner!) recognized him as Levanthi. This dolt hailed from the Empire of Levastya, which, unlike Madura's other ally, at least had a semblance of high culture. Albeit inferior to the Ayuri.

Dhananad glared back. "Do you find something funny?"

Benhan laughed. "Do not assume Cathayi women are as easily cowed as those in Madura."

Dhananad cast him a disdainful glance. It wasn't worth acknowledging the comment. "Her meeting with them means nothing."

Piros scoffed. "Don't you find it suspicious that she also met with the Vadarans, Bijurans, and Daburans? While not your enemies, they certainly aren't your friends."

The Altivorc King let out a yawn a lion would envy. "I would be more concerned with her visit to the Paladins' Crystal Citadel in two days."

Dhananad was about to respond, but found himself uncharacteristically at a loss for words. His mouth hung open as the others afforded him patronizing grins. When he found his tongue, his voice squeaked. "Your Nightblades are following her, then?"

Piros shrugged again. "Of course. We must know what she is up to. It is ultimately our goal to bring Cathay into our alliance's sphere of influence, though our plan could take a decade to accomplish."

Dhananad stomped his foot on the marble tiles. "Then you must see the importance of my marriage to her? Our son would have a claim to rule Cathay, which could move up your timeline by many years! Imagine, my infant son on the Dragon Throne, with me as Regent! It would give us access to more and better guns, and limitless firepowder. Not even the Paladins are fast enough to avoid a bullet!"

He glanced back to see his Scorpion shifting on his feet, in denial of the truth.

The Altivorc King cackled. "Humans! Always concerned about short-term gain. It is ironic that the Bovyans, the shortest-lived of your kind, seem to be the only ones who understand the effectiveness and subtleties of long-term planning."

Lord Benhan shared Dhananad's scowl, but before either of them could speak, the King wagged a finger at the Levastyan. "Don't try to deny it. Even though your ruling priests in Levastya now worship the Ancient Gods of Tivara, they do not seem to have embraced the wisdom of long-term thinking that we teach. Otherwise, you would not be threatening Korynth without having fully subjugated Selastya."

Prince Dhananad regarded him curiously. "What do you mean by *short-term*, oh wise King of the Orcs?"

The Altivorc King waved a dismissive hand. "Your entire plan rests upon the princess agreeing to marry you. You are obviously not going to accomplish that with your good looks, so you resort to the threat of force. Yet she is evidently befriending those who might be your enemies, and more importantly, those who can attack you on another front. Your threat of force will be neutralized." He smirked. "What part of your plan is it that you consider good?"

Heat rushed to Dhananad's cheeks. Nobody mocked him! Had he carried his *talwar*, he might have attacked the King, even though he would certainly have no chance of surviving if the legends of the King's physical prowess were to be believed. "Then it is quite simple. If the Paladins do not agree to help Cathay, then Bijura, Vadara, and Dabura will not be in a position to oppose our Scorpions. All we have to do is prevent her from meeting the Paladins."

The altivorc's yellow eyes narrowed as they locked on Dhananad's. "What do you intend?"

Dhananad turned his back on the altivorc to face Ambassador Piros. "Your Nightblades have surely noted that Princess Kaiya travels with little guard?"

Piros responded with a slow, dubious nod.

"My Scorpions say that her best protection is an ancient elf wizardess, five imperial guards, and a half-elf girl."

"Half-elf?" The Altivorc King leaned forward and turned toward Piros, who nodded. Dhananad knew the Tivari had tried to exterminate the elves millennia ago, but the King's sudden interest seemed to go beyond mere hatred.

He ignored the altivorc's query and continued. "When she departs from the safety of her embassy, a force of my personal guard, assisted by several of the Scorpions, will take her. And then she will be mine. Cathay relies too much on their Great Wall and does not have the seasoned soldiers to attack Madura and take her back. In due time, we will have a son, and when that happens, we will lay claim to Cathay."

Piros stroked his chin thoughtfully. "You would take her by force and despoil her against her will?"

Dhananad snorted. "I would think the Teleri would appreciate such measures."

"And if your men fail to capture her?" Piros asked.

"Then they will be disavowed. They will not wear the markings of Madura or the Scorpions. We will leave no evidence that we were ever involved."

Piros and Benhan both seemed to be in deep thought (at his brilliance, no doubt!), so much that he swore he saw smoke coming out of their ears.

The Altivorc King clapped. "Ingenious, Prince Dhananad! It is a sound plan, one that I am willing to support. I will supply several of my soldiers to assist you. Perhaps Cathay will fall within your alliance's grasp sooner than we expected."

Dhananad beamed at the compliment. He would be gracious and forget the previous insults. "Thank you, King of the Orcs. I will take my leave to prepare the specifics of the attack. Have your men come to the Maduran embassy under the cover of darkness."

After Prince Dhananad had spun on his heel and left, Piros sighed. He lamented spending the twilight of his allotted thirty-three years of life stuck in this city, dealing with fools like the prince.

He looked toward the beneficiary of his short lifespan, the Altivorc King. The ancestor of all Bovyans had made a deal with the altivorc gods, surrendering the collective life force of his descendants to sustain the Altivorc King's. The King promised to end the curse when the Bovyans gave him control of the three remaining pyramids in the north. That was not likely to happen in Piros' lifetime.

In the meantime, they remained strange bedfellows. Piros could not fathom why the Altivorc King decided to throw his weight behind a brash attack, especially after sparing no expense to stay unannounced in Vyara City. He had remained holed up in the Teleri embassy since his sudden arrival a few days before. Perhaps suffering clowns like Dhananad was easier than fathoming mysterious allies like the Altivorc King.

"It is a foolish idea," Piros said to the King. "One that has too many ways to fail."

The altivorc laughed. "Of course it will fail. Prince Dhananad does not realize the power of the old elf who protects the Princess of Cathay. But whether his plan succeeds or fails, it will not interfere with our goals. Let the prince put on a show; it will distract the Paladins from my work here."

What work, Piros could not guess, nor would the Altivorc King tell if asked. Piros had a hunch that it related to Lord Benhan's Levastyans, who sought to bring about the return of the Orc Gods on their flaming chariots.

Piros regarded Benhan, doubting the wisdom of the Levastyan's zealotry. Before their gods were vanquished, the Tivari wielded powerful magic which they used to enslave humanity. Worshipping those gods did not seem like the brightest idea.

Yet when it came down to it, they were all just using each other toward their own ends, ready to abandon alliances if they became too burdensome. Of the Levastyans, altivorcs, Madurans, and Teleri, only his own people had a truly noble goal: lasting peace for the world.

Lord Benhan smirked. "Perhaps we should inform the Paladins about an anonymous threat on the princess, to ensure Prince Dhananad's failure. We just have to know when."

The King bared his fangs. "I will let you all know the timing of his ill-advised plans."

CHAPTER 38:
Ulterior Motives

As the princess dressed with Meixi's help behind the screen, Jie considered the coincidences. The last time the Black Lotus had conducted a mission in Vyara City, they had a secondary assignment, executed under the guise of diplomacy. Following the Architect's plan, the Beauty had seduced a Maduran official, allowing her access to the young Prince Dhananad.

At least this time, their party's ulterior motive was noble. Today, they would cross the river to Vadaras to visit the government-in-exile of the Sultanate of Selastya. Selastya had been absorbed by its neighbor Levastya two decades before, after the Akolytes of their Sun God Athran lost their power to channel Divine Magic. Rumor had it some of the faithful had regained their abilities, and the princess hoped to convince the deposed sultan to send one to Cathay in hopes they could cure the *Tianzi*.

As noble as their intentions were, Jie questioned the timing. The princess had shown remarkable resilience after learning of Rumiya's deception, and gone on four days of whirlwind negotiations.

She'd charmed each of the maharajas of the Ayuri Confederation nations with charisma and wit, and received several wedding proposals, which she graciously deflected. In addition to arranging several trade agreements, she secretly secured mutual protection pacts. It now rested in the hands of the

Tianzi, who would ratify Cathay's side; and the Paladins' Council of Elders, with whom she would meet the next day.

Calling from the anteroom, Chen Xin said, "*Dian-xia*, we still lack sufficient protection. I humbly suggest this visit wait until after your full complement of imperial guards arrives. There is no need to recklessly expose yourself to danger."

Jie nodded, though the decision was never in question. They'd rehashed this argument each day, before the princess' meetings, always with the same result.

The princess' voice sang out from the other side of the screen. "We do not know when that will be. In any case, with the Paladins' omnipresence, there is virtually no petty crime in this city, let alone violence."

She wasn't wrong. Still, Jie sighed and recited her rote response:. "Teleri Nightblades are constantly following us. And in any case, we will be taking the ferry over to Vadaras, where the Paladins' presence is less evident. If Madura or its allies suspect your audience with the Paladin elders in two days, there is no telling what they would do."

Hushed whispers and giggles emanated from behind the screen. Meixi came out, beaming.

Then Princess Kaiya emerged. "You are worrying needlessly."

Jie sucked her lower lip. If anyone should worry, it was the *Tianzi*. His daughter, dressed like *that*, with a degenerate Maduran prince lurking around somewhere. The white silk outer robe, embroidered with green dragons, hung from her shoulders. Open in the front, it revealed a sleeveless, strapless inner gown of light green silk, whose neckline dipped just low enough to suggest the curves beneath. A blue silk sash tied tightly around her slim waist accentuated the contour of her hips. Intricate gold pins held her obsidian hair tied above her ears.

By comparison, Jie's own flat body would've made that dress look like a war banner on a windless day. "I would remind you, Prince Dhananad tried to poison you at your last meeting."

The princess' lips quivered as she maintained her smile. Her tone turned indignant. "I appreciate all of your concerns.

However, my father's health is now my priority. We will proceed with our trip to Vadaras. Prepare the guards for departure."

Chen Xin and Jie exchanged worried looks. "As the princess commands," he said.

Within a half-hour, the five imperial guards and two dozen embassy guards formed up around the princess and Ayana, who rode side-by-side on horses. The skies were overcast, and the hot and muggy air hung in her lungs. Jie knew the route well now, and watched every convenient place to lay an ambush.

Just ten minutes from the Cathayi embassy, the procession ground to a stop as an argument between a merchant and a miffed customer drew a crowd of spectators ahead of them.

The procession's crier yelled, his voice booming louder than his size would suggest: "Make way! Make way for Princess Kaiya Wang of Cathay!"

Despite his appeal, nobody cleared the streets. Instead, more bystanders crowded in to point and gawk at the beautiful princess in their midst. The soldiers, despite a week of drilling from the imperial guards, still lacked discipline. They broke their attentive stances, and instead bobbed and weaved to get a better view of the argument.

From her position next to the princess' horse, Jie noted the location: in a long lane between rowhouses. A perfect spot for an—

Several metal discs sliced through the air toward the first rank of embassy guards. Screams. Blood. Jie was on her feet at once. Her eyes tracked the discs back in the direction they came from. People ran every which way, yelling and pointing.

Sitting side-saddle on her horse, the princess now clenched its mane with both hands as it shied. Her mouth hung open in a silent scream as it reared.

Avoiding flailing legs, Jie reached up, snagged hold of the princess' long sleeves, and yanked. The two tumbled way too close for comfort to the horse's stamping hooves. The princess covered her head with her arms.

Above them, Ayana's horse panicked and shoved its way backward despite the elf's protestations, crushing several of the guards who had been to slow to react.

Jie sprang to her feet. She took the princess' quivering hand and pulled her up. Face pale, with the eyes of a startled doe, Kaiya trembled.

Chen Xin's voice boomed over the commotion. "Form up your lines! Move forward! Protect the princess!" He and the four other imperial guards backed in around them with naked *dao* swords.

The clang of metal on metal mingled with the cries of wounded men and the screaming crowds. The embassy guards fought valiantly, streaming forward to move between the princess and the pack of rugged assailants in front of them. Ayana yelled something from behind, her voice trailing farther and farther away.

The princess straightened and motioned back in the direction they'd come. Voice calm, she said, "Pull back, back toward the safety of the embassy."

Jie shook her head. Not without knowing what was in that direction. Tall men blocked her view. Being short came in handy sometimes, but not now. Added to which, this confounded dress hindered her movement. She tugged on the princess' sleeve. "Let me go first. They might be trying to flush us into the open, out of the ring of guards."

The princess nodded, and Jie slunk through the few rear guards. On the other side, the streets blurred in chaos as citizens ran for the cover of shops and homes. The road continued for several hundred feet before intersecting with a cross-street. Two-story rowhouses lined either side, providing no escape routes.

Something was wrong; danger lay in that direction. Or at least, that's what every instinct screamed. Jie scanned windows, doorways, and rooftops. Sounds of skirmishes approached from the direction she'd just come, and she stole a glance back. Their front line of soldiers had collapsed under the onslaught. No choice now. She motioned for Chen Xin to fall back.

Chen pointed with his sword. "Zhao, help hold the line! The rest of you, surround the princess and head back toward the embassy."

Jie took one step. Six turquoise-skinned humanoids charged toward them. Protected by chainmail, they brandished heavy broadswords in their left hands. Orcs. The intelligence gleaming in their eyes suggested altivorcs, not their stupid cousins, the tivorcs.

She whipped out a handful of throwing stars and flung them. The first altivorc fell to his knees, clutching his throat, but the next was on her with a downward chop of his blade.

Jie sidestepped the blow. In the same motion, she thrust the heel of her palm under his outstretched arm and into his unprotected chin, while stomping through the back of his knee.

Even as the second altivorc collapsed, two broadswords swept at her, one toward her neck and the other at her waist. Jie sprang between the two blades while hurling two spikes at each of the orcs' flanks. She landed in a forward roll, but tripped on her hem as she tried to regain her feet.

Stumbling to the ground, she twisted over, just avoiding the hack of another sword. It sent showers of sparks by her head. Yet the roll positioned her prone in front of the sixth altivorc. He cocked his broadsword back, ready to run her through.

Jie hooked his ankle and leaned into his shin with her shoulder. He sprawled backward, and she used her momentum to flip over him. The dress prevented her from straddling him in a controlling position, so she continued her roll. Finger-jabs in his eyes vaulted her back into a stand.

She took two steps back to reassess the situation. The first altivorc lay dying, the second was incapacitated by torn knee ligaments. The second pair appeared undamaged by her spikes, regrouping with the fifth altivorc to continue their attack. The sixth staggered to his feet, clawing at his black-bloodied eye sockets.

Past them, the guards still formed a protective ring around the princess, and pressed toward Jie. Luckily—at least as far as duty and not personal safety was concerned—the altivorcs seemed more concerned with her than the princess.

Jie whipped out a pair of knives and sheared slits down her dress to allow more mobility.

The altivorcs closed in a coordinated attack, cutting in three different directions. Jie twisted away toward their phalanx's left flank, putting one between her and the other two. As he spun at her with a backhand chop, she sank her knife into his exposed throat.

Before either of the remaining two could attack, the imperial guards came up from behind. Ma Jun decapitated one in a spray of black blood, while Chen Xin drove his *dao* through the other, punching through the chain armor as if it were cloth.

The escape path was clear—

Two figures with curved *talwar* swords stepped in and blocked their way. They wore plain brown *kurtas*. Scarves wrapped around their faces, revealing only their eyes. One leapt past Jie before she could react and began cutting through the guards with blinding speed.

The other fixed her focus on Jie. Those eyes… they belonged to the female Golden Scorpion who'd tried to slip poison into Princess Kaiya's wine.

The last time she'd faced a real Scorpion, Jie'd been knocked out in under a second. Needing to keep her distance, she unleashed her last spikes and stars with a single sweep of her hand.

Impossibly, the Scorpion evaded most and deflected the rest out of the air with a flash of her *talwar*, then lunged forward to close the distance. The speed with which she covered fifteen feet bordered on the unbelievable.

Jie flipped her knife into an underhand grip. There was no chance she could survive against such a skilled swordfighter.

In that second of resignation, the Scorpion attacked. The intention behind the dozen superhumanly fast slashes was as clear as if the Scorpion had whispered them beforehand. Pressed back, Jie suffered only a few nicks, though the sleeves of her beautiful gown were shredded to ribbons.

The Scorpion disengaged, her gaze flicking behind Jie.

In that direction, Ayana's voice growled, followed by the sound of dozens of weapons clattering to the ground. Jie didn't dare risk a glance back.

When they set out, Kaiya's stifling court gowns, more suited to a cool spring in Cathay, had made the hot and humid day downright miserable. That was a mundane concern now. She should've listened to Jie and Chen Xin's advice.

A blindingly fast swordsman darted back and forth around the perimeter of her own protective ring, stabbing and slashing with a rapid tittering of clashing blades. He engaged Li Wei and Ma Jun, who fought in unison. Neither the swoosh of one blade nor the clanging of another deterred his onslaught. A flash of his curved sword would've ended Li Wei's life had he not deflected it with a last-second clank.

Li Wei reeled back, his boots pattering on the pavement. The enemy closed, stepping toward Chen Xin's thrust and the swish of Ma Jun's horizontal slash. He spun out of the attacks like a gush of air, and the pommel of his sword met Ma Jun's skull with a crunch.

Xu Zhan's sword tolled as it received the blow which would've finished off Ma Jun. The assailant's foot brushed through the air, thudding into Xu's temple. He tumbled into Zhao Yue, and both clattered to the ground.

Chen Xin backed off, keeping himself between the assassin and her, while Li Wei pressed the attack on wobbly feet. The man slammed his fist into Li Wei's nose, sending him sprawling.

"Princess Kaiya." The attacker raised his blade over Li Wei's inert form. "Come with us peacefully, and we will spare your guards."

Far behind her, Ayana's voice sang in the melodic language of elven magic.

Chen Xin lunged forward, his sword whipping through the air; but the man evaded the attacks and elbowed Chen in the temple, knocking him to the ground. He looked to make good on his threat, raising his sword and chopping down.

Kaiya swept out the long sleeve of her gown, entangling his blade before it finished Chen Xin.

The attacker twirled the sword, wrapping the priceless fabric around his weapon. He jerked her forward, but she spun her way out of the gown and grasped the other sleeve in her hand.

As he stood and gawked at her bare shoulders, she coiled the gown around his sword and swept it from his hands and onto the street. His eyes widened further for a split second.

Moving faster than she could see, he lunged. His fingers clenched around her wrist.

Years of Praise Moon Fist training allowed her contact reflexes to take over. She turned her wrist out of his grip, and he reached with his other hand toward her neck. Without conscious thought, she covered the opening with her free arm, intercepting his hand and guiding it downward. Still, her tactile responses couldn't keep up with him.

Ayana's voice sang out again, closer now, and the man's speed slowed to almost normal. With this change, Kaiya gained the advantage. She pinned the man's hands close to his body while delivering an onslaught of punches, strong enough to send him reeling back. He ducked into a roll back toward his sword, still wrapped up in the remains of her outer gown.

A warm palm pressed on her shoulder at the same time a single, guttural syllable echoed in her ears. Her head swam with blurring colors before all went black.

The female Scorpion launched another flurry of attacks at Jie, making her give more ground than she had left. She would be bumping up against the princess soon. She started to reengage.

Behind her, Ayana uttered a foul-sounding word. The air popped.

Her opponent lowered her sword, eyes wide in the slits of the cloth. Jie shot a quick glance back.

Princess Kaiya and Ayana were gone.

Recovering from her surprise, Jie reached down and claimed Li Wei's *dao*, easily hefting its balanced weight in her right hand while brandishing the knife in her left. She grimaced at the pain in her flank—only now did she realize she'd been cut across the ribs. Her legs wobbled and her vision blurred for a second.

She raked her gaze over the area.

Besides spectators who kept their distance, only the two Scorpions were left standing. The Cathayi guards and several other attackers lay on the ground, incapacitated, killed or… sleeping?

Both Golden Scorpions advanced on her.

Even the improved reach the *dao* gave her would do little to help her against one, let alone two, of these astounding warriors. She resigned herself to the inevitable. Regrets threatened to break her already-fading concentration. Never learning who her parents were. Never telling Zheng Tian she loved him…

"Paladins!" The words passed from mouth to mouth among the distraught crowds. When the Scorpions looked past her, Jie glanced back as well. A dozen men in white *kurtas* with gold embroidered necks ran at astonishing speeds toward them, their curved *naga* swords drawn.

The two villains ran off, leaving Jie to curse herself for thinking such silly thoughts. She bent down to check on the closest imperial guard, Xu Zhan.

He was alive. Thank the Heavens.
When she started to stand, everything faded to black.

CHAPTER 39:
Interlude

Kaiya was cold, and her head ached. Her forearms stung and her knuckles burned. The soft surface beneath her was cool and damp. Grass. A sweet and nostalgic smell of evergreens hung in the air. Nearby, water rustled over rocks. Beyond the stream, beautiful voices spoke softly in a wondrous, musical language.

Her eyes complained as she forced them open. Gradually, the dappled sunlight peeking through the spindly tendrils of pine needles came into focus above her. What had happened? Where was she?

Her head protested at the effort to ease herself up, but she at last managed to sit upright. She looked toward the voices. A stone's throw away, a short, lithe silhouette gesticulated. The size, her voice... Ayana.

The ambush, the fight with the Scorpion. Her guards, fallen. Her priceless outer gown, lost. Maybe that's why it was so cold. Though it certainly hadn't been so chilly outside before.

"Ayana," she called. "What happened?"

The shadowed form moved toward her, revealing a second thin figure, who remained behind. Ayana stepped into the sunlight, which cast her face in a pale sheen.

Her voice sounded weak. "Princess Kaiya, you are finally awake. You fainted and have been unconscious for three hours.

It is a typical reaction, the first time you travel through the ethers. I imagine your head must feel as if it were split by a dwarf's axe."

Travelled through the ethers! Like Lord Xu, though she had never expected to ever do it herself. They could be anywhere. "Where are we? Where are my guards?"

Ayana pursed her lips. "I have sworn not to reveal our location, and in fact I am not entirely sure. I used an emergency spell that transported us to an anchor held by a friend of mine. Suffice to say, we are safe for now."

Safe! But what about... "The guards, Jie... we need to get back to them."

"I don't have the energy." Ayana sighed. "The Shallow Magic incantation is very taxing, especially when I transport someone else. Not to mention all the energy I used to protect you in your ill-advised escapade."

"We need to get back." Kaiya's voice sounded like a petulant child's to her own ears, but her retinue was her responsibility. Her fault.

"I am sorry, Princess Kaiya, but it is just not possible. We will have to wait until this evening, after I have rested."

The second shadow spoke in a mellifluous male voice. The words sang like a chorus of nightingales, reminiscent of Lord Xu.

Ayana shook her head adamantly, but he protested. She harrumphed. "My friend has agreed to send us back to Vyara City, although not to the same spot. He can only transport us somewhere he has been before. I would advise against it, since I am too weak to protect you now."

"I cannot just wait here and do nothing."

Ayana's brows furrowed. Despite the angry expression, her tone remained calm. "It is that self-assured attitude, that foolhardiness, which got you into that ambush in the first place. How many people have died because of your vanity?"

Kaiya's face flushed hot, partially from anger at the audacity of the rebuke, but mostly from shame. The elf was right. So concerned about Father, Kaiya placed too much faith in her own abilities of persuasion, never considering that that alone might be insufficient.

Ayana continued, merciless. "Do you realize what could have happened? Had I not been able to get back to you in time, the Golden Scorpions would have captured you. Prince Dhananad would be deflowering you right about now."

Hugging herself, Kaiya shuddered. She pushed the image of the musky prince's leer out of her mind.

The other elf emerged into the clearing. A longbow hung over his shoulder, and a thin straight sword, similar to Xu's, dangled at his side. Handsome, with fine features and shiny golden hair, he wore a poncho of forest-green.

No, not handsome; he was gorgeous. Kaiya straightened out her inner gown and ran a hand through her hair.

When he spoke in Arkothi, it was tinged with a sensually exotic elvish accent: "Ayana does not speak out of maliciousness. You will not find a more caring person."

Ayana's eyebrows sunk into a scowl. "I—"

He flashed a devilish grin at the matronly elf. "She has been alive since before the time your ancestor General Shyaotian established the Wang Dynasty, and carries three centuries of experience on her shoulders. She knows the human strengths that lead to the rise of nations, and the human weaknesses that have led to their collapse. Take her wisdom to heart."

Kaiya shuffled in place. "I understand. But my retainers are my responsibility. I cannot just sit here and do nothing."

He held her gaze. "Think carefully about what you can do in your condition. I can tell you firsthand that Vyara City is not as safe as you think. You should know this already. But if you believe it is that important to go back, I will send you."

Kaiya nodded. Still, she had to do *something*. "It is. Please send me back."

He shrugged. "Very well, if you are so insistent." He chanted several whimsical words of elven magic.

Kaiya's eyelids grew heavy, her head faint. Just before she slipped out of consciousness, he reached over with elegant grace and caught her.

Ayana frowned at Thielas Starsong for a dozen reasons, past and present.

He was too busy admiring Princess Kaiya to notice her scowl.

"Always a fool for a pretty human face," she said.

Thielas lowered the foolish girl to the ground at Ayana's feet. He then looked up with the grin that had disarmed so many in the past. Herself included. "The ephemeral nature of their beauty makes it all the more precious. I don't think you would understand."

She rolled her eyes. "I don't. Are you chasing that redheaded princess now? The fetish for headstrong human girls runs in your family."

His lips twitched. "You almost broke me of it, so long ago."

Ayana paused to think back on her middle years, when the strapping elf prince had reminded her of what it meant to be *young* again. A smile quirked on her lips, unbidden.

He locked his gaze on her, then looked away. "I have not been to Vyara City in thirty-two years. I don't have fond memories. It's the site of one of my two greatest mistakes in life. However, I will send you back to the Crystal Citadel. It is the safest place I know there."

Ayana chuffed. The Crystal Citadel might be safe, but returning this headstrong princess to the city was just enabling her impulses. At this rate, she'd never learn from her mistakes.

He studied the silly girl. "She is strong-willed and has a lot to learn. She may or may not remember much of this brief interlude, though I hope your lecture sticks."

Grinning, he sprinkled flower petals in a circle around her and the princess. His eyes flashed up to meet hers. "It was good to see you again, Ayana. Don't you find it interesting how often our paths have crossed in the last year, after a hundred years of separation?"

She shrugged. "Our involvement in human affairs has led to these unexpected reunions."

"We elves are too few. We must guide the humans so *they* can prevent the Tivari from reconquering Tivaralan."

"Nonetheless, I never expected nor hoped to see you again."

Thielas laughed. "You would hold the indiscretions of my youth against me?"

"No, only that I would hope you always remember me when I was as beautiful as she." Ayana lifted her chin toward Kaiya's sleeping form.

He laughed again. "You have always been older than I, and although you were wildly stunning then, I was mostly attracted to your wisdom." He winked suggestively at her. "I have to admit, that has seemed to grow only more in the last century."

Despite her many years and resistance to such charms, Ayana still felt the flush in her cheeks. She stared down at the ground, and then lifted her eyes to speak.

Thielas began a long chant in the flowery words of elf-magic. She knew not to interrupt his song, lest they reappear before the Altivorc King's throne or a Teleri breeding site. She fell silent, waiting patiently for the scenery to shift around her.

As he inflected the last syllable, her body began to slip through the ethers. The colors coalesced and reformed into an enormous chamber of marble with light blue streaks of istrium. A magnificent dome above swirled with color, like the Iridescent Moon itself. Princess Kaiya slept peacefully at her feet.

Gasps of surprise echoed through the Crystal Citadel's audience chamber, followed by the rasping of a dozen swords sliding from their sheaths.

CHAPTER 40:
Awakenings

Birds chirped in harmony with the low hum around her. Cool and light, the soft touch of fine linen sheets brushed across Kaiya's bare skin. The refreshing sensation stood in stark contrast to the humid heat hanging in her lungs. Muffled sounds of a distant conversation coaxed her into consciousness.

Though feeling fully revitalized, she eased her eyes open tentatively. They focused on large windows from which sunlight streamed in at a low angle, casting long shadows across the white, undecorated room.

Kaiya bolted up into a sitting position on a soft, unfamiliar bed. Her chest tightened. There was something eerily familiar about waking up in a strange place. Her brow scrunched up as she tried to recall her last memory… the ambush.

Guilt flooded over her. She looked frantically around the white-walled room. First locating the heavy wood door, her gaze then settled on a red *sari* draped over a simple wooden chair. The only other furnishings were the bed and a basin of water.

The breeze on her skin… She was naked, save for underpants and some musky-smelling gauze wrapped around her forearms. Kaiya pulled the sheets up to cover herself. Had she been captured? An image of Prince Dhananad's foul hands on her sent a cold shiver up her spine. Quickly banishing the notion, she eased herself from the bed, pulling the sheets along to stay covered in the event some rogue barged in through the door.

The window would give an idea of where she was, but it would also give anyone walking by a good look at her bare skin. She went to investigate the red fabric on the chair. Unsure of how to drape the *sari* correctly, she put on the *choli* shirt and *langa* petticoat first. Its open back, low neckline, and bare midriff was too immodest, resembling undergarments, but it was certainly better than exploring a strange place in nothing more than bandages.

Now dressed, if it could be considered dressed, she walked over to the window. She gasped. The red sun perched not far above the Shallowsea, which in turn merged into a bustling waterfront far down in the distance. The canals and streets fanned outward in a tangled web, cutting through flat white buildings cast in the setting sun's red sheen. Without a doubt, this was Vyara City. Given the vantage point, higher than anything else, this was the Paladins' Crystal Citadel.

Had the Paladins rescued them from the ambush? And if so, why had she awakened almost completely undressed?

Kaiya padded across the room to the heavy door and pulled it open a crack. The muffled sounds transformed into conversations in the Ayuri language; talk about the Cathayi wounded.

Her men, injured because she insisted on a trip that could have waited.

Without hesitation, she strode out of the room to find herself in a hallway, dimly lit through several windows by late afternoon sun. A dozen feet down the hall, a Paladin and an older Ayuri man stopped their discussion and turned to face her.

The young maid, Meixi, was sitting quietly on a wooden chair just outside the door. Her eyes widened. The girl dropped to the floor and into a bow. "*Dian-xia*, I'm so glad you are awake. I was so worried." The girl stood and adjusted Kaiya's *sari*. "I'm so sorry about your outer robe; it was lost in the attack. Your inner gown was filthy, stained with grass and dirt. I sent it back to the embassy."

Grass and dirt? Kaiya cocked her head.

The Paladin approached and pressed his palms together. "Good afternoon, Your Highness. I am glad to see you awake."

Forgetting her manners, Kaiya blurted, "How did I get here? Where are my men? How long have I been asleep?"

"About seven hours ago, your procession was ambushed. By all accounts, the elf woman Ayana Strongbow sequestered you away through time and space, reappearing almost three hours ago in the audience chamber of the Crystal Citadel. You have been asleep this whole time, unresponsive to the healer's attempts to wake you."

Time *and* space? How was that even possible?

The older man added, "We received an anonymous tip about the attack. The Paladin patrols came to your rescue, but we were too late to save all of your guards. Several were killed, and most of the rest received wounds of varying severity. Because of your status as a foreign dignitary, the Paladins took the extraordinary measure of bringing the wounded here for treatment and protection."

Several killed! Kaiya bit her lip, feeling a pang in her chest. She pressed her hands together. "Thank you for your kind consideration. Please take me to them."

"I will take you to the half-elf." The Paladin gestured for her to follow.

As they walked down the hall, she asked, "Who was behind this?" As though it wasn't evident.

"We captured several of the assailants who were put to sleep by the elf's magic. They claimed to be sellswords, but we are investigating their backgrounds."

Kaiya had a good idea where that trail would lead. "Two of the attackers were Maduran Scorpions."

The Paladin shrugged. "Perhaps, but witnesses did not see the telltale mask and sting. There are also some disaffected former Paladins who work as independent mercenaries."

Kaiya fell silent, mulling over his words as they came to another door. An Ayuri woman emerged from the room just as they were about to pass, pulling up short before she ran into them.

The woman's voice sounded too cheerful. "Your Highness! I am glad you are finally awake! Let me look at your arms." Without waiting for permission, she took Kaiya's wrist and unwrapped the bandages, revealing yellowing splotches. She rewrapped the gauze. "Good, good. You are healing quickly. You had no major wounds that I saw, just bruises on your arms that the liniment is taking out nicely. Are they painful at all?"

For the first time, Kaiya considered her own physical condition. Her arms did hurt a little, but the pain was a minor compared to her guards' injuries. She shook her head.

"Good. Your other maid and the elf are inside." The woman gestured toward the door she'd just exited. "Won't you come in?"

Kaiya nodded.

The woman guided Kaiya into another plain room. Two beds with simple wooden frames flanked a single window. Beneath the sheets of one, Ayana slept peacefully; on the other, Jie laid with her bare shoulders and arms above the sheets. Like Kaiya, her arms were wrapped in gauze, though black splotches peeked out through the white mesh.

Jie bolted up, holding the sheets up around her. Her face contorted into a wince. Kaiya's fault. "*Dian-xia*, I heard that you had been brought here, but they wouldn't let me visit you. Or even tell me where you were. Where did you go? Ayana didn't say anything, she just came in and tumbled into the bed."

Kaiya ignored the question. "I'm so glad to see you are alive. Are you hurt badly?"

Jie shrugged, evincing another grimace. "It's just a few scratches. I've been hurt worse."

The Paladin healer's lips squeezed tight. Her tone was stern. "You were cut across the side. Had the angle been more oblique, it might have sliced between your ribs and punctured your lung. You are either very lucky or very skilled."

Jie pouted, mouthing *skilled* in the Cathayi tongue.

Kaiya suppressed a smile. "How long will she take to recover?"

"We have stitched the wounds and wrapped them in a liniment that will speed the healing process. If your handmaiden is strong, she should be mobile in a few days and fully recuperated in two weeks. In the meantime, she should remain on bed rest."

Not likely. Kaiya bowed her head. "Thank you. How about my guards?"

"They are in other rooms, and I am not allowed to enter," the woman said. "But from what I have heard, their injuries vary in severity."

"I would like to visit them. Would you please let them know to make themselves presentable?"

The woman hesitated before nodding and leaving the room.

Kaiya turned back to Jie. Before she could even ask her question, Jie answered it: "All of the imperial guards have concussions. Chen Xin also has a broken nose, Xu Zhan a dislocated shoulder, and Zhao Yue a sprained knee. Of the twenty-four embassy guards, six were killed and another thirteen wounded, three seriously."

Her fault. Remorse gripped her chest. Kaiya's voice cracked. "The Paladins don't think the Madurans are involved."

Jie shook her head. "It was undoubtedly the Madurans. The woman I fought was the Golden Scorpion who tried to poison you. I suggest you call off your meeting with Prince Dhananad."

"If my audience with the Paladin elders tomorrow goes well, then we will be in a very strong negotiating position with Madura. We will take extra care. I will even ask for a Paladin escort if need be."

Jie glared at her for a second of insolence before turning to Meixi. "Can you find me some clothes? I must accompany the princess to the men's room."

The girl flushed. "The Paladin healer explicitly ordered us not to bring you any clothes, until your wound was better healed."

Kaiya covered a laugh. Maybe, just maybe, the embarrassment of nakedness would keep Jie from trying to return to duties. "I am going to visit the others. If I see a healer, I will persuade them to bring you clothes." The lie would keep the half-elf in one place, at least for a while. Kaiya spun and glided out of the room, Meixi on her heels.

Outside, the male healer waited. With him stood a young Paladin not much older than herself, and a dignified-looking older man, with a darker complexion and graying black hair and beard. His white *kurta* had gold embroidery not just on the neck, but along its borders as well.

The older man put his hands together. "Greetings, Your Highness. I am Devak of the Paladin Council of Elders. I was told you were awake now, and came immediately to inform you that the council wants you stay in the citadel under our protection until we learn more about who attacked you and why."

Kaiya pressed her palms together. "Thank you for your consideration, but I do not wish to intrude."

He shook his head. "It is our honor to host you here. The Oracle of Ayudra sent us a message that your personal safety is of the utmost priority. There is no safer place on Tivaralan than the citadel."

They had said the same of Ayudra. She stifled a snort. "That, I am sure. However, I can certainly tell you the identity of the likely culprit, as well as their motivations. In the meantime, I would rather return to my country's own embassy to prepare for our audience with you tomorrow morning."

The elder shook his head again. "Although I cannot force you to remain here, I can only hope that you see the wisdom in staying."

His voice rippled into the space between them. Meixi and healer shuffled on their feet.

Wisdom. The word weighed on her like a dwarf anvil. "Very well. However, I must send my maid back to our compound to retrieve some things that I will need for the night. I request that you assign some of your courageous Paladins to escort her."

"Of course. It is our honor to have you with us," the elder said. He motioned toward the young man with him. "This is Sameer Vikram, who has just recently finished his apprenticeship and awaits his final tests. He will take you to your quarters in the guest wing tonight, and also assist you with anything you might need during your stay." With that, he spun on his heel and strode down the corridor, disappearing around the corner.

Kaiya turned to Sameer. Handsome, with a light-brown skin tone, he had perfectly coifed long black hair and a short pointed beard. His eager expression would have put a puppy to shame.

He pressed his palms and bowed his head in salute. His voice purred, "I am at your command."

Kaiya smiled graciously and clasped her hands together. "Thank you." She then turned to the Paladin healer. "Before we go, I would like to visit my guards who are in your care."

The Paladin healer motioned for her to follow and guided her down the corridor to another room.

It was significantly larger than the two other rooms Kaiya had been in, but just as plain. Two dozen cots were laid out, almost all occupied by her guards, some quietly talking among themselves. So many wounded! All her responsibility. The guilt made her head spin more than the musky smell of herbal medicines that permeated the air.

News of her arrival circulated through the room. Some soldiers jumped to their feet before sinking to one knee. Others crawled off their cots and stumbled to their knees. All were in extreme stages of undress. Poor Meixi flushed bright red and excused herself from the room. Kaiya averted her gaze.

Chen Xin, his nose covered with plaster, spoke sonorously. "Men, cover yourselves."

Her own face must have glowed as bright red as Meixi's. Still, the men had paid for her foolhardiness with their lives and health. She raised her hand. "As you were."

Chen Xin bowed. "I was afraid you were… We are overjoyed to see you are safe."

"I am glad to see you are, too." She glided over to one of the men, who struggled through his injuries to rise. Hesitating for a split-second to touch an almost-naked man, she nevertheless placed a gentle hand on his shoulder. "At ease."

"We failed to protect you," Chen Xin said. "If it is your command, we—"

Kaiya silenced him with a shake of her head. "My dedicated guards, I want to express my gratitude for your hard work… and also to apologize. My own recklessness brought about this disaster. I promise not to risk your lives so callously in the future."

She bowed low at the waist. It was unheard of for a member of the Imperial Family to admit fault or apologize to guards, let alone bow so low.

The men returned to their knees.

Xu Zhan looked up. "It is our honor to serve you."

"It is our honor," all of the men repeated in unison.

Kaiya wiped away a tear. "We will stay here overnight, under the protection of the Paladins. Rest well and await my orders."

She turned to leave, and Chen Xin and Ma Jun quickly rose to follow her. She raised her hand again, giving them a silent order to remain. "As the Paladins told me, there is no safer place on Tivaralan. Focus your energies on recovering."

Kaiya glided out of the door. Hiding in the threshold where no one could see her, she hung her head. All the injuries. And the dead. Hot tears slid down her cheeks.

Meixi cleared her throat.

Kaiya wiped her eyes and straightened. As unfair as it was to those who suffered for her, she couldn't afford to dwell on it right now. With her audience before the Council of Elders, tomorrow would be an important day, one which could affect the lives of millions. She would need as much rest as the men injured in her defense.

CHAPTER 41:
Victory without Fighting

K aiya woke to light drizzle pattering on the outer walls. The refreshing scent of spring rain wandered in through the latticed window, mingling with the aroma of fried twisted bread, rice porridge, and hot soy milk—all brought by young Meixi from the Cathayi embassy.

With a few hours before her appointed audience with the Paladins' Council of Elders, Kaiya ate at a leisurely pace, mentally practicing her speech and formulating answers to the questions the elders were bound to ask. If she succeeded in winning the endorsement of the Paladins, it would go a long way to deterring the Maduran threat to her homeland.

She donned the multiple layers of a Cathayi court robes with Meixi's assistance, and wrapped the broad sash around her waist. The maid arranged her hair with fine jade pins, while Kaiya preened in a full-length mirror so that everything down to the last eyelash was perfect.

When at last a page summoned her to the main audience chamber, she was fully prepared. Rumiya's fake lotus jewel caught her attention, beckoning from its place on a table. Its audible hum, louder than ever, assailed her mental armor. One hand on Zheng Ming's kerchief, the other on Tian's pebble, she afforded it a last glance and left it there.

Ambassador Ling joined her outside the door. She glided through the Crystal Citadel's white marble hallways, admiring the breathtaking beauty of the carved columns, painted ceilings, and elaborate scrollwork.

At last, she came to a pair of doors made of the same light-blue metal as the Paladin's *naga* and Golden Scorpion's mask. With a deep breath, she composed her expression into one of serenity, to hide her nervousness.

A collective gasp from the numerous Paladin masters and Ayuri lords greeted her on the other side. Several craned their necks to get a better view.

Yet if they were admiring her beauty, Kaiya couldn't help but marvel at the grand chamber. White marble floors, streaked with pale blue imperfections, stretched the length and width of the enormous room, with smooth columns vaulting toward the ceiling. A dome soared high above, its colors swirling like a soap bubble. How small she was compared to this.

The room emitted a faint, pulsing hum. Could anyone else hear it? Kaiya's heartbeat echoed its call, sending a cool sensation through her body.

She made her way through the crowd to the front of the room. Thirteen chairs faced her, arranged in a semi-circle on a dais. All but the center were occupied by middle-aged and older men. Most had long, narrow beards and fine mustaches, and each wore a white *kurta* with a gold embroidered collar and border, denoting their status as an elder.

She nodded toward Elder Devak, whom she'd met the day before.

A page announced her in a clear, resonant voice, carried by the perfect acoustics of the hall. "Princess Kaiya Wang, representing the Empire of Cathay."

Kaiya brought her hands together and bowed her head in typical Ayuri fashion. The elders did so in return.

One with a split beard spoke. "Greetings, Princess Kaiya. We are honored to have you as our guest today. I believe it is the first time that a representative of your nation has spoken before the council."

The resonance of the hall magnified her voice. "Thank you for your generous hospitality, and for granting me this opportunity to speak."

Elder Split-Beard favored her with a curious expression. "The Oracle of Ayudra sent word that you would seek audience with us and recommended that we listen. Yet, as is his wont, he did not explain your business. Your activity in the city hints at a request. Please, speak."

She swept a demure smile over the assembled elders, satisfied they all seemed sufficiently captivated and speechless. When she began her long-rehearsed speech, each syllable echoed back to her as music. "I come to you on behalf of my father, Emperor Wang Zhishen, who has ruled Cathay for three decades of unprecedented tranquility, stability, and prosperity. We are a peace-loving nation, one which respects its neighbors and builds lasting friendships through mutually-beneficial trade."

Several of the elders nodded, while whispers tittered through the chamber.

Kaiya shook her head in choreographed sadness. "Yet there are those who seek to subjugate our people and plunder our wealth. They threaten us unprovoked, rattling their sabers at our borders. While our Great Wall and guns will surely repel an invasion, my ancestor once said, *vanquishing an enemy without fighting is the pinnacle of skill.* We do not wish to needlessly draw blood, even from those who seek to spill ours."

She peeked up through her lashes. Was the preamble working? Cathay had committed unconscionable actions in the name of free trade and the Mandate of Heaven. Surely they knew that. One elder stroked his beard; another's brow crinkled.

She kept her voice level, letting the acoustics magnify it. "It is for this reason that I have come to Vyara City: to negotiate directly with one of the aggressors, Madura. Yet our overtures for peace were met first with an attempt to poison me, and later an ambush on my entourage."

Murmurs passed among the assembled guests, many bobbing their heads. Madura's historical aggression toward its neighbors, though held in check since its occupation of Ankira, had earned it enough mistrust.

The youngest elder raised an eyebrow. "Those are serious charges. Do you have proof?"

Kaiya smiled defensively. Since when did Paladins defend Madura? This young one might prove troublesome. "Only what my guards have told me about both attacks. My people have no motive to implicate the agents of Madura."

"Nonetheless," the youngest elder said, "it is a serious accusation to make without evidence. But please, continue."

She lifted her chin. "With these incidents, and also its history of aggression and betrayal, we realized that Madura did not negotiate in good faith. Therefore, I have spent the past week meeting with those who might put pressure on them to curb their hostilities."

Kaiya paused momentarily, brushing her gaze across the room to gauge the elders' reactions as her words sank in. Behind her, murmurs of approval rippled among the dignitaries.

She turned and gestured toward the representatives as she named their countries. "The maharajas of the Ayuri nations of Vadara, Bijura, Dabura, Sanura, and Ebura have all provisionally committed to stand with Cathay. We have agreed that an attack on one is tantamount to an attack on all, and we will use all means—economic and diplomatic, military if necessary—to contain the Maduran threat. I humbly ask the Paladins, as guardians of the Ayuri Confederation, to endorse our mutual defense agreements." She bowed her head and held it, clasping her hands together.

The youngest elder cleared his throat. "Princess Kaiya, although I see the wisdom in your actions, I wonder if you have considered this: Madura has allied itself not only with the Teleri Empire far away in the North, but more importantly the Levastyan Empire which stands at our doorstep." He spread his arms wide. "This level of brinkmanship could very well throw Tivaralan into a chaos unheard of since the Century of War between the Ayuri and Arkothi Empires. Is that something peace-loving Cathay really wants to risk?"

Such sarcasm. Kaiya shook her head. "Of course not, Elder. The rulers of Madura may be brash, but they are not foolish. They certainly know that the Cathayi guns, Ayuri swords, and Paladin righteousness will lead to their expedient defeat, before their friends in Tilesite and Levastyas can come to their aid."

He laughed. "Paladins are protectors, never aggressors. Our mission is to maintain the peace, not to escalate war."

If the elder's logic became any more circular, she would rip her hair out. Nonetheless, Kaiya raised a hand to her mouth to cover her own laugh. "Forgive my idealism, but I believe that it is merely the perceived strength in unity that will deter Madura and hold its aggression in check. Is that not a means of keeping the peace?"

He smirked. "That may be so. I certainly admire your idealism. Where was your righteous enthusiasm when Ankira fell to the Madurans?"

Elder Devak raised his hand. "Peace, Elder Mehal. I can appreciate your courage to express yourself, especially for someone so new to the council. However, the princess speaks wisely: it is our cloak of protection over the Ayuri Confederation that has prevented a Maduran invasion of Vadara thus far. Furthermore, it is our responsibility to keep careful watch over the Golden Scorpions, who use the powers of the *bahaduur* for their own personal gain instead of for the betterment of all."

Elder Mehal pursed his lips and leaned back in his chair.

A balding elder lifted his chin toward her. "Although I admire your wisdom and poise, especially for someone so young, I must admit my disappointment." He nodded toward the empty chair. "The Oracle suggested that you will play a very important role in the fate of this world."

An important role in the world? The Oracle had never said such a thing. Kaiya opened her mouth, but no words came out.

"And yet," Balding Elder continued, "you do not look beyond the borders of your own nation, to see that our world is in a state of flux. We teeter on the precipice of a new Age of Empires. It threatens to set us back three centuries, into an era of perpetual war." He squared his jaw at her. "You come asking for protection, yet offer nothing in return."

Kaiya gazed at the floor to emphasize her remorse, before looking up and meeting his eyes. "Cathay honors its agreements. If it is within our power—"

Elder Devak silenced her with a raise of his hand and smiled at his balding colleague. "It may be. We will retire to deliberate your request. In the meantime, I implore you to consider what Elder Kairav has said."

The elders rose and withdrew to their meeting chambers atop the citadel. When the last one left the audience chamber, applause broke out. Several lords approached to convey their respects.

Kaiya smiled so many times, her cheeks hurt. Through it all, she dwelled on Elder Kairav's words—what role did she have to play, beyond the protection of her own country? What would they ask in return? She glanced back at Ambassador Ling, her eyes tacitly begging him to help her withdraw from the mob of admirers.

She didn't have to endure the adoration long. In short measure, the elders returned. The room fell into silence. Kaiya examined each of their faces as they took their seats, yet they hid their intentions better than a Golden Scorpion mask. She placed her hands together again to salute them.

Balding Elder Kairav spoke. "Princess Kaiya. After an unprecedentedly brief deliberation, we have decided to provisionally endorse the agreements between Cathay and the Ayuri Confederation. At this time, our endorsement does not necessarily mean that Paladins would be deployed for punitive action. It is our hope that the united front amongst our nations will be enough to deter Maduran aggression."

Such a lack of commitment! Kaiya bowed her head. Hopefully, it would hide her disappointment. "I appreciate your consideration. Is there something I might offer to demonstrate Cathay's sincerity toward this pact?"

"There is." Elder Devak gestured toward the back of the hall. Kaiya turned to follow his motion. The room rose into nervous chatter as the gathered dignitaries parted down the middle, starting from the rear, as if a giant dagger sheared the audience in half.

A slow vibrating wave pushed forward, sluggish but powerful, clashing with the low pulsating of the room. Fighting her curiosity and wanting to maintain a dignified countenance, Kaiya forced herself not to stand on her tiptoes to get a better view over all of the heads.

The last row of men split, revealing a tall figure in armor of red scales from shoulder to toe. A matching horned helm revealed only luminous light blue eyes. A black cloak hung from his shoulders.

Never making eye contact, the man strode to her side. He pulled off his helmet, tucked it into the crook of his elbow, and lifted his chin toward the Paladin elders.

She tried to get a good look at his side profile from the corner of her eye; but when he turned toward her, she felt compelled to return his gaze.

Prince Hardeep.

Rumiya.

CHAPTER 42:

Ultimatums

Anger. Sadness. Self-doubt. Kaiya could hardly sort out her conflicting emotions over the rapid pounding of her heart in her ears. The sluggish pulsing that Hardeep—no, Rumiya—emitted clashed with the low hum of the chamber, adding to her internal chaos.

"Princess Kaiya," Elder Devak said, interrupting the chastising voice in her mind. "I introduce the Last Dragon's Envoy, Girish, who wishes to convey his master's message to you."

Girish? How many names did this deceiver go by? Kaiya clenched and unclenched her fists.

The Last Dragon's Envoy flashed a feral grin. His canine teeth extended past his incisors and ended in sharp tips. To think she'd once been hopelessly in love with whomever this man was.

When they had first met, Prince Hardeep's voice had sounded like honey spilling from his mouth; Girish's tone slithered like a snake's tongue wrapping itself around her. "Princess Kaiya, I *knew* this day would come."

Discarding all sense of poise, Kaiya wrapped her arms around herself, as if that could provide armor against an evil wizard. She had to know how deep his ruse went, even if it would make her look silly in front of the elders and dignitaries. "Prince Hardeep, for two years of separation, I *hoped* this day would come. My hope was kept alive by your letters."

The elders leaned in and whispered among each other; the audience around them chattered in a low voice.

"Letters?" Girish's conceited smile slipped for a split second.

So it was true, the suspicions raised after her meetings with Ankirans. The ones she didn't want to believe. Rumiya had nothing to do with the letters. In that, at least, he was innocent. Her chest tightened and she placed a hand over it.

So if not Hardeep—Rumiya—then who?

Peng, who kept up the charade. How easily he'd duped her! She didn't even want to fathom why. It was too painful. Too fresh. Almost as fresh as the pain of Zheng Ming abandoning her. She was a fool, but at least she was now a fool with eyes opened wide.

"Never mind," she said. "You expected me. How did you know I would be here?"

The lotus jewel materialized in his hand. "This token I gave you, a flower carved from Avarax's scale It sparked the magic within you. It even made you beautiful. Everything you have done over the last two years has been put in motion by *me*, culminating now with our inevitable reunion."

Was it true? Did she owe her power, her very beauty, to a piece of an evil dragon? It'd formed the soundboard of the Dragon Scale Lute, which they'd left beneath the rubble of Wailian Castle. A shard, though, had gone missing.

Around her, the dignitaries echoed her thoughts in hushed whispers.

Her voice choked. "Why?"

"I knew you were the one," Girish said. "When I first heard your voice, and then when you played the Dragon Scale Lute."

Kaiya forced the indignation in her tone. "My voice?"

Girish's head swayed as he nodded. "It had a unique quality, though raw, in need of tempering. And you had a potential teacher in the elf Lord Xu."

So Girish had manipulated her, and possibly tricked Lord Xu, as well. Doctor Wu, the Oracle, and Master Sabal had all deepened her understanding of sound manipulation. Perhaps he'd caused all of it to fall in place. "What do you need with my voice?"

"My master wants you to sing the song promised to him by Aralas."

What? Kaiya brow furrowed. "Yanyan's song? Does Avarax *want* to sleep for another thousand years?"

Girish stared at her, and then laughed. "Silly girl. The song Aralas promised and the one Yanyan sang were different."

Kaiya's eyebrow rose, unbidden. This little detail never appeared in the histories. "Where am I supposed to find this song? Aralas returned to the Heavens a millennium ago."

"I have it." The wizard patted his chest. "But only your voice can sing it correctly."

"What does the song do?"

"I don't know." Girish shrugged. "Dragons are fickle beings."

Didn't know? Or wouldn't tell? After all the deceptions, his words stank as a lie. "Why should I comply?"

Girish turned to the audience. "As I told the council yesterday, if Princess Kaiya does not sing for him, Avarax will burn the city of Palimur to the ground. He will melt the stones to magma and immolate the hundred thousand souls living there."

Murmurs erupted throughout the hall. The elders sat in silence, regarding her with knowing eyes. They knew about this ultimatum. They needed a political agreement as much as Cathay, yet acted as if they were granting her a favor.

They'd tricked her, too. Still, Kaiya shuddered. All those people would perish in dragonfire, the horror recounted in ten-thousand-year-old elven legends of the Fall of Istriya. Dragonfire hadn't been seen since. After nearly wiping elves from the face of Tivara, the orcs had betrayed their dragon allies in the Dragonpurge. Only Avarax survived, his immense power such that the orcs, even armed with the magic of their gods, had no choice but to come to an uneasy truce with him.

Until Yanyan sang him to sleep with a Dragon Song. There was no record of Avarax using his fiery breath since awakening thirty-two years before.

Kaiya hung her head. "Where is this song?"

"Actually, I had a different song in mind." Girish tugged off his scaled gauntlets, revealing leathery hands. He reached into his cloak and withdrew a few sheets of paper, all ripped at one of the long edges. "This is the music Yanyan sang at the start of the War of Ancient Gods."

That song. Kaiya's heart thudded. A betting princess would wager the tears lined up with the lost pages of Lord Xu's book. But why did Girish want Avarax to sleep? Perhaps so that he, himself, could rule over the Dragonlands?

There was more to the story. "Won't Avarax recognize it?"

"The differences are subtle. When Yanyan sang, Avarax did not notice the treachery until it was too late." He passed the sheets to her.

She received them in two hands and flipped through them. There were four pages in all, detailing a song the likes of which she'd never seen before. Rapid changes in pitches. Vocalized chords. An extreme range in keys. It might very well be beyond her ability to sing, let alone invoke the magic involved.

"Try it." Girish's blue eyes searched hers, mesmerizing in the way they danced—like she'd danced for Prince Dhananad, like his irises danced when they'd met two years ago.

Heavens. Just like then, his eyes compelled her. Against her will, Kaiya sang the first three notes. The blue streaks in the hall's marble surfaces sparkled faintly. The Paladins' *nagas* shed a dim light. Even Girish's eyes pulsated, the slow resonance he emitted quickening. His grin widened. Power, like a jolt of lightning, energized her arms and legs.

Something wasn't right. She feigned exhaustion, staggering back a step and tumbling to the floor. He'd seen her faint from channeling a Dragon Song thrice before; would he believe it this time? In the corner of her eyes, Girish's smile faded.

She cleared her throat and coughed. "I need time to practice this. Maybe weeks, if I am to have a chance of singing it correctly."

Girish counted on his fingers. "You have four days before Avarax casts his shadow over Palimur."

She shook her head, pretending shame. "Even if I can learn it, I am not Yanyan. I was not taught by the elf angel Aralas. Even those three notes drained me."

He leaned over her, so close that his hot breath washed over her. "I don't believe you."

His proximity felt like centipede feet crawling over her skin. Yet perhaps there was an opportunity here. A chance to see her future, with the Oracle's help. "If Avarax wants to hear me sing, I want the Lotus Crystal from the Ayudra Pyramid, which he stole."

Murmurs roiled throughout the hall again.

"Palimur City is in no position for you to make demands." Girish roared with laughter.

Kaiya could claim a foreign city of a hundred thousand people didn't matter to her, but could she bluff a wizard nearly two-hundred years her senior?

Those blue eyes would see right through her.

Jie had crept into the audience hall, surprised at how easily it'd been to escape confinement in the medical ward and sneak through the corridors of the Crystal Citadel undetected. Perhaps the pure white robe she wore blended in with all the goodness around here. Or maybe it was because most of the Paladins were now crowding the audience hall.

Beyond the wall of their tall backs, Girish's power had screamed louder than the energy of all the Paladins combined, and even greater than the energy of the citadel itself. His voice raged like a wildfire as his patience with her princess waned.

For Princess Kaiya's part, she had dared to face down an evil wizard and make ultimatums. *Now* who was insolent?

Jie winced at the pain in her ribs as she rose to her tiptoes, trying to see over all of the Paladins and Ayuri lords. Meeting with little success, she slipped through the cracks in the wall of human bodies in hopes of getting a better view.

The princess' tired but melodic voice called from the front of the hall. The fatigue in her voice sounded off, almost contrived. "You want me to sing to him, you convince him to bring the Lotus Crystal."

Jie made it to the front just as Girish gripped the princess' face with a hand and chanted three foul-sounding syllables.

Reaching for her throwing weapons, Jie found none. She liberated a curved dagger from a bystander's belt while the Paladins surged forward with *nagas* in hand. The Paladin elders jumped to their feet, some leaping toward the evil wizard.

The princess tore at his arm; but then her body wilted, arms drooping to her sides. Girish wrapped his arm around her and guided her limp form to the floor.

As the Paladins encircled Girish, Jie edged behind them toward his back for an easier killing blow.

Girish's cackle sounded like flint striking steel. He stomped the floor. Jagged blue light flashed up from the imperfections in the marble to form a wall of energy around him.

A cold wave shoved Jie back. Around her, Paladins staggered away.

Looking around the room, Girish lowered his hand. The blue light dropped back into the stones. "At ease. I was merely confirming the princess' energy for myself. She did not tell the entire truth. No, she is not powerful enough on her own to sing my master to sleep, but she has more vitality than she claims."

With visible strain, the princess eased herself up on an elbow. Jie padded to her side and knelt.

Girish wagged a finger at them. "Feed her well, make sure she rests and cultivates her energy. And practices the song. The resonance of the world is strong at the Temple of Shakti in Palimur. She had better be there in four days, when the Sawarasati's Eye is open."

He must be referring to the Blue Moon, which would be at its largest for the year. He spun on his heel and stalked back toward the doors. People made way, flashing ward-evil *mudra* hand symbols.

Jie gave his back one last glance. The unarmored spot at the base of his neck made an inviting target, and indeed, there was an oval scar there from a previous wound, but… Jie turned back to the princess, whose eyes fluttered and closed.

CHAPTER 43:
ENEMY OF MY ENEMY'S ENEMY

Proud Prince Dhananad trudged into the Teleri embassy's audience chamber, his minions keeping a safe distance behind lest they become targets of his temper. Enraged at the audacity of Ambassador Piros' curt summons, he had considered not coming at all. When he became maharaja, he would cut off relations with the Teleri on the day of his coronation. In the meantime, he would suffer through this indignity.

Dhananad skidded to a stop in the middle of the room. He raised his hand to shield his eyes from the sun streaming in through the west windows. If only his vision hadn't adjusted. The patronizing grins from the ambassador, the Levastyan Lord Benham, and the Altivorc King greeted him from their cushions. Even the motley collection of guards did not bother to hide their smiles.

Without bothering to rise from his seat, Ambassador Piros beckoned him over, as if he were calling a servant. Or a dog. "Come, Prince Dhananad."

Damn Bovyans. Dhananad spat on the floor in front of the Teleri ambassador. "What was so important that you interrupted my dinner?"

"We received news from our couriers." Piros frowned. "The Paladins have endorsed a pact of mutual protection between Cathay and the Ayuri Confederation."

Shifting into a relaxed stance, he modulated his tone to amused boredom. "Yes, yes, my own agent was there at the time. Surely you understand that I know everything that goes on in the Paladin Council."

Benhan glowered at him from his cushion. "And you are not disturbed?"

"Why should I be?" Dhananad cocked his head. "Madura never had any plans to attack Cathay. *That* was the Teleri Empire's goal once your expansion reached their Great East Gate. As per our many redundant agreements, Madura has maintained a semblance of a threat, to keep Cathay's attention on our shared border."

Piros jabbed an impudent finger at him. "Your clumsiness has set us back. First, the futile attempt to kidnap the princess—"

"It was not futile!" If the Bovyan wanted to engage in a shouting contest, Dhananad could play. "We timed it perfectly, so the Paladin patrols would be nowhere nearby. It was just bad luck."

"And bad planning, and even worse execution." The Altivorc King taunted him with a laugh. "After that fiasco, Cathay won't see your vaunted Golden Scorpions as a credible threat."

Behind him, the two Scorpions' anger was palpable, even if hidden behind their expressionless masks. Dhananad shuffled in his place, waving an annoyed hand at the King. "It might have worked if your stupid altivorcs hadn't totally ignored the princess."

"It was poor communication." The Altivorc King returned his glare, the deadly glint in his eyes making Dhananad second-guess his insult. "A competent leader would ensure his allies understood the plan."

Dhananad shrugged. "What is done is done. A good leader adapts."

The Altivorc King grinned, revealing his fangs. "I agree. With that in mind, you will delay your meeting with Princess Kaiya tomorrow. Wait until after she sings to the Last Dragon."

"Bah." Dhananad spat in the altivorc's direction. "You are not my king, you are not even Madura's ally. I will dine with whom I please, when I please."

The Altivorc King leaned deeper back into his cushion. "Then you are a fool, walking into a diplomatic trap. Your father will disown you, and your stupidity will go down in the annals of Tivara."

Heat rushed to Dhananad's cheeks, and he could only imagine what shade he must be. This insult would not go unavenged. With a jerking motion of his hand, he ordered his Golden Scorpions to arms. "Kill the Altivorc King's guards, and then disfigure his pretty face."

The Ambassador and Lord Benham's jaws dropped. Their shock would have pleased him had the Altivorc King not worn an amused look—the kind that screamed at Dhananad's instincts of self-preservation.

The pair of Golden Scorpions jumped into action, their stings flashing as they closed the gap and cut through three of the altivorc guards before their weapons even left their sheaths. The two survivors had managed to draw their own giant broadswords, but fell before taking a swing as the Scorpions slashed through them. Black blood sprayed on the floor and walls.

They closed toward their final target, but the Altivorc King did not seem the least bit concerned. He leisurely shifted on his cushions as he withdrew a grey metal wand, pointed it at one of the Scorpions, and spoke a guttural syllable.

A bolt of blue lighting sizzled from the tip, hurling the man back a dozen feet through the air with a scream of agony.

In that split second, the other Scorpion reached him and stabbed. Dhananad barely registered the motion, but the final result stood out clearly. The Scorpion screamed and clawed at the King's hand, which seized his wrist in a bone-crunching grip.

Rising to his feet, the altivorc drove the would-be assailant down to his knees and plucked the weapon away. He threw it at Dhananad's feet. "I am very forgiving, and will forget this reckless transgression." He released his hold on the Scorpion's wrist. "Your life is spared... for now. Go ahead and meet with the princess if you are still so thick-skulled. You will see I am right."

The Scorpion gasped, clutching his hand, which bent at a strange angle. He fared better than his companion, who lay in a smoldering heap near the entrance.

Dhananad cringed, deciding once and for all he would never tempt the Altivorc King again. He turned on his heel and left, his entourage scurrying after him.

Ambassador Piros watched Prince Dhananad storm out of the room. Once his angry footsteps had faded out of the embassy, Piros motioned for his men to deal with the bodies of the five slain altivorcs and the Golden Scorpion. "Why did you goad the prince like that? Look at this mess... and your own men."

The Altivorc King laughed. "My soldiers will lay their lives down for me without question. It was a necessary measure, to remove that royal fool from the picture. Tomorrow, you will send word to Madura to demand Dhananad's recall. It will make our plans much easier."

"But the damage is already done." Lord Benhan threw his hands up. "The Ayuri Confederation and the Paladins will now be keeping a scrutinizing eye on Madura, and by extension, the rest of us."

Piros hid his scoff. Benhan had much more to worry about because of Levastya's proximity to the Paladins.

"As the Cathayi say, we must seek opportunity in adversity," the Altivorc King said. "When the timing is right—maybe not this decade, even— we shall incite an incident that implicates Madura. All of the mutual protection pacts the princess arranged will draw the Paladins' efforts in that direction. That will give your sultan the perfect opening to move into Ayuri lands."

Piros doubted the Altivorc King had Levastya's best interests in mind, and wondered what the altivorcs had to gain. "Madura has always been the weak link in our alliance. Sacrificing them for the sake of creating other opportunities will be of no consequence."

"And they will not go down easily," the King said. "Contrary to your taunts, the Golden Scorpions are a formidable force that will keep the Paladins occupied. It will provide a chance for you to attack Cathay and for us to capture Ayudra."

Piros chewed on the inside of his cheek. From a human perspective, Ayudra was a strategic port, controlling commerce into the Ayuri heartland. Yet to the altivorcs, who cared little for trade, it was a rock full of ruins. Perhaps it had to do with the King's obsession with the pyramids, the ancient monuments to their departed gods. "Avarax once attacked Ayudra. We should send an envoy to see if he might join our cause."

The Altivorc King burst out laughing. "Avarax is a shadow of his former self, still weakened by the Cathayi girl's song from the War of Ancient Gods. He can't use his breath. When he attacked Ayudra thirty-two years ago, all he wanted was the Lotus Crystal, and he bluffed to get it."

Piros nodded slowly, wrapping his head around the idea. Trickery was such a foreign concept to him, but apparently one that worked.

The Altivorc King yawned. "In any case, even if Avarax were a real threat, he serves only his own cause, which has minimal benefit to us. Let him rule over and expand the Dragonlands. It will keep the Paladins busy. Our goals would be better served if he never sets claw on Ayudra again. And my instincts tell me, this ploy to get Princess Kaiya to sing is another attempt to strengthen himself."

CHAPTER 44:
Pieces of a Puzzle

The four pages taunted Kaiya from where they lay neatly on her bed in the Crystal Citadel's guest chambers. She could see the notes, hear them in her mind, and yet the underlying power escaped her. The City of Palimur, along with all of its hundred thousand inhabitants, depended on her grasping the music's secrets.

Her languid legs protested as she traipsed back from the dresser to the bed for another look. After she woke from Rumiya's magic, her energy guttered in her belly. Fog shrouded her mind. It seemed like dwarf anvils hung from her shoulders. She looked down to confirm that it was, indeed, her own slim arms there.

Ayana leaned back in the plush chair. "You should sleep, especially after the way the wizard drained you. Maybe you will see the answers clearly when you are rested."

The door whispered open behind her, and Jie's soft but distinct footsteps treaded in. Ayana didn't seem to notice the half-elf's arrival, reassuring Kaiya that at least her hearing still served her well, even when the rest of her body did not.

"*Dian-xia*," Jie said, her voice strained. Her forehead furrowed. "As you commanded, I checked on the men. They are recovering well. The imperial guards are in no condition to protect you, but still wish to stand watch outside your chambers."

Kaiya turned and held her Insolent Retainer with her gaze. "While I appreciate their dedication, I would be happier if *all* my guards focused more on their own recovery."

The message seemed lost on Jie, who just sucked on her lower lip— a telltale sign the half-elf was thinking something she wouldn't say.

Unless prompted. "Speak your mind."

"Perhaps your guards' princess should heed her own words. She is having dinner with a rake of a prince tomorrow, after all."

Kaiya sighed. "I will sleep when Meixi returns with the magic mirror. I want to speak with Lord Xu about magic."

"*I* am pretty well-versed in magic; perhaps I can answer your question." Ayana's wounded pout belonged on someone a hundredth her age.

With a contrite nod, Kaiya smiled. "It would save me from the embarrassment of groveling before Lord Xu, thank you. I was considering something. When I invoke a command through my voice, short wording tires me. Yet when I lulled Prince Dhananad with a two-hour dance, I felt energized. Why would that be?"

Ayana put a finger to her chin. "I am afraid that my grasp of Artistic Magic is poor at best. Perhaps your voice is similar to Shallow Magic, which is quick to invoke but draining; while the dance is like Deep Magic, time-consuming and ritualistic, but less tiring. My friend you met in the woods might have been able to tell you more."

Jie sucked her lower lip again. "In the woods? What friend?"

A musical voice, along with gold hair and eyes of molten purple, flashed through Kaiya's mind, and she swore she could smell evergreen needles. The fleeting memory disappeared before she could grasp it. She shrugged.

Meixi burst into the room before Jie could complain, embracing the wrapped-up magic mirror as if it were her first lover. She bowed before Kaiya, proffering the bundle in two hands.

At last. Her body screaming for rest, Kaiya unwound the silk wrappings and found her reverse reflection looking back at her. "Lord Xu, I have questions about Avarax and Artistic Magic."

Ayana crowded in behind her, an expression of wonderment showing on the reflection of her face. "What is *this*?"

How could she not know? Kaiya turned her heavy head back. "A magic mirror."

"I have never seen one so... small and portable." Ayana's usually wise and knowing voice held a child's fascination.

To think that something could amaze even the old elf, who must've seen countless magical artifacts. Kaiya looked down to find her reverse reflection still staring back at her. She sighed and flung herself onto the soft bed, her legs dangling off the side. "Lord Xu keeps his own schedule."

Jie snorted. She slunk over to the side and peered at the pages of music. Her eyes bobbed up and down. "*Dian-xia*, can you summon the image of the book, to the torn-out pages?"

"Book?" Ayana asked excitedly.

"I guess he will appear if he decides to answer." With another tired exhale, Kaiya brushed her hand over the mirror's cool surface. The book shimmered into view. With several rapid brushes that made her tired wrist ache, she came to the ripped-out pages and lifted the mirror up.

Jie held the first sheet up to the image. The story of Yanyan's mastery continued from the picture on one half of the mirror to the sheet. "See? The tear line is close, but not exact."

"What?" Kaiya sat up as quickly as her complaining body would allow and looked. Jie was right: the tear lined up, but not exactly. A gasp escaped her. She turned to Ayana. "What do you know of Yanyan's story?"

Ayana shook her head. "Not much more than you, I assume. It occurred some seven centuries before I was born, and our written records emphasize the heroism of our own people during the War of Ancient Gods. Our Sun God Koralas sent his Archangel Aralas down from the heavens to teach the remnants of our people how to invoke the *Wrath of Koralas*, a ritual spell that would turn the air to fire and kill all animal life."

"Wouldn't that kill the elves, as well?" Kaiya shuddered at the idea of mass genocide.

Ayana shook her head. "During the years it took for our ancestors to sing the spell, Aralas travelled the width and breadth of Tivaralan, planting Trees of Light. Our people were to gather under the canopies and remain protected when the magic took effect."

Jie plopped down in a chair. "What does this have to do with Yanyan?"

"In his journeys, he encountered humans. Not wanting to murder guiltless sentient beings, he called off the ritual spell. Instead, he bade our people to teach humans different forms of magic, according to their ethnic affinities. The most talented of the Cathayi, Yanyan, went to sing Avarax to sleep so he could not ally himself with the Tivari."

Kaiya nodded. "Our own official history comes from several oral accounts told in the small states that made up modern-day Cathay before the first unification of the Yu Dynasty. To us, Yanyan was Aralas' lover."

Ayana's coughing objection rivaled Jie's eye-rolling protest in drama.

Kaiya peered at the old elf. "Do you not believe an elf can love a human?"

"Oh, no, that's not what I meant." Ayana waved both hands defensively. "Aralas' daughter became the first ruler of Aerilysta, the Queendom of the Moon. His son was the first sovereign of Aramysta, the Kingdom of the Sun. We call them high elves because of the divine ichor flowing in their veins. Yet Aralas', um, *interest* in human women has appeared in a handful of those descendants."

Jie rolled her eyes. Again. By now, she likely knew what the inside of her skull looked like. "I don't see how any of this has to do with Avarax, or the fact that the pages Girish gave you don't line up."

Kaiya twirled a lock of her hair. What had Lord Xu said when he gave her the mirror? "When did he say Doctor Wu obtained the book?"

"Thirty-two years ago." Jie shrugged.

"A lot happened thirty-two years ago," Kaiya thought out loud. "He said it was retrieved by the *Tianzi's agents*. Could that be the Black Lotus? Do you know if they might have been involved?"

The blood drained from Jie's face. It was hard to imagine anything surprising her. "I… it did not occur to me until now. There was a mission—famous among our clan because of the secrecy surrounding it, even now—by three of the most promising young masters: the Architect, the Surgeon, and the Beauty. Besides taking the young Prince Dhananad as a hostage, they retrieved a secret artifact. Maybe the book?"

So the Black Lotus had taken Prince Dhananad hostage. Perhaps it explained the man's quirks. Kaiya set the thought to the side, returning to more pressing questions. "And the missing parts of the book are in either Avarax's or Rumiya's possession."

"Grand Vizier Rumiya disappeared from history right around that time," Jie said, "only reappearing once over the next three decades: two years ago, to meet with you."

Ayana scratched her chin. "Rumiya says he wants Avarax to sleep again. He planted a seed in you so that you would be able to do it, and now produces the music that can accomplish that goal."

Kaiya's cheeks burned at the mention of planting seeds, since apparently, that was all anyone wanted of her.

"But he gave you a fake song." Jie held up the pages and poked them.

"What does this music do, then?" When she'd sung the first three notes, the energy of the audience chamber crackled with power.

Ayana stared at the pages. "Most importantly, what will the music do to Avarax?"

"It doesn't matter. I don't even have the energy to invoke the power of the song."

"In four days," Ayana said, "the Blue Moon's Eye is larger and more open than at any other time this year. The resonance of the world also wells up on the hill of the Temple of Shakti. That should help you."

Kaiya sighed. "That must be why he insisted on four days. He has already waited thirty-two years, I don't see why—"

"Thirty-two years!" Jie jumped to her feet. "Avarax woke up thirty-two years ago. He went to the Pyramid on Ayudra to steal the Lotus Crystal, which magnifies the energy of the world."

All of the details began to make sense, coming together like a web of interconnections. Thirty-two years ago, Rumiya acquired the book of music for Avarax, who was looking to magnify his power. Kaiya's voice droned slow and hollow in her own ears. "Rumiya wants to make Avarax *stronger*."

Jie's brows furrowed. "Why would he want that? What does Rumiya get in return? Besides maybe a trip down a dragon's gullet?"

The real missing pages of the book likely held the answers. However, it was unlikely she would see Rumiya—Girish—again, let alone convince him to give her the *real* song. Kaiya was on her own, with only four days to figure out those answers and get to Palimur in time to save the city and its people.

CHAPTER 45:
Checkmate

Prince Dhananad held his chin high as he sauntered through the ranks of Paladins guarding the entrance of Cathayi embassy. Even if they knew he was behind the attack on the princess, they would not dare touch him with the proverbial flag of diplomacy fluttering above his head. Two of his Golden Scorpions marched behind him. He imagined them grinning beneath their masks, their very presence a taunt to the Paladin Order that had abandoned them.

His third Scorpion, the pretty girl, whatever her name was, walked at his side, shedding her maroon *kurta* and mask for a *sari*. Her beauty would make Princess Kaiya jealous.

Because no matter what the Altivorc King and his yes-men said, Dhananad would win the princess over. The dinner tonight would help her remember his charm and seal their betrothal.

Cathayi Ambassador Ling greeted him with hands pressed together and guided him through the first house into an adjacent building. Servants knelt beside the double doors, on which two long scrolls hung.

Though the wavy script might have been gibberish, it felt as if someone had lodged a spear of ice down his spine when he looked at it. His knees wobbled and hands trembled. When the doors opened, he had to gasp for air.

He turned slightly to see one of his Scorpions through the corner of his eye, likewise quivering. With a deep breath, he stepped into an anteroom.

Princess Kaiya waited there, the long sleeves of her translucent outer gown hanging to the floor. Jade jewels pinned up her hair. The pink inner gown, stitched with white plum flowers, exposed her delicate collarbones, while accentuating the perfect divot at the base of her neck. It just barely hinted at the softness of her bust. Even her austere *choli* from a week before had revealed more.

The impertinent little maid stood by her side, looking no thinner from the punishment the princess had promised. She locked eyes with his companion, and both reached for their hips. He shifted his head from one girl to another, enjoying the duel of their razor-sharp gazes.

The princess bent slightly at her waist, and Dhananad stole a glance at the luscious valley between her breasts.

"Greetings, Prince Dhananad," she said, voice as placid as the Shallowsea. "Please be my guest tonight, in appreciation for your hosting me a week ago."

Dhananad clasped his hands together. "Thank you for your hospitality, My Orchid. I hope that after what promises to be a delectable Cathayi meal, we can conclude our discussion from last time."

She raised a perfect eyebrow, playing coy confusion. Such a cute girl. "Of course. I also invited some friends to share dinner with us, since it would be a waste to share our best cuisine with just one person. I hope you do not mind."

Friends? It was supposed to be a private dinner. Dhananad kept his expression jovial nonetheless. "Certainly not! It is always enjoyable to share a meal with many. Though I would have far rather had you all to myself." For the first several months. After that, perhaps other beauties could join them.

She smiled demurely and motioned for him to follow as she glided through the doors. He kept his eyes fixed on the elegant sashay of her hips.

His Scorpion drew in a sharp breath.

Dhananad looked up and raked his gaze across the room to find friendly grins on the faces of those he would not consider friends.

Fire raged in his face, but he remained silent as Princess Kaiya gestured toward a rectangle of embroidered silk cushions, each with a small table in front of it. The maharaja and queen from each of the three largest Ayuri Confederation states sat on one side, and three Paladin elders in white *kurtas* on the other. Most galling was the presence of the exiled old maharaja of Ankira and his plump queen near the head.

Princess Kaiya guided him to a cushion across from the Ankirans, next to her at the head of the table. Was it a place of honor in their culture? Or subservience?

He hesitantly sat. His own girl Scorpion stared at the floor, turning her head so her cascading hair screened her face from the Paladins. They, in turn, whispered among themselves.

The princess had such poor taste in guests. Things couldn't get much more awkward. With a wave of her open hand, she motioned for food to be served. Servants hurried in and out, bringing in trays filled with aromatic foods on exquisitely thin white porcelain dishes.

She gestured toward the first dish: a soup, made of a fish stock and soybean paste, with bean curd cubes and seaweeds, garnished with chopped green onions. "This simple soup was a favorite of my ancestor, Wang Xinchang, who founded Cathay as you know it today. He served this on the occasion of his first great alliance with the elf Lord Xu on Haikou Island, sealing their security pact. Tonight, our cook used seaweed from the Shallowsea around which Madura and the Ayuri Confederation lie."

Dhananad turned the porcelain spoon over in his hands, his heart racing. *Sealing of security pacts* suggested she had already decided on marriage! His rivals must have been sweating!

A porridge of black rice and golden grain, split in half to resemble the Cathayi yin-yang symbol, came next. "We call this

Yin-Yang Porridge: it symbolizes the fusion of the disparate elements of nature," she said. "In Cathay, we prefer to use a special short-grain rice grown in the southern province of Yutou, with millet from the northern province of Dongmen to signify the unity of disparate places. Today, we have chosen a black rice grain from my home province of Huayuan, and wheat grains from Dabura."

Daburan wheat? Though the servant offered a new spoon, Dhananad's fingers would not loosen around the first. If the princess was serious about marriage, she would have used Maduran wheat.

Heavier dishes began arriving. Servants brought in a large steamed fish with a reddish skin, covered with ginger, scallions, and peppercorns, and garnished with fruit slices. From the middle of the rectangle, they carved up individual portions and presented them to each guest. And what was this? The Ankirans were served first! They wondered at the straight sticks supposedly used for eating. Others struggled with the awkward utensils as they ate.

"A whole fish symbolizes prosperity," the princess said. "When served among new friends, it represents the hope that by working together in harmony, we will reap bountiful rewards."

Reaping bounties. Perhaps a child who would rule Madura and Cathay. Soon, soon enough Dhananad would need to start the arduous work of making that baby. In his excitement, he fumbled with the bizarre sticks the Cathayi used to eat with.

Then, a roasted turkey, skin brown and crispy and permeating the room with a savory aroma, was placed in the middle of the rectangle, its head pointing at Dhananad. Exotic squashes and root vegetables ringed the bird. It smelled wonderful, but such a hideous face staring at him! Surely this was inappropriate! Servants began slicing it.

"To us," the princess said, "chickens represent opportunity, and it would typically be served on such an auspicious occasion. But today, we were very lucky to find this wild turkey from a Kanin merchant. In our language, we refer to it as a *wild fire chicken*, and we dip it in a tangy sauce made from its own juices. To us, it means that if we wildly grasp for all opportunities, we will end up consuming ourselves in our own passions."

What? Dhananad almost snapped the chopsticks in his hands. Was the princess insulting him? The symbolism of the turkey left little ambiguity. Maybe she was *not* considering marriage, maybe all of these enemies—

A sliced barbecued pork loin, with a pungent sauce, came last, surrounded by stir-fried leafy greens. It was a commoner's dish, well below the expectation of royalty.

Princess Kaiya smiled. "Late in the Yu Dynasty, before the Hellstorm, the armies of Cathay defeated a small army led by an Arkothi Empire general who invaded and occupied some of our land. Far from the capital, the soldiers feasted on barbecued pork provided by the local farmers who were happy to be freed from the tyranny of that general."

Normally, the aroma would make his mouth water; but his appetite had fled. She was comparing him to a tyrant. Dhananad turned his nose up, not deigning to taste the pork.

As the distinguished guests finished the main course, the princess motioned for the dessert, it too bearing an unsubtle message: cut melons from each of the nations of the Ayuri Confederation, mixed together, lay in the hollowed rind of a Maduran melon.

Dhananad stared at the bowl. All of them, filling Madura. The Altivorc King had been right. The girl had set a diplomatic trap for him. The identity of the guests alone sent the explicit message that Madura's neighbors stood against it; the blatant selection of dishes, delectable as they probably would have been under different circumstances, had merely hammered home her point.

He blanched. The only uncertainty he held was whether Madura faced imminent invasion, or if his rivals had merely formed a defensive alliance.

Kaiya watched Prince Dhananad from the corner of her eye. He wasn't the only one not enjoying their meal. The Golden Scorpion woman, stunning in the rust-colored *sari* that complemented her light brown skin, demurred. The ruthless warrior who'd nearly killed her Insolent Retainer now looked less like a daunting foe than an ashamed and embarrassed young girl who had just been castigated by her parents.

Coming from a culture that emphasized proper etiquette, even when treating with enemies, Kaiya worried she'd overreached with her message. Prince Dhananad held his lips tight, his expression reminiscent of her own seasickness on the *Invincible*. She leaned over and whispered in his ear, careful to keep any hint of malice out of her tone. "Prince Dhananad, are you not well?"

"Unfortunately, I am afraid that something has not agreed with me," he answered in a low voice. "I will have to retire early tonight."

She'd gone too far. It would reflect poorly on Cathay. "And our talks that were to conclude tonight?"

The prince raised his voice. "I believe you have made your position abundantly clear. But know now that Madura will not suffer an invasion quietly. Those who dare tread on Maduran soil uninvited will meet the Scorpion's sting!"

Kaiya leaned back, hand on her chest. Nothing in the choreographed dinner party had been meant to suggest an invasion of Madura. "Prince Dhananad! Cathay is a peace-loving nation, we have no intention of infringing on Madura's sovereign territory."

"Yet it is obvious you do not recognize the province of Ankira as an inseparable part of our nation." The prince jabbed a finger in the direction of the Ankiran rebels.

She lowered her hand from where she'd been twirling a lock of her hair. "It is my concern—and I imagine that of all those present today— that a certain dignity be afforded all people. I am concerned about the women living in Ankira who, at your behest, are subjected to the depravations of Bovyan soldiers and their country's breeding program. I believe if you were to cease this cooperation with the Teleri, then your neighbors would think… more highly of you."

The prince leaped up and stormed out the room. The female Scorpion looked up for the first time that night, and then quickly dropped her head again as she staggered to her feet and shuffled out after him.

The room fell silent. All attention turned to her, some in admiration, others in disbelief.

The Queen of Ankira broke the silence, her eyes glinting. "What have you done? Have you sold us out?"

Paladin Elder Kairav, who'd criticized her the day before, scowled. "You still have not learned to look beyond your own borders."

Kaiya fiddled with her hair. Jie placed a reassuring hand between her shoulder blades.

Despite her embarrassment, she straightened her carriage. "Now that Prince Dhananad has seen that his neighbors oppose Maduran aggression, they will be more circumspect about meddling with any of us. I did this for the benefit of all." She turned to the Ankiran queen, hoping to appease her. "I did what I could for you. It is beyond our capability to liberate Ankira. At the very least, there will be fewer Bovyan soldiers garrisoning your homeland in the future."

The queen climbed to her feet as quickly as age would allow and stomped out of the room. The one Paladin elder stood up and departed as well, leaving his two companions behind.

Elder Devak afforded her a reassuring smile. "I believe you had the best intentions. I think you will prove it when you sing for Avarax in three days."

CHAPTER 46:
INTERVIEW WITH EVIL

The enthusiastic twitter of birds roused Kaiya from a fitful slumber, one where she dreamed of Rumiya's glowing blue eyes, snakes entangling her, and the gush of beating dragon wings. She sat up in her bed and dabbed the sweat from her neck and face. Looking down, she found Zheng Ming's kerchief in her hand, damp with her perspiration.

Despite her restless sleep, energy coursed through her limbs, at last recovered from Rumiya's draining two days before. The fog clouding her mind had fully lifted and her focus returned.

Jie's chirpy voice mingled with the excited birds outside her window. "*Dian-xia*, good morning. Hurry, get dressed; the river barge for Palimur departs soon."

Images of her childhood nursemaid, now replaced by the half-elf, danced in Kaiya's mind. Tucking the memory away, she smiled and kicked her legs over the side of the bed. She had little time to react when her Insolent Retainer tossed travelling clothes into her lap.

As she tugged on the cotton pants and squirmed into the shirt, Jie chattered away nonstop. "The Paladins have assembled quite a flotilla to escort us. There will be a hundred knights and masters travelling as honor guard, though I am not sure Avarax will be impressed. Speaking of Avarax, I talked with Minister Yi, my clan brother, last night. His hometown legends claim the dragon flew over the night of the Hellstorm."

Having just started to fasten her cloak, Kaiya paused. "If it was Avarax, why did he wait three centuries to reclaim his lands? He could have taken advantage of the Long Winter to seize more territory. Maybe it was another dragon."

"Avarax was the only survivor of the Dragonpurge." Jie sucked on her lower lip.

Kaiya finished pinning her cloak. "Then maybe it was just a fanciful story. There are so many legends and myths surrounding the Hellstorm." She bound her voluminous hair into a pony tail and strode toward the door.

Jie opened it, revealing Elder Devak with Sameer at his side. The young knight's ear-to-ear grin suggested he was happy to rejoin them, after not having accompanied them to the Cathay embassy the night before.

Then his eyes fell on the Insolent Retainer. His jaw dropped. "Jie. It's been a long time."

Jie grinned and wrapped him in an embrace. "Not long enough. You've grown."

"In two years?"

Kaiya looked from one to the other. There was a story here, one that would warrant a melodramatic novel or two given the unspoken conversation in their eyes.

Clearing his throat, Elder Devak pressed his hands together. "Good morning. I am here to escort you to your boat. And to apologize." He bowed his head lower.

Kaiya had a good idea of what he was going to say next and stayed silent, waiting.

"We knew of Avarax's ultimatum and we still made you present your case before the elders. We also knew that Girish was once Rumiya, Grand Vizier of Madura, though we did not know he had visited you in the past. Otherwise, we would not have granted his demand to have us introduce him as Girish."

It was no use being angry. Kaiya returned his salute, pressing her hands together. "To save so many people, I would have chosen to sing, regardless of our agreement."

The elder's lips twitched. "I believe you are well on your way to becoming the hero the Oracle foresees." He then beckoned for her to follow.

Hero? The Oracle had said nothing of the sort to her, nor did she want such a burden. A quiet life in a peaceful country seemed much more appealing. Her hand strayed to Zheng Ming's kerchief in her sash. Maybe he would be part of that picture.

Still, now wasn't the time to think of love or marriage. A city depended on her. She looked up from her thoughts to see her five imperial guards, each on one knee before her.

"*Dian-xia*," Chen Xin said. "I object to this ill-conceived quest. It puts you in needless danger and gains nothing for Cathay."

Kaiya had expected resistance from her loyal guards. "Chen Xin, is the *Tianzi* the Son of Heaven, who rules with the Mandate of Heaven?"

Chen looked among his comrades before turning his gaze back. "Of course, *Dian-xia*."

"And the agreements he endorses are the Will of Heaven?"

Chen Xin nodded.

She lifted her chin. "I am the Granddaughter of Heaven, and negotiated with the full faith and backing of the *Tianzi*. My words are his." It wasn't *exactly* true, since only an imperial plaque— presumably carried on the *Golden Phoenix*—could unquestioningly represent the *Tianzi's* word.

The imperial guards looked among themselves, their lips pursed and brows furrowed.

They weren't convinced. She cleared her throat. "Chen Xin. Li Wei. Ma Jun. Zhao Yue. Xu Zhan. You are my senior-most guards. Some of you have protected me since I was a babe in my mother's arms. I have trusted you with my safety. Will you trust me?"

More dubious expressions. She continued anyway. "Ayana will whisk me away to safety if it looks like I will fail, though unfortunately, she will probably not be able to save you as well."

Smiles bloomed on their faces.

Kaiya straightened her carriage. "We will go to Palimur, and you will protect me. That is my command."

The five guards lowered their heads in unison. "As you command, *Dian-xia*."

Countless Paladins greeted them outside of the Crystal Citadel, escorting them down to the river quays. Dockworkers and sailors finished preparing flat-bottomed barges, just wide enough for three men to sit abreast, for departure. A lizard the size of an elephant was hitched to each boat.

With Li Wei's assistance, Kaiya boarded the assigned boat. She turned back toward the quay, where Meixi bowed. When the girl rose, her lip quivered. "*Dian-xia*, it has been an honor to serve you. I wish I could accompany you."

The girl's dedication—and bravery—was heartening. Nonetheless, failure meant condemning a thirteen-year-old to death by dragonfire. "I thank you for your service here in Vyara City. Your knowledge of the local customs provided invaluable expertise to our mission. Not to mention much needed help with my hair and make-up when I had none." She ignored Jie's poke in her back and continued. "I will require your aid again when we return from this quest."

Meixi flushed a scarlet that would have made the setting sun jealous.

Holding the image of the girl in her heart, Kaiya took a seat toward the front, looking inland up the river. The boat slid forward, imperceptibly building speed as the lizard tacked in effortless zigzags through the waters. The hitching mechanism barely whispered, its mesmerizing undulations converting the beast's swaying into forward momentum. Dwarf-made, in all likelihood.

After two hours, during which Kaiya paid more attention to the scenery than deconstructing Rumiya's song, they stopped at a small port upriver. Without coming to a complete stop, the pilot unharnessed the lizard, which dockworkers guided into a corral, while other workers hitched a fresh lizard. The whole process took just a few minutes.

Time to focus. Kaiya pulled the pages of the song from her pack. With her head clearer, the music made much more sense than any time over the last two days. At times she would hum it, only to stop when the Paladins' *nagas* began to glow.

A sluggish but powerful surge, like a deluge held back by a weakening dam, emitted from the Paladin sitting in front of her. She looked up as he turned around and lowered his hood.

Rumiya.

He still wore the scaled armor, and his eyes glowed blue.

Kaiya sucked in her breath, while at her side, Jie whipped out a knife. Paladins rose with drawn *nagas*. Whatever good that would do.

He grinned, sending snakes writhing across her skin. "Greetings, Your Highness. I come in peace. I thought you might need help with the song."

In peace? Not likely. Kaiya motioned the Paladins back. She lowered Jie's hand and forced herself to smile. "Thank you for your offer. But first, may I ask a question? About you?"

He laughed. "Come now, princess. Do you still have feelings for me, even though you now know I am Grand Vizier Rumiya of Madura, and Girish, the Last Dragon's Envoy?"

Heat pounded in her cheeks. "Where have you been all of these years? Not from when we last met, though I would like to know, but from the time you left Madura."

As he considered the question, Rumiya's hypnotic gaze seemed more like snake's eyes than those of the beguiling beauty from two years before. "Control of nations and men was of little consequence when the power over cosmic laws lay at my fingertips. When I had a chance to learn from the most knowledgeable and powerful being on Tivara, I took it. For years, I gleaned his secrets. In return, I went where he could not, in search of the one who could please him with her voice alone."

His boasts coiled around her like a serpent, forcing her to choke her words out. "And in all of your travels, I am the only one who saw you in the last thirty-two years?"

He cackled like metal on flint. "I have more than one face, though this is the one I grew used to. I am ironically quite fond of it."

"What will you do to advance your power once your mentor sleeps? Assuming I am able to accomplish that."

His eyes searched hers. "I have learned all I can from him, and he only has one thing left to offer. Let me tell you a secret about dragons. Do you know how in your people's depictions of dragons, they are always chasing a flaming pearl?"

Kaiya shook her head, not to answer his question, but in denial of his comparison between the harbinger of death and destruction and the auspicious protectors of Cathay. "Our dragons are creatures of good. They are nothing like Avarax."

Rumiya growled, a low rumble that shook the boat. "Ever seen one to make a comparison?"

Kaiya lowered her head, chastised. Though she'd never seen Avarax, either.

Vindicated, he continued in a smug tone. "Though only legends, your images hold a grain of truth."

Rumiya's rough hand took her chin. He held her in the slits of his terrifying gaze. *No! Not again!*

Kaiya's chest ached, as if he'd ripped her heart out. From the corner of her eye, she saw Jie jump to her feet. Swords rasped from scabbards, where the imperial guards stood behind her.

Leaning in, the wizard let go and thankfully broke eye contact. His hot voice burned in her ear. "The pulsations of a magical dragonstone in a dragon's belly are the source of his power. When Avarax falls asleep, I will slay him, cut him open, and take his."

Kaiya shuddered. *If* he were telling the truth, her actions would replace one evil magical being with another. At least the Last Dragon was ostensibly predictable. There was no fathoming what a human with so much power would do.

Metal snapped with a clink. Beside her, hand shaking, Jie gawked at her knife, broken at the guard.

Rumiya laughed as he stood and raised his right hand. A blue flame flared in his palm, burning without a sound.

Kaiya rose and interposed herself between him and Jie. "Please. Stop. She won't do it again."

The wizard seized her shoulder in his left hand, sending heat searing into her body. He shoved her back into her seat, even as he glared at Jie. "Foolish girl, a mortal weapon has no chance of penetrating my armor. Now die."

"If you harm her," Kaiya shouted, spreading her arms, "I won't sing for your master. You will have to resume your search for someone with the right voice."

Rumiya stepped back, again locking her with his serpent eyes. "Would you sacrifice hundreds of thousands of lives and Cathay's mutual protection pacts for one stupid girl?"

Kaiya pulled the black-lacquered hairpin from the base of her pony tail and pointed the tip at him. "For my blood-sister, yes."

He'd seen through her bluff in the Crystal Citadel; or rather, tested her with his magic. Yet this time, he closed his hand, snuffing out the flame. He sat back down. "You, half-elf, are of little consequence. If I killed everyone who tried to slay me over the years, their bodies would litter the length and breadth of the Shallowsea. Now, princess, tell me how the song escapes your puny intellect."

Kaiya let out the breath she held. "I understand how the notes' modulation can affect the resonance of things. I just don't know how to magnify it to impact something as immense as Avarax."

Rumiya's brows furrowed. He spoke as if the answer was childishly simple. "Focus not on the dragon, but on his dragonstone."

What was that supposed to mean? Kaiya shook her head. "What if I don't have enough energy? How do wizards use powerful spells? How is it that magic which drained them when they first learned it becomes easier as time goes by?"

He gave her a blank stare. "Power is innate. The more you need, the more you draw from your surroundings. But I see now that even though you have the right voice, you just aren't talented enough on your own. Perhaps Avarax will consider *loaning* you the Lotus Crystal."

A chance to see her future. If she survived. She bowed at her waist. "I thank you for that."

"I shall be off. In the meantime, practice well." With a harrumph and a scathing glance at her, Rumiya blinked out of existence. The air popped as it filled the space he'd departed.

Kaiya slumped in her chair. If she never saw him again, it would be too soon.

Ayana sidled up next to her. "I have never heard such an explanation for how magic becomes easier to use. It just takes time and practice. And I have never seen anyone teleport without using words to manipulate magic."

Jie held up her shattered knife. "I stabbed into the bare spot on the back of his neck. I am sure I was nowhere near his armor."

When they'd first met, Jie didn't take the princess' talk of blood-sisters seriously. Hairpins or not. Yet time and time again, from shielding her from Prince Dhananad's rage to allaying Rumiya's threats, the princess proved herself a liege worth serving. Two years ago, she'd offered herself as a bride to Lord Tong to avert a civil war, and then later secretly joined the expeditionary force tasked with capturing the rebel's castle. Perhaps a moral compass, and not mere flightiness, guided her impulsiveness.

Now left undisturbed, the princess immersed herself in two days of meditation and study. Convinced she could deconstruct and alter the song to really sing Avarax to sleep, she experimented with the sounds to see the effect on Paladin *nagas*.

She paused only to eat, drink, and rest. Her dedication rivaled that of a Black Fist initiate.

In spite of all the effort, it was unlikely the princess could actually succeed. Their journey to Palimur could very well be a one-way trip.

At least Jie could learn something during their travels. It was pleasant catching up with the Paladin Sameer, He'd been so disillusioned when they'd last parted, but appeared enthusiastic and lighthearted now. Perhaps he'd turned his love away from the Golden Scorpions, though he deflected questions about her.

At times, he would point out places of historical or architectural interest along the riverbank. They passed famous temples, battlefields, and even a maharaja's old palace.

The moons rose and set, though it was Guanyin's Eye that Jie watched the most. If only she could slow its inevitable approach, to delay their confrontation with Avarax. Perhaps with more study and practice, the princess would actually be able to accomplish the task at hand.

Early on the second day, their travel upriver slowed. Boats clogged the waterways as refugees fled Palimur. Apparently, she wasn't the only one who doubted the princess' abilities. A torrent of people crowded the riverbank highway; some in horse-drawn carts laden with all their possessions, some on bare feet with babies slung across their backs. Many stared and pointed at the princess and whispered.

By midday, the hill of the Temple of Shakti in Palimur loomed into view.

Kaiya turned to Ayana. "I can hear the energy radiating from the hill."

Sameer nodded enthusiastically. "Palimur is a holy site, built on the delta where the Kaveri River washes into the Palimur River. The former is fed by several other rivers, including three flowing out of the Elf Kingdom of Aramysta, the valley of the old Kanin Pyramid, and Avarax's mountain. The area resonates strongly with the vibrations of the world."

Ayana added, "The hill is one of the Glittering Caves sites. During the Twilight of Istriya, our ancestors uncovered a Starburst there. Starbursts magnified the power of elven magic and turned the struggle for supremacy over Tivara in our favor… until the Year of the Second Sun, when the Orc God Tivar appeared in the heavens as a Red Sun, burning day and night, and rendered our magic useless."

Jie realized her mouth was hanging open. Elven legends had never interested her, yet she dwelled on Ayana's every word. She rearranged her expression into detached boredom and stared at the hill ahead.

They docked not far from the temple. The procession of a hundred Paladins marched through broad avenues of block buildings with domes and spires. It would've made for an impressive sight had anyone been present to watch.

The hill sloped up on a gentle incline. Its rocky ground harbored a few sparse shrubs and short grasses, but was otherwise devoid of trees. Jie scanned the flat, oval top, which she estimated to be a third of a mile wide, one milelong.

She held in a gasp. The size and shape resembled Elbahia Island, where she'd visited with Sameer two years before. A single mound rose some thirty feet above the rest of the hill near its east end, in the same place Elbahia castle stood

The Temple of Shakti mirrored the mound at the opposite end. Made of white marble, its multilayered steppes formed a dome supported by arched columns. As Jie understood it, Shakti represented the female energy of healing and creation. Though her own dismally flat chest was far from the perfect specimen, the symmetrical domes perhaps symbolized the female form.

She turned a jealous eye toward the curvier princess, who somehow made a squat appear graceful. Her eyes were closed, and her hand touched the hallowed ground. She opened her eyes, her previous look of doubt gone. "I hear it. The energy of the world bubbling in this point. I might be able to do this."

Jie flashed her an encouraging smile she didn't believe. This was such a lost cause.

Then, the hairs on the back of her neck stood rigid and her legs began to shake. Around her, Paladins and Priestesses of Shakti gathered, pointing toward the north. Jie followed their gazes.

An ugly blotch of red marred the horizon, floating inexorably toward them.

Avarax.

CHAPTER 47:
Verbal Jousting

Kaiya winced as the air roared with the slow bursts of Avarax's beating wings, even at a distance. Perhaps the dragon was in no hurry to hear her sing, since he was taking his time. Or maybe his enormous mass could only travel so fast. His slow approach gave her several minutes to listen to her surroundings.

The priestesses of Shakti chanted mantras to their goddess, their voices cracking under the fear Avarax evoked, even from so far away. The Paladins breathed in unison, slow inhalation followed by a slow exhalation, balancing out the priestesses' trepidation. Jie's heart beat calmly, palpable through the half-elf's hand on her shoulder. Ayana hummed to herself. The hill itself droned a serene, steadfast canticle.

Kaiya drew strength from the others, calming her own nerves. She could do this. After these last couple of days, Rumiya's song made sense, and altering it should be easy. If Lord Xu had ever contacted her, he would've surely confirmed that her alterations to the music would send Avarax into a deep slumber.

Down in the city below, horns blared, their low keen a background to the percussion of heartbeats and breaths around her. People who lacked the means or foresight to flee Palimur ventured into the streets, only to run back into their homes upon seeing the dragon. Her stomach tightened. Their lives, and the livelihood of all those who had escaped, depended on her.

Avarax loomed closer, a shard of cinnabar flashing in the blue sky. He grew unbelievably larger each minute, the slow pounding of his beating wings threatening to drown out all other sounds.

Around her, even the Paladins began to shuffle, the synchronicity of their breaths choking into disarray. Jie's hand pulled back. Ayana's hum faltered.

Her own heart galloped, cold fear crawling up her back and turning the blood in her arms and legs to ice. She shook her hands out, fighting the primal urge to panic. Death. She, and everyone else would die today.

Of all the sources from which she drew strength, only the hill's resonance remained.

Now, focus on your breathing, anchor yourself with the energies of the earth. Doctor Wu's words, repeated over and over again throughout her childhood, rang in Kaiya's mind now. She straightened her spine and gripped the ground with her toes.

It wasn't working! Her eyes locked on the dragon in dread fascination. His red scales and white talons came into focus. The glinting claws and teeth promised death. Every fiber in her body screamed at her to flee.

Close your eyes. Focus on the sound. Lord Xu's first lessons on the magic of sound repeated in her ears. The chorus of the hill rose into her soles, chanting in slow rhymes to her heart. With a deep inhalation, she sucked in the energy of the air. When she let the breath out, the Paladins' breathing lurched back into harmony.

The sounds around her slowed. The presence of Avarax loomed above. She opened her eyes.

His immense size blotted out the sun. From snout to tail, he might be even larger than the grounds of Sun-Moon Palace. His eyes glowed bright blue, boring into her soul. Death on wings, able to kill her a dozen different ways with less effort than it took for her to draw a breath.

Keeping her toes gripped to the ground, Kaiya bowed her head. "I am here, as you commanded."

"Then sing for me." Avarax's voice bellowed slow and powerful, his breath hot and reeking of charred flesh. "I have waited a thousand years to hear you."

Had she deconstructed Rumiya's music correctly, rearranged it to repeat Yanyan's feat a thousand years before? If not... No, better not to sing at all. Avoid the risk. She dared to meet the Last Dragon's gaze. "I do not think you want to hear the song your envoy provided. He seeks to betray you."

Hovering high above, Avarax regarded her for a few seconds. "All this is known to me. Little did Rumiya know that I tricked him, and he gave you the correct song. He will suffer his due punishment soon enough. Now sing."

Hardeep... Rumiya, evil as he was, didn't deserve that. And what punishment *she* might face if her plan failed? She summoned all her courage to make her own demand. "Only after you deliver what I asked for."

The weight of a hundred stares fell on her. The priestesses and Paladins must think she was insane. Maybe they were right.

Avarax echoed the sentiment. "Foolish girl. Sing, or you will burn in fire hot enough to melt stone."

Could he see her legs trembling beneath her gown? Hear the anxiety in her voice? Smell her terror? Drawing on the energy of the earth, Kaiya forced herself to project confidence. Now if only her queasy stomach would play along. She laughed. "Then you will have to wait another thousand years to hear the song you requested."

The dragon snarled. The slow vibration shook the ground, which resisted with its own tune. Around her, several priestesses and Paladins struggled to keep their feet.

Avarax opened his maw and bared his teeth, each sharper than a *dao* and as large as the imperial guard who wielded it. He extended a claw and flicked something from his jaws.

Though only a flake of snow compared to its enormous dragon backdrop, the object pulsed with a deep sound, stronger than any Kaiya had ever heard. It glittered as it escaped the shadow of the dragon and caught the rays of the afternoon sun, growing larger in its descent.

Jie stepped forward and caught it in two hands, her eyes wide with wonder. She knelt and proffered it.

Kaiya drew a sharp breath. Had she just bluffed a *dragon*? Maintaining a straight posture to hide her surprise, she received the jewel.

It was a colorless crystal, the size of a man's fist, but light as air. Round at the bottom, tapered toward the top like a lotus. The number of tiny facets was beyond fathom. It sang in her hands, forming a symphony with the sounds of the hill, the chanting of the priestesses and the breathing of the Paladins.

Avarax roared again, sending the air cackling like sparks. "Now, mortal, sing."

Can you feel the change in vibrations? Lord Xu had asked her the night before her departure for Vyara City. Avarax's voice had modulated. It echoed with something deep in his chest, sluggish yet powerful. Different yet familiar, now that the Lotus Crystal was in *her* hands.

Kaiya bowed low, holding the position as she contemplated the sounds. Before singing her planned modifications to the music, she had to first test her theory.

Raising her head, she lifted her voice in song, the exact melody which Rumiya had given her. Each note reverberated into Avarax, the frequency of the dragonstone at his core increasing. The dragon's eyes glowed a brighter blue, though the shade remained the same... the same as...

Those vibrations. Lethargic, with immense power behind them. Like a mighty river held back by a dam. Exactly matched to Rumiya's. The blue of his eyes, which filled her dreams, were the same. The scales of Rumiya's armor hummed at the identical frequency as Avarax's. Rumiya had disappeared when Avarax awoke.

Rumiya was Avarax.

Avarax was Rumiya.

It all made sense now. Two years before, he'd tested her voice. Tried to get her to sing. And when that didn't work, he conveniently recovered the Dragon Scale Lute and restrung it for her to play in the acoustically perfect Temple of Heaven. When he realized it wouldn't work, he probably shattered the instrument himself and made sure it remained buried beneath Wailian Castle's ruins.

And now she was making Avarax more powerful with the song, just as she'd feared days before. He'd tricked her once, two years ago.

Not this time.

She just had to undo what she started, using the variation she'd devised over the last three days. She transitioned into her new hymn. As long as he didn't notice...

Avarax's dragonstone buzzed a little faster, like a swarm of angry bees. No! It wasn't working! Maybe she'd misinterpreted the music. Or perhaps he *expected* her to make the modifications, shaped her actions. Just like with the fake lotus jewel years before.

What can we trust more than that which comes from within ourselves? The Oracle had said as much. She had to trust herself. If her music could make Avarax stronger, it could also make him weaker. She renewed the effort, pouring her heart into the next notes.

The steady rise in Avarax's energy wavered. Maybe...

Then it redoubled, even stronger than before. Inexorably building toward a crescendo. His triumphant roar echoed across the plain, shaking the city below. Her voice cracked. If she couldn't reverse what she'd started, they would all die here.

Harder. She had to try harder.

Trying is the first step to failure, Master Sabal had taught on the Shallowsea. *Your conscious mind cannot be moved... Do not just feel. Be moved.* She abandoned the song she'd meticulously planned over three days and now let Avarax's pulsations guide her voice, just as when the music had propelled her during her perfect dance for Prince Dhananad.

The Lotus Crystal glowed bright blue in her hands, and all the courage of the Paladins joined with the energy of the world and surged into her. Power welled up in her chest.

She sang new notes, and his immense body answered with a symphony of its own. Dozens, if not hundreds, of different sounds worked in concert inside of him, like the cogs of a dwarf clock. She was still making him stronger! Better to give up now than unleash Avarax on the world.

But wait.

The torrent of vibrations hid a quiet sound: Yanyan's lullaby, soft and soothing like falling cherry blossoms dabbing into placid water. Its residual echo held a tenuous check on Avarax's energy.

Strengthen those, and he would sleep. Kaiya slowed her tone, softer and softer to match the ancient verse.

Another rhythm flared somewhere inside of him, blocking the impact of her voice. No, worse! It weakened Yanyan's lullaby, diffusing it around them. A grin, if a dragon could grin, formed on Avarax's face.

Many of her honor guard cowered, some even throwing themselves into the dirt and covering their heads. The Lotus Crystal's glow guttered. The power inside her dwindled. The barrier of sounds constraining Avarax's energy began to collapse. It was hopeless.

Jie's hand pressed against Kaiya's back, evoking an image of the half-elf in her mind. Resolute. Courageous. Dedicated. Abandoning Yanyan's song, Kaiya sank her voice into a deep bass.

Around her, the faltering imperial guards and Paladins straightened in a wave radiating out from her. Young Sameer was first to recover.

"Form up, form up!" he said, even if he must be among the most junior compared to the masters.

The Lotus Crystal flared back to life, sending power coursing from her hands into her core. Yet despite the surge, how could her tiny voice possibly affect all of those interacting songs within him?

Focus not on the Dragon, but on his dragonstone. As Rumiya, he'd revealed the key to his own defeat. Kaiya sang directly to his dragonstone, his very source of vitality, using a different frequency to reinforce the remnants of Yanyan's lullaby.

Again, the same vibration flared inside of him, dispersing the effect of her voice. Yet this time, another verse revealed itself, whispering from deep within. Just like the stanza which kept her from renewing Yanyan's song, this was some sort of defense... but against what?

Listen. Sing. Be moved.

His defensive verse mingled with Ayana's hum, disrupting it. Had an elf voice vanquished him sometime in the past? Inverted, the sound would have an erratic beat and rapid changes, like nothing she'd heard before. She modulated her voice to create it...

The dragonstone responded with a sudden jolt.

She had him.

Subtle note by subtle note, she unwound Avarax's vibrations and bound them up with her own. Slower and slower, weaker and weaker, until he would be no more powerful than a manipulative, deceitful man who preyed on naïve princesses.

The dragon snorted. His brightly glowing eyes faded to a dull blue, lids sagging around them. He bobbed in the air as his wings echoed his dragonstone's slowing beat.

He opened his maw, teeth bared to roar, yet only music came out.

Her music.

His eyes widened, but the remaining blue within shimmered and then faded. With two rapid wingbeats, he pushed himself back half a mile. His wings cocked one more time... and withered. The hulking muscle of his forelegs and hindquarters shriveled, the limbs compressed.

As Avarax plummeted, his entire form shrunk and shifted. Red scales smoothed out and melded into soft flesh. His snout rounded and his horns shortened. Looking human, he splashed into the river—naked, foundering, writhing. The current carried him away.

Around her the Paladins rushed down the slopes toward the splash.

"Capture him!" a Paladin master yelled.

Kaiya gasped and brought both hands to her neck. What had she just done? How was it even possible?

Jie squinted, her sharp elven vision straining to get a better look at the man who was Avarax before the river swept him away. It happened so fast, it was hard to make out his features. She turned to Ayana. Maybe the elf had gotten a better view, even with her decrepit old eyes.

Beside her, the princess' legs wobbled. Before Jie could react, her charge collapsed.

Sameer, chivalrous as always, jumped and caught her before she crumpled to the ground.

Predictably, the imperial guards stepped forward to intervene.

As soon as the princess found her feet, the Paladin retreated three steps, head bowed and hands pressed together.

She afforded him a grateful smile. "Sir Paladin, thank you for your assistance."

Sameer bowed. "Your Highness, it was my honor. But I am not yet a full-fledged Paladin, just an apprentice."

The princess smiled. "Yet I could feel the power of your *Qi* supporting me as I sang. Surely you are one of power. Jie, give the apprentice the gemstone."

The Lotus Crystal! They had re-liberated it from Avarax and would now apparently be returning it to its rightful owners. Jie bobbed her head and presented it with two hands.

Sameer looked toward a Paladin master, who nodded. He received the stone in both hands, his eyes wide.

The master bowed toward the princess, hands pressed together. "Your Highness, young Sameer was wrong. He is a Paladin now. "

If Sameer's mouth could hang any wider, he would be able to stuff the Lotus Crystal in it.

"We have another visitor at the Crystal Citadel," the master said, "an Aksumi Mystic who is well-versed in the lore of the pyramids."

Jie and Sameer both gaped as they exchanged glances. It couldn't be! Not thousands of miles from where they'd parted.

The master continued, "Once she confirms the authenticity of the Lotus Crystal, you will complete your mission by delivering it to the Oracle of Ayudra, and return it to its rightful place at the pyramid."

The princess' breath caught in her throat. "The Pyramid. The Oracle. Sir Sameer, when will you take it back?"

Jie sighed. Perhaps the princess would now get a better view of her future. Hopefully, it would be one she wanted.

CHAPTER 48:
Return to Ayudra

Cheering crowds greeted Kaiya in every village and town the Paladin procession passed through on their way back to Vyara City. Returning refugees showered her with gifts, all of which she politely accepted, but then made sure were donated to those in need.

None of the fanfare compared to her reception in Vyara City, where they toasted her as the Dragon Charmer. She received more marriage proposals in a day than she had in four years back home, all of which she politely deflected.

Her unlikely quest accomplished, she didn't linger long in Vyara. With a continued heavy Paladin guard, she spent two days meeting with prominent Cathayi families in the region, and looked for gifts to bring back to her family as was the Cathayi custom.

Most importantly, a week after her encounter with Avarax, she made it across the bay to Vadaras, to complete the task which Madura's ambush had cut short. Unfortunately, in her meeting with the deposed Sultan of Selastya, she learned that the senior-most Akolyte of their god Athran had recently died. None of the other Akolytes had regained the ability to channel divine power into healing.

Maybe that was the *Tianzi's* last chance. In this, her journey was a failure.

With a heavy heart, Kaiya, along with Jie and the imperial guards, headed back across the Shallowsea to Ayudra Island. Going with the gentle currents, the voyage took half a day less than the inbound journey. Their barge arrived mid-afternoon on the second day. The familiar synchronicity of sounds echoed in her ears. The *Invincible* remained in port, towering high above all of the barges.

The same official who had made a fuss about her lack of identification papers the first time now received her entire entourage with a broad smile. "Welcome back, welcome back!" He gestured into the city. "The Paladins have opened Ayudra to you. This is an unprecedented honor. Though there is not much to see beyond the central boulevard."

Young Gayan skipped down the street toward them, reminiscent of the time she'd disembarked from the *Invincible*. He greeted her with a toothy grin. "Please come! The Oracle instructed the guest house to expect you."

He seemed even more carefree than the last time. After the experiences of the last two weeks, those days were forever gone for her.

Kaiya smiled back. Though the answer would be the same as always, she asked, "How did he know I would arrive today?"

The boy cocked his head. "He is the Oracle, after all."

"Then he would also know I would like to see him at once." She flashed him a playful pout.

Gayan giggled. "The Oracle said you would say that, word for word. He suggested you come first thing in the morning, when you are rested and your thoughts are clear. He said, *less haste, less emotion* would mean something to you."

Thoughts of the Praise Moon nun admonishing her young cousin Ziqiu came to mind. Apparently, the Oracle knew not only of the future, but the past as well. She bowed her head in acquiescence to the boy. "Very well. Please guide us."

The imperial guards and Jie followed Gayan down the street. Once they passed the wall separating the waterfront from the Paladins' district, they stopped at the surprisingly quiet smithy.

A different pair of teenagers sat outside, sharpening their *nagas* while the young dwarf Ashler peered over their shoulders.

He glanced up as they approached, a broad smile forming across his bearded face. The dwarf turned and entered the smithy, beckoning her to follow.

Inside, the heat sang its own song, billowing out in waves from the anvil, where a thin ring glowed blue-hot. The old dwarf paused from stoking the bellows and lifted his goggles. "Welcome back, lass. Ye come t'sing for yer Focus?"

Kaiya looked to Gayan, who bobbed his head enthusiastically. She tentatively repeated his nod.

"Very good then, lass. Listen t'its purr, and sing back t'it." Ashler gestured toward the band, glowing ever brighter with the rising temperatures.

The ring's hum echoed the rhythm of the island, vibrant and alive. So unlike the sluggish pulsing of Avarax's dragonstone. She sang back to it, letting her heart fall into beat with the rest of Ayudra.

The metal glowed brighter, as did several of the rough *nagas* hanging on the walls. Both dwarves stared with wide eyes and wider mouths.

"By Dirkan's Beard," muttered the old dwarf. "The God 'imself must've forged yer pipes. N'er before 'ave I 'eard the like."

Ashler beamed. "Aye. Let 'er cool down. I'll etch a symbol in'er, make 'er yers, though I'm sure she knows already. What be yer fancy, lass?"

Several images flashed before her mind. Dragons. Phoenixes. Musical notations. None of those seemed fitting anymore. Kaiya took up a piece of charcoal and drew the ideograph for Heaven, *tian*. Surely it was the Will of Heaven that had brought her there. *Tian* for *Tianzi*, and ironically the same word as her childhood friend's name. If only she could write it as beautifully as her sister-in-law Xiulan.

"I'll bring it to yer lodgin' t'morrow, when I'm done," Ashler said.

Kaiya placed a fist on her chest and bowed her head. "Thank you, Master Blackhammer. I look forward to seeing you tomorrow."

Tomorrow couldn't come soon enough, not because of the ring, but because of her appointment with the Oracle.

They returned to the guest house. Despite her command to rest, the imperial guards took turns standing watch outside her room instead of enjoying a full night's sleep in a comfortable bed. Jie, apparently, had no such compunctions.

Nonetheless, the half-elf was awake and by her side when Kaiya again woke to the harmonious interplay of morning sounds. Energy surged in her heart from what must've been the most restful sleep in a long time.

"*Dian-xia*, the *Golden Phoenix* arrived in port late last night. Young Lord Zheng Ming," Jie said the name as if she'd just sucked on a lemon, "was aboard and asks to see you."

Zheng Ming. Part of her, the one which longed to disengage from court life, yearned to see him, regardless of his shortcomings. No matter how much he disappointed her, his wit always made her heart race; his smile made her stomach flutter. Unlike the magical charm she'd felt with Hardeep, this was *real*. She could grow to love him as Sister-in-law Yanli, ever practical, suggested.

Nonetheless, a visit with the Oracle came first. "I am not ready to receive him."

Jie grinned. "The Paladins wouldn't let him past the wall."

"You don't like Zheng Ming, do you?"

The half-elf's lips snapped shut.

"Speak freely. Not that I have needed to give you permission in the past."

Jie shrugged. "My expertise is protecting you, and you do not tend to heed my opinions anyway. I see no need to comment on matters of the heart."

Kaiya held up the half-elf's lacquered hairpin. "As my sworn sister, I *ask* you to sp—"

"You will never be first for him," she blurted, like pent-up waters breaking through a dam. "Young Lord Zheng is in love with himself." Jie's sigh sounded like she'd just set down a load of bricks.

Kaiya suppressed her own sigh. When had she ever been first with anyone? The monster posing as Hardeep had only wanted her voice. All of the young lords in line to marry her wanted prestige. As for Prince Dhananad… she shuddered. Perhaps the only time when she had been first for anyone was with Ming's brother Tian, and they had just been naïve little children. Nonetheless, Father's deadline for her to choose a suitor fast approached.

"What about you, my sworn sister? Where is your heart?" Kaiya met Jie's gaze, knowing the half-elf would never confirm her suspicions.

True to form, Jie's face went blank for a second. Her eyes then sparkled with a mischievous glint. "I am in love with serving you, *Dian-xia*."

Kaiya covered a chuckle. Some questions might be better left unanswered. "Come, we must hurry to morning meditation."

They left the guest house, all five imperial guards in tow. Kaiya collected a handful of yellow flowers and set them by the statue of Acharya as they passed.

Gayan greeted them when they arrived at the semi-circle of megaliths at the Temple of the Moon. "Your entourage may join the meditation, but the Oracle bids you come to the Font by yourself."

Her guards grumbled, predictably, but obeyed her command to wait. They all remained outside the megaliths, save Jie, who worked her way through the crowds of seated Paladins.

Following Gayan up the steps, Kaiya arrived at the landing near the Font.

The Oracle looked into her soul as he welcomed her with palms pressed together. "You have grown in these short weeks."

Kaiya bowed. "If so, it was only with the help of the Paladins."

He beckoned her toward the bridge to the Font. "Come see... no, *hear* the fruits of your labor."

She crossed over to the mesa column. Unlike the first time, when faint blue light sprayed out of the font, the ray now seemed to suspend the Lotus Crystal several feet above the hole. Its facets refracted and dispersed the light, bathing the entire area in a dim blue. A single beam emerged from the tapered tip of the gemstone, shooting straight up to the Iridescent Moon.

He nodded. "Your Paladin friend Sameer returned the stone last night. I can feel the energy of the world more strongly than ever. Can you?"

Kaiya closed her eyes and listened. The symphony of sounds rang louder than the first time she visited. The waves seemed almost palpable.

The Oracle beamed a smile at her. "I look forward to feeling the difference in today's morning meditation. As for you, it is my understanding that your people practice a form of moving meditation, similar to our culture's yoga."

Kaiya had taken lessons in *Taiji Fist*, the *Supreme Ultimate*, from Doctor Wu, though it certainly wasn't her forte. Nonetheless, when the Oracle folded his legs into a lotus position, she assumed a high stance, rooting her feet to the ground. She closed her eyes and cleared her mind, letting the song of the island lull her into emptiness.

Do not move, *be* moved. Master Sabal's admonishment formed the first verse of the song in her head. The series of waves lifted her out of her stance and sent her feet teetering across the top of the mesa. Her hands moved of their own accord, much like when she danced for Prince Dhananad. Gravity seemed to release its hold on her as she accomplished feats of balance that should not have been possible.

When the Oracle clapped once, she found herself twirled into a cross-legged squat, back arched and arms bent like weeping willow branches. The Iridescent Moon had moved a phase, though unlike the first time, she didn't recall any images or visions.

She turned to the Oracle. "I... I don't understand. Everything *sounded* perfect. My movements *felt* perfect. But I didn't see anything this time."

The Oracle peered at her, his face wrinkled as his eyes, nose, and mouth all scrunched up. "Your movements articulated your future. You may not want to know how I interpret it."

Why had she come, if not to learn her future? She returned his stare. "Please, tell me."

He sighed. "You will be tested. You will suffer. You will lose a part of yourself. Yet in the end, you will gain more than you ever lost."

Kaiya found her lips pursed. The Oracle spoke in such broad generalizations; his words were more a riddle than the answers she sought. "Is there anything specific?"

"As I explained the first time, everything is symbolic. But what I can tell you from watching your dance is this: you will find love, hot and fierce enough to melt snow and ice. You will lose love, nay, have it burned away as if by the sun itself. Your homeland, weakened from within, will be invaded and occupied. You will be faced with a choice that can free your country, and the impact of that decision will ripple throughout Tivara."

Cathay, invaded and occupied. Like Ankira. Maybe she'd end up as bitter as Ankira's exiled queen. Her own choices would figure into the outcome. The inexplicable despair Kaiya remembered from her first visit to the Oracle flooded back over her now. "How will it happen? What choices must I make to avoid this future?"

The Oracle gazed at her as if she were asking how to switch day and night. "Your expression of the world's vibrations are only symbols. It becomes clearer and more exact the sooner into the future, and the cloudier the further you go. Remember, the future is not carved in stone, but rather billowing in the mist. The collective choices we make blow it into new shapes. What you manifested were merely possibilities. Sometimes, the decisions we make to avoid a certain future bring it about."

Kaiya frowned. If this was the type of guidance the Oracle gave the young Paladins, how could they possibly base their life's work on it? "Then what should I do?"

"Remember, a vision comes from within yourself. It is for *me* to give you guidance and for *you* to reflect on. Continue meditating on it, using the ring the Blackhammer Clan forged for you. It is a part of Ayudra, for you to take with you."

Kaiya wasn't sure of her own sincerity as she bowed low before him. "Thank you for your guidance. Farewell."

As she crossed back over the bridge, the sound waves of the Temple amplified his whisper. "The Bovyans as a race are very susceptible to the vibrations of the world, yet they cannot harness them. Therein lies the weakness of the Teleri Empire."

Since he'd whispered, perhaps he hadn't meant for her to hear him at all. As such, she didn't acknowledge his words, but continued down through the plaza.

Jie waited expectantly. Whatever vision she'd seen apparently made her beam ear to ear.

Kaiya nodded a greeting. "Where is Young Lord Zheng?"

"I understand that he has been waiting at the gate to the Paladin district all night and into the morning." The half-elf's lip twitched.

Kaiya sighed. How Jie could dislike the brother of the man she liked so much? "Let us see what Zheng Ming has to say for himself."

They continued back toward the harbor, their walk to the barricades taking just a few minutes. Zheng Ming sat quietly on the wall, mutually ignoring the Paladin sentries. His gaze met hers, sending her stomach into a routine of twists and tumbles that rivaled her latest dance. The girl she'd left behind in Cathay decided to replace the Dragon Charmer.

He jumped down from the wall and sank to both knees, pressing his forehead to the ground. "*Dian-xia*, please forgive me."

An apology. He probably didn't even know how he'd wronged her. "Young Lord Zheng, rise." Her voice came out as a timid squeak.

He lifted his head, his crooked grin making her heart race.

It was only when Jie poked her in the back that Kaiya realized she was playing with an errant lock of her hair. She let go of the tress and folded her arms together.

Zheng Ming climbed to his feet. "*Dian-xia*, allow me to explain my very late arrival."

So he did understand at least one of his offenses. She raised an eyebrow. "In front of everyone?"

His cautious smile sent her head spinning. "It seems due penance." Then his expression turned grave. "However, there is more pressing news I must tell you. The *Tianzi* fell deathly ill nine days after your secret departure from Cathay. The Crown Prince, too, was bedridden. Both poisoned by Lord Peng. Prince Kai-Wu sits on the Dragon Throne for now."

Nine days after… The pleasant dizziness disappeared. In its place, shock and confusion. Blood rushed from her head. Father, Eldest Brother almost dead. Poisoned by Cousin Peng, whom she'd trusted for so long. Perhaps he had his eye on the throne all these years. She reached out with a hand, as if it would keep her from fainting.

Jie's firm hand pressed on the middle of her back, supporting her. Zheng Ming took a step forward to catch her arm. If she weren't so concerned for Father's health, she'd be embarrassed at Ming seeing her so vulnerable. She couldn't worry about that now. She could be the Perfect Princess later, when she returned to Hua. Right now, she afforded herself a brief moment to be daughter.

"What… what happened?" The tightness of her throat clawed at her voice.

Ming held her in a sympathetic gaze. "The *Tianzi's* heart weakened and his entire body swelled up."

Wise and gentle Father, so strong when she was a child, now laid low by a traitor's ambition. Why hadn't she heard of this until now? Her mind tried to count the days between Father's illness and now, yet failed to grasp any number. Even the current date escaped her. "The *Golden Phoenix* is the fastest ship in our fleet. It could have been here within six days. Why are you just arriving now with this news?"

He bowed. "Lord Peng's men captured the *Golden Phoenix*. We thought they planned to whisk him home to Nanling. The crew refused to sail and were slain, to the man. It took us several days to recapture it, repair their sabotage, and redeploy new sailors."

Peng again. He'd deceived her time and time again, poisoned her family, murdered so many. Maybe even had Tian banished when they were children. The man knew no limits to his evil. Her only consolation… "I trust Lord Peng was brought to justice?"

Zheng Ming sighed. "He escaped over the Rotuvi border."

Her hands trembled as she tried to contain her anger and keep the desperation out of her voice. "We must return to Cathay at once. When will the *Golden Phoenix* be ready to depart?"

Zheng Ming shook his head. "We took a beating in a freak storm off Haikou, which caused further delays. The captain says repairs will take a week or more."

Kaiya looked to her handmaiden. "The *Invincible* was in port. Do you know where Prince Aelward is staying?"

The half-elf nodded. "Follow me."

CHAPTER 49:

Journey's Bounty

A cacophony of surprised gasps buzzed in Kaiya's ears, while the colorful court robes of hereditary lords swirled before her eyes. Head spinning from the disorientation Ayana's magic caused, she might have fainted right there in front of the kneeling ministers and nobles. She lifted a hand to cover her mouth and stemmed the rising nausea, her other hand reaching out for support.

Two images of her brother Kai-Wu, sitting around the central spot of the dais, undulated back and forth. Several imperial guards behind him drew their *dao* and advanced.

"Kaiya?" His voice combining incredulity and relief, both Kai-Wus lifted their hands and stayed the guards.

"*Dian-xia.*" A baffling chorus of voices spoke in unison. A mob of oscillating colors surrounded her.

With a few blinks, the ringing in her ears subsided and the images around her came into focus. Instead of a mob, four ranks of seated men held low bows in a semicircle around her. They raised their heads in a wave rippling out from the inside ring. Over half the lords of Peng's Nanling Province were absent.

As she suspected, there was only one Kai-Wu, and he wore a broad smile which didn't match the *Tianzi's* dignified yellow robes. "Kaiya, you appeared… quite suddenly."

She nodded toward Lord Zheng Han, Ming's father. "Young Lord Zheng told me of the situation, and I came as soon as possible."

Which was quite fast. She bowed toward Ayana. The old elf, after a ten-minute song which sounded like angels singing, had transported the two of them through the ethers back to Cathay. It worked out much better than the weeklong sea journey she'd asked of Prince Aelward.

Kai-Wu sighed. "The *Tianzi* and Crown Prince are both on their death beds. Doctor Wu is with them, delaying the inevitable."

The lords' expressions betrayed loyalties and ambitions. All had kowtowed before Father, sworn oaths when he was in his prime. Kai-Wu, while liked by all, did little to inspire confidence. Would they swear fealty to him?

Expansionist Lord Lin of Linshan pursed his lips. The people of his rugged forest province were well known for an independent streak. Lord Liang of Yutou, friends with the snake Peng, smirked, perhaps counting the hours. Cathay was about to throw itself into civil war.

Kaiya bowed, showing deference to Second Brother as she would the *Tianzi*. "With your leave, I would like to visit Father."

"Of course, of course. They are in the solarium." Kai-Wu made to stand, stopping when she gave a slight shake of her head. His place was here, in front of the hereditary lords.

She turned around, heads again bowing low. Pages slid the doors open and she glided through and strode toward the residential wing of the castle. Two imperial guards fell in behind her, along with Ayana.

They passed through Jade Gate and onto the covered bridge separating the castle from the residence. Halfway over the bridge, Ayana's pace slowed. "What magic is this? I have never seen wards so powerful."

Kaiya smiled, but preferred to keep the secrets of the castle to herself. She walked through the gate and continued into the residence.

Just outside the archway to the solarium, the usual guardians of the sleeping quarters' wing greeted her. Eight imperial guard sentries stepped to the side, allowing the old nun to approach with light bauble lamp raised.

Her wrinkled features creased further in surprise. "*Dian-xia.*" She then switched to the secret imperial language. "How old was the Founder when he arrived in Cathay from Heaven's Gate?"

"Forty-nine. He came from Great Peace Island, not Heaven's Gate."

The nun nodded. "Where was the portal on Great Peace Island?"

"Original Mastery Temple."

"What was his castle's name on Great Peace Island?"

"Pacified Lands Castle."

The gatekeeper switched back to Cathayi. "Welcome home, *Dian-xia*. I apologize for my impertinence, but your friend may not accompany you into the solarium." Her narrowed eyes showed no sign of apology.

The imperial guards stepped forward, barring Ayana.

Kaiya frowned. "Lady Ayana has helped me on numerous occasions. I—"

"It is all right, Kaiya," Ayana said. "I must be returning to Prince Aelward... just have someone get me outside of this magic bubble, and I will be on my way."

"Then, thank you for all of your help and guidance." Kaiya bowed at the waist to express her gratitude. She straightened only when Ayana made her way back through the residence with an imperial guard escort.

Kaiya studied the archway. How would Father, already ravaged by age and the burdens of rule, look now? And Eldest Brother Kai-Guo, just twenty-five... could she cope with seeing him near death? She took a deep breath and strode in.

Sunlight streamed in from the half-dome of glass, bathing the room in brightness. Despite shining on the dark-tiled floor, the sun couldn't warm the cold presence of impending death.

Xiulan, leaning at Kai-Guo's bedside, and Yanli, standing behind her, both gawked at her.

"Kaiya," Xiulan said, while Yanli beckoned her.

Beyond them, Eldest Brother laid motionless, his chest struggling with labored breaths. His ashen pallor stood in contrast to his usually healthy complexion. Kaiya's heavy heart weighed her steps, and she couldn't will her feet to move.

Sitting in a chair beside Father's bed, Doctor Wu held one of the *Tianzi's* limp wrists in her weathered hands, taking his pulse. She turned her head, her blue eyes delving deep into Kaiya's. "You have returned. Your journey bore fruit."

Indeed, if only Doctor Wu knew the whole story. She would undoubtedly appreciate hearing how her lessons helped vanquish the dragon. But now wasn't the time to tell the tale.

Doctor Wu smiled, the creases on the side of her eyes radiating out. "Come, child, bid your father and brother farewell."

Bid them farewell... it was that bad. Kaiya choked back a tear and stumbled forward. She fell to her knees by Father's frail form. Once, he'd been young and robust. Carried her on his back and threw her up in the air and caught her. But now... when she took his free hand in her own, the cold almost caused her to drop it.

"Sing to them. Let your voice escort them into the next life." Doctor Wu placed a surprisingly soft hand on her shoulder.

Warmth radiated into her from the doctor's hand, giving her courage. Kaiya started humming a lullaby, one Father had once sung to her. Slow and comforting, the words all but forgotten.

The *Tianzi's* eyebrows fluttered, their arrhythmic pulses threatening the harmony of her hum. His frail and stuttering heartbeat protested, jerking feebly at her melody. Behind her, Eldest Brother's faint and wobbling breaths magnified the amplitude of Father's imbalances.

"The combination of toxins," Doctor Wu said. "It breaks the natural resonance of their bodies, weakens them."

Perhaps it was no different than the vibrations of Avarax's dragonstone. Maybe she could influence their health and the toxins as well. Guanyin's Eye had already receded, however, and there was no army of Paladins, no priestesses, no elf wizard, no Lotus Crystal to lend her strength.

No. The power of two dying men did not begin to compare to a mighty dragon.

Kaiya rose from her kneel and gripped the solarium floor with her toes. With a deep breath, she cleared out all the other sounds besides her own hum, and the reply of her father's and brother's life forces. In the distance, the pulses of the Temple of Heaven reached even here. Doctor Wu, too, still projected immense power through the palm on Kaiya's shoulder. At her sides, Xiulan and Yanli breathed in harmony with each other. Her Ayudra ring. Kaiya might be able to borrow all of these, using her body as a conduit.

Continuing the lullaby, she raised her voice, accepting the irregular vibrations from Eldest Brother and Father's life forces, and harmonically nudging them closer to their correct course with musical notes.

Father's resonance was weak. Too weak. The toxins in both pushed back. It wasn't working. Despair threatened to overtake her, and she stuttered on her words.

No, she couldn't give up. A poison was nothing compared to a Avarax's dragonstone.

She let the toxin move her, pulling its vibrations to her instead of pushing them within Father and Eldest Brother's bodies. Their healthy energies filled in the space between the venom's wave pattern.

Behind her, Eldest Brother stirred. When she turned, his eyes were open and color was returning to his face. He propped himself up on his elbows and spoke, voice rasping. "Kaiya. You are home."

Continuing her hum, Kaiya nodded at him and shifted her attention to Father. The frequency of his vibrations remained feeble and irregular, though improved from when she'd started the song. Her energy, on the other hand, began to flag. Listless and heavy, her arms and legs protested the effort, and her concentration waned. She wouldn't be able to keep it up much longer.

"*Dian-xia*," Doctor Wu said. "Enough. This is far beyond the scope of a Dragon Song. Any more and it could cripple the power of your voice. It might even kill you."

Kaiya forced her voice louder. Just a little more, for Father, for the nation that might very well tear itself apart if he died today. All on her shoulders. She was alone.

No. Not alone.

Maintaining the melody, she sang to her sisters-in-law. "Eldest Sister, write… the words for health, power, and harmony. Second Sister, perform a tea ceremony."

Xiulan and Yanli exchanged dubious glances.

"Do it." Doctor Wu nodded toward her brush and prescription paper.

Xiulan took the brush and wrote the character for *power*.

The authoritative strokes of her hand invigorated Kaiya, sending a surge through her body. Her flagging energy provided one last push in her voice.

The *Tianzi's* eyes flew open and drifted onto her. A wan smile formed on his face. "My daughter. I did not expect to see you again in this life."

Kaiya gasped out the last note. The weight bearing down on her shoulders pushed her toward the floor. With supreme effort, she forced herself to remain standing.

Xiulan grasped her elbow, providing support, while Yanli brought a chair.

"Although he is still weak, he will live." Doctor Wu released Father's wrist and turned around to take Elder Brother's pulse.

The *Tianzi* pushed himself up into a seated position and beckoned a page. His voice still sounded weak. "Summon Kai-Wu, the *Tai-Ming*, the *Yu-Ming,* and the inner ministers. I will receive them here now."

The page dropped to his knees, then stood and hurried out of the room.

Doctor Wu finally came and took Kaiya's wrist in her hands. Her lips pursed as she held Kaiya's gaze with a stern glare. "Silly girl. Almost killed yourself, only to delay the inevitable."

The inevitable? Kaiya's heart tightened in her chest. "They will still die?"

Doctor Wu's expression softened into a grin. "Everyone dies. From the instant you leave your mother's womb, you are beginning to die. Yes, child, everyone dies."

"Even you?" Kaiya flashed a coy smile.

Doctor Wu harrumphed and stood. "*Huang-Shang*, I am going to prepare another herbal medicine for you. Do not exert yourself." She pushed her way through the stream of hereditary lords, brushing them aside like an autumn breeze through leaves.

To think a doctor could command the Son of Heaven...

All the lords, starting with the *Tai-Ming*, dropped to a knee as they approached the *Tianzi's* bed. Soon, they crowded the solarium.

The *Tianzi* cleared his throat and spoke with a stronger voice. "Great lords of Cathay. The nation prospers, yet we are not at peace. A rebel, one who once sat among you, hides on the other side of the Great Wall while his province descends into chaos. I command you each to provide soldiers to assist the imperial army in its pacification."

The lords all answered in rote unison. "As you command, *Huang-Shang*!"

Such resolve, such obedience! A tingle of excitement surged up Kaiya's spine. Even so, the idea of potential hostility was disheartening.

"In the meantime, I command you to concentrate your efforts into maintaining stability in your own provinces to ensure they do not follow Nanling into insurgency."

"As you command, *Huang-Shang*!"

Father lifted the Founder's Broken Sword. "Peng Kai-Long, once my treasured nephew, must be brought to justice, to be made example of lest others follow his lead. Now, reaffirm your oaths of loyalty to the empire."

"I swear!" All repeated.

The chorus of voices reverberated in the room. Kaiya smiled. For now, the hereditary lords would hold the line. Now if only something as simple as a vow could secure the return of Cousin Peng. Who could convince the Kingdom of Rotuvi to extradite him?

Father's eyes fell on her.

EPILOGUE:
All Good Things

The sounds of Sun-Moon Lake lapping up against the castle walls comforted Kaiya with their familiarity. She sat atop the ramparts, letting her feet dangle over the edge as she listened to the waters' song.

Whereas none of her personal imperial guards would dare protest, her current detail of dour men virtually ordered her to come down before night made it too dark to see.

Convincing them otherwise gave her more opportunities to practice the power of her voice.

She needed the quiet time to contemplate what had unfolded, and her unlikely and mostly unwanted place in this world.

In the two weeks since her return, the *Tianzi* and Eldest Brother had continued to improve, with Doctor Wu's constant ministrations.

Court life resumed as usual. Her sisters-in-law welcomed her home with open arms.

Yet nothing was the same.

The hesitant girl who left Huajing had returned a confident young woman, scarred by multiple betrayals and wiser because of it. Court gossip seemed trivial compared to the story of facing down a dragon.

The only ones who could understand that—Jie, and her guards Li Wei, Zhao Yue, Chen Xin, Ma Jun, and Xu Zhan—all remained behind in Ayudra until the *Golden Phoenix* could bring them home.

Zheng Ming—the one she most wanted to hear her story—was likewise stranded with the others.

Kaiya reached into her sash and withdrew Tian's pebble. As always, the cool smoothness reminded her of a carefree childhood, one that she could never relive.

Her innocence was dead. She started to cast the stone into the lake, sending it back to whence it came, but pulled her arm up short. With a sigh, she returned it to its place at her side. Some ideals were worth holding on to.

Her other thumb toyed with the Ayudra ring on her index finger. Its vibration mingled with the lake's waves, neither synchronized nor discordant.

"May I?" An open palm, like a beggar's, appeared before her, blocking the view of her lap. "I would like to see the ring that sings the song of Ayudra."

Kaiya's heart must've skipped three beats. She twisted to find Lord Xu sitting beside her on top of the wall, his legs hanging over the edge. His sad smile replaced the impish grin she'd grown accustomed to.

Angry questions welled up from her heart. "Why didn't you tell me? When you said someone would hear my song, you *knew* it would be Avarax, didn't you? Did you know Avarax was Hardeep? Why didn't you answer me when I called for you in Vyara City?"

His eyes searched hers for a few seconds, stirring her impatience. He then lifted the magic mirror and held it up to the skies. With his other hand he pointed.

She followed his finger, to a spot in the vast expanse of speckled night sky where a tiny red dot blinked.

"What can you tell me about that star?"

His question did nothing to answer hers. She responded in hopes of coaxing a reply from the fickle elf. "It represents the God of Conquest, Yanluo."

"Or in the language of the orcs, *Tivar*." He pointed to another a twinkling blue star. "How about that star there?"

"Wu-Long, the Dragon Guardian of Cathay." Curiously, it shined brighter than usual.

"She has appeared twice since the War of Ancient Gods, when great generals in Cathay's history reunified the nation." The elf's finger shifted to the nine-star constellation facing the blue star. "And who does Wu-Long oppose?"

"E-Long, the Evil Dragon."

"Now receding. Who do you imagine that represents?"

A spark of understanding dawned on her. "Avarax."

"The Powers of Good are on the rise, though Evil always seeks opportunity. The Oracle of Ayudra is not the only one who can divine the future, though he is infinitely better than an Estomari tarot-card reader." A hint of mischievousness twinkled in his eye. "Or an elf astrologer."

Had Lord Xu arranged her meeting with the Oracle? Or set it in motion as Hardeep had influenced the path of her life? "So you can divine the future?"

Shrugging, the elf laughed. "Perhaps. The dilemma of knowing the future is our desire to change it. Sometimes, an attempt to alter our destiny only hastens its arrival. If you had known you would confront Avarax, would that have influenced your choices?"

Kaiya twirled a lock of hair. It was one of the many questions which had weighed heavily on her these past few weeks. Even as people hailed her as the heroic Dragon Charmer, she might not have willingly confronted Avarax if she'd truly had a choice in the matter.

She was no hero. Her hand caressed Tian's pebble.

Lord Xu's eyes were on that hand until he looked up and smiled wryly. "To answer one of your questions, no, I did not know Hardeep was Avarax, though I knew he always watched Cathay in hopes of finding someone to sing to him. I told you as much, when you played the Dragon Scale Lute. I suspect he was responsible for the deaths of past magical music masters, who might've presented a threat to him."

Yet he'd spared her. Used her. And more troubling, "Is it true that his Lotus Jewel awoke my magic and made me pretty?"

"You were born with the magic of music, as well as the intuition to face the Last Dragon. That is why I did not respond to your summons. Sometimes, you have to find the answers within yourself."

He'd avoided the whole question, specifically the more troubling half. She placed a hand on her cheek. "And my beauty?"

All mirth disappeared from the elf's expression. "You were not meant to be beautiful."

Her heart sank. It sounded a whole lot like destiny again. "So everything that happened, and will happen, is my destiny?"

Lord Xu shrugged again. "You fulfilled your destiny when you vanquished Avarax. From here, you make your own. The stars just predict it. Resist the temptation to know it, since it may not always unfold as you hope. Worry not about what might be; concentrate on the present, the task at hand. That task now is to demand Lord Peng's extradition from Rotuvi."

With a melodic word, he disappeared, the air popping as it filled in the space he'd departed.

The future may not unfold as hoped. Ominous words, made all the more so coming from both an enigmatic elf and a mysterious oracle.

Threads of an Embroidery

Hong Jianbin stroked sleeping Leina's cheek as they lay in her new Floating World abode. He had purchased the single-story wood building with his greatly increased stipend as Chief Minister.

It was well worth it.

The secret entrance from the adjoining Jade Teahouse allowed him surreptitious access to his mistress, away from prying eyes.

To think, without the encouragement of a foreign refugee and the help of a renegade spy, this fishmonger's son would have never risen to the exalted position of Chief Minister.

His native Nanling Province now lacked a *Tai-Ming* lord to rule it. Once the imperial armies rooted out minor lords loyal to Peng and pacified the countryside, the *Tianzi* would replace the province's leadership with those he could trust. Faithful generals and ministers would be elevated to hereditary lords.

Which would be better? To become a hereditary lord would improve his chance of marrying Princess Kaiya. As Chief Minister, he would have plenty of influence beyond the reach of a single province.

He gazed at Leina. Perhaps he already had everything he needed.

Leina feigned sleep, hoping old Hong would soon unwrap his leathery arms from around her. His proposed celebration for his promotion to Chief Minister was something she did not enjoy.

He'd been particularly virile tonight, and she feared his old heart might not be able to keep up with his manhood. His death, just when she'd gotten him to a position where he could influence national policy, would be disastrous. Everything she'd endured in her assignment as his mistress would have gone to waste.

As always, he surprised her. Just like when he outlasted Peng in their game of power. Or talked his way into Prince Kai-Wu's good graces.

The Chief Minister, hers to manipulate.

At the cost of her body and pride.

It was too much to bear.

Besides the herbs which poisoned the *Tianzi*, she knew of others that would kill quite quickly. One of those, hidden in her nightstand drawer, would be tempting to take right now.

But then there was her mother, trapped in Ankira, relying on Leina to succeed in her mission to undermine Cathay from the inside. The house's secret entrance would allow her to covertly meet with the surviving insurgents and other lords and ministers she could bend to her will.

The most important key was to keep the imperial armies bogged down in Nanling Province. Then, the northern borders would be less defended once her employer was ready to invade. But how to sustain a provincial uprising without good leadership?

Peng Kai-Long.

She would think of a way to sneak him out of exile in Rotuvi Kingdom and back home where he could cause the most damage.

Geros Bovyan XLIII, First Consul of the Teleri Empire's ruling Directori, paced back and forth. The stone floors of his stark quarters in Tilesite were cold beneath his feet, in contrast to the anger which raged hot in his head.

The unlikely alliance of Eldaeri Kingdoms had recaptured some of the lands his armies occupied in Serikoth. The Bastard Prince Aelward of Tarkoth had broken his ingenious blockade of Bullhead Lake, allowing the cowardly Eldaeri to harass Teleri supply lines from the safety of the waters.

Apparently, Geros' commanders could not win a war without him.

The face of one such incompetent appeared at his door and thumped his fist against his chest. "Your Eminence, an official message from Cathay."

Cathay was a pig he planned to roast later, after sufficient marinating. He ripped the folded rice paper out of his underling's hands and whipped it open with a flick of his wrist.

To the Directori of the Teleri Empire:

Your vassal state, the Kingdom of Rotuvi, currently harbors the criminal Kai-Long Peng, former Great Lord of Nanling Province, within its borders. We will be dispatching Princess Kaiya Wang to meet with you and discuss terms of his extradition and continued trade between our great nations. We would request this meeting to take place in the port city of Iksuvius at your earliest convenience.

From Zhishen Wang

Son of Heaven, Emperor of Cathay

Geros harrumphed. How ostentatious a title for a pathetic nation of merchant princelings. Nonetheless, it would be a chance to meet the Dragon Charmer herself, who had foiled some of the Altivorc King's plans. Princess or not, Dragon Charmer or not, she was just a girl. And supposedly a beautiful one at that.

Geros turned to his lieutenant. "Have the rest of the consuls seen copies of this letter?"

"Of course not. You were first."

"Good. Draft my response, to be presented for the Directori's approval. I will personally meet with Princess Kaiya, on the occasion of the Northwest Summit."

His crowning moment, and one rife with underlying messages. To have her meet with him, in front of the eyes of foreign friends and foes, would symbolize Cathay bowing before him.

Now he just had to find out why he had not heard of Lord Peng Kai-Long seeking asylum in Rotuvi. And also get an update from his spy in Cathay.

Orchestra of Treacheries

Stirring the dying embers of his fire, Peng Kai-Long gazed out onto Guanyin's Tear Lake. After a month of travelling disguised as migrant farm workers with two of his most trusted guards, he'd reached the halfway point home in Nanling Province. To avoid a checkpoint in the staunchly Royalist Fenggu Province, they had veered off the main roads and now camped in the shadow of the old orc pyramid.

Despite what his officers aboard the *Golden Phoenix* had confessed under the *Tianzi's* agents' persuasive techniques, he never slipped over the border into Rotuvi. He hadn't even gone to Jiangkou, instead revealing himself to the insurgents in the capital as their anti-imperial benefactor. After a month of letting his hair and beard grow roughshod, he headed south, trailing the expeditionary armies meant to quell any resistance in *his* province.

The lake stretched for several *li*, glowing a light blue. Legends claimed it was the single tear of the Blue Moon Goddess Guanyin, shed when the Sun God Yang-Di presented the mortal world to her as a gift. Many people visited each day in hopes that the holy waters would cure their ailments.

Kai-Long snorted. The *Tianzi* had drunk twice his bodyweight in the water over the years and still never recovered from his poisoning.

Yet Kai-Long did believe one legend.

Cathay's guardian dragon once appeared somewhere in this valley. Though one local legend reported her sighting during the Hellstorm, most stories said she hibernated through the orc's Dragonpurge and would serve whoever woke her.

Kai-Long spat into the water. Who was to say hateful Cousin Kaiya couldn't charm *that* dragon as well?

No, he would have to rely on his own wits if he were to reconsolidate his power. The satisfaction of watching the Dragon Charmer suffer a slow death was motivation enough.

Liang Yu leaned against an Eldarwood tree, keeping watch over the funerary potter's shop. The rhythmic clanging of metal in the nearby blacksmithy all but drowned out the spring chirping of songbirds.

His search for Lord Peng, which had taken him to the border of Rotuvi and back, had proved fruitless. The devious lord had sunk so low as to feed his own loyal men disinformation. Despite what everyone believed, Peng had to be somewhere in Cathay.

Which brought Liang Yu here, to one of the information relay points for his former clan. Even with a Black Lotus renegade at large, they didn't think the location was compromised. Of course. They never considered that the Architect, one of the few masters who knew of this drop spot, might still live.

The latest message he'd intercepted accused the renegade—him—of treason, for helping the Teleri Empire train spies.

Treason!

He clenched his fists. He was no traitor. If the ruling elite weren't so corrupt, they'd recognize his patriotism. And the only two people whom he'd trained in Black Fist ways were Young Song and—

There was a light tug on his pouch.

Liang Yu spun around, curved knife ready to slash the young lady's throat.

She raised a metal hairpin, stopping the arc of his cut, and then bowed her head. "Master."

His special pupil, Lin Ziqiu, daughter of a *Tai-Ming* lord. Her skill had improved so much. She had tracked him here, and even succeeded in sneaking up on him. Used the noise of bell-making to mask her approach. Clever. Or maybe his hearing declined with age.

Though she was still not smart enough to realize his deception. He smiled. "Have you tracked Chief Minister Hong's mistress?" he asked.

She nodded. "Yes. He bought her a house in the Floating World."

The Floating World! It might be a better place to gather information than even the bell foundry. Liang Yu reached over and brushed hair out of her pretty face. "Pose as a Night Blossom, get close to her."

Her lip curled. "But I wanted to accompany Princess Kaiya on her mission to demand Lord Peng's extradition."

It was a pointless mission. A dangerous one, too, since the barbaric kingdoms to the north might not take kindly to accusations of harboring criminals.

Liang Yu shook his head. He couldn't expose his student to needless danger. But if he told her Peng was still in Cathay, she might warn the princess. "Hong's mistress is more important. My control over him is nominal at best, but if we can find a way to manipulate her, it might give us extra leverage."

Her expression lit up and she clapped her hands together. Always in search of adventure, this one.

Colors flashed in the corner of his eye. He pulled the girl back behind the cover of the tree and peered back toward the potter's shop. The mute worker from the bell foundry dropped several messages into a worn funerary urn.

Within a quarter hour, a Black Lotus trainee, hypnotized to forget his task after completion, would retrieve the specially-folded messages. Which gave Liang Yu a quarter hour to send his student on her way, and then find out what his former clan knew.

Jie rested her head on her closest clan sister's shoulder. Yan Wen had come to Ayudra on the *Golden Phoenix* with Zheng Ming, and joined her on an unplanned journey.

For what must've been the hundredth time, Jie opened the small magic pouch Ayana had given her, marveling at the massive interior space. If only she could fit Zheng Ming through the opening, she wouldn't have to listen to his constant complaints about the heat and humidity.

She looked up from the pouch and toward the back of the river skiff.

The imperial guards sat back in their seats, their rigid discipline softened in the princess' absence. They chatted and joked with Sameer, revealing actual personalities. The belligerent Levanthi mercenary, on the other hand, sat apart, always staring ahead toward the homeland he hadn't seen for two decades.

The chocolate-skinned Askumi Mystic Brehane, with whom she'd shared an adventure two years before in the Teleri Empire, also kept to herself. She ostensibly studied her sheaf of magical scrolls, but was more likely trying to avoid Zheng Ming's flirtatious banter in his ever-improving Ayuri tongue. By now, he must've heard a dozen different ways to say *no*.

Rounding out the motley crew was the dwarf Ashler Blackhammer, who constantly tinkered with some contraption he planned to market.

Rumor had it that Avarax, now limited to two legs, was making his way to Selastya. With the repairs to the *Golden Phoenix* expected to take much longer than the initial estimate, she'd convinced the imperial guards that the princess' future safety relied on foiling whatever nefarious plans the dragon had.

They now travelled with Sameer, on his quest to investigate the magical dead zone surrounding the Levanthi Pyramid.

Orchestra of Treacheries

Eight Cathayi warriors, an Ayuri Paladin, a Levanthi mercenary, an Askumi sorceress, and a dwarven weaponsmith in a boat. There had to be a punchline in there somewhere.

Avarax huddled among the beggars near the docks of some river city. It had taken him weeks for his two legs to bring him here, and he was not sure how much farther he had to go to reach Selastya.

Princess Kaiya's music still reverberated through his dragonstone, holding his immense reserves of energy in check. Though he was still virtually invulnerable, his magic remained locked away. Somewhere in her song, the tapestry of musical notes had destructively interfered with the frequency of his dragonstone. It was something only her voice could do.

Two years of planning, only to have a naïve girl grow into an insightful woman and deconstruct the fake song he'd given her. No, she could *not* circumvent the magical ward designed to protect a human voice from singing him to sleep, as the slave girl had a thousand years ago. But she had reverse-engineered the other ward, the one set to prevent an elven voice from forcing an involuntary transformation.

Xu had done so during the Hellstorm, trapping him in human form for nearly three hundred years. Only when he tricked one of Aralas' descendants into playing the Dragon Scale Lute had he been able to regain his dragon form, if not all his power.

Never did he imagine that a human whelp—not even one with the voice of the slave girl—could accomplish the same as Xu. It should not have been possible.

Though fond of Rumiya's form and all of the entertaining adventures it afforded him when he chose, he was not pleased at the prospect of being stuck as a human for another three hundred years.

Decades were not long for an immortal. Another chance would present itself. Maybe not today, maybe not in a century. But it would happen. If one thing was reliable, it was that mortal beings had failings which his fifty-thousand years of experience could find ways to exploit.

The first step would be tapping into the energy of the pyramid to restore his magic. Now if only he could find his way to the closest one, in Selastya. It wasn't that easy. Everything looked a lot different at ground level.

It didn't matter. Soon he would look down on the world again, and make Kaiya his own.

These stories continue in Dances of Deception and Finding The Faith

Appendix

Celestial Bodies

White Moon: known as RenYue in Cathay and represents the God of the Seas. It's orbital period is 30 days.

Iridescent Moon: known in Cathay as Caiyue, it is the manifestation the God of Magic. It appeared at the end of the war between elves and orcs. It never moves from its spot in the sky. Its orbital period is one day and can be used to keep time.

Blue Moon: known in Cathay as Guanyin's Eye, it is the manifestation of the Goddess of Fertility. It sits low on the horizon. Its phases go from wide open to winking.

Tivar's Star: A red star, a manifestation of the God of Conquest. During the Year of the Second Sun, it approached the world, causing the Blue Moon to go dim.

Time

As measured by the phases of the Iridescent Moon:
Full = Midnight
1st Waning Gibbons = 1:00 AM
2nd Waning Gibbons =2:00 AM
Mid-Waning Gibbons = 3:00 AM
4th Waning Gibbons = 4:00 AM
5th Waning Gibbons = 5:00 AM
Waning Half = 6:00 AM
1st Waning Crescent = 7:00 AM
2nd Waning Crescent = 8:00 AM
Mid-Waning Crescent = 9:00 AM
4th Waning Crescent = 10:00 AM
5th Waning Crescent = 11: 00 AM
New = Noon
1st Waxing Crescent = 1:00 PM
2nd Waxing Crescent = 2:00 PM
Mid-Waxing Crescent = 3:00 PM
4th Waxing Crescent = 4:00 PM
5th Waxing Crescent = 5:00 PM
Waxing Half = 6:00 PM1st
Waxing Gibbons = 7:00 PM
2nd Waxing Gibbons =8:00 PM
Mid-Waxing Gibbons = 9:00 PM
4th Waxing Gibbons = 10:00 PM
5th Waxing Gibbons = 11:00 PM

Provinces of Cathay

Province	Ruling Family	Resources
Dongmen	Zheng	grain, stone, guns
Fenggu	Han	Timber, rice, grain
Huayuan	Wang	Livestock, rice, wheat, lumber, firepowder, guns
Jiangzhou	Liu	Timber, wheat, silk
Linshan	Lin	Wheat, millet, timber, porcelain
Nanling	Peng	livestock, steel, stone, gems, crossbows
Ximen	Zhao	Fishing, rice
Yutou	Liang	Fishing, rice, iron, copper, fish paste
Zhenjing	Wu	Ships, rice, fish

Human Ethnicities

Aksumi: Dark-skinned with dark eyes and coarse hair. On Earth, they would be considered North Africans. They can use Sorcery.

Ayuri: bronze-toned skin with dark hair and eyes. On Earth, they would be considered South Asians. They can use Martial Magic.

Arkothi: olive-skinned with blond to dark hair and light-colored eyes. On Earth, they would be considered Eastern Mediteraneans. They can use Rune Magic.

Bovyan: The descendents of the Sun God's begotten son, they are cursed to be all male and live only to 33 years of age. They are much taller and larger than the average human. Their other physical characteristics are determined by their mother's race. They have no magic ability.

Cathayi (Hua): honey-toned skin with dark hair and eyes. High-set cheekbones and almond-shaped eyes. On Earth, they would be considered East Asians. They can use Artistic Magic.

Eldaeri: olive-skinned with brown hair. Fine features and small frames, they are shorter in stature than the average human. In a previous age, they fled the Orc domination of the continent and mingled with elves. They have no magic ability.

Estomari: olive-skinned with varying eye and hair color. They are famous for their fine arts. On Earth, they would be considered Western Mediterraneans. They can use Divining Magic.

Kanin: Ruddy-skinned with dark hair. On Earth, they would be considered Native Americans. They can use Shamanic Magic.

Levanthi:— Dark-bronze skin and dark hair.— On Earth, they would be considered Persians.— They can use Divine Magic.

Nothori:— fair skinned and fair haired.— On Earth, they would be considered Northern Europeans.— They can use Empathic Magic.

Acknowledgements

First, I would like to thank my wife and family for the patience they have afforded me as I pursued my childhood dream of fiction writing.

A shout-out goes out to my old Dungeons and Dragons crew: Jon, Chris, Chris, Paul, Conrad, and Julian, for helping to shape the first iteration of Tivara twenty-five years ago. Huge thanks to Brent, who contributed so much backstory to the new literary version.

A huge thanks to my sister Laura for her spectacular job with the maps.

Thanks to the readers and writers on Wattpad for their encouragement and feedback.

And finally, to writers over at critiquecircle.com who motivated and helped me along the way.

Jason, for patiently providing countless ideas. Kelly, for amazing input, character development and all the other advice. Victoria, for showing me how to layer scenes. Andy, for unparalleled wordsmithing. Ernie, for teaching me the fundamentals of fiction writing. Lindy for your sharp eye. Taylor, Darryl, and Rick for the numerous suggestions. Laurel, Joyce, Tracy, Traci, Kathyrn, and Ardyth for beta reading; and all the others who critiqued.

Special Thanks

This special edition of Songs of Insurrection was only made possible by many generous pledges and donations.

From Patreon, I would like to especially acknowledge Elena Daymon and Samantha Mikals. I'm humbled by your support; as well as Dianeme Weidner, Spring Yang, Nicholas Klotz, Scott Engel, Mary Luu, Dexter Bradley, and Lindsay Shurtliff.

From Kickstarter, many thanks to Dyrk Ashton, Wraithmarked Creative, Zach Sallese, Dian, Ben Nichols, Rich Chang, Henrik Sörensen, Dan & Robert Zangari, Philip Tucker, Steven Hall, Jan Drake, Michał Kabza, Cody Allen, John Idlor, Kathy Jones, Nic Guinasso, Doug Williamson, Susan Voss, J. Zachary Pike, KE Sizemore, yesterspectre, Bobby McDonald, Andrew Barton, Michael Tabacchi, Emmanuel MAHE, Nicholas Liffert, A.Y. Chao, Artgor, Michael Mattson, Alexander Darwin, Krystal Xu, Caroline Atkins, Angela Engelbert, Shawna Dees, Nicolas Lobotsky, Justin Gross, Joey Hendrickson, Sarah Polk, Lawrence Wight, Eddie, Graham Dauncey, Jennifer, Virginia McClain, Christian Holt, Christopher Kranz, Leanne Yong, Kanyon Marie Kiernan, Scott Engel, Ivor Lee, Dan K, Mike Filliter, Ryan Kirk, James Yu, JC Cannon, Michelle Rapoza. Craig A. Price Jr., John Jutoy, Derek Freeman, Gerald P. McDaniel, Mat Meillier, A. Hakes, Helena Jones, Ashley, Charlie Gipson, Lapiswolf, PurpleSteamDragon, Laura E Custodio, Megan Mackie, Ashli Tingle, Stacy Shuda, Anna Lee, Don Quaintance, Anne Kinney, Jessica Stone, Stanley, Derek Alan Siddoway, Ting Bentley, Ernesto, Gary Phillips, Dianeme Weidner, Timandra Whitecastle, Paul Cassimus, Paul, Walt Mussell, JohnYu, Chris, and Andre.

About the Author

JC Kang's unhealthy obsession with Fantasy and Sci-Fi began at an early age when his brother introduced him to the *Chronicles of Narnia*, the *Hobbit*, *Star Trek* and *Star Wars*. As an adult, he combines his geek roots with his professional experiences as a Chinese Medicine doctor, martial arts instructor, and technical writer to pen multicultural epic fantasy stories.

Made in the USA
Columbia, SC
13 March 2025

9412448b-a3b0-42d0-8b7a-46db1ada258eR01